THE IRISH PRINCESS

This Large Print Book carries the
Seal of Approval of N.A.V.H.

THE IRISH PRINCESS

KAREN HARPER

THORNDIKE PRESS
A part of Gale, Cengage Learning

GALE
CENGAGE Learning™

Detroit • New York • San Francisco • New Haven, Conn • Waterville, Maine • London

30555 8668 R

GALE
CENGAGE Learning

LIBRARY OF CONGRESS CATALOGING-IN-PUBLICATION DATA

Harper, Karen (Karen S.)
    The Irish princess / by Karen Harper.
      p. cm. — (Thorndike Press large print core)
    ISBN-13: 978-1-4104-3703-7 (hardcover)
    ISBN-10: 1-4104-3703-5 (hardcover)
    1. Clinton, Elizabeth Fiennes de, Countess of Lincoln,
1528?–1589—Fiction. 2. Princesses—Ireland—Fiction. 3.
Elizabeth I, Queen of England, 1533–1603—Fiction. 4. Henry
VIII, King of England, 1491–1547—Fiction. 5. Clinton, Edward
Fiennes de, Earl of Lincoln, 1512–1585—Fiction. 6. Great
Britain—History—Henry VIII, 1509–1547—Fiction. 7. Large type
books. I. Title.
PS3558.A624792I75 2011b
813'.54—dc22   2011000828

Published in 2011 by arrangement with NAL Signet, a member of Penguin Group (USA) Inc.

. . . Foster'd she was with milk of Irish
breast.
Her sire an Earl; her dame of Prince's
blood.
From tender years, in Britain doth she
rest . . .
Bright is her hue, and Geraldine she's
named . . .
Her beauty of kind; her virtues from
above;
Happy is he that can attain her love!

From the sonnet to Elizabeth Fitzgerald,
"The Fair Geraldine,"
by Henry Howard, Earl of Surrey

CHAPTER THE FIRST

Whitehall Palace, London
January 25, 1547

I, Gera Fitzgerald, was going to kill the king. He was dying, but I was going to kill him anyway.

In the dim back servants' hall, I pushed the hidden panel that led to the king's bedchamber. It seemed I had waited for this chance my entire life. I had been forced to bide my time until the king was alone in the small back rooms so few knew existed.

Henry Tudor, king and tyrant of all England and of my beloved, battered Ireland, was living his last moments on this earth. I pressed the dagger I had secreted in my shawl to be sure it was still there. Yes, its sharp steel, warmed by the heat of my body, waited to strike with all the power and passion that festered within me.

My pulse pounded in my ears as I hesitated but one moment. I could bear up to it if I were caught, I tried to buck myself up. If I must, I could face torture in the Tower and bloody death by beheading like those I had loved. At my trial, I would speak out for my family and my country. The Geraldines had been the salvation of poor Ireland and must be again.

I stepped into the void, black as the pit of hell, for I'd not dared bring a lantern or even a candle. The air was stale, so this entry must not have been recently used. A cobweb wove itself across my sweating face and snagged in my eyelashes. No matter if I kept my eyes open or closed, it was the same deep darkness.

I went slowly, one hand along the wooden wall, one out ahead so I would not bump into the door at the end. A sliver jabbed into my finger, but I ignored it. My hand touched the door.

I froze, straining to hear. Some strange sound came from within, a rhythmic hissing. I pictured a fat, coiled serpent, the king of England I had so long detested and feared. Snoring — that was it. He slept.

I recalled the arrangement of the two rooms I had walked through nearly three years ago, the shadows, the silence. Not silent now. As I pushed the door inward a crack, I saw wan light, though it nearly blinded me at first. I felt I'd opened a long-sealed tomb: No air stirred and the very smell of death sat heavy here.

I shuffled along, giving my eyes time to adjust, though there was little to bump into but the oaken bed that dwarfed everything. I saw the source of light was a pewter lantern on a small table across the room.

He had gone quiet now. What if he were dead already? It would not be enough if he escaped me after all this time! But no, though the snoring had ceased, a sharp rasping for breath resounded from the big, curtained bed. Had he hidden out here like a wounded animal — or was he ashamed to let others see him as he was? Did he really want to cleanse his soul and risk dying alone? *Ah, well,* a little voice in my head seemed to say, *in the end, cobbler or king, we all must die alone.*

Though I knew the king was hard of hearing and the heavy brocade curtains separated us, I tiptoed into the small adjoining room to be certain no servant or guard slept there. No one. Just shadows, like dark ghosts from Henry Tudor's past and mine, those who had been murdered, those who cried out for justice, even from their graves.

A single fat candle burned on the table here, illumining a short stack of parchment.

9

The candle diffused the sweet scent of expensive ambergris and threw flickering light on the rows of rich parchment-and-leather-scented books shelved on all four walls. Hoping no one would wonder how the obese, crippled king could rise from his bed to lock the door to his more public chambers, I went to it, listened with my ear to the carved and gilded wood, then twisted the key in the lock.

As I passed the table again, I bent to look at the documents lying there. In fine script, the king's will! I longed to burn it all, at least the parts about the Tudor heirs being bequeathed my Ireland. Somehow I must find a way to restore my brother's rights and title, for that would benefit our people more than Tudor power. I pushed the papers aside to get to the back of the document. He had signed it already, so its decrees and bequests were final.

I could barely keep myself from slashing the royal will to pieces with the dagger. Instead, I fished the weapon out and, as carefully as I could, sliced off the bottom inch of the last page that bore the signature. Let them think the king had done that before he did away with himself. I hoped to make my deed look like suicide instead of regicide. I would leave the dagger in the hand of the king's corpse.

I bent to stuff the narrow piece of parchment in my shoe, where it crinkled in protest. A thought hit me with stunning force: Should I be taken and executed, no one would ever know my wishes, my story, my legacy. I should have made a will or written my life's events. If I survived and the king was dead and buried, I would not let my life and loves and reasons for my deeds be buried too. I would record my own story and entitle it *The Irish Princess,* for what could once have been.

Nodding at the decision I had made, I tamped the papers into place. Keeping the dagger out, I trod as quietly as I could back into the bedchamber.

The king was breathing easier now. I took off my heavy outer shawl and tied it around my waist, lest I would need to flee, for I must leave nothing behind that could be traced.

The bed was not only huge but high. At least it had a three-step mounting stair, which the king himself or those who lifted him up had needed. I climbed the first step and knelt upon the third. It creaked, but then, at the last moment, I hoped to wake the king so he knew why his life was forfeit. But if he called out for help, would his voice carry clear to his guards or to someone who might be just beyond in his formal bed-chamber? Was this gigantic but ill man yet strong enough to stop me?

I parted the bed curtains so I could see within. At first, I thought I saw only a pile of pillows, but the king was propped upon them. After all his harsh breathing, he was so quiet now. Was he awake, watching, or had he just died?

I cleared my throat to see if he would move. Finally — now or never, I told myself. Let him die in peace, some would say, but I would never have peace that way. In my mind, I heard the shouted, futile but bold words of my family's battle cry: *A Geraldine! A Geraldine!*

I knelt upon the mattress, dragging my skirts and the shawl. I crawled closer, my fingers gripping the handle so hard that my entire frame shook as I began to lift it.

I held my breath and positioned myself better to strike. I would awaken him now, to pass judgment on his brutal life.

Then a wheezing voice came from the depths of the black bed and the huge, fleshy frame: "You've come to bed at last, my dearest love, my angel."

■ ■ ■ ■

Part I

■ ■ ■ ■

My Youth

Love that doth reign and live within my
   thought
And built his seat within my captive
   breast,
Clad in arms wherein with me he fought,
Oft in my face he doth his banner
   rest . . .
And coward Love, then, to the heart
   apace
Taketh his flight, where he doth lurk and
   'plain,

His purpose lost, and dare not show his
   face.
For my lord's guilt thus faultless bide I
   pain,
Yet from my lord shall not my foot
   remove, —
Sweet is the death that taketh end by
   love.

   — HENRY HOWARD, EARL OF SURREY

Chapter the Second

*Maynooth Castle, County Kildare, Ireland
June 4, 1533*

I, Elizabeth Fitzgerald, called Gera by my family, descended from the famous and infamous Geraldines of Italy and Normandy, enjoyed early years of a protected, even pampered childhood before catastrophe came calling. The first day I can recount when my sweet security began to fall apart, I was barefooted and boating with my siblings on the River Lyreen in a craft of lath and tarred canvas called a *naomhóg,* as ever under the watchful eyes of our guardians Magheen and Collum McArdle. I loved to sail, even at that age, and rowing to me was so slow.

Born in January 1523, I was but ten years of age that day, the middle child of our brood of five, though I was ever being told — and scolded — that I was the most willful and talkative of us children. Mayhap that was to make up for my dear sister Margaret, age twelve, the eldest of us all, for she was deaf and dumb. Next came Gerald, age eleven, who would have been the heir to Father's earldom but for our older half brother, Thomas. Then came Cecily, age nine, and Edward, almost eight.

Oh, yes, my parents loved each other dearly in every way, to have a child nearly each year, but that was oft the way of Irish families. Why, even the poor folk, who could hardly feed their brood, had large ones. My mother, Elizabeth Grey, was the second wife of our sire, for his first, Elizabeth Zouch, a well-connected Englishwoman as was my mother, died young, leaving him with two children, including Thomas, Lord Offaly. He would someday be the 10th Earl of Kildare and, so we thought then, would also inherit his father and grandsire's title, lord deputy of Ireland, given by the English kings. Gerald and I — though I was younger than him and a female to boot — were the leaders of our little band.

"Row harder!" Gerald ordered as if we were Roman slaves and he emperor. Even Margaret could follow along easily today. She sat next to me and copied my pulls on the oar. We had a score of little hand signals we used between us, since she was deaf and dumb. She was learning to read, but that was slower going than we were rowing.

"No, you beef-wit!" Gerald shouted at his younger brother. "You're splashing me, Edward!"

"Leave off!" I challenged Gerald. "You are the one who wanted the tiller, and the helmsman always gets wet. You're acting like Thomas, always thinking of keeping his fancy garb clean and dry."

Despite Magheen's and Collum's coaching from the bank of the stream, we somehow managed to ram the prow into one of the swan nests made of mounded sedge and reeds. The big male swan appeared from out of nowhere, hissing and snorting at the McArdles. They shouted back in Irish at their fine, feathered attacker. My dear Magheen, who had ever been a nursemaid and second mother to me, flapped her skirt at it, then had to run. Finally, my lanky gray wolfhound Wynne came tearing down the path and chased the swan out into the middle of the water. We nearly fell overboard, holding our sides and screeching with laughter until we saw we were drifting away as fast as the angry swan.

"Row, me hearties!" Gerald shouted again, pointing back toward the tall tower of Maynooth Castle that we could barely see over the foliage of the beech forest. "Row or we'll be swept down to the Liffey and then clear to Dublin Harbor and so to England!"

"Stuff and nonsense," I muttered. "We'd crash over the falls at Leixlip Castle and have to swim for our very lives. All right, I'll count and we'll all pull together." I nodded to Margaret to encourage her. She always watched my lips when I talked, but I knew she could not have taken in all that, so I started to row as I counted, and she soon caught on. It wasn't fair, I thought for the thousandth time, that she could not hear and talk, when I liked nothing better than to eavesdrop and chatter. Everyone said that I was the pretty one too. Yet Margaret was the best friend to me in all the world, next to Magheen, because my sister Cecily was always going off in corners to read and sulk over I knew not what.

A deep, distant voice called to us as Magheen and Collum caught up to us again and we struggled against the current. It was Father waving from the bank near the lawn of the castle! He had come home from his duties in Offaly and had come to fetch us himself.

"*Slainte mhaith!* Good health to you!" The McArdles greeted their liege lord with a bow and a curtsy. Magheen and Collum were the keepers of the Irish brogue and ways, for our tutors were all English, though I more than the others loved to hear Magheen spin her tales of the little folk and the old Gaelic ways. Truth be told, our family, which ruled the Anglicized Pale, was more English than Irish in manners, speech, and dress. Still, Father's motto was, *Ireland for the Irish,* though I doubt he told such to the king and his court when he visited London.

But when this tall, broad-shouldered, handsome man — Father to us, but to kin and country Gearoid Og Kildare, Garrett Fitzgerald, 9th Earl of Kildare — spoke, everyone listened, and not just from fear, for we adored him. We promptly put the prow into the riverbank at his feet and scrambled out to greet him, though he'd been away but three days this time. Barking and cavorting, Wynne jumped about in mad joy at our excitement.

However powerful Father was in Ireland and England, too, he was above all warm and charming. He drew people to him not just by his position but by a natural esteem. I think that won him friends at first in the Tudor court. It was his downfall later, but I shall save all that for what is to come. Only our family knew Father's physical strength was not what it used to be. He had been wounded more than once in battle with Irish rivals, and that had taken a sore toll on him. He tried hard not to limp from a wound in his left leg from the last fray with the O'Carrolls, and on damp days he had trouble breathing from the long-healed slash of his chest by some would-be Gaelic assassin's *scian*.

It was said Garrett Og's first marriage was a love match, and I know his second was, for he and my mother were what Magheen called lovebirds. Father always had gowns made for his Bessie to match his court finery and even when he was away on business in his realm or when he'd been summoned by King Henry VIII to give account of himself in London, I know Mother slept with a small portrait of him beside her and kissed it each night he was away. I tell you true, for I had seen it.

In many ways, besides their fine faces and forms, my parents were well matched. Mother was the granddaughter of a queen of England, Elizabeth Woodville, wife of the Plantagenet king Edward IV. So she was intricately related to the influential Grey family of England, which descended from the royal Tudor sister of the current king. Indeed, my mother was a second cousin to

King Henry VIII, and Father, too, was connected through his first marriage as a cousin to the king. I tell you, whether we children were tutored in English or Irish, we were taught that we were the uncrowned royal family of Ireland.

"Father, we have missed you!" Gerald cried as we surrounded the big man.

"But you must not miss putting the boat back where it belongs," he said. No matter the occasion, he always pressed us to do our duty. We quickly shoved the boat back up into its hiding place, where a rain-swollen river or a passing fisherman would not take it from among the low-hanging willows. Then our raucous welcome truly began, with everyone talking at once.

"Gerald cheated when we played Skiver the Goose," Edward said as Father ruffled the boy's hair and patted Margaret, Cecily, and me on our flushed cheeks.

"If that is so," Father's voice boomed out, quieting the jumbled greetings, "I am sorry to hear it, for the Geraldine Fitzgeralds do not cheat, but they do speak their minds and are ever ready with an answer or a defense. Gerald?"

"I only peeked once before I poked him, Father, and if I hadn't I might have hurt him with the stick."

"Gerabeth?" he asked me, using my pet name that only he and my brother Gerald used anymore. As ever, I thrilled to have his attention, but I know now he reckoned I would always tell true, even to my own disadvantage. Margaret, of course, had never spoken, and Cecily would tat-tale everything Gerald and I had done amiss while he'd been gone. I tried to throw the best light on my brothers' spat that I could.

"They had a bit of a disagreement, Father. We all had our eyes closed, so I can't say. But we all pulled together in the boat."

"As it should be. Now," he said, seeming distracted and looking back at the McArdles, "I have news for my family and retainers, so you are to join your mother and Lord Offaly in the great hall to hear of it. Your uncles have ridden in with me too."

An entire family gathering of the Fitzgerald males, I thought. Father had five brothers, all younger than he, of course, since he was the earl. Lord Offaly, our half brother Thomas, our elder and our better, was oft here, but what was this occasion? I wondered. I straightened my skirts and pushed back my flyway red hair, which had come loose in a torrent, and tried to remember where I had put my shoes.

I should have worn a straw hat, I suppose,

for my skin was milky and freckles could pop out on my nose and cheeks in a trice. And Thomas, even more than Father, believed in looking one's best at all times. I'd overheard Thomas tell Mother I'd be a raving beauty someday, but she'd best watch that I didn't turn into a saucy hoyden. It had taken me nearly a fortnight before I dared ask Magheen what a saucy hoyden was, because she would pry out of me where I heard it and I feared that it was something frightful.

We children stretched our strides to keep pace with Father as we, all barefoot, ran along in the grass just off the gravel lane toward tall, gray-stoned Maynooth Castle, our main residence in Kildare County. It stood — still stands, though much the worse today — like a stone sentinel amidst almost six hundred acres of fields, forest, and the largest deer park in all Ireland. We were eleven miles from Dublin, at the gateway of what was called the Pale, the civilized area over which Father ruled — with permission of the English kings, of course, though we'd all have much favored independence and equality. But Father's power kept the best peace to be hoped for with the Gaelic chieftains still so warlike. As for pirates oft pillaging the coastline, well, that was more trouble.

When Father whispered something to them, Magheen and Collum rushed ahead of us, Collum pulling Wynne along by his collar as they climbed the staircase from the first-floor entry, probably to fetch Mother or our guests from the living quarters overhead. Maynooth was already centuries old and had been built for fortification, so the rooms were stacked in a tall tower. The Church of St. Mary's and the College of the Blessed Virgin Mary of Maynooth, the latter which Father had founded, were attached to the castle. Within the courtyard behind the castle were domestic buildings where servants slept and supplies were kept.

The castle itself was richly furnished in fine style. The chamber I shared with my sisters had rich, imported hangings and Turkey carpets and overlooked the forest to the river and fertile fields beyond, some planted in rye, some peppered with black sheep. Out the other side we could see the market town of Maynooth, which also supplied many of the castle's needs.

But on this ground floor we entered, cool and vast and usually peopled only by Father's reeves and reckoners, lay the great hall, the place of ceremony and administration of Fitzgerald power, a place that awed us all anew as we followed him toward it today. We had dined here ceremonially on a dais and we children had stood at the side sometimes for investitures or pronouncements, but never had we been summoned so suddenly. Others were gathering too, from some of our kin to squires and even a smattering of liveried *galloglass*, Father's armed foot soldiers who guarded him when he traveled but seemed to melt into the walls at Maynooth.

Our still-bare feel felt the cold stone floor as we walked through the eastern side of the great hall, which oft served as a waiting room for petitioners, then as we entered the formal area with its wall buttresses and central line of pillars. There our five uncles joined us and, despite the evident solemnity of the occasion, bent or knelt to give us hugs and greetings. Uncle James, the eldest, who was most like Father, and whose Leixlip Castle was barely four miles away, was my favorite. They were all wed; what fine times we had at yule or on St. Patrick's Feast Day, when our families were together. Such strapping, fine-looking men, James, John, Richard, Oliver, and Walter — I can yet see their ruddy faces, their blue-green eyes, and hear their boisterous voices, though muted for this mysterious occasion. Too soon their smiles from seeing us sobered that day at Maynooth.

A shiver snaked up my spine when I saw Thomas, his handsome face marred by a frown as he looked everyone over as if he would bid on a new horse at the fair. He stood off to the side, finely arrayed in half armor and a rich green surcoat, one booted foot upon the elevated dais with the two carved chairs set under the crimson-and-white silken banner with the Fitzgerald crest. Thomas had soundly smacked Edward once for laughing at the chained ape upon the crest. We had all learned well the story of how a tamed ape had once preserved the Geraldine line by snatching the infant son of Maurice Fitzgerald, a thirteenth-century Earl of Kildare, from his crib during a fire.

But, Father had said, the ape then dangled the baby over the parapet of the castle. Father said the story should warn us that one who seemed our savior one moment might turn to traitor, though we could trust the Lord Jesus himself and Mother Mary. And, I always added silently, certainly Saint Brigid of Kildare, whom Magheen said watched over us all. Ah, I could recite entire prayers to Saint Brigid, the saint of healing and fertility and protector of unwed maids, my favorite prayer to her being, *Saint Brigid, spread above my head your bright cloak for protection.* Little did I know then how much I would need that and how much she would betray me.

An expectant hush fell that day in the great hall as Father and Mother came in and took their high-backed, ornately carved chairs. In the hush of concern and anxiety, Father stood and motioned Thomas closer to him.

"The king of England, His Majesty Henry the Eighth by grace of God," Father's voice rang out, echoing . . .

I dared for one moment to think we would have a royal visit. Or surely the king had not died and left his kingdom with no heir but a daughter, Mary, whom my mother had once attended before her marriage. Besides, King Henry had dared a divorce — hardly popular in Ireland — and to wed a Protestant. Now everyone awaited the birth of his hoped-for son by that second queen, the seducer and shrew Anne Boleyn.

". . . has summoned me to England to give account of my duties here and in the Pale," Father announced. "The king is most displeased that I have seen fit to move his ordnance and armaments from Dublin Castle to be stored here at Maynooth, which

I believe is my right, and sound judgment too." He cleared his throat, suddenly looking nervous instead of confident. "I am praying," he added after a pause, "that I will not be detained in England, as has happened before, while I explain my strategies and rights to the king and his chief minister, Thomas Cromwell."

Twice Father had been held against his will while answering such a summons, but then I'd heard him jest that he would never have met either of his lady wives had he not been kept about the court there. Before any of us were born, he had been years away at times, as if King Henry held him hostage for the Pale's good behavior.

"Is Mother going too? All of us?" Gerald whispered beside me as we watched Father draw Thomas closer to his side.

"And so, in my absence, I am naming my heir, Thomas Fitzgerald, Lord Offaly, as deputy governor of Ireland, and overseer of all Geraldine affairs."

"Oh, no," Edward muttered at my other side. "He'll order us about and slap us too."

"Sh!" Cecily hissed.

Thomas made a flowery speech about how he would uphold Geraldine pride while Father was away and keep us all safe from outsiders. I suppose he meant the Gaels beyond the Pale, but he might have actually meant the English too. Everyone listened raptly, including one man I saw shaking his head. It was Christopher Paris, our foster brother — not because he was adopted but because he had been fostered out to our family by his own.

Fosterage was one way, Magheen had told me plain, that powerful families kept the loyalty and control over lesser ones, who then owed them money and fighting men. Foster brothers were treated as family members, for the relationship was an honored and almost sacred one. Christopher was nearly thirty, older even than Thomas, and had been with the Fitzgeralds long before I was born. He was the constable of Maynooth Castle, with the duty to keep us supplied and safe. But I knew he had dared protest to Father that the extra firepower on the premises made Maynooth less safe, not more, though I had not the vaguest notion how he could reason thus.

As both Father and Thomas spoke, I saw Mother's lower lip quiver. She blinked back tears and kept her head held high, so I did too. All of us, but my dear Margaret, of course, soon swelled the hall with the shouted battle cry that Thomas, soon to be deputy of Ireland in Father's stead, himself led: *A Geraldine! A Geraldine!*

Father summoned each of us children to him separately that evening, in order of our birth. Mother sat beside him in his favorite room, the library, which boasted one hundred and twelve fine volumes or manuscripts in Latin and, of course, mostly Irish or English on all sorts of subjects. With the college he had founded and this library, Father hoped to raise the level of education in our land. We had oft sat at our lessons in this room. The library was a special place, for it housed in a filigreed silver box *The Red Book of Kildare,* a precious family heirloom kept current regarding our history and lists of land and household possessions and the names and records of those loyal to the cult of Kildare, as Christopher Paris had called it once.

As I approached the door to the library, I heard Father telling Mother in the sweetest voice, "Bessie, Bessie, my love. This too shall pass, and I will be back home before you know it. I've dealt with Henry Tudor before."

"But I've seen him turn on those he once favored. The years I served the princess Mary — before she was declared bastard and exiled from court and his affections —

30

CHAPTER THE THIRD

It was but a month later that the next stone fell from the protective wall Father had built around us. It was high summer, and the rain had stopped for once. Magheen and I, with two armed *galloglass* trailing us as always, were riding back from Maynooth village, where her sister lived, wed to a cobbler. We rode sidesaddle, of course, as was proper, though I'd have liked to mount like a man and ride like the wind. Riding fast and sailing — the loves of my life, and I a mere colleen.

I recall that it had recently struck me — for I daresay I was a precocious child both in body and brain — that the village of Maynooth was more than just a forest and a field away. By that I mean its merchants, smiths, and shepherds seemed aeons back in time. The village folk still left milk out at night for the little people, scraped hoarfrost from the fields to cure headaches, nailed horse-

he had coddled her, favored her, even spoiled her."

I knocked and was bidden to enter. The room was lit by a large lantern and several candles; their flames flickered as I passed. I knelt before Father for his blessing, as I had done many a night before bed. Dry-eyed but pale, Mother clasped her hands hard together and bit her lower lip. I bent my head and closed my eyes.

"My dear, quick, and bright Elizabeth, our Gera," he said as his big hand rested on my head before he lifted my chin so I looked up at him. "Never forget the proud heritage of the Fitzgeralds, who stand tall for all Ireland. Guard your tongue and your maidenhood over the years, for you will be the beauty of us all, the best of those who have come before. Rise now, child, for you must never give obeisance to anyone but the Kildare earls — and to the Tudor kings, of course. Never forget that if only Ireland could truly be for the Irish, you would be an Irish princess, and worthy of the title."

He said all that in a rich, soothing voice but for the mention of the Tudor kings, and then his words were bitter, like nettle juice curdling milk.

"Obey your mother and help with the others," he continued. "When you are able, protect those less fortunate and blessed than we. And pray God I will be home soon, before all the rogues in Ireland come knocking on Maynooth's door to court you."

He smiled as he said that, his teeth flashing white against his brown beard and mustache before he got a bit of a coughing fit. I thought he would dismiss me then, but as I curtsied and turned reluctantly to go, he seized my wrist and pulled me to sit on his knees in a hard hug. He smelled of wind and forests and freedom.

"There," he said with a kiss on each of my cheeks as he held my face between his huge hands. "Bessie," he told my mother, "I know you think she favors your family, but she's a russet-haired, green-eyed Fitzgerald through and through." As I got to my feet again, his voice broke into what we always called "the brogue." In a way it was our family's second, secret language. "Ay, I'll be telling meself while I'm away, 'tis sure as rain our Gera be doing us proud; there's no denying it." The speaker's voice always lilted through the words and went up at the end as if asking a question, and I had a hundred questions I dared not ask that night.

My feet felt like stone as I walked away. Father's voice was hoarse and almost breathless as he gave the old Gaelic farewell,

32

"Go raibh maith agat," which meant, "May it go well with you." At the door to the library, I looked back at them, holding hands, but with their eyes still shiny on me. I forced a smile and made a jaunty wave. But I would have screeched like a banshee had I known I'd never see my father again.

shoes at their thresholds, and fell on their knees before a new moon, however staunch attendees of Mass they were. Holy wells abounded, with pennies and pieces of metal tied with scraps of rag dangling above them, some the little people had supposedly dug, so what was really holy and what old pagan practices? Slowly, I knew, the power of the Fitzgeralds would bring even the poor folk to prosperity and peace.

"Mother of God," Magheen cried, crossing herself as she pointed ahead at a wolf that slunk across the road from the beech forest up ahead. Our mounts shied, but we calmed them. "Bad luck, and that's for certain," she muttered. Magheen always pronounced *mother* as if it were *mither.* She was full of old folktales too, which could entrance me for hours. Cecily had no use for such but was always sneaking chivalric romances, which she had been forbidden to read until she was at least twelve. So Gerald would not tat-tale on her, she bribed him with her share of sweets.

I was grateful I had not brought my wolfhound, Wynne, today, for he would chase a wolf until he dropped. "Bad luck only if the wolf is hungry," I said, "though he looked beset too."

"Too, aye," she said, crossing herself

35

again, and, shaking her head, added, "and the leprechauns in the ditch have gone silent."

I knew she meant the frogs, but I wondered what had affrighted them, for they oft croaked day and night this time of year. It was as if something dire floated in the morning mists off the rye field. Yet we saw no more wolves in the stretch of forest, and soon the gray stone tower of the castle came into view. As we turned up the lane, Edward came running toward us across the lawn, scattering the sheep cropping grass.

"He's in the Tower!" he shouted, gesturing like a windmill with one arm as if we were to hie ourselves inside. "Father's in the Tower!"

"Oh," I said, bursting into tears of relief, "he's come home! No wonder we didn't hear from him. He was busy telling the English king to mind his realm and let us alone, and then he had to catch a ship to hurry home."

I had dismounted and turned to run into the castle when Edward grabbed my arm and spun me back. I saw his tears were not ones of joy but of terror. "No, sister," he said. "I mean Father's in the Tower of London, where the crown criminals go and sometimes get their heads cut off, so I heard

36

Thomas say."

I gasped. Thomas was here. And Father locked away like some wretched traitor in a deadly place. Mother had told us about the Tower of London when she'd explained how large and impressive that city was. I tore inside and took the stairs up to the solar two at a time. Mother's voice, strident and sure, not broken as I had expected, mingled with our half brother Thomas's angry tones.

"I can help by going to the English royal court, I tell you," Mother argued as I hesitated just outside the solar door. "I have contacts there, the Greys, especially my brother, Lord Leonard."

"Father had intimates there too, and what did it get him?"

"But I'm the king's second cousin by blood —"

"Blood — that's what they're after," he interrupted, but she went on.

"Thomas, I'm pure English too, so mayhap they will listen to me. How dare they say Garrett Og, Earl of Kildare, grows too powerful! He needs to be strong if he is to keep the Gaels at bay and control the Pale. He's helping Ireland, not harming it!"

"The Tudor will stop at nothing to have his way, mark my words. My lady, by this move King Henry has tried to cut Father off at the knees so —"

"Don't talk like that! The Tower's a hell-hole of torture and cutting off more than legs. No, I must go to my brother, leave the children safe at his country house in Leicester; then at court I can —"

"You must not take your children out of Ireland, away from Maynooth. The king would surely like to get his hands on them too, just to keep Father and me in line. I say you should not even go, and I'm the one in command now. Action needs to be taken here, though, to show them that they can't cow us. I've ordered Christopher Paris to double-provision the castle and set up more guard posts, lest the English send an army looking for me or even little Gerald. I trust them not — any of them."

"Thomas, please do nothing rash. Calm negotiation, that's what's needed, not some sort of defiance your father would be blamed for, please!"

I leaned against the wainscoted wall in the corridor, my legs shaking, tears dripping off my chin, my stomach ready to heave up the buttered biscuits and blackberries I'd over-eaten in the village. I slid down the wall and huddled there, my arms clasped around my bent knees, pretending Father was hugging me like he did the last night he was here.

Magheen found me and tugged me away to my room, where we told Cecily and even Margaret about Father, through acting him out being locked in a room and pacing there. I played Father's part, pretending to stroke my beard and frowning until I was certain Margaret understood. But, by Saint Brigid, I did not understand, except that I was on both Mother's and Thomas's sides. To get Father back, we should sail to England, ask the king nicely for his release, then, if he refused, storm the Tower of London to rescue him, all of us together: Thomas, my five strong uncles, and those loyal to the Geraldines.

It was a wretched winter, waiting, hoping, praying. Mother pleaded with the king by letter through her brother Leonard, while Thomas fumed and cursed and rode about the Pale with a growing band of men, stopping at Maynooth now and then to confer privily with Christopher Paris.

We were desperate for word from London, though we did hear that King Henry's wife, Anne Boleyn, had not fulfilled her queenly duties any better than her predecessor, Queen Catherine of Aragon. For the Boleyn had been delivered not of the desired son, but of a girl, Elizabeth. So I shared with that princess of England a first name, and had Father been crowned king here as he should, I'd have shared her title of princess too. I was fiercely glad the English king was disappointed in her birth, for, like me, she was not one to hold the promise of future power.

Then too, word came once that Father was dead, but — thank the Lord — it was but rumor. Still we heard he was gravely ill in the dank, dark Tower, coughing up blood, while we all felt guilty for enjoying the splendid tower house he had made for us. Father's declining health convinced Mother she should go to England in the spring of 1534 to visit and intercede for her beloved husband, no matter what Thomas said. She was defiant and nothing could convince her else. She planned to take her children with her and leave us at her brother's estate, called Beaumanoir, but the week before her departure both Gerald and I fell gravely ill.

'Twas feared we had the dreaded small-pox. Mother called to me from out the door of my chamber, lest she catch the pestilence, which would keep her home. Gerald was in another room, both of us tended by villagers who had survived that oft-fatal scourge. Physicians were summoned, and we were dosed. I knew naught of all this until later, for my fever was so high I was out of my mind. When it was certain we had some sort of spring sweat and not the pox, Magheen tended me, and Collum stayed with Gerald. I was barely strong enough to hug Mother farewell when she left for England with Margaret, Edward, and Cecily, with promises that Gerald and I would join her soon. I was grief-stricken to see them go. Yet if she could free Father, it would be worth anything.

But two months after Mother left, about the time when Gerald and I thought Thomas would send us and the McArdles to England, our world shifted again. Thomas, unbidden and unbridled, stomped into the Irish Parliament in Dublin and sealed all our fates. June 11, 1534, it was, a dread day, though we foolishly cheered, "A Geraldine! A Geraldine!" at first when we heard what our bold brother had dared. Our uncles came to tell us that Thomas had ridden into Dublin with a force of nearly eight hundred foot soldiers and a hundred and twenty horsemen who sported green silk fringe upon their helmets, a favorite flourish on our half brother's garb. And for that, Thomas was forever after called by the nickname Silken Thomas.

Word of the next events came to us from various messengers or from one of our uncles riding in to confer with Christopher. Striding into Parliament, Uncle James said, Thomas had thrown down the Sword of State and, because of King Henry's attacks on the Catholic Church in England and his divorce of Queen Catherine, declared the English king a heretic who did not deserve Ireland's allegiance. And he had defiantly proclaimed, "I am none of King Henry's deputy. I am his foe. I will render Ireland ungovernable unless the Earl of Kildare is sent back to us forthwith!"

Instead, God help us, the king of England sent an army of twenty-three hundred men under the command of Sir William Skeffington, a hated former lord lieutenant of Ireland. Because he had been lately in charge of King Henry's armaments, he was known as "the Gunner." Though I was yet still young, I could reckon one thing in this tightening noose of events over which I had no say or control: If someone called Silken Thomas had to fight someone called the Gunner, who would be the victor then?

14 December 1534
My dearly beloved children Gerald and Gera. I deeply regret to share dreadful

42

news that your father has passed on to a better life two days ago. It was of natural causes, my brother assures me, and my lord has been buried within the walls of the Tower in a small church called St. Peter in Chains. I shall think of Saint Peter and Saint Patrick greeting my beloved at the gates of heaven, though nothing comforts me. At least I was allowed to visit and tend him in his last days. At court, I desperately tried to plead his cause. And, of course, he took all of our love with him and knew we would carry on and support Thomas, now 10th Earl of Kildare.

Children, I fear your sire, my dear lord, lost heart from his imprisonment and from fretting over the current rebellion in the Pale. I have asked again, in letters both to the new earl and to your uncles, that you two be smuggled out of Ireland, if it comes to that, and sent to me and safety at your uncle Leonard's estate here in Leicestershire. Edward, Margaret, and Cecily send their love and miss you sorely too. Uncle Leonard says we all are welcome here. He sends his regards and deepest regrets to you.

This letter must be sent by secret means, so I pray it reaches you before word of your sire's passing. I am devastated by my loss but will go on for all of you.

Your mother, Elizabeth Grey
Countess of Kildare

I burst into tears when Christopher Paris read the letter to us. He too looked grieved. "I feared such," he muttered, almost to himself. "I'd be sending you both to your mother today, that I would, but the new lord won't allow a bit of it."

Gerald and I, both crying, held hands. "Thomas — I mean, the earl — won't let us leave?" Gerald asked.

"Too dangerous, he says. Then, too," Christopher added, his voice taking on a sort of mocking tone, "says he, 'Now that I am Ireland's uncrowned king, we can't have the Irish prince and princess fall into the English king's hands, now, can we?' After all, anything happens to Thomas, the new Earl of Kildare, till he has a son of his own, you are next in line, Gerald — the heir. A clever one, Thomas is, though a bit of a headlong hotspur, eh?"

I could not believe Christopher would dare to criticize Thomas, though now I see through more mature eyes that our foster brother did resent our half brother's high-handed ways. And I had heard Christopher say once that but for a mere accident of birth, he too could have been a powerful man's heir. But then I was also shocked when I heard that two of our five uncles refused to raise men for or join the uprising of Silken Thomas and just stayed home.

At St. Mary's Church next to the castle, we held a quickly called memorial service for Father, yet it was packed with retainers and local gentry as well as most of Maynooth village. After the priest's closing benediction, Thomas stood up and added, "My father, Garrett Og Fitzgerald, the ninth earl, was the second coming of Brian Boru, Ireland's brave eleventh-century warrior who won kingship of Ireland. Boru died at the Battle of Clontarf after shattering the Viking hold on our beloved land. Though my father died in a foul English prison and left his task undone, I shall shatter the English hold on our beloved land."

Everyone cheered and applauded him, but I was angry with Thomas that day. New earl or not, leader of the rebellion or not, granted, firstborn son of my father's first family, why did it sound as if only he claimed our father, when Gerald and I mourned for him too?

If the so-called Fitzgerald rebellion and

Father's loss were not enough to grieve us, it soon became clear that the arrival of the English army showed who was truly for the Irish cause and who was not. Despite Thomas's army numbering seven thousand, his siege of Dublin Castle, where many loyal to England were holed up, failed, mostly because many of the so-called Anglo-Norman families of the Pale took one look at the English might and were only too happy to stay neutral or even loyal to England.

Thomas's main force was made up of family members, retainers, and tenants of our lands and those kin loyal to them. In short, it was most of those listed in *The Red Book of Kildare*, which had been moved for safety's sake out of its silver box in the library and hidden with several sacks of silver coins in an empty vat in the wine cellar below the great hall. At least the inland Gaels, whom Father had managed to keep in line, delayed "the Gunner" Skeffington's army with their raids. Thomas's forces fought the king's invaders too, but the Irish loyal to him kept falling back in a hard-fought campaign through the bitter winter and into the spring of the next year.

As I was approaching my eleventh year, Magheen said I seemed much older. I tried to take on the mistress's duties in the castle, copying things I'd seen Mother say and do. But then, in mid-March it was, from the top tower rooms we saw the English army swarming toward Maynooth like a plague of black ants.

It was just skirmishes and light arms fire around Maynooth at first. Sometimes Thomas, who knew the area far better than the invaders, still sneaked in and out at night by a tunnel that connected the wine cellar to the river near where we had hidden our boat. He had recently ordered the tunnel redug, for it led to the river water supply that had helped the castle survive a siege in the fourteenth century, before the inner courtyard well was dug.

But when the English army encircled the castle, Christopher told us he had blocked and obscured the river entrance and Thomas came no more, though we knew he had gone to raise reinforcements to defend Maynooth. Christopher was fully in charge now, even of the garrison here that owed allegiance to Thomas. I could see Christopher reveled in his power, despite the dangers. He ordered Gerald and me about much more than Thomas ever had. But at least we had some firepower to fight back, guns and ammunition Father had seen fit to bring here from Dublin Castle.

I felt deserted and scared, but I was also a Fitzgerald and kept my head held high. I was helping my half brother and three of my uncles, who were commanding the Irish troops, I told myself. During those days when our tutors and most of the castle musicians had fled and I hadn't seen Mother for so long, Magheen was my teacher, and I became more Irish, more fiercely independent, and, however terrified, more bold.

"I'll be telling you, your mother wouldna approve of you wearing your hair loose all the time, that she wouldna," Magheen scolded me one day while we worked side by side, making beds. "Nor are you wearing the proper petticoats, and your skirts drag."

"Magheen, just take a look at how we're living," I said with a sweep of my arm around the room. We had moved the living quarters for the castle's women to the top tower room, for we hoped cannon fire could not reach us here. Our wool-stuffed mattresses on the floor were cheek by jowl, and we had extra foodstuffs piled everywhere. Outside, sheep, cattle, and horses had been brought into the inner courtyard, and the smell of them drifted clear up on the breeze at times. The castle's fine furniture had mostly been made on site in the rooms below, since the staircases were too narrow for them to be carried up or moved. I told myself and others we were doing our part to live a bit crudely, for weren't our Fitzgerald forces sleeping on the ground?

"I just wish I knew what was going to happen next, and I wish I could help fight," I told Magheen as I leaned my elbows on the narrow window ledge, looking out over the lawn and fields where the siege cannons were being set up.

"Stuff and nonsense. Women don't fight — at least that way."

"I would like to find a way. Won't Thomas attack them from the rear before they start pounding us to pieces? And are my uncles safe?"

"Did you never tell her of the prophecy then?" Sinead, one of the chambermaids, who was helping, asked. "About the ship to England?"

"What ship? What about a ship?" I demanded, rounding on Magheen. I loved ships, and my dearest delight was to sail in one of any size. "Have you heard something of an escape that Gerald and I weren't told?"

"No, my colleen. Just a prophecy from the

old days, nothing to fret for, and Sinead can just learn not to flap her lip, that she can."

"If it's just a story, no harm in telling me," I insisted. "You know I love the old tales."

"By Saint Brigid!" she muttered, but she gave me an answer anyway. "Just that someday five earls will be carried to England in a cow's belly and never return."

"In a cow's belly? Though my uncles be earls in their own regions, Thomas said last time they are being careful never to be together these days so they cannot be rounded up like cattle — in a cow's belly, indeed!"

It was then, that very moment, and I can even recall what I was looking at — Magheen swatting Sinead out of the room — that the first cannon blast against Maynooth battered all I had ever held dear.

CHAPTER THE FOURTH

March 22, 1535

"If Lord Thomas doesna come with more troops soon," Magheen muttered, "Maynooth will be rubble."

"You must not say or even think so," I protested from my perch on a wooden barrel where we all huddled in the cellar below the great hall. "Thomas — the earl — said the castle withstood a long siege a hundred years or so ago."

Collum said, "Not against King Henry's new artillery, overseen by the Gunner. And not with no reinforcements on the horizon."

"We must all be brave," Gerald put in, trying to keep his voice steady. It had not yet lowered to a man's tones and sometimes came out reedy and shrill. "Thomas will surely come with an army and make them leave us be."

The crash of cannonballs had tormented us day and night, nigh on a week of it. My wolfhound, Wynne, had barked at each blast at first but now, brave stalker of game though he was, he kept close to me and whimpered. The early, defiant cries from our castle garrison of "A Geraldine! A Geraldine!" had become more sporadic and finally silent as our supplies of powder and cannonballs dwindled.

Christopher had been dead wrong about the guns not reaching where we women had been living high in the tower. Amidst rubble, dust, and the acrid smell of gunpowder from a direct hit, we had lugged what foodstuffs and bedding we could salvage to the dim, dank cellars. Yet even down here, the rumbling of cannon seemed to shake our very bones while our nearly one hundred men fired back. During the day, even Gerald, guarded by Collum, sat with us women, waiting, wondering what would happen next.

Though but thirteen years, Gerald was feeling the burden of being the heir of Silken Thomas, the rebel 10th Earl of Kildare. Christopher had informed us more than once that he had orders from Thomas to help Gerald escape to safety through the tunnel if the castle walls were in danger of being breached. At least the fact that Gerald was still here made me feel better.

"I think," Gerald said, rising to his feet as if that would make us heed his words the more, "I should be able to parley with the English in my brother's place, or at least help fight."

"I am constable here," Christopher announced, appearing behind us before we saw him. "And I outrank the heir or the absent earl right now; there's no denying it. We are cut off by an impressive force, if I do say so mcself. I had not fathomed the might of the English king to send so great an army and armaments against us. Perhaps we be more important to him than we had learned to think," he added with a bit of a swelled chest. "But, Gerald, I shall be sending you off straightaway when it gets dark, or the earl might have my head, and I hope to find a way to preserve it and all we have left. Collum, best be packing some things for the lad, as you'll be going with him to my kin in Donore till the coast be clear of the English and we can spirit you away to the continent."

"Clear to France or Italy from whence the Fitzgeralds came?" Gerald asked, looking awed, while my stomach twisted to think of being separated from him. I saw Magheen and Collum exchange a quick look. As far as I knew, they had never been parted and, like my parents, were a love match. But neither said one word in protest.

"Will I not go too, and with Magheen?" I asked, jumping off the barrel and standing next to Gerald to face Christopher, who shook his shaggy head.

" 'Tis enough of a gamble, two escaping into the night when we're surrounded, but not four — and not two females to slow them down. The English be wanting to get their hands on the earl and the heir, Gera. Should they ever take Maynooth, you'd be but sent to your mother; I am certain of it." He dismissed me with a wave of his hand and stalked out before I could argue further.

That very night Christopher's plan — the part of it he had admitted — came to fruition. Gerald donned a shepherd's hooded cloak and carried a staff and a pack of food on his back, and Collum much the same, though he had a knife and a matchlock pistol. Gerald waited at the door to the tunnel while Collum said a quick farewell to Magheen. I tell true, I had not shed tears since the bombardment of Maynooth began, but I cried now, silently, for my dear guardians' and my parents' separations, and for my being parted from Gerald. For as I have written here afore, though Gerald and I had our spats from time to time, we had forged a friendship too.

"I will see you when I can, Gerabeth, when things simmer down a bit," Gerald promised, blinking back tears and holding tight to my hand. He was trembling, just as I. "Christopher is going to put out the word I have the pox and have been sent away to be tended at an undisclosed site to avoid panic."

How foolish to think our people — and our enemy too — would not panic when he came up missing, I thought, but I said only, "I wish you were being sent to our uncles or kin, not to Christopher's family."

"Collum said the same, so mayhap . . ."

Gerald raised both reddish eyebrows and put his finger to his lips, as we had so oft done to avoid saying something in front of Cecily that she could tat-tale to Mother. Gerald squeezed my hand before Christopher pulled him away. In the wan lantern light I saw tear tracks glistened on Magheen's face as she gave a final wave to her husband. She came to me, and we stood arm in arm to see our dear ones swallowed by the maw of that dark tunnel. One of Christopher's most trusted men, fully armed, led the way, and Christopher himself, stooped down, thrust a cobweb away and brought up their rear.

About an hour later, I realized with wonderment that the siege guns had gone suddenly silent, as if mourning the loss of not only Father and Mother, my sisters and Edward, but now Gerald too. Despite Magheen, the others around me, and the garrison defending us overhead, I had never felt more alone.

"Wake up! Gera, wake up!" Magheen whispered, and shook my shoulder. She was on her knees beside me. I ached all over from sleeping on thin straw and floor stones, but I came instantly alert. And realized the guns were still silent on both sides. Bodily and emotionally exhausted, I had fallen into the first solid sleep I'd had in days. Then I remembered — Gerald and Collum were gone.

"What is it?" I asked, my pulse pounding as I elbowed myself to a sitting position. Wynne raised his big head as he lay beside me.

"Some sort of truce, I hear. One of the garrison told a cook 'tis some sort of arrangement between Christopher and the English."

"He didn't give them Gerald as a hostage, did he?"

"Sh! I'll be getting in trouble for so much as warning you, but no, wasna that. A strange man just came through here with a lantern, looking in every corner of the cellars, searching for Gerald, I think, so the English must be searching the castle for him. The stranger said with a snort, 'Only women,' and went back upstairs."

"You should have wakened me. Maybe it was a man brought in to talk about Christopher's terms to get Thomas a pardon, and he wanted to see whether Gerald or Thomas was here."

She shook her head. "By Saint Brigid, there's worse news."

"What then?" I whispered.

" 'Tis not yet dawn, and the fog's thick as pudding outside, but 'tis said Christopher indeed got Gerald and Collum away, then sent his man with a white flag to speak to the English general."

"That's what I said. He's found a way to parley with the —"

"No. He's invited more than just one of the English in, that he has."

"It was a flag of surrender?" I gasped. "To the Gunner?"

"We've let you sleep several hours, but we've been praying Thomas gets word and that there's to be pardons all 'round. But

57

the garrison man told the cook that our braw constable Christopher be taking money for it too, as well as the enemy's promise that he can remain in command."

"Better Christopher than the whoreson English!" I hissed, using one of Father's curse words. Ignoring Magheen's gasp at what I'd said, I shoved my feet into my shoes.

"Wherever are you going? You must stay hidden here."

"I'll not. Only a girl, not the heir, I know," I said, getting to my feet and pushing past Magheen, who made a grab for my skirt. I could hear Wynne's claws scrabbling on the floor as he fell in behind me like my shadow. "Stay here!" I ordered Magheen instead of Wynne, and let the dog follow me upstairs. I looked tousled and wrinkled, but I had to know what was going on.

I climbed halfway up the narrow, twisting stairs to the great hall and, with a sigh of relief, saw a man in Fitzgerald livery on guard there. Torches set in wall sconces blazed above him, throwing dancing lights.

"Where is the constable?" I asked him. "I am the last Fitzgerald here of the family he is pledged to protect, serve, and obey, and I must speak to him."

"I'll send word soon," he told me, frowning. "Now 'tis not the time."

"It is the time!" I insisted, not backing off. "It may be past time." I didn't give a fig if this man was now loyal to Christopher and not my father or even to Thomas. "I demand that you call my foster brother here at once."

Christopher must have heard my raised voice, for in full body armor — but no longer in Fitzgerald livery — he clattered down the stairs toward us, his sheathed sword scraping the curved stone wall. His shadow cast by the torches loomed long over me.

"I'll not have you unsettling the ceremony being prepared upstairs," he told me, and pointed with his mail-encased right arm down the steps the way I'd come. "Look at it this way, Gera. You'll be leaving here and seeing your mother and the others soon, no denying it. Everything's arranged. We're to be pardoned, the earl too when they find him, though I warrant he'll be cooling his heels in England for a time. I've arranged it all, and I'll remain in command of Maynooth."

"And you believe them?" I demanded, hands on my hips. "After they've been trying to blow us to bits, you believe them?"

He put one foot up on the stair above

where he stood just as Thomas had on the dais the day Father passed the control of Maynooth and the Pale to him. I could tell Christopher's choler was up, for a telltale vein beat in his forehead. He gritted his teeth. I knew he wanted to cuff me down the stairs, but I didn't blink an eye, however much I was forced to look up at him. He said, his voice mocking, "Since you be a saucy meddler in men's affairs and a military field commander now, think on this. Are they wanting to consume more time, money, and munitions? The Gunner is an old man now, and ill too."

"You've seen his face? You met with him? Did you really let Gerald go, or did you hand him over too? Everyone knows the English like hostages for surety."

"Now it's reminding me of a howling woman you are, mourning at someone's funeral, when I've saved the day for all of us. If the earl had arrived with troops, it might have been different. Now get below, and I'll be sending for you when I make plans for your departure to England."

He pointed again as if I were Wynne, who stood beside me growling low in his throat. For one moment I wished the wolfhound would spring at Christopher, but I took the dog's collar and pulled him back down the stairs. Our foster brother had become someone I didn't know, someone lusting for power and control, just as Mother had said of King Henry.

I reveled in the fact that the English tyrant must be distraught that he had a second daughter but no legitimate son, only a bastard by one of his mistresses, a Bessie Blount — which showed the Irish what a lecher Henry Tudor was, gossip said. Worse, six years ago that son, Henry Fitzroy, Duke of Richmond, had been but ten when he'd been named viceroy of Ireland, with Skeffington as deputy. And the ultimate insult: Rumors had been about that King Henry would name his bastard son king of Ireland, an outrage and a sham, Father had said. And after all these years, with no strong son to inherit his throne, perhaps King Henry lusted even more for power and control, and that was why he wanted to subdue our Ireland. But I must write down what came next at Maynooth before I lose heart.

It was the wee hours of the morning, a dark and rain-swept one, according to the same garrison guard who now stood at the bottom of the stairs to our cellar sanctuary. Even the walls of the castle, I thought, seemed to weep. How had it all come to

61

this so soon, Father dead, Thomas who knew where? Mother and my brothers and sisters far away . . .

We heard trumpets overhead, then a shuffling followed by sudden cries, shouts, and running feet. A bit of clashing steel — swords on armor? Our guard ran up the stairs, his armor clanking. Had Christopher at the last decided to resist? I told Magheen to hold Wynne and peered up the stairs again. Our Irish guard was nowhere in sight, but a tall, half-armored pikeman stood at the top of the twisting staircase, his back to me, facing the great hall. I could hear an echoing hubbub. I darted back where the stairs made the turn, pressed myself against the stone wall, and listened. Wan, flickering light from moving torches above made it seem the stone walls and stairs were shaking.

A voice I did not know — not an Irish voice, an old, crackly one I had to strain to hear — was giving orders. I gasped when I took the words in, falling to my knees on the stone stairs and pressing my hand over my mouth to keep from screaming or vomiting.

"Yes, every fourth one of the lickspittle rebel Irish to be executed, the traitor Christopher Paris first!" the speaker shouted.

"Hang the bag of Judas silver 'round his neck so he takes it to hell with him. What he has done would sicken any brave soldier, and they'll all be made example of. We'll call it 'the Pardon of Maynooth' when we write King Henry. Line them up; get it done. Hang him and leave his body there; then behead the others. We'll show the entire Pale that the king of England means business with traitors — traitors to us and even to their own kind, the damned double-dealing Irish curs!"

Christopher had surrendered the main stronghold of the earls of Kildare into English hands, and yet they meant to execute the constable and one-fourth of the garrison, nigh on twenty-five men? And beheadings? That was what the English king did to enemies in the Tower of London, and now in our tower here.

I heard shouts overhead, protests, armor clanking. Men's voices cursing, some crying for mercy, perhaps the very sounds of doomed men in hell itself. That man's words — no doubt "the Gunner" Skeffington himself — were so dreadful that, after the initial shock, they could not quite sink in. Curse the English king!

What of us women, then, huddled in the cellars? When word of this got out to Irishmen, would they not all rise to arms or would they cower in submission? For once, I was almost glad that the women who had been seen and dismissed downstairs were apparently of no account. Perhaps they thought the third Geraldine daughter was also with her mother in so-called civilized England.

Not to panic the women, I went back downstairs and pulled Magheen aside and told her what I had heard. She turned ashen, crossed herself, then walked away to tell the other women only that they must kneel and pray that the earl and his forces came quickly. But once they began to mumble their prayers and I started back for the stairs, she nearly dragged me into the darkest corner of the wine cellar, a separate vaulted area where Gerald and Collum had slept lately.

"Despite what Christopher has done, I am going upstairs to plead for their lives," I told her, trying to free my wrist from her grip. "Surely they will not hurt a mere girl, and maybe I can shame or stop them."

"And see all that? At the least, you'll not let them be taking you too, the murderous wretches. What if they try to trade your life for Gerald's, or even for the earl's? They're heathens, cursed of God. You and I, my child, be going out that tunnel lightning-quick to the village, where my sister can hide us."

Something struck me then — an awareness, a certain clarity. It was as if I emerged from the fog of childhood, or as if someone had pulled a hood off my eyes so that I could see the sky, to soar like a falcon, for that was Saint Brigid's sacred bird. Even in my hatred and horror, I saw Magheen was right: that I had to flee, to fly away, not only for myself but for the future of the downtrodden Geraldines.

"Yes," I told her, amazed at the sudden calmness of my voice despite the great weight upon my heart, "we must flee so we can tell the truth, maybe find Thomas. But we can't risk going into the village, because Christopher said the English were quartered there. Fetch our cloaks and anything else you can quickly gather. And give me your apron, because I'm going to take *The Red Book of Kildare* with me under my skirts, lest they find it. If they get their bloody hands on that, they'll know exactly who to hunt down and execute in the entire Pale."

Looking both proud and terrified, Magheen untied her apron, yanked it over her head, and thrust it at me.

"And fetch Wynne's leash," I told her as I

65

started to pry the lid off the vat that held the book.

"Gera," she said, turning back. "No — from now on 'tis Lady Fitzgerald," she said, emphasizing each word. She had never called me that before, nor had she curtsied to me when it was just the two of us, as she did now. "But, milady, two women fleeing with their heads covered might make it to your uncle James at Leixlip or to Dublin and find a boat to reach your mother, but not with an Irish wolfhound in tow. Wynne is too protective, a barker, and folks hereabout know he's always at your heels."

She spoke truth. Another bitterly hard decision: I must leave Wynne too. Only Magheen and I must go on the run like criminals, mayhap with a hue and cry out for us soon. We had no time to waste, though no doubt all above were concentrating on the bloody executions. Damn Christopher Paris, once one of our family, constable of our castle — a fool, covetous for power, now paying the price.

I tried to tie the apron around my waist in a sling up under my skirts, but I saw the book would bang against my knees, so I bound the crimson-covered treasure to my chest and swirled the cloak Magheen brought me around my shoulders. One bag of coins lay in the vat; perhaps Gerald and Collum had taken the other. I thrust the bag in Magheen's hand and she put it in our food sack. Clasping the book to me, I led her behind the group of praying women toward the tunnel.

Wynne padded over to me. I bent and, one-armed, hugged my beloved pet around his neck, then for one quick moment buried my face in his thick hair. It was like saying farewell forever to my pretty, pampered past again. "I love you, my Wynne, so much," I whispered, and choked back a sob, for that was so true of all I was forced to leave behind.

I saw Magheen had summoned Shauna, her own cousin, from the women praying fervently with bowed heads. Magheen must have chosen her to tell the others to keep our secret. Magheen pressed Shauna's fingers around Wynne's collar, and I whispered to that alert, eager face, "Wynne, stay. Good lad, stay!"

Dear God in heaven, how I wished that I could stay and relive my days and dreams here. Magheen pulled my elbow and swept aside the hempen curtain covering the tunnel entrance. We had no time for candles or a lantern and could not risk drawing attention by a light.

It was black as Satan's soul inside. I had been through here several times, once when all five of us were pretending we were pirates, but we'd had a lantern. Magheen went first as we both felt our way along the damp, earthen length of it. Cobwebs laced themselves across my sweating, tear-streaked face. It smelled more fetid than a bog.

"What if they know about this escape route because of Christopher going out to parley with them?" I whispered. "They might have a guard at the other end."

"Our only chance," she said. "Oh, Saint Brigid, spread above our heads your bright cloak for protection."

I had to keep talking. It helped me beat back the blackness to face my fears. "We may be trapped in here, if he boarded it up again," I said.

But from this stale, rank place — had it been like this for Father, with his labored breathing and fatal coughing fits in the Tower of London? I wondered — we began to smell fresh air. And from the lack of all light, I saw grays emerge. Could we be at the river entrance? Already the dark journey seemed eternal, but it had just begun.

CHAPTER THE FIFTH

Though dawn was just pearling the sky when we emerged from the tunnel, at first it seemed midday to us. Blinking at the brightness, as Magheen started down the path I whispered, "No! We'll take our boat."

"But they used barges to drag supplies up the river," she protested as she turned back. Like me, she kept her voice low, fearful someone would spring at us from behind the big beeches or the shrubby wood beyond.

"But that was before the siege, and now they are intent on their bloody work at the castle. It will be faster to float to Uncle James at Leixlip, if he's still there and not under siege too, but they must have wanted Maynooth above all."

Indeed, the English must be concentrated at Maynooth, for no one walked the river path at this early hour, and we children's *naomhóg* awaited under the newly sprouted willow boughs. It saddened me to see the double sets of oars we had used and the tiller Gerald had steered. I carefully placed *The Red Book of Kildare* in the boat's belly before we shoved the craft into the river and clambered in. As ever, the current took us away. Sitting side by side on a wide seat, Magheen and I rowed together to go even faster.

With tears in my eyes, I saw Maynooth's tall silhouette swallowed by the fog. The sedgy banks of the Lyreen, the familiar fields, the few crofts and cots between the castle and the village seemed to rush past. Despite our speed, I felt stunned, mired in the unreality of it all as if my feet were stuck in a bog. But I needed to think — think clearly!

"We should both lie down in the boat when it goes past the village," I told Magheen. "English soldiers may still be there, or someone may recognize us and call out."

We pulled our oars inside and lay in the bottom of the boat, staring up into the mist as the spring sun ate slowly through the fog. It was but four miles northwest to Leixlip, then twelve beyond that to Dublin, if we needed to go that far.

What to do? Though Magheen was much

my elder and had been my nurse and guardian, I was the Geraldine, the one who
needed to make adult decisions now. Should
we stop at Leixlip and inquire for Uncle
James? Father had a town house in Dublin,
but that could be ruined or overrun by the
English. If we could get our boat past the
small waterfalls near my uncle's estate, we
could reach the point where the Liffey burst
into Dublin Bay. But with the English fleet
anchored there, could we find safe passage
to Uncle Leonard's estate in the English
shire of Leicester? And once we were across
the Irish Sea, how would we travel to Beaumanoir, which lay not on the water, but
almost in the heart of enemy England?

As we passed under overhanging tree
boughs and saw the familiar swallows and
kittiwakes going our way too, the sky grew
ever brighter. I imagined I smelled the
gorse-scented air of early spring, though we
were barely past mid-March. I pictured the
glens near the Lyreen and the Liffey with
golden furze breathing out its clove scent,
my favorite out-of-doors aroma. I fancied I
smelled peat fires from the village, for I
wanted to take every memory of Maynooth
and Kildare County with me and —

Magheen sat straight up in the boat. "Do
you smell that on the breeze?" she de-

manded, craning to look back toward the village. "Smoke. A fire. The brightness we just passed. The village is burning! The English bastards have put it to the torch! *Antragh, Antragh!*" she kept keening, rocking with her head in her hands. "Too late, too late!"

Our boat swept on, but I could see she was right, for gold and orange flames slashed into the early morning sky behind us. Magheen's sister and her family — all those she and Collum knew and loved. The market square, the shops, the houses of wattle and thatch. Did the English have to ruin everything? Did they intend to obliterate all the Fitzgeralds had owned and commanded? And without our family to keep the peace, would Gaelic raids increase or would civil war split our land? The Fitzgeralds had been able to keep the English out, and now here they were, stomping on all of us with their brutal boots.

As if I were her nurse and comforter, I held the sobbing woman to me as the current pulled us on. I knew how desperately my dear friend wanted to run the boat ashore and rush back to see if her family and friends had escaped, to help any way she could. But I also knew she would stay with me to the very gates of hell, and I loved her all the more for that. High- and low-born barriers be damned; Magheen McArdle was more my mother in that moment than my birth mother, granddaughter of an English queen, had ever been.

That afternoon, as we passed through the glens of the Liffey with their mossy rock ledges leaning overhead, I felt closed in by fear. We were sitting in the boat but not wearing ourselves out with rowing in the brisk current. When necessary, we pushed away from rocks with the oars. But where were we really going and what must we do to escape the Gunner and his men?

"Saint Brigid has let us down," I told Magheen, who was still wiping her eyes and nose with the hem of her skirt.

"That be blasphemy! We're alive and away from the fiends, are we not?"

Eager to keep our strength and spirits up, as if I were a child — which was not possible ever again — I asked her, "Will you tell me anew the story of Saint Brigid's cloak?"

She nodded and sniffled. Her voice was muted at first and, after all her tears, she hiccoughed through the first of it. "There be dozens of stories of miracles and wonders the blessed Brigid did after she received the veil from Saint Patrick himself. Like you, milady, she was a chieftain's daughter, and young when duties first fell to her."

I let her talk, perhaps the best diversion from her pain, and mine too. As ever, she went off on side stories now and then as I watched streams pouring into the river, swelling its width and depth.

"Though she traveled far and wide as abbess in her nunnery," Magheen went on, "Brigid hosted gatherings of important people and intervened in disputes and brought peace to warring factions."

Which made me think, if she did all that, why did she not do the same now for those who venerated her? But I held my tongue and nodded to urge her on.

"As you recall, she accepted a site near Kildare for her small community from Dunlang MacEnda, king of Leinster, and built a church there. But she required extra land for farming to support her people. When the king refused, she said ever so sweetly to him, 'Just give me as much as my cloak will cover,' and, of course, he agreed to so simple and small a request. But as she laid her cloak upon the ground, it began spreading till it be covering the entire plain. 'Tis amazing what a lot the Lord can do with what little we give Him."

"And she was bold enough to risk challenging and besting a king," I said almost to myself. Yes, our Saint Brigid of Kildare would not have gotten what she wanted if she had railed at him. She was clever to the core. And so would I learn to be if I ever met the vile English king or any of his reeky, hedgepig, murderous lackeys.

We had more trouble than I'd thought getting the boat safely out of the water and up on a stony bank just above the waterfalls where our gentle Lyreen joined the Rye Water to birth the big River Liffey. I secured the *Red Book* to my chest again and hid it under my cloak. We ate what soda bread we had left and drank from the flask of ale Magheen had brought. The roar of the falls was soothing, almost luring, and that gave me time to think.

"We have two choices," I told Magheen as she bent to fill the empty flask with river water. "One, I follow the rocky path and you let the boat loose over the falls, and I try to snare it on the far side so we can get clear to Dublin town to find an Irish ship to England. Or we go on foot from here, first to Leixlip Castle, hoping to learn whether my uncle or some retainer of his we can trust is in the area and can assist us. And," I said, getting to my feet and shaking out my skirts, "I think we need to go on foot. With our village put to the torch, there may be women on the roads now anyway, or those put out of their houses by the quartering of English troops."

"Thinking clear you are, milady. All right then, off we go. May Saint Patrick and Saint Brigid be our guides."

I knew the path from the falls to the castle, for we had visited here many a time and played about the grounds. Leixlip Castle somewhat resembled Maynooth, a gray stone structure, but it perched on a rocky outcropping of limestone in the wide valley. It too had a crenellated tower, but a round one, and not so high as ours.

Though I was tall for my age, surely a mere girl mingling with some local folks to overhear what had happened here would not be overly suspicious. But we went not twenty strides toward the castle gate when I saw that the English soldiers were here too, though not the swarms of them we'd seen outside Maynooth. Their horses were bigger than our Irish breeds, and that gave them away, as well as the horrid pennants flying from the castle walls. In place of the usual crimson-and-white Fitzgerald banners, I saw green-and-white pennants with Tudor roses and some sort of mythical beasts.

"Beasts, all of them," I muttered.

"What's that, milady?"

"Best go back to calling me something else hereabouts. Call me Shauna."

At least other Irish were about, some pulling carts, evidently provisions for the castle. When we approached the guarded gate to the castle's inner courtyard, I walked slowly past as my bravado evaporated. I could not let them take me or my precious book. But then I saw a face I knew, a rhymer who had been at Maynooth but whom Father had loaned to Uncle James, since he liked the epics of the Irish past so dearly. Liam, I think. Liam the rhymer.

"Magheen, go talk to that man there with the green cap. See if his name is Liam, a rhymer, and what he can tell you about Uncle James. But tread carefully. If Christopher sold out, who knows who else has done the same."

"Aye, I remember him, a bawdy one with the kitchen maids, he was," she muttered. While she sauntered after him, I stood against the outer castle wall and watched her talk earnestly to him. To my disappointment, without so much as a glance my way he walked toward the path she and I had come up from the river. Taking her time, though I was so impatient I could have screamed, Magheen strolled back my way.

"It wasn't him?" I demanded, crestfallen.

"Oh, 'twas, and don't you be telling me Saint Brigid be letting us down again," she scolded. "It seems since your uncle didna take direct part in the rebellion nor put up a fuss when the English demanded use of his castle, they merely turned him out and took over. He's sent his family to relatives in Meath, but he's secretly living in that very forest by the falls we just came through, though deeper in, at his hunt lodge, and Liam knows the way."

I sucked in a sigh of relief. So easily accomplished? Had the tide turned for me? But what dreadful news I had to tell Uncle James. I beat down my anger that he'd handed this area over to the bastard English, but he had no armaments with which to fight, and we'd heard he'd pledged all his men to Thomas's army.

"Will Liam take us there now?" I asked. "Do you think what he said can be trusted?"

"Do we have a choice?" she countered. "Come, then." She began to whisper even more, so I almost had to read her lips. "He's awaiting us just off the path to the falls, and I tell you again, Lady Gera of Kildare, that Saint Brigid of Kildare is holding her cloak above us."

It was all I could do to walk slowly instead of run. I could have hugged Liam the rhymer, for he led us directly to a place where one of Uncle James's men dropped from an oak tree and blocked our way, then led us on into the thickening forest. Father and Gerald had been to the hunt lodge, but never any of us women. After we told the two men what had happened at Maynooth, Liam said but one thing. I have always remembered it, though it meant naught to me at the time: "Even Ireland's little people — leprechauns and fairies — are not immortal or important, but they too weep and die."

More men guarded the small hunt lodge. Someone summoned Uncle James, who burst through the front door with his arms open wide when he saw it was truly me. Thanks be to God — and yes, Saint Brigid — I was in the strong embrace of my favorite uncle, telling him the terrible tidings from our castle and the village too.

Living in a small but cozy hunt lodge in the woods, I saw three months blur by. It was a blessing to be with Uncle James, who sorely missed his family too and reminded me so much of Father. He sent secret word to my mother that I was safe and would be delivered to her as soon as possible. Finally, we heard through Uncle James's covert communications that Gerald and Collum were not with the family of the traitor of Maynooth — part of Christopher's plan to betray us all, I feared — but that Thomas's sister, Mary O'Connor, was hiding them at her home, from whence they would be passed on to others until they could escape to France. Magheen and I rejoiced when we heard that good news.

We also learned that Silken Thomas, whose name was on everyone's lips, had been bested in battle and was in hiding too. Once things had turned against him, many had deserted his cause and crept to their homes, hoping to claim they were loyal to England. Yet we heard nearly a hundred were tracked down and imprisoned or executed. I felt so torn about Thomas: I admired his defiance and bravery — or was it all foolhardiness and bravado? He had not been patient or planned well enough. Father had used his personal charm and negotiation skill for years, and Thomas had exploded it all in one brash act.

In the sweet summer weather — for the green, green beauty of Ireland blossomed no matter the perils of politics — a letter was smuggled in from Mother, bemoaning that the English were calling our uprising not the rebellion of the Irish but of the Ger-aldines. She wrote that she feared for all of us and was endeavoring to earn our way back into the English king's good graces.

When I read that, I thrust the letter into the flame of the single lantern at the hunt lodge. No matter how chilled we were, we lit no hearth fire that would send up smoke. I frowned as the letter turned crimson-crisp on its edges, then burst into flame as I dropped it in a pewter dish on the small table.

"Best to burn covert correspondence, I suppose," Magheen muttered as she bent over her needle and thread to take in the seams of a plain russet gown for me, one Uncle James's men had brought us over these long weeks.

I almost told Magheen that Mother had turned traitor too, to want to appease England's killer king, but I held my tongue even with her. Uncle James had also preached peace to me, insisting that the English might was too forceful to fight. But he had praised me for taking *The Red Book of Kildare* when I fled. It lay wrapped in a thick sheepskin under the floorboards of the lord's bedchamber he had given to me and

Magheen the first day we'd arrived.

I was ready that very warm mid-June day to take a walk in the woods, guarded by a one-eyed man of Uncle James's retinue, when a knock sounded on our door. "Enter!" I called out, and my uncle swept it open to rush in. He held in his hand another letter, one that must have come for him in the same packet as Mother's. His smile lit the room as he picked me up and spun me about madly.

"What? What? Tell me!" I shouted as Magheen clapped and jumped up to dance a little jig. "Gerald is free in France? Everyone is pardoned?"

"Maybe neither or maybe both — soon!" he said, and put me down. "The Gunner has died of some disease, and in his stead King Henry has named your mother's brother and her host, Lord Leonard Grey, as the new deputy of Ireland! A man of the Kildare clan by blood ties will soon be here in the Gunner's place, God curse his black soul!"

"Is King Henry mad, or has he changed his mind toward us?" I cried. My pulse pounded, and I could have soared.

"It seems he's extending an olive branch," Uncle James said, as he bent over the letter to skim the words again. "Of course, Lord

Grey knows Ireland, for he was here over twenty years ago as marshal of the English army. This appointment has been made by the king's henchman Cromwell. Perhaps the loss of life at Maynooth was the price Thomas paid for his rebellion, and Lord Grey will patch things up now."

"Oh, I pray so. No doubt Mother has beseeched him and even the king to make amends for us." I regretted that I'd just burned her letter. After all, I'd recently decided clever, covert ways might be the best path to revenge.

"But here's the next thing," Uncle James went on, his handsome face aglow. "A truce with your five Fitzgerald uncles in attendance! All five of us have been invited to meet your uncle Leonard at Kilmainham Castle in Dublin next month as soon as he arrives. So, my pretty, your Irish and English uncles shall be there to put things aright."

"And Thomas?" I asked.

"I don't know. I hear he's holed up somewhere, but perhaps at Kilmainham we can sue for favorable terms for him. Everything is possible now, including a safe way to send you to your mother. We'll take you with us to the castle, and Lord Grey can send you to her. Finally, finally, a way out of this wretched situation!"

"See, Magheen," I said that night in bed, quite late, for we had all sat up to celebrate. "That is sheer superstition about five earls going to England in a cow's belly and never returning. I warrant Mother did manage to pull some strings to at least pretend to mend things with the king who as good as killed her husband and ruined her castle. She no doubt used her court connections, clever deceit, even feminine wiles; I just know it."

"Best you not think such, milady, for it would be too easy and too dangerous with your fair face that's blooming to maidenhood now and will flower full over the years. Beauty is as beauty does, you know, so best leave both the peacemaking and plotting to men."

I still felt I was spinning with joy and, for once, didn't fear I'd have my frequent nightmare of being trapped in Maynooth's cellar in a small boat afloat in a river of blood with heads bobbing in it. Nor was I in the mood to heed Magheen's subtle scolding or superstitious stories. Five earls in the belly of a cow upon the water, indeed! And Saint Brigid's cloak growing so large it covered acres of land?

Nor did I believe in turning the other cheek when one — and one's entire family and people — were sore smitten. Even if the king of England gave us back Maynooth on a silver platter, made reparations for those slaughtered, and pardoned every last Fitzgerald to boot, someday, somehow, I was going to make him pay.

CHAPTER THE SIXTH

July 1535

I was so thrilled that I could hardly sit still on my horse as we six Fitzgeralds with several retainers and guards were passed through the English-guarded gates into Dublin town. Dressed in a fine peach-hued velvet-and-brocade gown trimmed with golden ribbons and a gauze cap lined with pearls, I felt like the princess Father had always said I should be. My attire was a bridal gown that belonged to Uncle James's daughter, one of my many cousins, one who had been wed at age fifteen. With its tight bodice and tiny waist, it fit my slender form perfectly.

I only fretted that my cloak concealed the gown's grandeur from the people who recognized us or heard we were coming and carefully, quietly, from alleyways or upstairs windows, cheered us on our way with the familiar cry, "A Geraldine! A Geraldine!"

They dared not make much ado, since English soldiers were about in the cobbled streets. But one man's voice called out as if in warning, "Remember the Pardon of Maynooth!"

Dublin town always amazed me with its tall, protective walls and cheek-by-jowl tumble of buildings overhanging narrow streets. I could smell the sea from here, and terns and gulls screeched overhead. The big bay lay beyond, sadly, we had heard, now crowded with English ships. How I had loved the several times Father or Uncle James had taken me sailing on the bay. I had reveled in the toss and sway of the big ship and wished I could help steer her myself. Now I wondered how Father's fine town house had fared, but I dared not ask.

"Today at the banquet we are to attend," I had heard Uncle Walter tell his brothers, "peace will be bargained for and the future of the Fitzgeralds and of all Erin settled for years to come." We could only pray that, since our family had helped keep the peace for nearly a century, it would be settled in the Fitzgeralds' favor.

Our party clattered through a great park and up a gravel lane toward the venerable old castle of Kilmainham with its nearby Saint John of Jerusalem Knights Hospitallers' priory. Lying on land south of the Liffey, the castle had long been the residence for the English viceroys in Ireland, so it seemed the right place for this conference today.

But above all, I was excited to be with my five Fitzgerald uncles, for they were the ones who now represented my father, the former earl, and Thomas, the current earl, albeit he was in hiding with a price on his head. Surely, all of that would be rectified today. Uncle Leonard had recently arrived with English reinforcements and several more ships, yet I had no doubt he would want a truce. I knew full well that Christopher had been rash and wrong to be overly certain that the English would parley at Maynooth so they would not have to spend more money and time in what I had heard they called "wild Ireland." But with the Gunner dead and Uncle Leonard charged with calming the Pale, praise be, the outcome now partly hung on family loyalty, not just politics and power.

Yet something else made me feel important today. For the first time in my life that I could recall, Magheen was not with me as if I were some child to be tended and corrected. Although she was coming to Dublin later today, she was back at Leixlip, packing what things she could assemble for our voyage to join my mother, which had been arranged through messengers between my English uncle and my Irish ones.

And, with my petticoats wrapped around it, Magheen was enclosing *The Red Book of Kildare* in the false bottom of my specially made traveling chest. Even if the English knew of its existence, they might assume it was with Gerald and not with a young woman, a colleen, as the village folk would say. So that was one of the few benefits, as far as I could see, of my feminine gender. Although I did miss my family, I was loath to leave Ireland. Still, I had always wanted to sail the Irish Sea, so I tried to buck myself up.

As the six of us dismounted, Uncle James helped me off my palfrey and gave me a wink. "With our Fitzgerald brains and brawn and your beauty, Lady Gera, we shall win the day."

We were greeted by one of Uncle Leonard's lieutenants and escorted into a banquet chamber with a fine table laid out, even silver saltcellars and glass goblets. Servants and guards with yeomen's halberds stood about, and then we heard men coming, boots on the stone floor. Flanked by at least a dozen men, Uncle Leonard Grey — I as-

sumed it was he, and he did vaguely resemble Mother — entered through the
arched entry.

Yet as he looked us over, he seemed a
hawk of a man, with sleek brown hair and
slanted eyebrows over sharp, gray eyes. A
blur of bows and greetings followed; for a
moment I was lost in the hubbub of tall
men. Finally, Uncle Leonard, lean and
angular in physique, turned and looked
down at me. He clicked his bootheels and
nodded as his eyes took me in.

"Ah," he said, his voice a bit breathless, "a
lovely young Geraldine."

I curtsied, staying down until he raised
me. His fingers were thin but strong; he kept
hold of my hand. "Your mother has missed
you greatly, Elizabeth," he said. After being
called Gera for so long, I started at the
unfamiliar use of my real Christian name.
"You certainly favor her," he went on, turning me about once as if to assess my merits,
"but are even more . . . indeed, more radiant with that gold-red hair and your sea
green eyes. A rare beauty indeed, though
yet a maid, and I have promised your
mother, among other things, that I will
dispatch you to her forthwith."

How relieved I was — I warrant we all
were — to hear he had promised Mother

certain things. "Uncle," I said, smiling up at him, "we are glad you are here to make peace for us and with us."

"Ah," he said, loosing my hand. "My dear, would you be terribly distressed if I asked to speak with your uncles privily? I shall see you are feted in a chamber just off this one, and your Irish maid has been sent for. The very ship that brought me hence is returning on the morrow, and I will have you on it. Men's business, king's business, here now, you know."

I must have looked crestfallen, for Uncle James stepped forward and put his arm around me. "It's for the best, Gera," he told me. "Fitzgerald business too."

I did not want to leave them, but I knew I must obey. I curtsied to each of my Irish uncles and then to Lord Leonard Grey again. A tic jumped at the side of his narrowed left eye, where he had a puckered scar. Surely I could trust this man. He had taken my family in and given them safe haven and was sending me to them. He had the king's power on his side and had come to help mend a dreadful, bloody mess by negotiating with my Irish uncles.

Fighting back tears of disappointment at my dismissal, I followed a woman who had suddenly appeared from a side room and gestured to me. Why had not Uncle Leonard introduced us? He was speaking to the others already, and I had been as good as forgotten.

Inside the small chamber she led me to, a sumptuous table was set for one, so she must not be eating with me. She introduced herself simply as Alice, and I discerned at once from her voice that she was English. She was dressed too well to be a servant. Suddenly two long-eared lapdogs sleeping on small pillows in the room cavorted about her feet, which made me miss Wynne terribly, and for a moment I did not trust my voice. I sat at the table as she uncovered several succulent dishes for me.

I was amazed at the array of food for just myself but realized these were the same delicacies the men must be sitting down to, so their grandeur comforted me. Mackerel in gooseberry sauce, huge prawns, ale cake and carrot pudding and a Venetian glass decanter of ruby red wine.

"This is one of my favorites, milady," she said, indicating a small silver tureen. "Poached sea urchins, hedgehogs of the sea, we English call them."

Before I could stop myself, I blurted, "And *we* Irish call them *granneog na farriage*."

Alice's brocade gown bespoke wealth. Was she of my uncle's household? I had a spate of questions to ask, but she took the dogs, one under each arm, and left me.

And I heard her lock the door.

I jumped up to be certain I was locked in. Yes, curse it. The latch would not budge. I pressed my ear to the door but could hear nothing, not footsteps nor voices. Did Uncle Leonard think I would interrupt their king's business? I wanted — I needed — to trust him, but this reminded me too much of being shuffled off to the Maynooth cellars while horrible things happened. Someone had called in the street earlier, *Remember the Pardon of Maynooth,* and that was no pardon at all.

My blood hammered in my head, and I could hear my heartbeat. Breaking into a sweat, I darted back to the table and seized a fruit knife. Once Gerald and I had put one of his pet snakes in Cecily's sewing box in retribution for her telling Mother we had stuffed ourselves with pilfered yuletide comfits. And we had gotten into the pantry where Cecily had locked her box and books by sticking a knife point in the lock, then twisting and jiggling it.

I worked like one possessed to move the mechanism and free the lock. Finally, something clicked. The latch lifted. Would they have a guard at the door? I poked my head out and saw no one. Again, a female, and a young one at that, was of no concern to them, even if she be a Fitzgerald, fearful but spitting angry.

It seemed the nightmare of Maynooth again. Men's raised voices, the clank of sword on armor. Cries of protest: "Deceit! The worst sort of betrayal!"

I tore down the corridor toward the banquet room as Uncle James's voice rang out: "We came in trust and faith! Can you not honor family ties, or is there no honor left in England?"

And my English uncle's distinct voice cutting through it all: "Put them in irons! Their cells are prepared. The king has ordered you to London to face charges and —"

I had silently cursed Thomas, Earl of Kildare, for losing control and not biding his time and reining in his hatred, but now a raving fury took over my body and voice. Holding up my skirts, I ran into the hall where guards were dragging out my uncles. James and Walter were already manacled behind their backs.

"No!" I shrieked, and launched myself into Lord Leonard from behind. He did not go down but was thrown forward, nearly to his knees. A guard grabbed me about the waist and yanked me back, twisting my wrist until I dropped the knife I realized only then I still held.

But I wasn't to be cowed. "We came to you in peace at your invitation!" I screamed at him. "We are related by marriage and blood! Stop it! Let them go!"

My English uncle did not even deign to answer but, with a jerk of his head, had me carried away, thrashing and shouting. I was shoved back into the room where I was to have feasted — or be poisoned, I knew not — while the male Fitzgeralds were as doomed as my father had been — no doubt as Thomas would be. When the guard seized the other two knives from the table and slammed the door on me, I could not help myself. Cursing with every vile word I had ever heard my father or Thomas use, I threw dish after dish of food and Venetian glass against the door, then beat my fists upon the walls and fell to sobbing so hard I could barely breathe.

Later, much later, the guard opened the door and stepped in, nearly slipping in the mess I'd made on the floor. "Aye, milord, she seems ready to listen now," the man announced, and Uncle Leonard stepped past him into the room. His boots gritted through broken glass as he entered. I sat in the far corner from the door, a heavy pewter candlestick in my hand like a battle mace.

"Put that down and grow up, girl," he said. "Some things are not fair, but it's the way of the world."

"The way of the king of England and those who serve him, perhaps."

"Judas priest, do you not think your father and uncles fought underhanded when they had to? Do you think Gearoid Og Kildare or Silken Thomas just asked for power and it was given them — or that whoreson foster brother of yours who gave Maynooth over to Lord Skeffington? But I am sorry that you had to see all that — and act like a strumpet when you must learn from your mother to be a lady. It will take you much farther in life."

"I don't want to go to a land where your king rules."

He snorted and sat down, both warily and wearily, I thought, across the table from where I sat with the candlestick, a pitiable weapon against him and his men.

"Elizabeth," he said, sitting up a bit straighter and resting one arm on the empty table as if to prop himself up, "your maid will be here soon and you are sailing tomorrow and will be delivered to your mother and siblings, where I hope you will learn to be a good influence on them all and they on you. With your remarkable beauty and pluck — properly controlled, of course — you will do well in great Henry's England."

I wanted to curse great Henry, England, and this man, but, as I had reasoned out before, honey might catch more flies than vinegar. Sometimes I truly wearied of everyone remarking on or reacting to my physical form and face as if there were naught beneath all that. Yet both Magheen and this man had suggested I could use my fair countenance as a weapon over the years, maybe to climb high, maybe to reach the king and his family so I could finally have justice for my kin and country.

"I am not a monster, my girl," he went on, though his frown made him look like one. "I am a widower who would like to wed again. I am a good brother to your mother and enjoy having her children about my home. I care deeply for your fatherless family and want you to rise high, as befitting the royal heritage from which we descend. But let me add one thing, should you yet want to gainsay my orders." He sat forward in his chair and pointed a thin finger at me like a threatening schoolmaster.

"You did, you know," he said, "attack the

royally appointed deputy of Ireland with a knife in your hand, so I could make a fuss over an attempted murder charge and leave you here in a cell awaiting trial for, oh, who knows how long? That would be one alternative to your not wanting to go to England."

I hated this man, my uncle. He had dashed my fervent hopes for help and healing. But I knew when I was beaten — at least for now. I dropped the candlestick on the floor, where it thudded dully onto the sweet rushes strewn there.

"Good," he said, smacking his palm on the tabletop. "King's orders that the Fitzgerald men come to London for questioning and, hopefully, your half brother, Thomas, too, when he sees the futility of holing up like a trapped animal in the middle of a wood, just as I hear you and your uncle James did. Oh, yes, we are fully aware of where Silken Thomas hides within his moat and entrenchments. You know," he went on as he rose and went to the door, "I rather fancy a woman with spirit, but not when she gainsays me, and it's the same with Henry Tudor, so remember that. I'll send Alice for you again. She'll take you to a room, where I suggest you and your maid get a good night's sleep when she arrives."

Was he insane? After all that had happened here today, let alone since Thomas threw down the sword of state in the Irish Parliament and cursed the king? I wanted to say something dreadful to him, but nothing seemed bad enough — or safe enough, now that I had pretended to capitulate so I could learn how to play a woman's game. I was not yet grown, but maidens were contracted to wed at my age, though they were not bedded. Maybe I could eventually seduce or wed someone I could convince to help me kill the king.

"And, Elizabeth," he said just before he rapped upon the door for it to be opened by the waiting guard, "don't think for a moment that you can get word to Thomas or any other rebels that your uncles can be rescued from here. The five of them are going to England on the morrow too, earlier than you. At break of dawn they are sailing like precious, sent-for cargo in the hold of a ship called the *Cow*."

I gasped. *Five earls . . . in the belly . . . of a cow . . . upon the sea . . .* But that silly superstition ended, *never to return again*. For the first time in my life, I fainted.

■ ■ ■ ■

PART II

■ ■ ■ ■

My Maidenhood

The soote season, that bud and bloom
  forth brings,
With green hath clad the hill and eke the
  vale;
The nightingale with feathers new she
  sings;
The turtle to her mate hath told her tale.
Summer is come, for every spray now
  springs . . .
And thus I see among these pleasant
  things

Each care decays, and yet my sorrow springs.
— HENRY HOWARD, EARL OF SURREY

CHAPTER THE SEVENTH

As our English ship, the *Swiftsure,* bucked the waves, I insisted on tending Magheen myself. I wiped her sweat-damp brow and carried slop buckets, for she was sore stricken with mal de mer. I myself reveled in the tilt and roll of the great, creaking wooden vessel, for it made me feel alive again. Since I had seen my uncles dragged away, I had lived in a sort of shell, but this sea voyage, and now Magheen's needs, had brought me back to myself.

"Gera — milady," she whispered with a groan, "grateful I am for your help but I'd best be left alone. I had no notion sailing could be like this — aaah."

"I'll not leave you, for you did not desert me when I was —" I began, but when Alice came back in with fresh linens, I stopped in midthought. Though the woman was overseeing the care of both of us, I could not forgive her for locking me in the chamber at

103

Kilmainham while my uncles were penned in like cattle being taken to England in the belly of the *Cow*. And how did I know this woman was not a spy? I saw Alice had also brought another woman with her, who began to care for Magheen.

Alice Stinchcomb had finally explained she was from Uncle Leonard's household at his estate of Beaumanoir. She had been brought to Ireland with him to accompany me until I was delivered safely to my mother. Through Uncle Leonard's wife's long illness, Alice had been her maid. She was a comely woman with shiny black hair, dark brown eyes, and quick, birdlike movements. Perhaps to make amends for her initial treatment of me, she shared tidbits about my family, my mother's nervous fits, how my siblings' schooling was faring when, I must admit, my book education had been lacking of late. She thought Cecily "a bit standoffish," a novel way to put my sister's snippiness, I thought. My heart softened toward Alice a bit when she told me things she had done to amuse poor Margaret, who missed me dreadfully — that was Alice's very word for it — dreadfully.

I was surprised Alice was allowed to take her two spaniel lapdogs everywhere she went; my uncle did not seem the sort to have permitted that. Most lady's maids would not be allowed such, but perhaps they had been the pets of my aunt Eleanor. Posy and Pretty were ever underfoot and, once again, made me miss my Wynne, who could have covered those two little yippers with both front paws.

I had decided that being kind to the spinster — Alice admitted she was nigh thirty with no husband or family — would be good practice for what must come next. I must learn to tolerate, mayhap even cultivate the English so I could earn my way into their trust. That way I could climb the ladder to reach the king or his men — his vile henchman Thomas Cromwell, for example — and find a way to wreak justice for all the Fitzgeralds.

"Magheen just wants to lie there," I told Alice while the other woman changed the sheets on the narrow built-in bed that was to have been mine. "But I will go stark mad if I don't get some fresh air." That was God's truth and I risked the request, for it had seemed Alice must have orders from my uncle to accommodate me somewhat.

"We can take our guard and go up on deck for a little while," she said, wrinkling her nose either at the foul air in the cabin or at my request. "Now that we're out of

Dublin Bay, 'tis allowed."

I told Magheen where I was going, but she only moaned and gestured me away again, so I swirled a cloak around my plain blue gown and, with more excitement than I would admit, followed Alice down the companionway and climbed a set of stairs onto the deck. Bates, a brawny guard, the very one, I learned, who had seized me when I attacked my uncle, followed behind us as always.

My spirits lifted, and I sucked in the tang of crisp sea air. I saw what we called a mackerel sky, with rows of clouds like marching men. In the slant of morning sun, the Irish Sea was a restless, rich blue-green topped by whitecaps as bright as the big-bellied sails straining overhead. Aloft, royal sailors in their sky blue shirts clung to rat-lines as the great vessel plowed through the shifting waves.

I followed Alice to the railing, and Bates brought up the rear of our little band. I gripped the railing and steadied my stance to take the plunge and roll. The wind ripped back my hood and yanked my hair free. My cloak billowed back as if I had great, flapping wings to fly away.

For one moment, staring out over the vastness of the sea, I almost forgot my troubles, till sorrow sat hard on my heart again. Where, out there, were my uncles? My father had not survived the Tower of London, where they were being taken. Could they? And Thomas. The English knew where he was and how his haven was fortified.

But most of all, I feared for my dear brother Gerald, for I had overheard that the king's chief minister, Cromwell, had told Uncle Leonard that he must pursue Gerald, boy or not though he be, until he was caught or killed. I must not forget, I warned myself, that whatever pleasures came my way, I was now living among the enemy. And I must ever keep in mind that, since Thomas seemed doomed, my brother Gerald must be helped to return to Ireland and aid our fellow countrymen we all loved.

With Alice and Bates quickly falling into step again, I walked to the other side of the ship and gasped. Indeed we were far out from Dublin Bay. My beloved Ireland was but a thin green line on the western horizon. I sucked in a sob, but stemmed my tears.

I forced myself to look away and saw a tall, broad-shouldered man, as dark-haired as I was fair, standing alone at the very prow of the ship. Unlike me, he wore no cloak or cape but high boots, leather breeks, and a jerkin over a white linen shirt. Like me, he seemed to revel in the pitch and yaw of the ship as he looked ahead, not seeing or else not heeding us.

"Is that the captain?" I asked Alice.

"Not him. I'll introduce you to him later — the captain, I mean. That is Lord Edward Clinton, sent along to test his sea legs, so I hear. A ward of the king, rising fast at court and even in Parliament, they say. Tied to Lord John Dudley, one of the king's key men," she went on, sounding puffed up just to know all that.

I realized Lord Clinton would be a good man to know. However many steps he was away from the king's presence and power, I had to start somewhere.

"Am I forbidden to speak with others?" I asked, though if she said I was, I intended to make a fuss. "I have much to learn of England, and not only midland ways." Midland ways, for Beaumanoir was in the English midlands, Alice had told me more than once.

"He's from the far north, way up in Lincolnshire, almost to wild Scotland," she said, with another wrinkle of her nose. "And," she added, turning slightly away from Bates as if to shut him out from whatever tidbit of gossip she would impart next — I must admit I was all ears — "he helped himself immensely last year by wedding the king's former mistress, Bessie Blount."

I gasped, which seemed to stoke her fires to proceed. Did his marriage bring him closer to the king or build a barrier between them? I wondered. I knew nothing of mistresses, royal or otherwise, but I warranted I needed to learn that and so much more.

"You see," she went on, "that means Lord Clinton is stepfather to Bessie Blount's son by the king, a boy not much younger than Clinton, Henry Fitzroy, Duke of Richmond, the lad whom the king named viceroy of your country years ago and then wanted to make —"

"To make king of Ireland!" I blurted.

It hit me with full force then what a splendid opportunity this was. The man at the prow of this ship was the stepfather of King Henry's bastard son, the one the king had desired to make our Irish king instead of my father!

"But when Fitzroy caught consumption, and because you Irish have such a damp, boggy climate, His Majesty changed his mind on that," she informed me with a little shrug. "You see, the king's former mistress had years ago been married off to someone else, and when she was widowed, her lands adjoined Lord Clinton's — well, you know what I mean. And obviously, though she is older than her handsome husband — I hear he is but two and twenty — I believe she is still lovely and accomplished, or the king would hardly have given her a look in the first place."

I tried to remember everything she said, all her meanderings, for it could be ammunition for later. Surely somehow this Edward Clinton of Lincolnshire had been put in my path as the first step toward my revenge.

Before Alice could respond or say me nay, though she and Bates were soon at my heels, I walked quickly away from them and approached Lord Clinton from behind.

"Good day, my lord," I addressed him, then, with the sounds of wind and sloshing sea against the hull, had to say it louder. "Good day, my lord."

He turned and looked at me, his eyes widening in surprise. He smiled, flaunting white teeth in his sun-browned face, a handsome face with a strong nose and blue eyes like the sea and slashes of dark eyebrows that seemed to work independently when he so willed it. Compared to the whey-skinned, light-haired Irish, he seemed almost devil dark.

Though his collar-length hair was raven-hued, up this close it shone almost bluish in the sun as it whipped about his wide forehead. He had the slightest hint of stubble on his cheeks but sported no beard. He said nothing for one moment, and we seemed to hang suspended, sailing together, without even the ship or sea under us. It was the first time in my life my stomach did a strange little cartwheel at the mere nearness of a man.

I told myself that was simply from the fact that I might have found my first mark, as Alice interrupted our mutual stares with formal introductions.

"I knew the lady was aboard," he said to Alice, and took my hand in his large one with a little bow. "My lady Elizabeth Fitzgerald, I am pleased to make your acquaintance."

No one else aboard had shown me that sort of respect, so I bobbed him a quick curtsy, telling myself I really wanted to slap the king's man, however handsome and polite.

Lord Clinton and I turned in unison, as if we had planned it, toward the narrow, plunging prow thrust out over the sea, which forced Alice and Bates to stand not with us but behind. Without even looking, I felt the shrouds and sails thrum with their power as the ship strained forward, toward England yet unseen. On deck or clinging to ratlines, the sailors seemed to disappear. Fine salt spray flew at us, but I didn't mind, and he barely blinked at it.

"I think we're in for a squall," he said, pointing at some distant gray thunderheads. "But, you being Irish, I suppose you are used to rain. Your land would not be so green and fertile without it."

"I am half English. And does it not rain a great deal in England?"

"It does, and it is green and lovely too."

As he said *lovely too,* he looked at me and seemed to emphasize those words. I felt myself blush. I hoped he thought it was windburn on my fair skin.

"I am regretful for your troubles," he said, speaking just loud enough for me, but not my hovering keepers, to hear. His voice was deep and slightly raspy, and his intonation was a bit flatter than Alice's or even my mother's.

"I thank you. No doubt your family fares far better than mine these days."

"I miss my family," he said, as if I'd inquired about that and had not alluded to his rising star at the king's court. "I am father to a new daughter my wife and I have named Bridget, and my stepson has not been well."

Ah, I thought. *Then perhaps King Henry is agonizing over his boy's future, just as we fear for Gerald.* But my mind also snagged on the fact that Lord Clinton's daughter's name reminded me of Kildare's patron, Saint Brigid. Was that a sign from her — though I reminded myself I did not believe in miracles — that this was indeed the man I should use to get closer to the king? But how? He was young and I was younger, and he was wed and —

"Lady Elizabeth, you are showing your sadness on your beautiful brow, but I understand why. Again, my condolences."

I tried not to look at his mouth when he spoke, but it fascinated me. A taut lower lip but a fuller upper one. And his eyes, kind but probing, showed he was truly interested in my plight. When I blinked back tears, he evidently decided it was time to change our topic of conversation.

"I am on this voyage because my mentor, Lord Dudley, has suggested I might want to take service afloat," he told me.

"Command a ship?"

"Yes, or a fleet someday. His Majesty is most adamant about building up his navy.

We are an island, after all."

We are an island. His words echoed in my head, as did nearly everything he said. I was going to retort that Ireland, too, was an island, but I fell to thinking of myself, feeling — despite Magheen and certainly discounting Alice and Bates — I was an island at sea, soon to be adrift amidst English people and English power.

"If I were you," I blurted, "I would take service afloat, for I think it would be wonderful!"

I could have cursed myself at that. I sounded such a child, and presumptuous that my opinion would be of any account to this king's man.

"Then I shall weigh that in my decision," he said quite seriously, though a little smile lifted one side of his mouth.

It began to rain, big, plopping drops from the gray clouds clotted even closer overhead. I felt crestfallen that I could not converse with him more to learn about his lord Dudley and the king. Saint Brigid forgive me, but I would have liked to have stayed up on deck with him in wind and rain as the ship plunged on, but Alice and Bates hustled me back down below.

The *Swiftsure* landed us at Liverpool before

going on to London, much to Magheen's relief and my regret. I looked for Lord Clinton as we disembarked and mounted waiting horses, but I did not see him again. I wondered if I ever would, for Alice had said that Uncle Leonard's estate was at the edge of the deep forest of Charnwood, encircled by the River Soar, seven miles from the village of Leicester and three days' hard ride to London. I pictured myself in eternal exile there, an Irish island in a thick, river-girt forest, never able to reach the power wielders of the realm who might be convinced to spare my family or upon whom I could wreak vengeance.

After two days' jogging ride, I saw a grand mansion emerge from the trees of Charnwood forest. I gasped aloud. A long gravel lane led toward a massive gatehouse and two turreted towers that stood like sentinels over a distant, sprawling manor of rosy brick, with its windows blinking in the sun.

"No," Alice said to me from her mount with one dog in each saddle pack, "that's Bradgate, not Beaumanoir. It is the country seat of Lord Henry Grey, your kin, but more important, his wife, Frances Brandon, is niece to the king. They have a one-year-old daughter, Lady Jane, though I reckon they wanted a boy, as ambitious as they are, and rightly so, if the king does not have a legitimate son, but only his two daughters. I tell you," she added, lowering her voice even more and nearly leaning out of her saddle toward me, "little Lady Jane Grey, through her mother's royal blood, stands fifth in line to King Henry's throne, should anything befall his daughters, Mary or Elizabeth, but they are out of favor anyway. You see, 'tis said he's even wearied of Queen Anne now too and seeks another."

This time I was so weary that her prattle barely sank in. I warranted that if the king of England threw off his lawful first wife, he could dispense with another, the one I'd heard called "the Boleyn whore." But I already knew who Henry Grey was, for I had been schooled in Mother's royal relations as well as my father's. It was a veritable spider's web of Grey kin: Henry Grey's great-grandmother was also mine, so we were second cousins, and I would be a third cousin to their young child, Lady Jane Grey.

"But I'm sure you'll meet the Marquess of Dorset — that's Lord Grey's title — and the marchioness soon," Alice went on, "for they oft hunt deer in these woods and stop by Beaumanoir for sustenance or a respite. Oh, yes, they love to hunt."

My eyes sought the mansion at the end of

the other fork in the gravel lane, the home of my now hated enemy Lord Leonard Grey, but the place where my dear mother, sisters, and brother awaited. I could barely keep myself from spurring my mount onward. So close to my loved ones at last, I even forgot my hatred of the king for a moment.

We passed through a gate in a waist-high stone fence and rode on. Also built of rosy brick, though not as large or grand, Beaumanoir emerged from trees, hedges, and gardens. At least a dozen deer grazing on the lawn scattered as we rode in. My heart beat so hard it almost shook me in the saddle.

I looked up and saw Cecily's face pressed to an oriel window and waved at her madly. Edward, his legs so much longer than I remembered, came tearing out the double doors, screaming, "She's here! She's here at last!" Mother and Cecily hurried out, Mother weeping with her arms wide open. I dismounted and threw myself into her embrace.

"My darling girl. My darling, beautiful girl," she kept saying as even Cecily hugged me and Edward patted my back so hard he almost hurt me. Over Mother's shoulder, I saw Margaret run out, gesturing to me with our hand signals that meant, *Miss you, love you!*

And so I was really in England at last. Not home, not ever home, but now on the dangerous wilderness path I must somehow learn to tread.

CHAPTER THE EIGHTH

During the rest of that terrible summer, I tried to settle into life in rural England, but I felt pent up with frustration and fury. Overseen by our strict tutor in the schoolroom with Edward and Cecily, I missed Gerald wretchedly and worried for my Irish uncles and Thomas. Mother had nearly sealed herself away, frantically writing letters to Uncle Leonard begging him to show Thomas mercy, for he had surrendered with hopes of a pardon and was being sent to England. She also wrote letters to Thomas Cromwell to spare my uncles and Thomas; letters to Princess Mary, whom Mother served when the princess was a child and not cast off yet by the king; letters to her cousin Henry Grey, who was at court.

Alice Stinchcomb, to my amazement, contributed greatly to my worldly education. I gleaned from overhearing servants' chatter that, though she used to be my deceased aunt's maid, she was now Uncle Leonard's mistress! And they said she would no doubt be cast off when he returned from his duties in Ireland and wed again. Such discarding of once desired mistresses, I learned then, was the way of the world, England's noble and royal world, at least. Lord Clinton's wife, Bessie Blount, had been cast off by the king, and it was said Anne Boleyn had more power over King Henry before they were wed than when she was queen and bore his child.

Whenever I could get outside with Magheen or Margaret in tow, I took walks along the fringe of forest, for we were not permitted to go into it nor ride about the estate on our own. I had been told I must stay within the waist-high stone wall. Uncle Leonard's man Bates — Fulk was his given name — remained my shadow, though he kept a ways back.

Today, as I strode out with Margaret into the meadow rippling with thigh-high grass and white oxeye daisies, I remembered crossing the Irish Sea, standing at the prow of the ship with Lord Edward Clinton, the king's man. On this warm, late-autumn day, the shade of the tall oaks in the forest beckoned me. I turned to Margaret, pointed at the opening in the fence, and said, "That way."

She shook her head and made the signs for, "Mother, no," but I kept going. I knew she and Bates would follow. If he ordered me back, I was not in a humor to heed him, for I was desperate for diversion. The forest ahead of us adjoined the two Grey properties. Farther on lay an alabaster stone quarry, the recently vacated Grace Dieu nunnery, and a priory, one that, I'd heard, had fed nearly one hundred peasants last year during a drought.

That merciful act reminded me of some of the charity our own family had extended to Irish cotters and villagers in terrible times. But now, with the Geraldines out of Ireland, we feared struggles for power would mean our poor people could have their crops ruined and towns raided. Irish families like the O'Donnels, the Butlers, the O'Briens, and the Desmonds resented not only one another but the occupying English soldiers, and the wild Gaelic chieftains were always out to plunder what they could.

Feeling trapped here, like a dog in a kennel, I heaved a huge sigh. I had not even seen any of the places near Beaumanoir, let alone the royal court in London, which was my true aim.

We evidently startled a family of rabbits, for they bounded off. No, they were hopping at us and past us, not away, and I soon reckoned why. Through the ground I felt then heard hoofbeats, a goodly number of horses, and the yipping of hounds. Someone must be hunting nearby.

Two stags with full racks of antlers lunged from the trees. At least six riders exploded behind them. Rather than leaping the stone fence, the two stags bolted through the opening I was heading for, and the riders funneled through after them as if they would mow us down.

Bates shouted something I could not discern. I pulled Margaret behind me, then waved my arms over my head and screeched like a banshee. The first stag barely missed us as he tore past, his eyes wide in his frenzy. The second veered away, running along this side of the fence. The barking pack of hounds rushed past, one knocking into my skirts, then bouncing off as they pursued their prey.

But the man and woman leading the hunt party reined in, as did their five liveried servants. I did not need to read the colors or the crests to know who they were. Henry and Frances Grey, the Marquess and Marchioness of Dorset, to use their proper titles, had returned from London. When Mother heard that, she would be in a fret about how long we should wait before paying them a visit.

I glanced over my shoulder to be sure Bates was all right. Then, as those who were our kin and yet our betters looked down on us from their lofty heights, I pulled Margaret into a deep curtsy beside me. I had not yet met the Greys, for they had been away at court since I'd been in England. They seemed a bit mismatched, she so stocky and he so thin. A rhyme I'd learned as a child pranced through my head: *Jack Sprat could eat no fat, his wife could eat no lean. And so between them both, you see, they licked the platter clean.*

He said to her, "Not the sort of deer we were wanting to catch, eh, my dear?"

She snorted a laugh, then muttered, "It's the mute Geraldine girl and the one who went missing."

"Yes, my lady," I said, squinting into the sun to look up at them and rising slowly from my curtsy. "This is Margaret, and I am Elizabeth, called Gera."

"She's a beauty," Lord Grey said, pointing at me with his riding crop. "Would that our Jane would turn out so well but be properly behaved. Such a shame about the rest of them."

I assumed he meant my family and felt insulted that they spoke of us as if they were assessing horses to be bought or sold. I stemmed a sharp retort and said, "Since you have new come from London, have you heard word of my Fitzgerald uncles in the Tower or my brother, Thomas, Earl of Kildare?"

"You've been attainted, all of you," Lord Grey said with a dour look, though mayhap that was ever his expression.

They both looked down at me so haughtily I did not admit I couldn't fathom exactly what that meant. I knew our family name was tainted with what had happened. I suddenly pitied their little daughter for having parents who were so cold that an icy breeze seemed to blow from them. And since this woman was King Henry's niece, I knew now what the Tudors must be like.

I swallowed my pride and forced myself to say, "I know my mother would be honored to receive you, my lord and my lady. Can you not come to the house for refreshment and talk to her of London and the court?"

"Not when we've been cooped up at Whitehall and Richmond for weeks on end," Lord Grey said. "But do tell her she should keep a better eye on such a pretty maid —

more than one guard and one other woman at least with you at all times, and not one deaf and dumb. Now you've cost us two fine stags, but I'd wager you will cost other stags much more than that over the years, eh, Mistress Fitzgerald?"

His wife laughed as he spurred his horse away with the other men in pursuit. For one moment more, the king's niece frowned down at me, then galloped away too. With her swarthy skin and manly jowls, she was not an attractive woman, but I warranted that with her royal blood, she was a catch for any man. Her mother, Mary, King Henry's sister, had been so beautiful that she'd been called "the Tudor Rose." She had once been the queen of France, wed to an old, sick man. But when he died, she'd married a man she desired, Charles Brandon, now Duke of Suffolk, a great friend of the king. So how, I thought, had the great love of two no doubt handsome people created this plain, rude, and frowning woman?

Pulling Margaret along and with Fulk Bates this time walking at my side, I hied myself back toward redbrick Beaumanoir. Bates did not scold me for heading toward the forest. Perhaps he pitied us for how we'd been treated or felt sad that our name had been tainted on top of all our other trials.

■ ■ ■ ■

"At least, at last, my Gera, you cannot say you have seen no one of importance," Mother said the moment we went in through the side door. "The gardener sent word to the house of the approach of the Greys and said they were speaking with you. I was most disappointed they did not stop here, but they are mad for the hunt."

I realized that Cecily and Edward must still be at their lessons. But Mother had evidently seen us coming back to the manor and rushed downstairs to greet us, for she was flushed and out of breath. "I intend to ask them directly for help, for it seems . . . it seems," she stammered, flourishing a letter I saw was not in her handwriting, "that your uncle Leonard has been pressed by debts incurred in the Irish insurrection and has seen fit to strip Maynooth of its furnishings and sell them to recoup losses."

"No!" I cried, balling up my fists at my sides. "Everything we had? I hope that doesn't mean Wynne! The library books too?"

"But they have searched high and low for *The Red Book of Kildare*," she went on, ignoring my outburst. "He asks if I know where it could have gone or been hidden. Dear God in heaven, if they find that, they will have the list of all our precious goods, our rental records, and the names of our kin and retainers. Oh, where could it have gone?"

"I believe it was hidden somewhere on the grounds," I told her.

"But who knows where? Would Gerald?"

I shrugged. I had never lied to my mother before and tried to tell myself it wasn't really such a lie because I had hidden the book on the grounds — these grounds, Lord Leonard's very grounds, under a big yew hedge out by the fishpond full of trout. I also had convinced myself that no one but Magheen and I should know of its location, for it might put others in danger, especially Geraldine loyalists listed in the book. Mother was desperate to protect her own family, so who knew what she might be willing to bargain for our safety, and I was coming to trust no one. If a foster brother and an uncle could turn traitor, such deceit must run rampant.

"But what news from our Grey cousins?" she asked me. "You should have asked them in for a visit, so I could learn the latest news from London."

"I did invite them and ask them. They said

we were tainted, or I think the word was *attainted,* all of us, but I knew that, so —"

Crushing the letter to her breasts, she swayed back against the wall. "Tainted or attainted?" she asked, her flushed face going ashen.

"Yes, that was it. Attainted."

"That means we all stand accused with the men, all of us," she whispered, and pulled Margaret and me to her so hard I almost could not breathe.

Margaret was making hands signals for, *What? Tell me!*

"Does that mean we are all going to the Tower?" I demanded. "All of us?"

"I don't know. Surely not, but . . . I don't know. I must write my brother and the Greys. I must write the king again."

Loosing us, she lifted her skirts and rushed up the staircase to the hall from which we heard her chamber door slam. Margaret patted my arm, leaned close, and mouthed nearly in my face, *What? What?*

"Nothing new," I told her, moving my lips deliberately. "Just that we are all Irish rebels."

But something cold had coiled in the pit of my belly, worse than how I'd felt before. Now that Mother took refuge in her rooms and in her endless letters to our enemies, and now that I had seen so much of Tudor evil, I must become a mother to Margaret and help protect Edward, whose life could be endangered as one in line to the Irish earldom — especially if Thomas were executed or Gerald was captured.

"Come on then," I told Margaret as she watched my lips make each word. "Let's walk inside so we won't be hit with rabbits or hounds or Greys."

I don't know if she truly caught all I said, but she nodded, and, until Alice summoned us to supper, we paced the oak-paneled gallery like the prisoners we soon might be.

During that autumn and winter, Uncle Leonard stayed in Ireland to settle things down, and the trial of Father's five brothers and Thomas began in London. Mother wrote her letters, which I imagined Beaumanoir's London messenger must be shredding in the forest en route, for she never received a reply, as if everyone had deserted our cause. The Fitzgeralds, all of us, were attainted, which meant we were accused of treasonous activities against the crown, so we were more or less under house arrest.

But, indeed, the outside world continued to revolve: Queen Anne was arrested for horrid sins against the king, such as adultery and witchcraft and even incest. In the sweet spring of May 1536, she was found guilty and beheaded in the Tower, where my uncles awaited their fate. Anne Boleyn's child, Elizabeth, was declared a bastard, while the king the very next day became betrothed to Jane Seymour. Ah, I could have warned Queen Anne and her daughter about that madman king, for I had seen such family treachery at close range — all spawned by the terrible Tudor.

In July of that year, we heard that the king's illegitimate son, Henry Fitzroy, Duke of Richmond, aged seventeen, had died of the wasting disease some called consumption. I hoped the king suffered sore from that loss, though, I must admit, I sorrowed that Lord Edward Clinton, who had mentioned to me that his stepson was ill, must be grieving too.

Meanwhile, for those long months I prayed, even on my knees, for someone to ride into our rural prison who could help me somehow gain access to that king so I could harm him in any way possible. And then, one cold, windy, and rain-swept day that year — early October, it was — my prayers were finally answered. Delivered to our doorstep was the very one, if I'd had the power, I would have chosen out of all the Tudor world.

While rain rattled against the window and thunder rumbled, we three girls sat before our bedchamber fire that evening. Cecily read aloud to us from *The Romance of the Rose,* one of several books she had sneaked into her travel trunk when she'd left Maynooth. Wouldn't it be something, I thought, if the books she'd squirreled away and *The Red Book of Kildare* were the only volumes saved from that vast library — and by the young women of the family, not the men? Speaking of which, Edward had just stomped out, pronouncing the romance was *drivel,* for it was about the attempts of a courtier to woo his beloved. So I was surprised when our brother burst back into the room.

"Two riders have come in fast!" he announced. "I heard it down the stairs when they told the house steward they are clear from London, and something about a rebellion! And Mother's down there too!"

"Our rebellion?" I asked him, but he darted out again, evidently to eavesdrop more. I left Cecily reading to herself, as Margaret only looked at the painted pictures, and followed my brother to where he was crouched by a carved balustrade at the top of the stairs. I peered carefully over but could not see much of the two visitors.

"You mean this isn't Bradgate?" A man's raised voice carried clearly to us. "The storm is so bad on the north road, all muck and mire, so we had to cut westward. I had hoped we could shelter here, then go north. I've important missives from Lord Cromwell and the king."

That news alone would have been enough to make me topple down the stairs, but the speaker's voice nearly jolted me from my perch. It could not be. Surely other men had deep, raspy voices. This speaker was upset and annoyed, not calm and kind.

"I must catch a glimpse of them," I told Edward, and, feet-first, slithered down several steps to peer beneath the banister. Uncle Leonard's elderly steward, Master Hemmings, was explaining that this was another Grey residence not far from Bradgate. Mother chimed in with some sort of explanation, but her voice was weak compared to the others, and I could catch little of what she said.

"Oh, Lord Leonard Grey's home," the visitor who was doing all the talking replied. I could see only his booted legs, wet and mud caked. And, hanging from one shoulder, a sopped leather satchel was held tight to his hip with one big hand. "We must have lost our bearings in the storm," he explained. "I went on Lord Leonard's ship to Ireland and returned with it. So the Fitzgerald family resides here, and you are the Countess of Kildare. I hear your brother has not yet returned from Ireland."

It was he, Lord Edward Clinton! But on a special mission for the king and Cromwell. I strained to hear whether he would mention my name. No doubt he had forgotten the young woman he had talked to, seemingly in earnest, that day at sea. But what were those papers he had mentioned, and how greatly would it harm the king's cause if they were stolen or destroyed? Would the loss of them help someone else's rebellion succeed?

"You must stay the night," Mother said, her voice rising a bit. "And if you would please take missives back to His Majesty and Secretary Cromwell from me, I would be so grateful."

"I am actually in service to Lord John Dudley, but he serves Cromwell and the king. Yes, I would do that for you, though my return to London may be delayed with this rebellion near my home."

I must be careful, I thought, if I sneaked downstairs when all were asleep and stole the royal letters, not to harm Mother's too. Or would she hand them over just before they left? Their voices were fading. I strained even harder to hear, going down another step.

Master Hemmings spoke: "Yes, the weather is so beastly, you must stay. I will call for hot food and bathwater. We will bring bedding in here for you by the fire and see that your horses are fed and watered."

Lord Clinton: "I am grateful. We would appreciate a chance to get dry and fill our bellies with something hot. Rain or not, I'll be on my way at daybreak, for I have papers to urge my Lincolnshire neighbors to stand firm against a peasant rebellion. The king calls it the Northern Rising, but the enemy insists it is the Pilgrimage of Grace."

"A religious rebellion?" Mother's voice finally rang out clearly.

I could not hear Lord Clinton's answer, only the hum of his voice. He must have turned away, gone into the solar. I turned to scramble back up the stairs but bumped into my brother, who had sidled down behind me. I'd been so intent on the men below, I had not heard him.

"Good," Edward whispered, frowning. "If the king has an uprising on his hands in the north, perhaps it will take his mind off destroying the Fitzgeralds for theirs in Ireland."

I had never shared my own pilgrimage of rage with my family, for they would have tried to dissuade me. "I'm going to bed," I added, "and I'm glad they'll be gone in the morning."

"Heave to," Edward whispered, almost shoving me ahead of him up the stairs. "Here comes Mother."

When we rushed back into the room where Cecily had been reading, Mother came quickly in, wiping her eyes. I could only hope Cecily didn't ask where we'd been.

"I had such hopes the visitors below had brought a message from the king himself, saying everyone was pardoned," Mother told us. "But I have an opportunity at least to write the king a letter, delivered by a northern lord. It will have to go north and then back to London, but that young man has vowed he will at least see it is delivered, God be praised!"

And, I vowed silently, God be praised if I could somehow sneak downstairs tonight and destroy those letters. Anything I could do to support rebels against the king — even if it meant someone who had once

been kind to me would suffer for the loss of
his letters — I would gladly do. Exiled and
nearly imprisoned as I was here in the heart
of England, I had found something I could
do to strike back.

CHAPTER THE NINTH

I lay in bed that night listening to the rain, Margaret's heavy breathing, and the beating of my own heart. My fear I'd drift off to sleep and miss sneaking downstairs was unfounded, for I was alert and tense. And I had a plan.

It would be foolish to try to steal Edward Clinton's papers, since he would know someone in the house took them and might blame Mother. But if they were ruined — smeared with rainwater, which surely could have seeped in during his wet ride — they would be no good to him or to the king. And with the vile weather, perhaps he would even escape some of the blame.

So when the great house fell silent, as far as I could fathom with its normal creaking of floors and the patter of rain on the windows, I slid out of the bed I shared with Margaret. Fortunately for my late-night foray, Magheen did not sleep in my room now but shared one with two other maidservants down the hall, or she would have come instantly awake. From a small table beside the bed I took the pewter cup with drinking water in it, surely enough to ruin whatever royal missives awaited downstairs. Did those papers from Cromwell and the king command arrests, imprisonments, beheadings of the rebels? Perhaps Lord Clinton and his northern neighbors were to seize fathers from their families or hunt down their heirs as if they were stags to be hounded to death.

I had not dared to keep my clothes on or take the time to don them now, but pulled a dark cloak about my linen night rail. I knew the solar well, but I prayed a candle or lantern burned low there so I could see my target. I could hardly be stumbling about in the dark while two men slept on the floor. And I prayed Lord Clinton and his companion were so exhausted that they slept the sleep of the dead.

Barefooted, holding the cup of water, which trembled in my hand, I crept down the wide staircase, nearly jumping out of my skin each time one of the treads creaked. Wan light silhouetted the dark door of the solar where the sun spilled in so sweet and warm most mornings. Surely the two men were not up this early or awake this late.

Saint Brigid, but the door was actually ajar! Without opening it farther, putting one eye to the two-inch crack, I peered in. A lantern sat on the far table where once in a while we took our breakfast. Both men — dark, sprawled forms — lay on bedding before the hearth, so I would not need to traverse the entire length of the solar. But I thought of something then: What if the leather satchel, which I assumed held the missives, was under Lord Clinton or somewhere on his person?

But fear, even if I risked much, could not hold me back, not after all I'd seen and suffered from the Tudor king.

Yet I hesitated. If I were caught, could it make things go worse for my uncles or Thomas, or even Gerald if they caught him? For all of us here? But what could be worse than an Act of Attainder, which had already been declared against the Fitzgeralds? It was now or never.

My pulse pounding, I pushed the door inward so I could slip through. It did not squeak. I blessed the rain, for its noise covered my footfalls. Which big body here was Clinton's? Oh, yes, that rakish, raven dark hair, mussed now by sleep and not sea wind, while his slightly smaller companion was blond. But no leather satchel in sight.

Then I saw it, hanging by its strap on a chair, which was also draped with drying garments. Everything looked shades of gray in the flickering hearth fire, near which stood two pairs of big boots. Holding my breath, I shuffled toward the satchel and lifted it from the chair but a few feet from the sleeping men.

My hand was shaking so hard I slopped some of the water onto my wrist. Should I take this out into the hall to smear the pages, then come back in? If Lord Clinton had examined the papers to be sure they were dry and then found them ruined in the morning, he would know they were tampered with. Or perhaps he would think the dampness of the leather had seeped into the parchment during the night.

Daring to leave the door ajar, I side-stepped through the opening with the satchel and sat down in the dim hall with my back against the wainscoted wall, where I could catch the meager light from the door. No turning back now. I would have to be quick.

Then a thought struck me, something I had overlooked. What if these important missives bore seals of state? Could I get the water between the pages without breaking the seals?

I opened the satchel and reached inside to find — nothing. My mere sliver of light fattened across my lap and on the floor. I looked up and gasped. A half-naked, sheet-draped man stared down at me.

I tried to scramble up but was lifted off my feet, bounced once, and held in a hard embrace against a muscular, naked chest. I heard the pewter cup tip onto the floor, so his feet must have gotten wet. I still held the empty satchel.

"How nice to see you again, Lady Elizabeth," Lord Clinton whispered, his mouth so close to my ear his breath heated the shell of it. "Do not scream, or you'll make this worse — if that's possible."

"I was only checking to be sure Mother's letters she said she was giving you were not overly pathetic or demanding. She's not . . . not been herself lately."

"And you were bringing me a cup of water to slake my thirst too? Now hold your tongue."

"Let me down. Where are we going?"

He elbowed open the door to the dark room across the corridor where Master Hemmings received visitors since Uncle Leonard was not home.

Though it was at first pitch-black in here,

141

in his linen sheet he looked like a Roman ghost in a toga. He left the door to the hallway partly open, so wan light from the solar sifted in. He sat me on the edge of the table, holding me there with his hard hands on my shoulders and his solid thighs against my knees. We were nearly eye-to-eye, so close I could smell cloves on his breath. I stiffened my backbone, but he seemed so big and threatening.

"Now let's hear it, Lady Elizabeth, the truth," he ordered.

"I told you. I know Mother wrote letters to give you, and she's so distraught and desperate lately, I did not want her to beg or say something . . . something amiss."

"Why did you not ask her what she wrote?"

"I don't want her to think I believe she's that way, of course."

I was amazed how easily I could lie, though I'd been doing a bit of it lately. I usually got in trouble for telling too much of the truth, but here I was with a nearly naked man, alone in the middle of the night. He shook me by my shoulders.

"Listen to me," he commanded. "Those missives are none of your concern."

"But my mother is so —"

"I mean the royal missives you were after

142

for some reason I'd not care to contemplate. Some pitiful retribution against His Majesty? We're all no more than replaceable spokes in the big wheel of state, with Henry Tudor at the hub, and you'd best learn to accept that, Irish rebel blood or not. You can't stop that wheel, Elizabeth; you can only contribute to its revolving as best you can and so profit from its progress."

"That wheel grinds people into the dust and mud," I told him, trying to shake his hands off. "High and low, even his own wives — and your wife."

At that he shook me again. "Hell's gates, I am telling myself you are only a maid, a naive but disturbingly comely one at that, so I don't need to be caught with you here — but then, it would be quite obvious you came to me, wouldn't it? Stranger things have happened between maids and men, even married ones."

"Let go of me! I had no intention of any of that. I just wanted —"

"I'm going to let you go back upstairs to a warm bed, but do not try such a stupid trick with any other man who stumbles in here — or especially if you are called to court. Despite your dangerous heritage, I doubt if you'd just be let go next time without some sort of . . . of compromise. Ours will be that you will agree to tell me the truth on all things next time we meet, or I will be forced to summon your mother now and write to your current guardian, Lord Leonard, as if he — and I — don't have enough on our hands right now."

As he said *on our hands,* he loosed his hard hold of me but ran his palms and fingers down my upper arms to my elbows, then back up, smoothly, strongly. It was like a comforting caress, only that, but it shot a shiver clear up my spine that almost made me dizzy.

"Do we have a bargain or not?" he demanded, and I had to struggle for a moment to recall what he had just said. Oh, yes, that I would tell him the truth about all things next time we met. I doubted if we would meet again, for I was cloistered here like a nun, and he was heading north to do his vile king's bidding.

"Agreed," I said.

He lifted me off the table, making a snatch for his linen toga as it nearly came undone — undone, that was how I felt. I wanted to curse and strike him, but I wanted even more to ask him if he had decided to take service afloat, tell him I was sorry to hear he'd lost his stepson. No! What was wrong with me?

"Ordinarily," he was saying, "I would insist on something to seal the deal, but not with a mere maid who has so much to learn, and sadly, from someone else."

What was he talking about? Did he know I would be sent where I would see him again? *And sadly, from someone else?* Such as whom?

With his hand in the small of my back, he pushed me to the door and out. I darted across the corridor to recover the pewter cup, then lifted the hems of my night rail and cape and darted up the staircase. At the top, I looked back. He was still standing there, watching. The light aslant from the single lantern or the glow of embers from the solar made his eyes gleam as if lit from within.

In the morning, when I woke after a restless night, he and his companion were long gone.

After a long, bitter winter, word came that my uncles had been declared guilty of treason charges and would soon be sentenced. Needless to say, Silken Thomas was chiefly blamed for the Fitzgerald rebellion and was also adjudged guilty. The most we could hope for, Mother said, was that they would all be kept in the Tower as Father had been, but that they would live to be released someday. We hoped and prayed that King Henry and Queen Jane Seymour might produce a son, heir to the Tudor throne — for it was said she was with child. But I only wished for them a son if it would mean the king would be more secure and magnanimous and permit Fitzgerald pardons someday, on the condition, of course, they return to keep Ireland under crown control, as they had for nigh on eighty years.

But a bit of good news: Somehow Mother had convinced Uncle Leonard that she could spend a fortnight in his London town house so that she could petition the king and Cromwell for at least a visit to her stepson and imprisoned brothers-in-law in the Tower. After all, she'd been able to visit Father there. Perhaps her deluge of letters finally wore the deputy of Ireland down, or he felt guilty for his traitorous arrest of the five Fitzgerald brothers. But the most amazing thing of all was that Mother was taking Cecily and me with her.

Edward was angered that he could not go, but she felt one of the spares to the heir was better off hidden away in Leicestershire. Though the family had been named in the Act of Attainder, it seemed we women were considered harmless and were free to leave

Beaumanoir — if we had permission. Poor Margaret was crestfallen that she would be without me for nearly three weeks, but Magheen vowed to take good care of her. Cecily hoped to visit the booksellers near St. Paul's Cathedral, so she was in whirls over our journey.

As for me, I had no hopes of getting near the court, especially when I heard we would be staying not at Uncle Leonard's town house but at Suffolk Place, the city home of Frances Grey's father, Charles Brandon, which was clear across London from the king's palaces of Westminster and Whitehall. Charles Brandon, the Duke of Suffolk and a close friend to the king, would not even be there, for he was "mopping up the northern rebel problem," as Henry Grey had put it when he'd ridden in to give Mother permission for our visit. At least perhaps, I thought, if I pleaded hard enough I could visit my uncles in the Tower of London with her, for she said it was but a ferry ride across the Thames or a ride ahorse over London Bridge.

London Bridge — whenever I saw that bridge, any bridge, I vowed it would be a sign for me to pray to Saint Brigid to build a bridge between me and someone at court, someone who would give me access to the king or his family. How dared Edward Clinton call me naive, however Irish, rural, and young I might be, I fumed as we rode with several guards in a pack train past the walls and through the gate of Beaumanoir in July. Despite the beauty of the day, Cecily read a book, even bouncing along ahorse. Fulk Bates was one of our guards, and Alice was attending Mother. And I? I was going to London to find a way to triumph over the Tudors!

CHAPTER THE TENTH

London
July 16, 1537

As we rode through the ornate Aldersgate entrance to the city, I was so excited that, for once, I could barely speak. Not only were we in London, close to the king, but we were to stay in a house once lived in by his sister, Mary, "the Tudor Rose," who had wed the Duke of Suffolk, and the house now actually belonged to the king himself! How I hoped that Henry Tudor might visit while we were there. Then I could enact my swift and sure revenge — though, of course, Mother and I would try humbling ourselves first to plead prettily for the pardoning of our family members. I was young then, so young and so foolish.

"Are we to pass the Tower itself?" I asked Bates as we turned from Cheapside onto Bread Street. He had lived in London in the service of the duke, so was a great source of information I hoped to put to good use. He had ridden beside me nearly all the way, as if his horse's flanks were sewn to my mare's.

He raised his voice to be heard over the hubbub of street hawkers. "No one of import or sense in London rides about the streets if they can take the Thames. We'll be ferried from the water stairs at the bottom of the street, but you'll see the Tower in the distance — and from the upper floors of Suffolk House. The house lies on the far side of London Bridge, nearly across from the Tower. And the bridge is cheek by jowl like this too, so don't you be begging to ride across it."

With all his scolding and fussing over me, Bates was starting to sound like my brother Gerald, whom I missed so much. We'd received glad news that Gerald had been safely spirited out of Ireland and was in France, probably heading for Italy. I recalled that, despite our dangers during the siege of Maynooth, he'd blurted out that he would be thrilled to see the continent. Well, I was thrilled to see London at long last, and that would have to do for a female Geraldine, one with a purpose if yet no plan.

All the way within the city, three-storied houses and shops leaned over our heads as

150

if they would tumble down upon us. We passed livery stables, hostelries, and inns with fantastical names, such as the Serpent's Head or the Keys and Crowns, all with painted signs that bore the replicas of their names but no written words. Margaret would have found those signs a help to know what lay within. And the smells and sounds, sweet or rank, everything from yeast breads and herbal nosegays to swine being herded past and the contents of last night's slop jars thrown into the central channel of the street.

Bates pointed out apprentices in blue smocks darting hither and yon on errands for their masters. I could easily pick out gaudily garbed gallants who swaggered down the streets, elbowing others out of their way with a curt, "By your leave." Several strumpets with their skirts hiked up and breasts nearly falling from their tight bodices displayed themselves with the rest of the wares.

"Hot mutton pies!" came the continued cries from hawkers with ramshackle booths or wooden trays of items strapped to their bodies, including pick-tooths and pin cases. "Live periwinkles! Fresh herring! Seville oranges!" And where was Seville? I wondered. I had so much to learn. "Any wood

151

to cleave?" came the cry of a man with a hatchet. "What do ye lack? What do ye lack?"

"We lack the Fitzgerald men," I muttered with a glance at Mother and Cecily, who rode just behind. My sister had even put her book away to gawk. But all too soon we were at the water's edge of the broad gray Thames where the cries became, "Oars east!" or "Oars west!"

"East!" Bates shouted at a man with a barge that could also take horses, but then our party was large enough that he also had to hire a second barge for our other guards and luggage.

I liked being out on the wide river, with its panoramic view of shops, houses, and great buildings — countryside too. I knew we were headed for an area called South-wark, so I peered in that direction. The breeze blew brisk here, and the waves and four oarsmen rocked the craft a bit. The water was so crowded that they had to avoid wherries, galleys, and other craft I could not begin to name. A far cry, I thought, from sailing the sea. A great wave of home-sickness assailed me — for our little boat in the River Lyreen, for Gerald at the helm of it, and . . . and then Edward Clinton's face flashed through my mind.

Mother, Cecily, and Alice stayed seated on a crude single bench, but Bates came to stand by me where I held on to the railing. "There," he said, pointing ahead. "London Bridge —"

"Are those shops built right on it?" I asked, amazed.

"And houses. As for the Tower, you can only see its turrets and pennants from here, that monstrosity of pale stone."

"It's more than one tower," I marveled, squinting into the breeze. "I wonder which one Thomas and my uncles are kept in."

"And on the other side," he said, all too obviously to change the topic as he pointed again, "Suffolk House."

It was not a house at all, for it was larger than Maynooth or Leixlip castles, if not as tall. We had been told that the king had recently traded another London residence with Charles Brandon for it. No wonder Mother had been delighted that her cousin Henry Grey had arranged for us to stay there. Perhaps, she thought — for she was ever grasping at straws — our permission to lodge here was a sign the king was softening toward the Fitzgeralds.

As we alighted from the ferry, I saw that redbrick, sprawling Suffolk House dominated the surrounding shops and tiled or thatched houses. Only the Church of St. Saviour seemed to hold its own space, though beyond lay acres of fields. In the central cobbled courtyard, windows gleamed down at us like blinking eyes. After we dismounted, I pulled my gaze away from the vast expanse of brick, ivy, and glass just in time to see Mother waver on her feet.

Cecily and I leaped forward to steady her and seat her on the wide lip of the central fountain. Alice wetted a cloth in it and dabbed at Mother's forehead as the July sun beat down. The large door into the courtyard opened, and a man who announced himself as the house steward — wearing green-and-white Tudor livery, no less — came out to meet us and extended his hand. No, it was a piece of folded parchment for Mother. It bore a red wax seal with a looped ribbon stuck in that.

"Let us go inside," Alice urged, but Mother only nodded and opened the missive where she sat.

"A welcome from the king himself?" Cecily whispered, leaning close to catch a glimpse of the writing. "Or word you finally have the interview with him or Lord Cromwell that you have been so hoping for?"

"I regret to say," the steward broke in, "that it would be best for your ladyship and companions to return to Leicestershire on the morrow. We sent a rider to find you on the road and tell you to turn back, but he must have missed you. Of course, you may stay the night."

My stomach twisted in foreboding. I too hovered close as, with trembling hands, Mother broke the seal. Cecily and I helped her to hold the stiff parchment open. I could tell Cecily read it faster than I or Mother, for she gasped. And I . . . I wanted to scream and pull down this vast pile of bricks one by one and throw them at everyone in London, starting with the king's steward of Suffolk House.

For the paper we three women skimmed, signed *Henry R* in a big, bold scrawl with flourishes, was actually from the Privy Council and countersigned *Thomas Cromwell, Lord Privy Seal*. It read, in part (I have it yet today, though I cannot bear to look upon it),

Act of Attainder of Treason Declared and So Ratified by the Privy Council and here signed by His Majesty, King Henry VIII, by the grace of God, King of England and Lord of Ireland, against the rebellious and insubordinate and traitorous Irish family of Gerald Fitzgerald, 9th earl: to wit, Thomas, 10th earl and his five uncles, now prisoners of the realm adjudged guilty, having had a lawful trial, and against Gerald, 11th earl, and their close kin both in the English realm and the Irish realm. Seeing that the blood of the Geraldines is corrupted toward the crown of England, be it enacted and established by the authority of the present Parliament and the Privy Council that said rebels against the lawful English crown and their liege lord, King Henry VIII, by the grace of God, King of England and Lord of Ireland, listed above shall be executed for said treasons and rebellions at Tyburn on July 17, the year of our Lord, 1537.

"That's on the morrow!" Cecily shrilled, and burst into tears.

Mother swooned again, and Alice kept crying, "What is it? What?"

And I blurted to the hovering steward and to Bates, who was wringing his cap in his hands, "Where, in Saint Brigid's name, is Tyburn?"

It was sheer nightmare from then on in London. That night, in the house and city and realm of the king, our enemy, despite my exhaustion I lay awake. I churned my side of the bed to huge ruffles as if they were waves on the sea. We three Fitzgerald women slept in the same room, in the same huge bed, though three chambers had been appointed for us, and Alice slept in a trundle near the door as if to guard us. Cecily, gently snoring, lay between Mother and me.

It seemed not a breeze stirred, when I longed to feel sea wind and be rocked to sleep by the rise and fall of a ship, a ship heading home to Ireland. But I knew now that might never be. I could only pray my dear brother Gerald, who would unknowingly inherit the Fitzgerald earldom on the morrow, was safe and far away and could return someday. And I vowed to abet that any way I could.

At last I slept, or thought I did, swimming in fear and fury. My blood pounded in my veins and head. . . . *The blood of the Geraldines is corrupted toward the crown of England.* We Geraldine women were named in the Act of Attainder and order for the executions of the men only as *their close kin,* so were we safe? Back to confinement at Beaumanoir while my other uncle — the traitor uncle Leonard Grey — stomped about Ireland arresting others where he had already tricked and betrayed Thomas and my uncles.

The dream that haunted me drifted back. I tried to keep it at bay, the drowning, suffocating feel of it, but it was even worse. I was not in a boat this time but was swimming in the cellar of Maynooth while cannonballs shook the castle above me. Swimming not in water but in blood with heads bobbing past, not just Father's now, but Thomas's, Silken Thomas with green fringe over his head like a shroud, and Uncle James and the others . . . And one by one they raised their hands to try to grasp something before they were swept away, no — no, they were waving good-bye.

I tried to reach out for them, seize them, save them, but I woke with a start when Cecily hit my shoulder and whispered, "Loose me! You're hurting me!"

I saw I gripped her wrist and pulled my hand back, only to feel my face slick with tears. When Cecily groaned and rolled over, I whispered, "Sorry!" but I resented her ability to sleep. I got up and padded barefoot and sweating to the window.

Bates had been right. In the wan moonlight I could make out the dark silhouette of the Tower from here. To be so close and yet so far from our loved ones, yet not to be able to comfort them, to let them know that we — I, at least — would carry on and avenge their deaths and fight however I could to see Gerald returned to Ireland as earl someday. But Bates had said that Tyburn was far on the other side of the city, across the river, out in the country. That was good, I thought, though it meant there was no way then for us to glimpse our kin and wave them a farewell. At least men who loved green, green Ireland could gaze at meadows and trees and see the open sky away from all the hubbub of London before they died.

If only I were a man grown! I would try to free them, but if I could not, I would be there near them, to let them know —

Mother cried out in her sleep, and I saw Alice get up and go to her, as I did too. "Gera, I must hold him," Mother whispered, and at first I feared she'd caught a fever that made her senseless. Or like me, was racked with nightmares. "I must hold your father to me and tell him I tried."

"Oh, the portrait," I said, and went to her open traveling chest and felt through her unpacked things until I found Father's small painted and framed likeness she had kissed each night even in the good times when he was away. I took it to her, crossing through a patch of moonlight, where he stared up at me, handsome, stern, commanding. I kissed it too before I gave it to her, and she closed her eyes and cuddled it close.

I sat on the edge of Mother's side of the bed until dawn dusted the sky. All four of us women looked like ghosts of ourselves that morning. Mother's face had an almost greenish cast. We must start home right after breakfast, the king's steward had said. We must be away. What a devastating first trip to London, I thought, but I vowed I would be back with a vengeance.

The surprise of that dreadful execution day — the first surprise, that is — was that the king had sent a guard to be certain we left London and took the road toward Leicestershire. But we managed to get only as far as across the river and nearly to Aldersgate when Mother became nauseous and could not even ride.

"I can't go back across the river and cannot . . . cannot make it home," she murmured as Bates got her dismounted at the sign of the Keys and Crown I recalled passing on our way in yesterday.

"I'll see if there's a room where she can rest," Bates told the royal guard as he and Cecily helped her inside. God forgive me, but I stood at the edge of the busy street a moment, tempted to jump back on my horse and ride westward, for I had gotten out of Bates where Tyburn was. He'd even told me that the long procession through the streets of those to be executed — evidently, to act as a warning to other would-be criminals and traitors against the crown — stopped for a respite at a place called High Holborn, and I reckoned we'd just passed High Market Street that would take me in that direction. But I must not distress Mother more than she already was. Besides, I'd wager the king's guard would be up on his big steed and after me in a trice if I fled.

That king's man, frowning, took the reins of my horse and the others and handed them to our guards from Beaumanoir and told them to find a boy to hold them in the livery stables next door until he knew of Lady Fitzgerald's condition. I supposed horses were for hire there too, or at the stables just down the way. Evidently not seeing that I tarried outside, he followed the others into the inn.

Across the street I heard a ruckus, for a comely girl was shoving at a man and shouting loudly enough for everyone to hear, "If you touch me once more, I'll tell my da you coupled wi' me by force, and he'll have your head. Now leave off, or I'll tell him a pretty tale!"

I went inside and nearly ran into Bates, coming back out at a trot. He'd obviously realized I had not come inside and was in a fret. "She'll need some time lying down," he said. "Hopefully we can set out in the forenoon so we are well out of here when the crowds swell."

"More crowded than it is already?"

He shrugged, then nodded. I could tell I'd caught him at something.

"Say on," I demanded, grabbing his wrist.

"It's not only a main market day, but the crowds will be heading out toward Holborn and Tyburn, if you must know."

"To watch . . . to watch that? They don't just take them off alone into the countryside to . . ."

He shook his head. I should have known that would be the way of it in vile Henry's city. If they paraded condemned prisoners through the streets for folks to see, crowds would flock to the hangings or beheadings, out in the countryside or not. The blood . . . the blood in my nightmares, the tainted blood of the Geraldines . . . the shed blood of our Lord Jesus Christ, slain for us . . .

"Lady Gera." Bates's voice broke into my

agonizing as he grasped my arm to steady me. "You aren't going to be sick too, are you?"

"Sick to my very soul. Fulk Bates, you must help me. Of course I would not dare to go clear out to Tyburn, but I must glimpse the prisoners when they go past — near here, maybe at Holborn. Mother will be in bed, Alice and Cecily tending her, and we can slip away for a short while."

"Oh, no," he said, pulling me off to the side of the common room, greatly deserted now, even of the king's man, for perhaps he guarded Mother's chamber door. "I've been ordered to keep a good watch on you — keep you safe, I mean."

I liked Bates, despite the fact that he'd last served my uncle Leonard. He had a kind heart beneath it all. And he was a fount of information I needed. His wit was more for horses than for cleverness, but I knew he cared for me, and not only because he'd been paid or commanded to do so. Therefore, I felt almost guilty for what I did next, but I was desperate. And the fact that he'd let slip that he had been especially ordered to watch me gave me courage — and a certain insight.

"I swear to you we will only watch the prisoners pass and then ride back," I promised. "It can't be far — it isn't, is it? If you do not come with me, I swear I will tell them you have put your hands on me in a most untoward manner by force, and I a mere maid."

His eyes widened, and his jaw dropped open. "You . . . They'd not believe you."

"Really? Why do you think they said to keep a good eye on me? I wager it's because my mother's cousin Henry Grey said I need watching closely, either because I am pretty or wayward. And, heaven forbid, they must be thinking I'd make a bargain in the marriage market. Yes, I'll tell my mother and the king's man too."

Bates blanched, then blushed. If I had not just seen the young woman across the street tell a man to unhand her, I doubt if I would have thought of this ploy. I held my breath, thinking he might indeed try to stand against me.

"All right," he said, looking as if he'd be next to turn green at the gills. "But you, milady, got to swear you'll not make a fuss and tell no one — ever."

"Of course not," I vowed. Despite the tragedy of the day, I felt a tiny triumph that I had finally gotten my way.

It turned out the king's guard was next door

at the livery stable, so I peeked in at Mother, who was sleeping, and told Cecily I was going to take some air with Bates as a guard. Not exactly a lie, I thought. She urged me to take my cloak and wear my hood up, so I did. We slipped out the back door and, with a few pence of my hoarded coins from the money Magheen and I had fled Maynooth with, I leased us a horse from the livery down the street. Just one mount, for, at the last minute, Bates insisted I ride pillion behind him or he would not go, but how I would have loved to ride my own horse, and astride too.

We crossed the bridge over the River Fleet and clattered down Holborn Hill amidst growing, shoving crowds, with Bates nervously telling me where we were as if we were on a tour of the town.

"We must be in time," I interrupted his nervous chatter. "Surely we are ahead of the procession, not behind it."

"Heard tell they have a respite just beyond here."

Here seemed more a raucous fair than a sober crowd that was supposed to learn to obey the king today by viewing the condemned and their execution. Jugglers, drunks, dancing girls. Hawkers selling pigs' ears and trotters and all the other singsong chants we had heard upon entering London yesterday surrounded us. Men hunkered down around a grass ring by the roadside, wagering on a cockfight where two fierce birds pecked and kicked at each other with tiny spurs on their feet. Blood flew faster than in a fistfight farther down the way.

Bates reined in the horse and backed us into a small space between two shops from which people hung out the windows above us. I saw no church nearby but heard the slow, monotonous tolling of a distant bell, no doubt a death knell. The crowd hushed and heads turned and . . . there came the procession of the condemned en route to Tyburn. My stomach clenched; it was like a triumphal parade, and headed by a man with a scarlet sash around his chest and an unsheathed sword in his hand, who seemed to be the grand marshal of this obscene display.

"Who is that man?" I asked Bates. "The constable of the Tower?"

"Only seen him once when he was the king's champion at a joust, but that's John Dudley. Climbing fast in the king's eyes, so's I heard. Kind of his henchman in all things now, but works with Cromwell too."

Dudley! The very man Edward Clinton had called his mentor when I first met him on the ship to England. The man he'd mentioned in the same breath with Cromwell and the king the night he stopped at Beaumanoir carrying commands to put down the northern rebellion. Dear Lord in heaven, what if Clinton was here too?

I saw no one else of such obvious import, but John Dudley's image burned into my brain, florid face and pointed beard, scarlet sash, and a sword that might as well have been a pitchfork, for he reminded me of Satan. I added John Dudley — Clinton too now — to my list of enemies to be dealt with. King's bootlickers! Killers, every one of them!

But then John Dudley and everything else faded to nothing. Sounds muted; my vision blurred with tears. The scene now became my nightmare in broad day, not with heads floating past in blood, but at first I could see only the heads of my uncles and my half brother going by above the crowd as they sat in two separate carts. It seemed so unreal that for a moment I just gaped.

The condemned — my dearly beloved — wore nooses about their necks, so were they to be hanged instead of beheaded or was that just tradition? Already they wore shrouds, which clung to their wasted forms. And then, as if someone were answering my unspoken question, I heard the dreadful words, "Hear tell they're to be hanged, then cut down and quartered, cut up in parts like a piece of beef."

I nearly threw up. Yet it was now or never. Trembling, I managed to stand behind Bates on the horse's rump and saw they sat on crudely made coffins, when Fitzgeralds were always buried with prayers and pomp. Guards rode before and behind, and constables ahorse were decked out in bright uniforms. Several guards were already eating meat pies and cheese as if on a countryside lark.

Thomas was in the first cart with Uncle James and Uncle Walter, and the others rode in the second. Though the crowd, like me, seemed awed at first, I could tell they were going to explode with noise again. Mere mutterings rose from the rabble, a few raised fists, but cheers were building. I would have given the rest of my life to have saved them, but I could only think of one way to help send them bravely to their unfair fates.

"A Geraldine!" I shouted our family battle cry and hit Bates's hand away as he tried to make me sit down. "A Geraldine!"

Thomas and Uncle James's heads jerked up; their eyes sought me. I threw back my hood and, with one hand on Bates's head to steady myself, cried out again, heedless of what the constables or guards would do, "A Ger-al-dine!"

Thomas looked struck by lightning. Chains rattling, he stood. His haggard face lifted in a thin smile. All my uncles stood, raising manacled wrists to wave as if they were riding out of Maynooth for just a little while. I could read Uncle James's lips; how much he looked like my father. I am certain he shouted to me, "Be brave! Stay safe! A Geraldine! A Geraldine!"

I saw Dudley rein in and turn back, scanning the crowd, looking furious — probably looking for me — but I ignored him. I knew not whether people realized what we Irish were shouting, but they picked up the battle cry, perhaps thinking it was calling down curses on the condemned. As the two carts rolled away with all six Fitzgerald men standing and looking back at me in wonderment with fists upraised, the crowd erupted with the cry, "A Geraldine! A Geraldine!"

Bates pulled me down behind him and urged the horse away before we could be singled out. Bucking the screaming crowd, we rode back in the direction we had come. Though racked with sobs, I felt I had won

the first skirmish in my war against the
Tudors and their lackeys.

Chapter the Eleventh

"It seems you hold all the cards again, Lady Gera!" Susan Clarencieux cried as she tossed hers down in defeat. "The luck of the Irish!"

My gaze met Lady Mary Tudor's across the little gaming table where four of us sat playing Primero. We were not to call her *princess,* for she and her sister, Elizabeth, had not been reinstated in the line of succession. But here at Hunsdon, we did at times address Mary as *Your Grace* and not just *my lady.* Mary gave a small shake of her head, and I knew she silently commiserated with me for that careless comment about the luck of the Irish. The fact that my mother had once served in Mary's household years ago, when Mary had not yet suffered so in the loss of her father's fickle attentions, made her, I think, almost

171

protective of me.

Besides, at age sixteen, I was the youngest lady in attendance here. Twelve used to be the minimum age for a girl to be accepted for a court position, though I had heard Queen Jane Seymour had raised that to age sixteen. I was fully aware I was not at court, but here with Mary in her rural exile. Despite how I was saddened that poor Queen Jane had died bearing the king a prince, I reveled in the thought that Henry Tudor was grieving for the loss of one he loved!

In the few weeks I had been at rural Hunsdon with Mary Tudor and her household of forty-two (which sounded large to me until I learned that, when she was considered heir to the throne, she had nearly three hundred), I had learned she was full of surprises. My expectation that she would be dominating and rude was wide of the mark. Indeed, she was fun-loving, gentle, and kind, though I could tell she, like me, had suffered much.

She was chestnut haired, and it was said Mary's coloring was a blend of her Spanish mother's skin and her pale-faced father's. She had recently turned twenty-three, but she looked and seemed older than her years. Quite nearsighted, she frowned to see at a distance, which gave her lines upon her forehead that aged her. Her petite stature and form seemed so at odds with her deep, almost mannish voice. But most surprising of all, I could see she too feared her royal sire's whims and commands, even from afar. How she had suffered with her poor mother, Catherine of Aragon, when the king had thrown them both aside to have Anne Boleyn.

In short, though I tried to detest her, I could not. I remained wary of her, as if feeling my way through the dark tunnel of Maynooth. My plan now was to befriend the king's daughter so that I might someday get closer to her father. I must strike at the root of the evil tree, not its branches — unless that could harm Henry himself.

Besides, truth be told, Lady Mary tried to entertain those of us living with her, and I had not had such good pastimes in years, not that it made me forget the Fitzgerald troubles. Mary was generous with her allowance, so much so that she was oft in debt and had to petition Cromwell, who held the purse strings for the king, for funds. She loved sharing things with her ladies and the few visitors she was allowed: good food and music, gambling money and beautiful clothes. She had ordered two lovely gowns made for me, so I now owned four fine ones and could change the sleeves, bodices, and skirts about to suit the day. My time at Hunsdon House in the rolling hills of Essex helped to heal my heart, but I was softened only toward Mary and not her tyrant father. When I managed to maim or murder him someday, it would be for me and mine — but for Mary too, I vowed.

"All right, ladies," Mary said, popping up from the card table, "time for our afternoon constitutional. I feel quite ready to walk for miles, so come along."

Despite sallying forth today, she was oft ailing and kept to her bed, sometimes with horrid headaches she called megrims, sometimes with painful menses or terrible toothaches. And, Lady Susan had told me, each November when the weather was sunless, Her Grace was assailed by such melancholy that she took to her bed for days.

"Lady Gera," Mary Tudor called, and gestured me to her as we went out into the sunshine for a brisk stroll.

"Yes, Your Grace," I responded, and hurried to catch up with her. She pulled me along and we walked together, leading the others down a narrow gravel path through full-blooming gardens.

"Susan was not thinking of your past,

which weighs so heavily upon you, when she said that about the luck of the Irish."

"I know, Your Grace. She was reacting to my luck with the cards."

"And I know your purse for wagering is not bottomless, so I was glad to see you win. There have been times when I too have been in households where I did not wish to be, and ill supported too."

"But I am happy to be with you for more than one reason, and you have been more than generous with me."

She nodded and took my elbow as if to steer me along. "But surely you would prefer to be with your mother," she said. "I . . . I understand that too, you see."

Yes, I missed my mother, but she shut herself up more than ever now, even when we needed her. And the day we'd parted, as pleased as she had been that I would enter Mary Tudor's household, she had made her plans for me plain at last.

"Gera, my dearest, Edward is still so young and Gerald a hunted criminal, so you are indeed our best hope for recovery right now."

"But won't Cecily be placed in a prominent household too, for she is only a year younger than me and —"

"And won't make her way in the world as

175

you, not with her solitary ways. You have the Grey and Fitzgerald good looks, if you can but learn to bridle your . . . your passions."

My eyes widened. "I am our best hope for what?" I threw Mother's words back at her, ignoring the sugared compliments.

"Why, to make a fine, important marriage, and as soon as possible — a betrothal at least. Keep your eyes open, a smile on your face, and your temper tamped down. We cannot rely on the generosity of my brother forever, so —"

"Forgive me, Mother, but I wish we did not have to rely on him at all, because he is more than unreliable — he is not to be trusted. How do we know he won't hand Edward over to them when he returns, or use us as hostages to make Gerald come home and give himself up?"

"Do not become political, my Gera! See what it gets us? Nowhere. In exile. Now, I have it on the best authority that about ten years ago Anne Bourchier — I used to know her mother — wed a man named William Parr when she was but ten, though of course they didn't live together for years. King Henry's own sister Margaret was betrothed at age twelve to the king of Scots, and went to live with him at age fourteen. And Catherine Willoughby, who is now Lady Suffolk, wed the duke Charles Brandon, a great friend of the king's, when she was but fourteen and he was forty-eight. Older men, allies with wealth and power — that is the best we can hope for since our Irish heritage is gone."

"It isn't gone, but has just been pirated from us for now! That's what the king of England is — a pirate, as daring and immoral as those who used to plague Ireland's shores! The last thing in the world I want is to be wed or betrothed to any Englishman. But . . . but I see what you mean . . ." I had to admit, for had I not dedicated myself to getting access to power and the king any way I could? Mary Tudor might be one way, but indeed, a man who closely served the king could be another.

"I just want to tell you," Mary Tudor said, bringing me back to the present, "that we shall have among us for supper this evening a visitor, a man I'm sure you have not met, one who rather likes the ladies, if you catch my drift. Since you are new and the youngest here, I thought it best to warn you."

I stiffened, for mayhap she implied instead that her father would visit here. Hunsdon was his house, and servants still talked of how many deer he had slain in its vast forests and how he had favored the place as a rural refuge from the plague. The king and Queen Jane had once visited Mary here, so one of her other ladies, Margery Baynton, had said, and it was only twenty miles from Greenwich Palace. So did she mean a suitor or a sovereign was coming?

Mary stopped abruptly on the gravel path in the knot garden, turned to me, and said, "No need to fear. Henry Howard, Earl of Surrey, is also a fine poet and a friend of your uncle Leonard Grey."

I nodded, though I was thinking his tie to my uncle was no recommendation for the man. "We call poets rhymers in Ireland," I said lamely, trying to cover the faux pas I'd made to look so alarmed. We started to walk again, this time passing through the water gate to stroll the inner edge of the moat.

"Dear Gera," she said, for Mother had written to her about my pet name and Mary liked to use it, "poet or rhymer — or rake-hell, for he has a bad reputation and vile temper — I warrant Surrey's been to Greenwich to try to cheer my father, so we'll hear if his spirits have lifted some in his loss of the queen. At least, praise God," she said, probably without realizing she was frowning deeply, "the king has his precious prince now, and Elizabeth and I have a brother —

a half brother."

The ravaged, gaunt face of my half brother, Thomas, flashed through my mind as I had seen him last on his shameful way to the scaffold. It was a miracle Mother had never found out what I had done, but I had told Magheen and was miffed at her for days when she insisted that I would bring bad luck upon myself by my defiance and deceit. But now I noted how Mary's voice quavered when she spoke of the new prince who had surely supplanted her in her father's affections and obstructed her path to the throne. Ah, the fate of women, who could never govern alone, never choose whom they would wed, never simply challenge an enemy to a joust or battle.

It turned out that our visitor was no one eligible as a suitor, for he was wed, but he was the powerful Duke of Norfolk's son and closely related to the royal Tudors in blood and service. New-fledged hope bloomed in me that I might use him to get nearer to the king. Besides, the Earl of Surrey seemed in collusion with my mother too, for that evening he spoke of how young he and his wife were when they were wed. I had perched in a window seat alone in the gallery to listen to Lady Mary play her virginals; the earl came to sit beside me, rustling my skirts so that I had to move over a bit into the curtained shadows.

"I heard our hostess call you Gera, so if I may presume . . ."

"You may presume, at least to call me Lady Gera."

"Ah, a sharp wit for one so young. Lady Gera, we hardly had a chance to chat after our introduction earlier," he whispered, leaning so close I could smell a rich pomade from his person mingled with wine on his breath. Attired in finest peacock blue brocade, and for a country visit too, he had been drinking a great deal and still had a goblet of wine with him now. Stretching out his legs as if to display his gartered hose wrapped around well-turned legs, he gave a satisfied — or a yearning — sigh.

When he just studied my face overlong, I decided to put him off a bit. "I believe," I told him, "Her Grace asked at table how your wife, Frances, was doing, but I did not hear your reply." He had been watching me all evening over supper, enough to make my face heat once or twice. I might be painfully young yet, but I did not want him to think I was a green girl — a wild Irish colleen — who could be taken advantage of.

"Ah, yes. Frances and I wed at the lofty

age of thirteen but have only lived together these last two years, when we turned twenty. And lately I've been away from her quite a bit, in service of God and king — perhaps not in that order, or perhaps they are one and the same," he said with a muted snicker.

I must admit I did favor the bitter undercurrent to his words whenever he mentioned His Majesty, as everyone liked to call the man, a term of worshipful adoration I tried to avoid using.

"Such a difficult way to begin a marriage, I warrant," I whispered back. "And I hear your sister Mary is the widow of the king's dead oldest son, Henry Fitzroy, Duke of Richmond."

"So you're a student of the spiderweb of titles and relationships," he said, "or at least a student of court gossip. Yes, keep your ear ever to the ground on that," he said with a smirk, and shook his head at something else he evidently dared not say.

He leaned back toward the window, set ajar, looking now not jaunty but most melancholy. Such quicksilver moods, I thought, but then Her Grace had warned me that he had a sudden temper. He frowned and sighed again, took another swig of wine, then stared down at his knees while I covertly studied him. His expression was somewhere between a grin and a grimace. His eyes, sleekly arched brows, close-combed hair, and a small, pointed beard were all of the same auburn hue. Lanky and loose limbed, he nevertheless carried himself with great pride, oft flinging flamboyant gestures when he spoke, however still he sat now. Magheen would have said he had his nose in the air.

I did not let on that I had inquired of his pedigree. The Howards had strong claims to royal blood. Though cousins to the Boleyns, they had smoothly escaped the downfall of that family. He sighed again and lifted his hand over his heart in the most affected way.

"You see, I was a boyhood companion of Fitzroy," he told me, still looking down. "The mere thought of his loss still makes me sad. In short, he was my best friend, and I yet mourn my equal friend, no grudge, no strife. His Majesty saw fit to have me share his son's schoolroom and travel with him to France in our youth. I knew his beautiful mother well, and his stepfather, Edward Clinton. Now poor Clinton's lost Bessie too, but he's a charmer and a climber, and he'll wed even higher, I've no doubt."

I sat frozen, trying to get my thoughts

back to the conversation, back to pumping this man for any information I could use about the king. But I kept seeing Edward Clinton, *a charmer and a climber,* at the helm of the ship with me on stormy waters and in the dark room at Beaumanoir when he held me with his hard hands and told me that strange things could happen between maids and men, even married ones. And now he might wed again.

"Lady Gera, what did I say? Are you all right?"

"Indeed I am. Your loss reminded me of mine; that is all."

I was aching to ask him if he'd seen Edward Clinton lately or if he had gone to sea. But Clinton was my enemy too, along with his malicious mentor, Dudley. So I said instead, "It must be both a blessing and a burden to belong to such a premier family so close to the king."

He sat up straighter; his chin lifted. "Why, who would credit how beautifully you have put that, my sweet, a burden and a blessing? As I wrote in a sonnet recently, 'I weep and sing, in joy and woe, as in a doubtful ease.' Yes, the Howards sat at the pinnacle of power when Anne Boleyn was in favor, and are a bit out of fashion right now, though the king still values our military prowess when it suits him." He took another drink of wine. I was amazed his speech was not slurred, for his eyelids seemed heavy as he assessed me, but then, this was a master wordsmith whether in his cups or not.

"Thank God," he went on, "Anne Boleyn did not take us down with her, for my father — her uncle — oversaw her trial and helped pronounce her guilty."

It frightened me that such a pronouncement of family betrayal no longer made me so much as blink an eye. It was the way of the world when it came to power, and I merely nodded as he plunged on: "And if that damned Cromwell doesn't drag His Grace into a foreign Protestant marriage for political reasons — passions and politics, a volatile mix — perhaps we can find His Grace a more pliable Catholic bride who is pure English, eh?"

I assumed he meant someone else in his staunch Catholic family, for Anne Boleyn's Protestant leanings had been an aberration for the Howards, Mary Tudor had said. With a snide smile and a quick elbow to my ribs, Surrey added, "My dear, fair Geraldine, if you weren't from a hotbed of Irish rebels, we'd dangle you before the king, eh, youth or not? He needs a fillip in his autumn years. You are one of the comeliest young women I have ever seen, and I shall write a sonnet saying so, I swear it. With my name upon it and circulated in high places, it shall fetch you a fine marriage."

He was slurring his words a bit now, so the wine must finally be affecting him. He nearly leaned on me, so I was glad Mary's ladies were intent on her playing, for I did not intend to pass up this chance for information I could use.

"But the king," I said, hoping to get him back on track. "Are you so sure he will wed again at his age after all his ill fortune with three wives?"

"Remember what I said about politics and passion, my sweet. For one reason or the other, Henry Rex will wed again, and under ordinary circumstances, he'd find you a tasty temptation."

At that, I could brook no more from him. "I believe our royal hostess is finished, and we will soon be at the gaming tables, my lord. So if you will kindly excuse me —"

I stood up fast enough that he almost rolled sideways in the window seat and spilled the last of his ruby red wine on his bright blue hose — it looked rather like blood, I thought, and felt a bit queasy at all I had heard and all I had dared.

■ ■ ■ ■

My days serving the princess Mary in rural Hunsdon came and went. The Protestant German princess Anne of Cleves, King Henry's fourth wife, came and went into English exile from court, because the king liked her not and refused to consummate the marriage and wanted it annulled. Base-born and -bred Cromwell, now Earl of Essex, had arranged that sad match. He had also climbed too high too fast and had a host of nobly born enemies, so he too came and went. He was arrested for treason (and for his supposed plans to wed the princess Mary, which everyone knew was just another trumped-up charge at his treason trial), and was beheaded in July of 1540, one year after I had met the Earl of Surrey, who still came to visit us from time to time with gifts for Mary — and for me.

Surrey's hotspur temper continued to get him in trouble; once the king ordered him locked up at Windsor for striking another courtier. While there, as he had promised, he wrote a poem in my honor, one he had dared to entitle "Description and Praise of His Love Geraldine." Yet I was honored, and my mother was thrilled to hear it had been circulated at court, much, I feared, as one might pass around a handbill of sale for a rare mare. I write here the sonnet, for it went like this:

From Tuscane came my Lady's worthy
    race;
Fair Florence was sometime her ancient
    seat.
The western isle whose pleasant shore
    doth face
Wild Camber's cliffs, did give her lively
    heat.
Foster'd she was with milk of Irish breast:
Her sire an Earl; her dame of Prince's
    blood.
From tender years, in Britain doth she
    rest,
With Kinges child; where she tasteth
    costly food.
Hunsdon did first present her to mine
    eyen:
Bright is her hue, and Geraldine she
    hight.
Hampton me taught to wish her first for
    mine;
And Windsor, alas! doth chase me from
    her sight.
Her beauty of kind; her virtues from
    above;

Happy is he that can attain her love!

The line about Hampton Court was pure poetic license, and why not? For I fear the rakehell, as Mary Tudor had called him once, took license with everything else — though our strange friendship was pure, despite his reputation and his flirting. He hardly needed me, for the Howard family had a great new triumph. Despite the disaster of the Boleyn marriage, they had managed to dangle (as Surrey had put it to me) another young, ripe Howard girl, named Catherine, called Cat, in front of the aging king's nose. Desperate to regain his own youth, the king had snatched her up. The lady Mary was much offended that her father would take a fifth wife and one four years younger than herself.

But she, like me, wanted to be in the king's good graces, so, after a rough patch where Queen Catherine openly favored the seven-year-old Elizabeth and ignored Mary, my royal mistress made peace with Cat Howard. Shortly thereafter, Mary and her ladies, including me, were summoned to Hampton Court to serve the new queen. Finally, I was going to meet — and somehow beat — the king.

CHAPTER THE TWELFTH

Hampton Court Palace
August 1540

You might know *he* was at court. I do not mean the king — I shall relate that next, for of course Henry Tudor was in residence, though he was out hunting when we arrived that warm summer day. Rather I mean that I heard "Captain" Edward Clinton was there and would not sit with the next Parliament the king called, for he was soon to go to sea. Clinton, a member of Parliament, king's captain, and king's lackey! And I overheard that, much like his monarch, the widowed wretch had wed yet again, this time to Ursula Stourton, niece to John Dudley, no less! I felt both Clinton and Dudley were the king's beasts, lined up to aid and abet him just as the carved and painted griffins, unicorns, and dragons lined the entrance to this vast redbrick palace along the River Thames.

I kept telling myself how much I hated Clinton, but I was angry with myself that my eyes oft sought him amidst the crowded tables of courtiers at midday meal in the great hall while everyone awaited the king's return. Clinton was engaged in conversation with the bootlicking villain Dudley, who had overseen my family's executions. Which of the ladies was Clinton's wife — if she was here at all — I knew not and cared not.

Upon our arrival, Queen Catherine had sent for my mistress to visit her apartments, while Mary's ladies were to stay nearby in the suite of rooms we had been allotted. They were quite pleasant, though small and not that near the royal suites, which were on the south and west sides of the Cloister Green Court, one of three interior courtyards in this monstrously large place I must learn to navigate. Still, our windows overlooked some gardens, a greensward, and the Thames a mere stone's throw to the south.

I felt quite overwhelmed that day. Who would credit that I had finally gotten myself this far? Though where I was exactly in a sprawl of buildings with one thousand rooms and two hundred eighty beds, all in use, since the entire court was here, I was not yet quite sure. (And, however much I hated the Tudors, I must admit I was impressed with the pure water that was piped in from springs at Coombe Hill three miles away and the privy water closets in most of the bedrooms. Why, at Maynooth and even at Beaumanoir, besides chamber pots that must be emptied, we had to walk to the end of the cold hall and perch our bums over jakes like drop chutes that led to a cesspit or rushing river.)

I peered out windows to get my bearings, but from here I could see so little of the eighteen hundred enclosed acres that made up Hampton Court Palace. At table, where food had been brought in from the vast kitchen block, I had heard chatter about the walled and towered tiltyards, three bowling alleys, shovelboard lanes, and closed tennis courts with twelve windows for spectators to admire the king's prowess. By Saint Brigid, everything here, from the chapel to the yew maze, from gilded ceilings to carpeted floors, was for the pleasure and passions of "His Royal Majesty," our "sire," as if he had begotten us all!

Unlike Mary's other ladies, I could not sit still embroidering or I would go stark mad waiting for her to return from her audience with the queen. I slipped out for a solitary walk, rehearsing how deceitfully I must behave here at court. At last I would meet and live near the forty-nine-year-old king, killer of the Geraldines, my target for justice and revenge. We had been told that His Majesty, now that he had wed his young bride, had returned to the first flush of youth, with early risings, much hawking, and hunting, though, because of an ulcerated leg, he merely watched his young queen, whom he had dubbed his "rose without a thorn," at her favorite pastime of dancing.

I tried to calm myself, but my unease was made far worse as I rehearsed what I would say and do when I met Their Majesties — I admitted I was going to have to call them such. But the other person I could not bear to be civil to sought me out as I paced the long gallery alone.

"I saw you in the great hall at dinner," Edward Clinton said with a tight smile. I felt a huge blush begin, heating my throat and spreading upward and downward. He looked sun-browned and windblown, even here at Hampton Court, where everyone else seemed combed and careful. He looked — damn the man — grand, with his broad shoulders tapering to his leather-covered chest and his narrow hips and strong thighs. Unlike most courtiers who wore soft shoes about the court, his legs were encased in black riding boots. So was he leaving now, and for where?

"Oh, did you see me? I did not notice you," I lied, forcing myself to look straight ahead and not into that intense and intimate stare. Somehow I managed to keep walking.

"You are much grown in all the right ways, Lady Elizabeth," he said, looking me over. "I believe I heard the Earl of Surrey say your friends call you Lady Gera."

"They do," I said, not breaking stride, "so you should call me Lady Elizabeth."

"Tart tongued too. That should serve you well at court, as long as you are not addressing Their Majesties. I regret I shall be leaving for a while to go to sea and will not be here to keep you out of trouble." He fell in beside me, his long legs easily keeping up when I stretched my strides.

I bit my tongue before I could blurt, *Good riddance!* Truth be told, I would have loved to go to sea — but, of course, not with this man. "You regret leaving because you have wed again," I said. "To a Dudley, I hear."

"Ah, you do care. Actually, I did not know Ursula Stourton — yes, John Dudley's niece — until she was named one of Anne of Cleves's maids of honor. Ursula is en route to Kyme, my Lincolnshire castle, for a while. It seems she's with child already, and now that her former royal mistress Anne of Cl—"

"Has been cast aside, as kings — this king, at least — are wont to do one way or the other."

He grabbed my arm and stopped my headlong strides, putting my back against the wall and blocking me in, just around the turn of the corridor in a dimmer, narrow hallway. "It seems I am ever to be giving you advice," he spit out, angry now. "I was afraid the Tudors would have to tangle not with Lady Elizabeth, but with Gera Fitzgerald of the infamous Irish Geraldines."

"I don't need your advice or your taunts. Leave off and unhand me."

"But you need a good shaking. Hear this, Irish. You will be walking a thin tightrope here, and you must beware or it could snag you, or worse — choke you like a noose if you take a tumble. The king keeps his friends close but his enemies closer, and which you become to him is up to you. But you must have no illusions that your Helen of Troy face or ripening body will save you, if push comes to shove."

I wanted to push and shove him away. He leaned closer; I could smell sweet cloves on his breath. Curse him, my knees felt weak as if I could topple into him, as if some magnetic north pulled me toward him. I had to lash out, say something.

"Will you hold it over my head that I tried to steal your precious Pilgrimage of Grace papers?" was all I could manage, and that a bit too breathlessly.

"That rebellion was put down too, and do not plan to start another. I'm not the one who will hold it over your head if someone reports to His Majesty or one of his council —"

"Someone such as your lord and master, the king's henchman, John Dudley? Oh, I can see why you wed his niece, just as you did the king's former mistress. Stepping-stones to power — to Parliament, to a command at sea."

"I am deeply honored you have kept up with my career."

"A pox on your career! Dudley oversaw the horrible execution of my half brother, Thomas, Earl of Kildare, and my uncles."

"Yes, I heard and rued the day. But your kin would not have even been in the king's clutches unless your uncle Leonard Grey had tricked them with promises or pardons and handed them over. And now he too has overstepped, and I don't want you to be next."

"He did? How?"

"You seem to have done well with court gossip but haven't heard that? Don't be warning your mother, as she'll hear the news soon enough. Grey has been replaced as deputy of Ireland by St. Leger —"

Amazingly, I thought of poor Alice first. My uncle would come home now and take a bride, and it wouldn't be her. She'd buried her sorrows, even as I had, but it still grieved her sore to lose him.

"Just heed me now," Clinton was saying. "Your uncle is being sent home to face charges of treason, with the main accusation being that he intentionally let your brother Gerald slip out of Ireland and flee."

I gasped and pressed my back and legs against the wall to stand. "The king will attack that uncle too?" I whispered. "Lord Grey was a traitor to us, but — him too? Then the king wants Gerald that much? Will he wipe out my brother Edward next and the rest of us?"

"That is especially why, fetching maid or not, you must take a care for your own safety. Now I must go before someone comes upon us, though I warrant everyone's lollygagging about the base court waiting for the king to return from his daily slaughter — of deer, this time."

I wanted to scream and beat my fists against the wall, against this man. Yet I wanted to cling to him too, his new Dudley wife be damned, for I needed someone to be strong with me. He did care for me somehow. His undertone was critical of the king, however slavishly he seemed to serve him and Dudley too. He rued the day he'd heard his mentor had overseen my family's executions. I was so very afraid, and yet I could tell no one what I intended to do, trust no one.

"Gera Fitzgerald, do not be a fool. I repeat: You must be wary; stay out of plots and trouble. You must not let others know your feelings. Hell's gates, Irish, you don't know the half of what can go on and go wrong here in the poison garden of court policies and politics. I hear someone coming. I'm off for Lincolnshire and then to sea. Keep your head down here, Irish, but keep your chin up too."

He lifted my chin in his big, calloused hand, so that I stared up at him. I held my breath, wanting to knock his hand away, but feeling we swayed and rocked in unison, as if we were at sea again. I felt capsized by the fierce look he gave me. Our mouths

197

were so close; it was the first time I had ever really wanted to be kissed, and I believe I was foolish enough to part my lips and breathe through them.

"And watch your beautiful backside too, because others will," Clinton muttered. He pulled his hand back, spun away, and was gone, striding down the dim corridor away from the long gallery to which I must return to find my way back.

I cursed myself for not berating him more, but I was still digesting all that he had said. I should at least have shoved him away, I told myself. But my heartbeat still thundered in my chest. No, that was the sound of hoofbeats, echoing in the inner cobbled court.

I ran along the gallery to a window in time to see a string of men ride in with hunt hounds yapping at their heels. And there in his huge saddle on a massive steed — it was easy to pick out which one he was — sat Henry Tudor, king of England, Scotland, and — curse his evil soul — lord of Ireland.

The first time I saw Henry Tudor up close that very afternoon, when I was formally presented to him, I wanted to spit in his face and claw his eyes out. But I gritted my teeth, curtsied, and braced myself as he touched my hand to raise me, and his sharp, sunken eyes went thoroughly over me. What would it avail me to be thrown into prison for defying him outright? Mother had been sore ill off and on, so it might be the death of her. She had forbidden me to so much as come home for a visit. I would like to escape with my life, even after I sought justice for the Fitzgerald fatalities, though if not, I would die for what I hoped to do. *But how to do it; how to do it?* repeated in my brain as Henry Tudor still looked me over and seemed to approve.

But, I noted, the queen did not. Her lower lip thrust out, she pouted. She even stamped a foot, mayhap because, for this moment at least, she was not the center of her lord's and everyone's attention. Yes, I learned that later about her — despite all she had and how heads always turned her way, she was ravenous for attention and affection.

And speaking of attention, it was the first time I noted how avidly her closest maid of honor, Lady Jane Rochford, of whom I knew nothing then, watched the queen's every move as she stood slightly off to the side. It was almost as if the middle-aged Lady Jane were living her life through the young queen of whom she was obviously so proud, for she hung on her every word and move. When Cat Howard smiled, Lady Jane did too. When Cat looked affronted, it seemed to me Lady Jane Rochford wanted to slap away the perpetrator, even the king. The woman's smothered passions made me almost understand her. She had, I thought, a fierce fondness for her royal charge, one that made me miss Magheen's affection for and loyalty to me.

"My dear lord," Queen Catherine said with a pert smile as she clung to his arm, even as he seated himself heavily in a massive chair, "I have told your daughter Mary that I shall take Lady Elizabeth Fitzgerald for my own maid, someone a bit closer to my age. Of course, Mary said she considered her — your," she said, nodding at me as I tried to cover my surprise at this turn of events — "services as a gift to me. Oh, my dear lord, I am so happy you were pleased with your hunting today, and the new necklace is so lovely — look!"

Despite at least twenty courtiers looking on — Lady Jane giggled and simpered when her mistress did — the queen tugged her taut bodice away from her breasts and leaned toward him so he could glimpse the rubies on a gold chain that plunged between her plump, pushed-up breasts. I could not but help think that if my mother or

Magheen had seen one of us girls do such in public, even to a husband or family member, we would have been soundly cuffed and scolded.

"How prettily it sets off my fair skin, see?" she shrilled with a giggle that was soon drowned by the king's guffaw of approval. I could tell he yearned to plunge his big paw down her neckline, and not to fondle the necklace. And so, in just a few moments, I learned that a lady-in-waiting — me — could be traded off to humble someone — a king's daughter — just as a pretty bauble might be given for favors or power.

Indeed, my first impression of the monarch I so loved to hate was that, as dangerous and wary as he was, he was stupid enough to be besotted with a silly girl. Yet he was no doddering fool, for his eyes, deep-set and small like a pig's in his jowly, florid face, were watching everything, even as Jane Rochford did. Despite his obvious happiness now and hail-fellow-well-met demeanor, I knew what he was really like.

As he and Cat — so they called her behind her back — walked away toward the royal apartments, Mary Tudor came up to me and took my hands. "Once she heard of your youth, she was determined to have you in her service, but if she'd seen you first, I warrant I'd still have you with me," she said, almost plaintively. "Surely she, like queens before her, has learned not to surround herself with fetching ladies-in-waiting. I shall miss you greatly, but she desires new things — and the young."

"But you are young," I protested loyally.

Frowning, she shook her head. "Too old at heart, after . . . after everything," she whispered, though the presence chamber had greatly emptied of people. "I shall write your mother to explain — a step up, really, to serve a queen, so I am certain she will be pleased. I hear she is ailing."

"It's an ailment that seems to come and go, Your Grace."

"Well, I have said it before, but I understand how desperate one can feel when kept away from one's mother who has lost much and is sore ill." Her eyes filled with tears. "And I asked if you might keep your maid, Alice, and the queen acquiesced, so that she won't be sent back and you will have someone with you from home."

Home, I thought. Home was still Ireland, and as much as I got on with Alice now, who was grateful she could ride along on my petticoats, I wanted Magheen with me.

Perhaps noting my sad expression, Mary squeezed my hands before she moved away with her faithful ladies sweeping along in her wake. I imagined Alice and I would be expected to move our things from Mary's ladies' chambers, but to where? I wondered. And what scolding and warnings would Edward Clinton have for me when he heard that in one fell swoop, through no effort of my own, I now served the person who was closest to the king?

As I turned away, I saw a girl, perhaps of six or seven years, in the doorway to the corridor. What had she seen and what was she thinking? As Mary Tudor had just mentioned, I sensed this girl was older than her years. She stood silhouetted by a late slant of sunlight that gilded her silken gown and red-gold hair and etched her slender body. Both maidens, we wore our hair — much the same hue, as if we were sisters — spilling from small, gabled French hoods that Cat Howard had made the fashion. We both stared at each other, and I noted we had worn the same hue of willow green. Only the color of our eyes seemed different, for hers were as dark as mine were light.

I felt I gazed in the mirror of memory, for the young woman looked so much like me — her face intelligent but restless. She was struggling for control, yet felt overwhelmed and afraid. Oh, yes, I recognized all that in her at once because it was so familiar.

Then in a rustle of skirts she was gone, with a matronly lady I had not seen following close behind her. It was the next day when my new royal mistress fussed over the girl as if she were a pretty pet that I learned who she was. The uncanny image of my past self was Elizabeth Tudor, the king's youngest daughter.

Despite so much going on that autumn at court, the winter months of 1541 dragged on. Everyone moped about inside with the inclement weather, first at Hampton Court and then at Whitehall in London, bored and melancholy. The king — the center of every courtier's universe — kept to his rooms, where his physicians cauterized his weeping leg sore. His terrible temper threw a pall on everyone, except me, who was glad he suffered in any way.

Those of the queen's household still chattered and danced and laughed in her chambers, before she sent us all away early each evening. Then, I took it, she dictated letters to family and friends. I saw she could barely write her name and never glanced at a book, but her young, handsome secretary, Francis Dereham, went in to take her dictation. Sometimes only her closest companion,

Lady Jane, who I learned had been wed to Anne's Boleyn's brother, George, tended her at night and put her to bed. But eventually Cat the queen became more subdued and moodier than before. Even visits from the Earl of Surrey, spouting poetry and compliments, lifted no one's spirits.

I did gather information that might be useful to me against John Dudley and the king, the best of which was that the king had a small, secret suite of rooms behind his presence chamber and state bedroom at both Hampton Court and Whitehall, and, I assumed, other palaces. These rooms were accessed by narrow passageways that connected to inner palace halls by hidden doors. 'Twas said no one but a few close comrades had access to those privy rooms. When the king was alone — unfortunately ever zealous for his own safety — he evidently slept in them, rather than in his grand state bedchamber. Carefully, surreptitiously, I tried to reckon where those hall entrances could be, but without success.

In March I was finally summoned "home" to Beaumanoir for the first time in twenty-one months, though not for a reason I had expected or wished. My mother had died.

CHAPTER THE THIRTEENTH

Beaumanoir
March 1541

I grieved not only for my mother's death, but that she had kept me away from her and my siblings for so long, however much I understood her passion to resurrect our family's good name and position. Cecily had written that Mother's world had shrunk to her chamber, where she ever kept my father's picture close. They had heard her speaking to him as if he were alive. I had written back that I would be home straightaway and that they should place the small portrait of our sire in the coffin with her.

She was to be buried in the chapel on the Bradgate grounds. As Alice and I reined in with our guards before the familiar facade of Beaumanoir, I told myself that perhaps she was better off in heaven with her beloved lord husband and the others she had fought so hard to save. Then too if her brother

Leonard was convicted of and executed for treason and his properties forfeit to the crown, Mother would have been cast on the kindness of Frances and Henry Grey — unless in the near future one of us had our own home to take her in.

As everyone came out to greet us, Magheen, Margaret, and I blubbered like babies. Magheen had silver hairs among her brown and told me that her dear Collum had written a short note on the last of Gerald's letters from Italy, which I could not wait to read. Edward and Cecily hugged me too. How they had all grown!

Margaret was twenty and quite pretty, but of course would never wed. If I only had my own household, I would take her with me. I wished our dear Gerald, 11th Earl of Fitzgerald, now aged nineteen, could be here for this reunion, however sad an event. One of my goals was to help him come home, not to England but to Ireland, to restore and claim the Fitzgerald earldom. Edward, sixteen, so tall now, obviously trying to grow a beard, was in the service of Lord Henry Grey, Marquess of Dorset. Cecily, newly betrothed to a ward of the Greys — who I hoped could abide a wife with her nose ever in a book! — was seventeen. I was finally eighteen, an entirely marriageable age, a favorite dancing partner, my company sought by many men at court, though I truly favored none of them.

On our way upstairs, Margaret clung to me, and Cecily pumped me for information about the courtiers and their ladies. Did she not realize what rulers and their nobles had done to us? I fumed, but I did not scold her. I saved my energy for my return to court, for so far I felt I had done naught but meet new people and help to amuse the spoiled ninnyhammer who was our queen, though I was ever searching for a way to bring our enemies down.

How happy I was to see Magheen and someone else who awaited me there. For, although Uncle Leonard had been sent to the Tower, he had done a favor for me I could never have imagined. That first day I arrived, I had no sooner gone upstairs with my family than I heard much ado in the downstairs hall that we had just come through.

"Whatever is that noise?" I asked them.

"Edward, don't you tell," Cecily said, but Margaret was signaling that I should go back downstairs.

"He was out for a walk on the back lawn with Hemmings when you arrived," Edward blurted.

"Who was?" I demanded, my heart pounding. Surely Captain Clinton had not come calling. Curse it that I had thought of him right now, even wished to see him. He had been making quite a name for himself at sea, and when he came ashore he went home to Lincolnshire, for he and his wife had an heir — named Henry, you might know.

As I rushed back down, with everyone behind me, I recalled the night I had sneaked down these stairs to try to ruin Clinton's papers. Though he was an enemy with ties to Dudley and the king, I longed to have him about the court to ask for advice. Somehow I trusted him, despite the devils he served.

Alice had greeted her two yapping, little lapdogs, Posy and Pretty — Margaret had happily tended them while we were away — but no other dogs were in the house as far as I knew. Yet I heard barking and then the scrabbling sound of dog paws skidding on the wooden floor, a big dog.

The elderly house steward, Master Hemmings, came hurtling into view with a big Irish wolfhound on a leash, pulling him along. Had my uncle brought one home? He reminded me of my long-lost Wynne, but this dog looked thinner and whiter-haired. He pulled his leash free and sprinted straight for me.

Wynne! I fell to my knees and held out my arms. The old dog bounded so hard into me that we both went down, rolling on the floor.

"Wynne, my boy, Wynne, my Wynne!" I laughed and cried, letting all the emotions loose I'd tried too long to hold within.

Madly licking my face, he remembered me. Since I had left him in the Maynooth cellars that night Magheen and I had fled six years ago, what a story he must have to tell. Perhaps, I thought, Uncle Leonard had brought him for me to say he was sorry for his treachery that night he arrested my uncles in Dublin. Could he really have let Gerald escape, as they had accused him? I had heard that they also held him responsible for not producing the precious *Red Book of Kildare,* so that retribution could be made against those who had supported the Fitzgerald rebellion, the very book I had buried under the hedge here at Beaumanoir.

"Lady Gera," Master Hemmings said with a wheeze, "my lord Grey brought your dog back — with some other things from Maynooth for your family. He said . . . he would see you when his name is cleared, and he is

returned . . . returned from the Tower. . . ."
The old man faltered.

My face buried deep in Wynne's hair, I shuddered, for who had ever returned to us from the Tower? Still hugging him, I choked out, "Thank you for tending him, and to my uncle for this too." It burned my mouth to say that, but I guess even traitors, especially those who were suffering just like those they had betrayed, could be a bit forgiven.

And so, besides Magheen and my remaining family, I now had two precious keepsakes from the past: my dear Wynne and *The Red Book of Kildare,* which our English enemies still desperately desired.

Whitehall Palace, London
May 26, 1541

"Ooh, this cloth-of-gold gown will glitter in the sun!" The queen cooed and clapped her hands as her mistress of the wardrobe displayed it for all of us to see. "When I took my motto, 'No Other Will But His,' I did not know his will included giving me such pretty jewels and gowns! His Majesty says he wants to show me off to the whole realm!"

"And he wants to be sure," I muttered to Alice as we stood in the far corner of the queen's crowded presence chamber while everyone but me fussed over each new gown, "that a massive display of might keeps the rebellious north under his thumb."

But everyone, even me, was excited, for the entire court was going on a summer progress out of hot, sweaty London on a visit to the north. The king's ulcerated leg was much improved, even though he now walked haltingly with a cane. My former mistress, Mary Tudor, was going along, though not the king's younger children, Edward and Elizabeth. Except for last yule, I had seldom seen Anne Boleyn's daughter after that first moment we'd come eye-to-eye.

"I've heard," Alice whispered as she brushed flecks of something off my brocade peach-hued double sleeves, "that His Majesty is so eager to be certain the northerners stay cowed that he's ordered huge pieces of artillery to be brought by sea and river to meet us in the north. And," she added with a smug smile, "your old friend Lord Edward Clinton is in charge of getting the pieces there by ship, some of the very same guns, so gossip goes, that were used to assault your Irish castle back when."

I gasped. Why did it ever seem that each thing I heard of Captain Edward Clinton made me hate him more? "Back when," I spit out, but caught myself before I blurted out the rest: *Back when is the present and the future to me.* Perhaps, I thought, on this progress where the entire court would be living in tents each night, at least when manors or castles were not nearby, I could somehow get close to the king. But what to say then, what to do to hurt him?

And now I must contend with Edward Clinton, whom I had assumed would not be on the progress, even if it would pass through his home shire. If only I could also find some way to bring him and Dudley down, but Dudley, now named Lord Lisle, with more advancements on the horizon, sometimes went to sea too. He was staying behind with several others to oversee royal business in London while we were away.

I sighed and watched the excited Cat Howard continue to ooh and ahh over each gown presented before her. Her little lap-dog peeked out from the hem of the growing pile of brocade and satin gowns. How I missed Wynne already, to have been reunited with him and then to leave him so soon, the story of my life somehow. But it gave Margaret something to do, for now she cared for Alice's midgets and my mammoth dog. Whom did I have to care for, whom I really cared for? I thought, feeling sorry for myself amidst all this fervid anticipation.

When the queen excused us, I went out into the Privy Gardens with their great, splashing fountain. On the other side of the high wall ran the Thames, and boatmans' cries oft echoed here. It was my favorite place in the king's favorite London palace, a haven for me. Running splashing water — boatmans' cries . . .

"Forgive me, Lady Gera, for following you outside, but is it not a lovely day?" a man called to me.

The sun was in my eyes at first, but I recognized the voice. It was Sir Anthony Browne, the king's longtime master of the horse, an intimate of the Tudor tyrant. Sir Anthony was nearly sixty but in good physique for his age, much better than his corpulent comrade the king, who was a bit younger. He was widowed, with a brood of adult children who were probably older than I, so at first I'd given no thought to the fact that he seemed to seek me out, for many did.

But since I had been back at court — especially since I had finally accepted that it would give me greater access to the king if I were with one of his comrades — I had taken to smiling at Sir Anthony. Mother, may God rest her soul, would be pleased I was finally harkening to the advice she'd given me the last day we were together. An older, powerful, wealthy man, she had said — yes, but at what price to me?

"It is indeed beautiful, my lord," I responded. "I thought you would be so busy preparing all the horses we will need for the progress that I would not see you until we were en route northward."

He smiled like a schoolboy who had been given a yuletide sweet, and offered his arm, which I took so that we strolled the gravel paths among the blooming rosebushes together. "I hope so much time in the saddle will not tire you, Lady Gera. My condolences again on the loss of your mother."

No thanks to your friend the king for making her life a misery, I longed to spit at him, but I said only, "That means a great deal from one who recently lost his wife."

"Well, not so recent that I have not picked up the reins of my life again. My family is all grown, you see, and wed, but for my youngest, Mabel, who will soon come to court. I am sure she will appreciate new friendships here, if you would be so kind."

"Of course, if you don't mind her friend coming from a rebel past," I said, unable to completely play the simpering maid. I had best get a reading right now of whether Sir Anthony was sent to keep an eye on me for someone else or for his own pleasure.

"My dear," he said, stopping and turning toward me, "you are here at His Majesty's court, so obviously that past, which is no fault of your own, is no impediment to your future. I know all that Irish sadness is behind you, and so much brighter lies ahead. I shall look forward to riding off and on with you on our journey through the northern shires and, dare I say, our journey of life." Then he added hastily, "Here at court."

He bent to kiss my hand, surprising me by turning it palm up before he did so. I studied him anew: Anthony Browne was an agreeable enough looking man, brown hair, with flecks of gray, brown eyes, brown beard and mustache, even brown garments today, though finely made ones. The other times we had talked, I had thought his bluff speech and manner a sort of brown too — bland and plain. But he had surprised me today, and the touch of his lips lingering on my palm was pleasant. As for that remark about life's journey, perhaps there was some potential here for closer proximity to the king through at least a friendship with Sir Anthony Browne.

Amidst the happy hubbub, as if I needed more reasons to detest the king, on May 27, 1541, Margaret Pole, Countess of Salisbury, was beheaded for championing her rebel family, especially her son Cardinal Pole, who had criticized the king. Luckily for Cardinal Pole, like our dear Gerald, now Earl of Kildare, he was living abroad, out of the king's clutches, though word was the king's minions were trying to track him and arrest him too. The executed countess had been a close confidante and governess of Mary Tudor when she was but a child, and I could imagine how Mary mourned her loss. This king thought nothing of executing women who got in his way, let alone men — a warning to me, but one I could not afford to heed.

For dire word came to the court from Ireland that Henry Rex had been declared not lord of Ireland, as was tradition, but its king.

On June 13, but a few days before we set out on the progress, under great duress, the Irish Parliament met to formally declare and proclaim the king's new title and power over the Irish. In a great company of Irish ecclesiastics and nobles, including the earls of Ormond and Desmond, the O'Brien and the O'Reilly — all at one time or the other allies or rivals of my father — everyone had been forced to give their approval. Of course, with the Fitzgeralds out of the way, or so everyone thought, the Irish were forced to accept this king and his heirs in perpetuity, as, I believe I later heard the decree was pompously worded, "Forasmuch as Your Majesty has always been the only defender and protector under God of this realm."

Again it was stated in Dublin that day, as in the Act of Attainder against my family, "The blood of the Geraldines is corrupted toward the Crown of England." On and on with outrageous lies and insults, forced on a free, proud people. None of the good things our family had done to raise the level of living, to help educate and prosper our beloved people, were so much as mentioned.

The very night before the court set out on the progress to flaunt the king's power to his own subjects, I sneaked into the chapel and, before the altar on my knees, vowed to myself and God — Saint Brigid too — that the so-called king of Ireland would not find a defender and protector to keep him from Fitzgerald justice through me!

CHAPTER THE FOURTEENTH

Despite all I had seen perpetrated on the Fitzgeralds, Ireland, and the king's own people, I did not fully grasp the awesome might of the Tudor king until that day the court set out from London. The great royal progress to the north, as it was called even years after, assembled and snaked its way northward, a massive, portable display of people, property, and power, with me in the midst of it.

One thousand marching armed soldiers led the way, followed by eighty archers with drawn bows. Then, finely arrayed with gorgeous trappings on their mounts that Sir Anthony had prepared, rode the king, queen, and his closest nobles — I rode behind the queen at the back of that group. Next came our servants, including Alice, mounted or in carts, then wagons drawn by huge draft horses carrying two hundred tents, followed by five thousand packhorses laden with tapestries, clothing trunks, and plate for the three hundred courtiers. And to think that when we Fitzgeralds had ridden out in the sweet Irish summers to survey our lands and greet our people, we had gone with but twelve guards, one Geraldine banner, and hunks of meat, bread, and cheese in our saddlebags!

But that was not all. More lumbering wagons and carts with food, staffed with enough servants to handle four months of meals in field kitchens, brought up the rear. They would be needed when we were not entertained at manor houses or castles. Along the way, the king and his men would hunt deer, and fish and fowl would be provided, enough to feed an Irish army on the move.

When I had heard the stops our huge entourage would make en route, I was disappointed we would not visit Edward Clinton's holdings of Kyme Castle or his new manor house I had heard he was building at some place called Sempringham. We would pass very nearby and go through Lincoln itself, the seat of his power in Parliament — so close but yet so far. It was only curiosity that made me want to see his lands, I told myself, for I was eager to take in every day's vistas and villages.

Although I loved being out in the country-side, away from London, the roads were so crowded with gawkers that we might as well have been prancing down London's busiest fairways. Only some of the guards and soldiers marching before us were mounted, but dust was always our companion. At least the weather was quite good, with rains only at night, drumming on our tent roofs through the midland shires, even as we passed quite close to Leicester and Beaumanoir. Hours in the saddle, as Anthony Browne had warned, and cots at night made me stiff by day, for only the king and queen slept on down mattresses each night in their separate tents.

We traversed more or less twenty miles a day, with all the stops for food and comfort. Endless hurrahs and "God save the king!" rang in my ears on this tour to what I'd heard both the king and Anthony Browne called the "brute shires."

But it did indeed begin to feel we were in the north when the temperatures dropped at night and the winds picked up, especially beyond Grimsthorpe Castle as we entered Lincolnshire, Clinton's home area, nearly two-thirds of the way to our destination of York. Grimsthorpe was a vast edifice owned by Charles Brandon, the organizer of this progress. After a comfortable single night there in real rooms in real beds, we pushed on and camped again in tents on a grassy plain surrounded by gentle hills.

The buzz in the cavalcade that day had been that Lord Edward Clinton's men would soon join us, after sailing the channel and coming up the great River Ouse with artillery for the king to flaunt in Lincoln and York. There bad feelings about the Northern Rebellion still seethed, though it had been put down five years before. So of course I was tense too, wondering if I would have to face Clinton again — and with some of the very guns that had blasted my beloved Maynooth and had convinced the traitor Christopher Paris to surrender our stronghold.

But far more disturbing news was the word that had come with the daily London messengers and quickly spread about the camp: When my uncle Leonard Grey's trial for dereliction of duty and treason had gone against him, he had cast himself on the mercy of the king. (The mercy of this king, the fool!) Thinking his holdings and life would be spared for the good services he had done the crown, he admitted he was guilty — and had been beheaded, a familiar fate for those I was kin to by now.

Despite how he had betrayed us Fitzgeralds and deserved to die for that alone, I grieved for the man who had taken my family in and had brought me Wynne. At least, I grieved for his being so stupid as to trust this king — and, of course, I grieved for Alice too, who had loved my uncle even when she knew he planned to wed another. But so far, she was holding it all in.

"You aren't ill, are you?" Alice asked me as she made certain I was settled in the tent I shared with five of the queen's other maids of honor. "You look peaked and you keep chewing your lower lip and frowning off into the distance."

"I grieve for him too, really, Alice. And, truth be told, it annoys me that they will parade through the so-called rebel brute north with the very cannons that blasted holes in my home in Ireland."

"I know. But my point is you jump like a startled rabbit every time his name is mentioned."

"Whose name? I spoke only of my uncle."

"Edward Clinton, of course."

She pulled my hands down and grasped them; I realized I'd twisted my single strand of pearls into knots. "My lady," she said, whispering amidst the bustle of the others in the tent, "I know how it is to long for the unobtainable. I warrant you know that I was your uncle's mistress after his lady died, but then he wanted to make another marriage . . . and now . . . look at him. . . ."

She drew in a sharp breath. "I did not mean to ever speak of that to you, and you so young, but now that you've been at court and have seen the ways of the world, I . . . I never speak of him and I thank you for giving me a life away from him. Forgive me, for I know I'm babbling. During his trial, I agonized for him, but now my memories are so dear and yet so painful."

Though she was holding my hands as if to comfort me, I tugged her outside and walked her back by the slope of the hill beyond the fringe of flags and tents. "I am so sorry for your loss and grief, Alice, truly I am," I told her, wishing I had better words of comfort, for she was crying freely now. "If it helps at all, please know that I am mourning my uncle too, for what kindnesses he did extend to me and to my family." What would Magheen or Mother — before she became so sad herself — have said to help her? I wondered.

"I-I know," she stammered, "you have mixed feelings about him, my lady, for . . . for what he — he and I — did that night in Dublin when your uncles were taken. I only wanted to please him then, hoping he would . . . would keep me." She tugged her hands free and produced a handkerchief from up her sleeve to blow her nose and wipe under her eyes.

"Stay here a moment," I told her. "I am going to tell the others I'll be to bed later — not that they would miss me, since some of them are meeting their lords or lovers. Then we will talk more."

Inside the tent, I made my excuses and one of the women, I recall, whispered, "Is it Sir Anthony? For I heard him tell His Majesty he favors you greatly."

"I'll not tell," I said with a little smile I did not feel and a wave as I seized a shawl Magheen had made for me and darted back outside.

Dusk was darkening into night. Stars were popping out overhead, and the northeast wind was picking up. Alice and I linked arms and walked away from the torches being lit and sat on the grassy brow of a hill where we could see the camp, especially the queen's large, beflagged tent, which was always pitched near ours. We looked at the back of it, but I saw shadows as a few people moved about inside. This late each day on the progress she had never summoned us to her, and oft said she was quite worn out.

Alice gave a sigh and wiped her eyes again. "It is hard to see others so happy in love," she whispered. "The queen has been radiant on this tour, His Majesty's centerpiece, his rose without a thorn. They seem a bit mismatched, but I wish them all happiness."

I didn't, but I patted Alice's shoulder. How much I had disliked this woman at first, but now I wanted to comfort her. In like wise, how much I had wanted to hate Mary Tudor, but found I could not. But no softening, no womanly weakening toward the king and his lackeys, Dudley and Edward Clinton.

We sat in companionable silence and somehow that was enough. We had both suffered, but what woman had not? I felt a stab of sorrow for my mother's plight, losing her beloved husband, her son Gerald, her brothers-in-law, and her home. And, silly girl that I was, I pitied myself.

"What's that ado over there?" I asked, pointing as mounted men and wagons lumbered into our camp, but as soon as I asked, I knew. Captain Clinton was here with the armaments he'd brought part way by sea. They would be carted the rest of the journey through the brute shires as a warning to rebels. I squinted into the growing dusk but could not make out which one he

226

was among the riders. Sir Anthony had told me that Clinton's duty was to deliver the artillery pieces here and then others would take over to get them the rest of the way. So would Clinton go on with the cavalcade or head home, not far away, as I reckoned it?

I insisted on walking Alice to her tent, instead of the other way around, as she had me each night. She curtsied deeply to me with, "I am grateful to be in the service of such a lovely lady — lovely inside as well as outside."

Though we had been both in and out of tents this night, I knew what she meant and was deeply moved. However much I missed Mother and Magheen — Margaret too — it was good to have a companion who was a friend, and I felt, somehow, we'd made that transition this day.

Still thinking of how young women needed the guidance of their elders, I saw the ubiquitous Jane Rochford, the queen's guardian, slip out of the royal tent. She darted away at first, but then I saw her circle back to the rear of the tent, where she pressed her face to the canvas. Was she peering within through some slit I could not see from here?

Watching the carts with cannons creaking in, I lingered on the hill where Alice and I had sat. At last Lady Jane moved, a mere dark form against the whiteness of the tent. But she did not go in the front entrance where she had come out, as I was expecting. Rather, she knocked on the taut canvas where she stood, then apparently unlaced a back entrance, when none of the other tents, as far as I knew, had such. Perhaps since the king had secret chambers and accesses in his palaces, the royal tents had a back entrance.

When Lady Jane opened it to look in and windmilled her arm at whomever was inside, in the wan light I glimpsed the queen in a white night rail in a man's arms, and not the arms of the king. Not even the arms of her secretary, Frances Dereham, whom she had summoned to her so many nights. It was a man who served the king in his chamber, one of his favorites, but not mature in years as were some of his staunchest comrades. It was the young and handsome Sir Thomas Culpeper.

I saw the man and the queen part reluctantly, for he darted back to kiss her again and whirl her once about before darting out the back of the tent with a nod at Lady Jane. While she laced up the opening, so I could not see so much as a slit there, he strode away behind several tents in the opposite direction, then toward the king's large tent across the grassy courtyard.

And so, amidst all my agonizing, finally a piece of dangerous knowledge fell my way that could, if not bring down the king, at least hurt the man and his manhood.

"Crazed and careless, don't you agree?" a man asked behind me in the darkness. I gasped and jumped up, though the voice was one I'd longed to hear. "But I can understand," he went on. "I would almost hazard all for a taste of forbidden fruit myself right now."

Edward Clinton! I was so shocked I hardly took in his words at first.

"How dare you seek me out!"

"Sad to say, Irish, I just found a privy place to relieve myself, and, as I returned to camp, there you were. So what did you see and what do you plan to do with such dangerous knowledge? Will the king kill others to protect his pretty bride queen, and will you be foolish enough to be in his gun sights? Or will he kill only her — and her lover, of course?"

"You . . . you saw it too?"

"I did, and thought you were another of the queen's ladies besides Rochford — which you are — but put here to keep an eye on others seeing what we just saw. But you are here to spy to get evidence against the queen to torment the king, aren't you?"

"You know nothing about anything, so leave off and leave me alone."

"I wish I could," he said, seizing my wrist as I started away. "But I can't trust what you might say that would implicate me too, when I want no treasonous complications. It's possible this will all be hushed up when the king finds out, but I doubt it — rather it will be a bloodbath. If the queen is being so foolhardy, she will be found out and suffer for it without your help, though I know you are passionate for revenge against the king."

"You think you know everything about me."

"Not nearly enough. But you did once promise me that when we next met — and that was months ago — you would tell me all the truth. Perhaps this time then."

My pulse was pounding so hard I could barely hear his low voice in the wind. "Why," he went on, "are you out unchaperoned to watch the queen, or do you have a tryst with someone else? Sir Anthony Browne, perhaps?"

"You, Captain Clinton, are the spy!"

"I keep abreast of court events even when I am away."

"I suppose your lord and master, Lord

Dudley, writes you all. I said, let me go," I repeated, surprised he still held my wrist as I tried to pull free.

"I'm afraid I can't do that, Irish."

"I will scream — English!"

The wretch dared to chuckle. One-handed, he untied the cape he wore. In the rising wind, which had made it flap like raven's wings behind him, I was surprised he took it off, for the night was getting colder.

"I admit I'm stalling for time," he said as he draped it open over one arm, "but I'm trying to reason out the best way to get us both away from here so that, when the queen's adultery —"

"It was but a kiss and a —"

"Grow up! I'd wager Kyme Castle that Culpeper's been bedding her — at her invitation — at least during this jaunt through the shires. And John Dudley says she keeps Frances Dereham with her at all hours dictating letters with only Rochford around — and Cat Howard's known Dereham for years. As for Jane Rochford, she's been poisoned by hatred ever since the Boleyns fell, and I won't have you endanger me or mine, or turn into the risk-her-neck fool the queen's become when she's had everything she ever wanted — except maybe someone to really love."

"You are risking your precious reputation — mayhap your own marriage — to be out here with the Irish rebel like this. I don't take it lightly that some of those guns you've been tending are the ones that were used to batter my home castle. And don't think you can get off by saying you rue the day."

"I'm starting to rue this day. Talk about taking a risk. But for some mad-as-a-Bedlamite reason, I've felt drawn to you ever since I saw you captive on that ship from Ireland to England, the very day you helped me decide to go to sea. Gera, I pray you'll someday forgive me for this, but you're going to have a little accident and go home with me."

"What? I —"

It was all I got out before he swirled his cape at me, over me, then put his hand over my mouth, forcing the material partway in as I opened it to scream. He hefted me into his arms, however hard I kicked and thrashed, and carried me up and over the hill. *Go home with me,* he had said. Home to his castle or his manor house?

He laid me down on the ground; I heard him ripping the ties from his cape. He tied my ankles together, then my arms down at my sides. When I tried to suck in a breath, I was so undone I could barely get air.

"Stop fighting," he said, and squeezed my shoulder. "I'll be back as soon as I fetch myself a fresh horse, since I was leaving anyway."

So calmly spoken. Was he helping me and himself, or the king from learning his royal wife was cuckolding him — yes, cuckolding the king of England! I knew not how long I struggled, even tried to roll away so Clinton could not find me when he came back, but it was futile. It seemed an eternity that I lay there, writhing, cursing him.

I heard a horse snort. "I'll loose you as soon as we are away," he said, and picked me up in his arms. He set me across a large saddle, then mounted behind me and spurred the horse away. I was both panicked and, God forgive me, thrilled.

But I would be missed. Though I had told one lady who shared my tent that I would be in late, surely they would set up a hue and cry for me, at least in the morning.

Clinton soon untied and unwrapped me, then just pulled the cloak back around my shoulders over my shawl. Indeed, my struggles and anger had made me quite warm enough. I sucked in sweet, cool air and looked around.

No hills now, for the land lay flat, much

like my own Kildare. Looking like a ripe peach balanced on the horizon, a full moon was rising. It bathed us in enough light to see the dirt lane, though I supposed he could have followed it in the dark, since this was near his home.

"They will find me missing," I told him while my shoulder and hips bounced against his hard body as we rode along.

"By then I will have a shepherd there to tell them that he found a red-haired woman unconscious at the bottom of a hill and sent her in a cart to Kyme Castle, his lordship's home. And that she has a badly sprained or broken leg and hit her head, so she doesn't recall her name or place — at least for now. Ursula and I will take you in, then get you back to London much recovered when the progress returns. And if you choose to gainsay that story later, you are a fool and will suffer the consequences, and, of course, bring me down too, if that is your wish."

"You cannot do all that!"

"I am doing all that. If the queen has been so suicidal in her actions, someone else will come forward to tell on her. You will get your wish to see the king suffer and not be ruined in the process."

"But —"

"Quiet. We're at the shepherd's house, a

good man, one of my retainers. I'm going to have to take you off the horse so you don't ride away from me."

He reined in by a small stone cottage, half timbered with a thatched roof, dismounted, then lifted me down. Holding my hand instead of my wrist, as before, he tugged me into the tiny front yard and sat me on a settle, then raised a hand to knock on the door, even as it opened. "Oh, yer lordship," came a man's voice.

Clinton went in. I could hear the buzz of men's voices through the open door. A blond woman with hair so light it looked white in the moonlight came out with a cup of cider for me and perched on the end of the settle as I thanked her and drank gratefully. "We've some cheese if you like," she said.

"No, this is fine. I thank you."

"Milady Clinton be glad for guests."

I had time only to nod as Clinton strode back out and we were off again, even as I saw the shepherd with a crooked staff striding back the way we had come, a black-and-white dog at his heels. So easily accomplished, Clinton's mad plan?

When we were mounted again, I was so nervous I had to say something. "Here I am being swept away to your castle. My sister

Cecily would love this, for she's daft about chivalric stories of heroes rescuing beset ladies from evildoers."

"But this tale is real. I am taking you to Kyme, though I'd rather Sempringham were finished to show you. Perhaps I shall show you anyway, my pride and joy."

He meant the house he was building, of course, but he'd made it sound as if I were his pride and joy. In truth, I had not had time to reason out how I would have used my information about the queen's infidelity to bring down the king's pride and joy. An anonymous note? A public announcement to shame him before others? Oh, yes, I'm sure Clinton was right that I would have been blown away in the blast of the king's disbelief and rage. But the sad thing was, no matter what, Henry Tudor would survive and thrive as he had in the past, and I did not want that. I wanted him to do more than suffer. But I reveled in the fact that the man who must fancy himself beloved by all women would be devastated by his own passions again.

"Perhaps they will send my maid to tend me," I told him, not wanting to admit I might owe him a great deal for spiriting me away.

"If so, I hope you can trust her, else I'll

have to really break your leg and knock you in the head to make it all seem the truth."

I knew he was jesting. My father had oft done that to lighten a terrible moment. "Yes, I believe I can trust Alice now," I told him. "But I'm sure your wife will not like playing hostess to two strange women."

"Ursula will do what is best for me and her family."

"Meaning the Dudleys too? I have no desire to help the Dudleys."

"John Dudley would love to have the Howards, including the pompous, poetry-spouting Earl of Surrey, brought low again, and if — when — Cat Howard falls . . ."

"I see."

I really did see things from more than just my viewpoint now. I must learn to reason out all the different sides, the struggles for power and revenge besides my own, so that I could play my cards better, perhaps use other people to get my way. Sir Anthony, loyal to the king to a fault, but, I would wager, willing to take on a beautiful young bride, rebel past or not. Even John Dudley, Lord Lisle, loyal to the king only to the extent he could rise in power and profit his own family. Surrey and his father, the Duke of Norfolk, out for their own family's elevation. But Edward Clinton — what did he hope to get out of this? Just that I would not name him as a corroborating witness if I ruined the queen? Or more?

In starlight I first beheld Kyme Castle. It sported a tall tower of light gray stone, three floors stacked with narrow windows, and a crenellated roof standing sentinel over the scattering of other buildings. It looked so much like Maynooth that I nearly burst into tears.

"A tall tower," I said. "My home castle was built that way against the raids of the fierce Celts."

"This was for defense against the Danes and then the Normans years ago. It serves us well enough, but I intend to make my seat at the new manor at Sempringham, not far from here."

The horse's hoofbeats echoed as we rode over a wooden bridge above a moat. He called out to the gatekeeper. A portcullis guarded the entrance, but it was up, and half a huge wooden door opened for us as if by magic. As we rode into a cobbled courtyard, again I blinked back tears, for, even in the arms of my captor, one of my English enemies, it seemed so strangely like coming home.

CHAPTER THE FIFTEENTH

I still hated the king and told myself I detested Edward Clinton, but I quickly learned to love Lincolnshire. Ursula Clinton was kind too, despite the late hour, as she came out of their suite of rooms to greet me. Though surprised to hear our tale, she saw the import of our news about the queen.

"Shall I write to my uncle?" she asked her lord. She was quite pretty in a pale, wan way and, to my surprise, her stomach bulged with a second pregnancy that even her loosely wrapped night robe did not hide. She had long, honey blond hair parted in the middle and a spray of freckles across her nose. Her eyes were dove gray with high-arched brows, and her lips and nose were thin.

"We can't trust this to pen and paper or a messenger," he told her. "I'll tell your uncle soon enough, if all hell doesn't break loose first. Queen Cat and that stupid, vindictive

Rochford," he added, giving me a quick glare, "have managed to doom themselves."

"Highborn or low, a man should be able to trust his wife and she him," Ursula said, not looking at me, but I took her message. When I had the chance, I would find a way to assure her that her husband meant naught to me.

Lady Ursula Clinton's own maid, rousted out of bed, tended to my needs that night with a bath and a clean night rail, a pretty one with ruffles, no doubt Ursula's own, for she loaned me a gown in the morning. I was quite resigned now to Clinton's plan and hoped they would send Alice to me with my own clothing. In Alice's private mourning, she might prefer to be away from the king and court. But I fell asleep late that first night thinking of Magheen and how she was longing yet for Collum, off in Italy with Gerald, who must come home to May-nooth . . . must come home here to May-nooth, where I slept safely in the tall tower, must come home to the place of our future and our dreams. . . .

I sat bolt upright in bed. Midmorn sun streamed in a narrow window. My heart almost thudded out of my chest. Where was I? Oh, yes, sequestered in rural Lincolnshire because I held in my hand a secret that would convulse the king's cavalcade and the king himself. Here, with Edward Clinton, his wife, family, and people, where I could not let him know that I had missed his voice and his touch and his damned advice, here in Lincolnshire.

Alice indeed was sent to me, delivered personally, to my surprise, by Sir Anthony Browne and two armed guards, so Clinton's shepherd had played his part well. And so, the hour Sir Anthony was with us in the sunny solar at Kyme Castle, I played the invalid with a wrapped, elevated leg and a slightly dazed expression.

"I'll send a physician from Lincoln the moment we arrive to set that leg," he promised. "It must be set right. Wouldn't do to have a beautiful young woman limping after it was healed."

"I thought it was broken at first, my lord," I replied, grateful he hadn't dragged with him one of the royal physicians who tended the king's leg. "I believe now it is only a bad sprain. Yet I still feel a bit light-headed from accidentally knocking my head. I might topple off a horse — and don't wish to be jolted about in a cart," I added, trying to outthink him.

"No, no, that would never do. How kind

of Lord and Lady Clinton to keep you and then send you back to us in London, and now you'll have your maid too. I shall miss you on the way and look forward to seeing you back at Hampton Court when we return from York in October."

I had noted how relieved Sir Anthony looked when he saw that Ursula Clinton was indeed in residence, with a toddler named for the king in leading strings upon her lap. And perhaps he had delivered Alice promptly to me so that I would have not only a nursemaid but also a chaperone. After all, in what he had called the brute shires, who knew what could happen to a maid, especially one he had his eye on?

He leaned down to kiss me soundly on each cheek and held my hands in his overlong before he bade me farewell. Clinton went out with him, where, Ursula reported, they were huddled in earnest conversation in the courtyard.

"He favors you and he's a powerful man," she said, looking more relieved than ever, for I knew she had watched her husband and me together like a hawk. "If he asks for your hand, what will you say?"

"I am not certain, though with my family to help care for, now that my uncle's lands are forfeit to the crown, I . . . I am not sure."

"Is there another who has your heart?"

"Only my love for Ireland and my loyalty to my brother, the Fitzgerald earl, who is in exile in Italy."

She nodded. "The blessings but the burdens of family. I understand, but a woman must take her joys when she can too — a good man, children . . ." she said as little Henry squirmed to get down from her lap and came over to me. "I am sure Sir Anthony would be a good choice for you."

"Horsie?" little Henry asked, pointing at the wrapped leg I had propped up on a cushion on a stool. "Ride?"

"No, Henry. No, no," Ursula scolded. "You see, he means . . ."

"I know. It is universal, isn't it? Well, my boy, as long as the king's man doesn't come back in and find me bouncing you on my broken or sprained leg, get on then and take a ride."

I helped the rosy-cheeked child up on my leg and bounced him a bit. He giggled with delight, a far cry from his father's expression when he came back in, though his face softened when he saw me with his little heir.

"Sir Anthony meant to also say that the queen will miss you, but she will have Francis Dereham write you here from time to time to tell you all the king's triumphs in the north."

"In the brute shires," I added, "these dangerous places where people dare to speak their minds and rebel. And it's obvious Sir Anthony doesn't know one whit of what's going on in the queen's bedroom with Rochford's pandering, so the king must not either."

"Yet. Or else your much-enamored suitor suspects but knows better than to be the messenger of such ill news. And, despite your ability to play horsie with our son, I just realized I'll have to put you in a cart or on my horse if we ride to see the new Clinton manor at Sempringham, because you have told Sir Anthony you dare not ride alone."

"And I dare not go along at all," Ursula bemoaned, patting her belly, "though I'd love to see the progress — actually the progress of the king as well as of our future home. You will take your maid with you, of course, Lady Gera."

"Of course," Clinton added for me, as he looked out the window toward the Kyme Eau, the stream that passed by and fed the moat. "And then, when it's time for me to head back to my ship that's sitting in the wash at the mouth of the Ouse, we'll go by boat from here, then by ship through the channel to the Thames."

I hoped my face did not light when little Henry finally dismounted, for it was not the return of my leg that pleased me so. I did not want the watchful Ursula to know I was thrilled to go to sea again — and with him — so I had to bite my lip to keep from cheering.

Again, as we rode out two days later, Lincolnshire reminded me so much of the Kildare area around Maynooth. I sat before Lord Clinton in his big saddle as we headed toward his new edifice abuilding there, near the little village of Sempringham, barely an hour's slow ride from Kyme. I was awed to silence by memories of home that flooded my mind. Thank heavens, Alice's chatting with two of Clinton's men and his pointing out certain sights kept me anchored in reality.

"This is fen country," he told me, pointing toward the tangle of shallow waters that looked much like the peat-filled Bog of Allen between Kildare and Dublin. The fields of waving, ripe grain, the meadows dotted with cattle but especially with sheep — a wave of homesickness almost laid me low. The little market towns, Sempringham so much like Maynooth, the solitary landscape, the ancient tracks that meandered off the lanes, the rivers running under small bridges — all moved me to silent tears. How had I managed to stay sane away from Ireland?

I nearly lost my hard-won control when we reined in at the churchyard in Sempringham, and he said, "See that well spouting from the ground?" I did indeed, for it so resembled one near Maynooth blessed by Saint Brigid, one of the holy wells of Ireland, where waters flowed freely from the ground. "It is said," he explained, "that Saint Gilbert of the Gilbertine order blessed its curative waters. Ha, we should dip your leg — and your head — in it." I elbowed him for that gibe, but he went on, "Some old folks nearby claim it was dug by fairies."

"By fairies?" I exclaimed. "We call them the little people, and they do all sorts of mischief if we don't appease them. I take it the fen people are tough and stubborn, living independently away from the crown's reach — at least, usually."

"Ay. Prideful and independent to a man — and woman. In short, you would fit in fine here, Irish. But I want to show you my future home."

I thought it a shame they would leave old Kyme Castle, that is, until I saw Sempringham Manor even half built. Ever careful to be certain that no one would see me walking unaided yet, on a pair of crude crutches Kyme's carpenter had quickly made I hobbled about behind Clinton on a tour of the vast place. He helped me get around piles of cut stones and lifted me up to another level when necessary. I thought we played our parts well, but in my heart I began to play another part: that I was his lady and he was showing me our future home.

A gatehouse and an inner courtyard of pale gray, the very hue of Maynooth stone, were mostly completed. A suite for family and separate rooms for guests overlooked both a distant green river with rowboats in it and gardens yet to be planted. I saw fishponds laid out by string and stakes in the ground, a place for a grassy bowling alley. We walked through the foundations of both privy rooms and public ones and a great hall for banquets, receptions, or dancing, or for retainers to come with their requests and problems, much like at Maynooth.

"You have not said much," Clinton — indeed, I believe I began to think of him as Edward that day — observed. "Do you not feel well, or are you having second thoughts about our plan?"

It had become "our" plan now, to keep us both safe from the wrath of the king when — if — Cat Howard came tumbling down. We were quite alone now, even amidst the hubbub of workers and the nearby presence of our companions. Alice was watching men hoist a stone aloft with a winch and pulley, and his guards were momentarily elsewhere.

"In truth, my lord," I told him as the two of us stood at the bottom of the grand staircase that, so far, climbed only to blue sky, "I am in awe and a bit envious. It is all so lovely, so very much like what I hold dear. All of it, your new manor house, Sempringham and Kyme — Lincolnshire in general, Edward."

"Then I am pleased and honored," he said, almost choking on those words in his emotion, much as I had barely gotten my thoughts out. His eyes glistened.

Standing in a shaft of sunlight, he took my hand. I pressed his too. So rapt were we, gazing at each other, that we ignored Alice coming closer and clearing her throat and the fact that one of my crutches fell to the ground. It was then I knew I loved Edward Clinton, but that was of no account, for I must continue to hate him too.

■ ■ ■ ■

I must admit, as excited as I was to go to sea, I regretted leaving Kyme and Lincolnshire in mid-August to head back to London and then onward from there to Hampton Court, to which the royal entourage would return in early October. Edward told Ursula he would be back in time for their child's birth. I thanked her sincerely for her kindnesses to me and Alice and gave a hearty hug to little Henry, who had begun to call me "Dee Jar," the best he could do with Lady Gera.

On an early August morning, we started out, Edward, Alice, and I and one guard, Simpson, in a craft not much larger than the canvas *naomhóg* from my childhood days at Maynooth. We rowed the narrow Kyme Eau, then unfurled the sail in the wider River Witham, which twisted and turned its way through fenland and then hills toward the sea. Late that afternoon, I saw a town in the distance.

"Is that Lincoln?" I asked.

"I see you need more instruction in the lay of the land here," Edward said with a tight grin. "Lincoln's inland and farther north. That's Boston, on the waterway called the Haven, and it will take us right to the wash and then the sea."

"I never heard of Boston, but then you would be a stranger in my land to all but Dublin, I wager."

"Will you take me on a tour of it some-day?" he said, his voice lower than before.

"If you help to get me home — home to Ireland," I whispered back, and heard Alice force a cough and clear her throat as when-ever we spoke only to each other.

No doubt she saw the warning signs in me, recognizing them from her own di-lemma with Lord Leonard when he was wed and she first began to adore him — that was what she had told me recently. She said she was so torn by her loyalty to her dying mistress, his wife, Eleanor, but so drawn to him and he to her. And, I thought, as I watched the silhouette of the town with its church tower emerge from the distance, perhaps it was what poor Cat Howard felt: torn between loyalty to the old, fat, ill king and a growing passion for her lover or lov-ers.

I must be careful, I scolded myself, not to fall into the same trap that had ensnared the queen. I must not let my growing desire for Edward Clinton, a married man and a king's man, overthrow me and my quest for justice against the king and John Dudley.

"Boston used to be called St. Botolph's Town," Edward was saying. "It's a huge wool exporter, but most ships are getting too large to approach it, else I would have put the *Defiance* in here rather than left her at the mouth of the Ouse. We'll have to sail a bit of the wash to get to her and my men."

"The *Defiance.* I like that name."

We shared a swift smile and soon were out into the vast expanse of the tidal harbor called the wash. "I timed this for high tide, or we'd be stuck aground, even in this little boat," he told me, pointing at the narrow beaches we passed. "At low tide there can be three miles of beach here. Except for the tides, it's often dead calm, but when a gale blows up, it can turn to raging water in an instant."

"Kind of like court life," I observed. "Hours of boredom and then a big blast — perhaps what is coming soon."

"Exactly. When you live in a place where people need to make their own pleasures, trouble is on the horizon. That's why I like the sea. Your skills can take you far, but a greater force to be reckoned with is always just over the next wave, and that is the challenge and the reward of it all."

"Like that day we met and the storm came

251

up when it was already rough," I said. I was recalling not only our first sail together but the wonderful times I had sailed with my father in Dublin Harbor or along Ireland's coast, watching the sailors, learning what I could about the tides and winds, but — small girl that I was then — never able to steer.

He only nodded, his lips pressed tight together as if to stop from saying more. And then I noted something else about the waters of the wash. It was so flat and calm, you could see forever, clear back into the Lincolnshire fens we had left but that now appeared so close. Sometimes I thought I saw a ship or a hill, but then it all disappeared.

"Mirages," I said, and Alice nodded.

"I thought I was seeing things too," she agreed, as she came back to sit beside me, and Edward moved more into the prow. "And," she whispered to me, "I am going to pretend some of the things — the looks, at least — I've seen between you and his lordship weren't there either. I said I wouldn't tell you, but on our ride from the progress to Kyme, Sir Anthony told me that he hoped you would consider him as a suitor — so there it is."

"So there it is," I repeated, and turned

away to study the shifting horizon.

As night fell, we climbed a ladder to board Captain Clinton's three-masted ship, the *Defiance.* I thought she was a real beauty, and all too soon, I knew what it meant to throw caution to the winds. A breeze had sprung up the moment his ship's master, the bluff Mason Haverhill, turned the prow toward the channel and the waves kicked up.

The sails filled with wind power, the rigging began its muted thrumming as the ship strained southward and the crew leaped to follow orders both on deck and above. Hoping Alice fared better than Magheen had at sea, I did not want to go down to the captain's cabin with her, so I stood amidships, both hands on the leeward rail.

"Remember to limp at least once in a while," she had told me. "That supposed leg injury wouldn't heal completely by now, would it?"

But at this moment, I didn't know and didn't care. I braced my feet a bit apart on the bucking ship in a bracing breeze, and how desperately I wished I could turn pirate, and command captain and crew to sail clear 'round the south of England to Ireland.

After a while, looking as salt-coated as I must be, Edward came to me and said, "Would you like to steer her? It's not easy going, but I think you can manage. Then I must insist you go below with Alice so my cabin boy can feed you and you two can get some rest before dawn, when we'll be in the Thames."

"Oh, yes. I would love to steer."

I leaned on his arm across the deck as we climbed a few steps and approached the man who held the big wheel. "Cap'n, milady," was all he said with a stiff half bow as he stepped away to let Edward take the wheel.

"I seldom steer her myself," he said, "but it does give one the ultimate feeling of power." He nodded that I should come closer. I did, ducking my head under his arm to stand between him and the wheel.

"But in the dark, isn't it more dangerous?"

"Of course, but we know the area and use our navigation devices. And, as I'm still fairly new to this, I rely on my excellent ship's master and crew. Put your hands on the protruding ends of the spokes."

"Oh, it pulls."

"And turns the rudder at the aft of the ship."

He put his hands above mine on the same

spokes, and it seemed to me we steered together. Waves and wind, kings and kingdoms be damned, we steered into the darkness together.

CHAPTER THE SIXTEENTH

Hampton Court Palace
October 16, 1541

"Ooh," Mabel Browne, Sir Anthony's daughter and my dearest friend, whispered to me as the king entered the Chapel Royal with the queen on his arm, "he's so big, and she's so small!"

"In his eyes, we are *all* small by comparison," I told her, both annoyed and amused by the reaction of her first glimpses of the king and queen.

"Hush!" Sir Anthony said as he sat down in the pew on my other side. "Before the service begins, His Majesty will make a speech."

I was impressed with how Anthony — for I was to call him by his Christian name now — always knew intimate details of the king's actions and plans. And I must admit, I was impressed that he had produced such a dear girl as Mabel. In the brief month I had known her — for her father had ordered her sent to court to keep me company until the king's progress returned — she had quite filled the hole in my heart from missing Margaret, yes, and Cecily too. At age thirteen, Mabel was really a bit too young to serve as one of the queen's ladies here, except for the fact that Catherine Howard loved to surround herself with young people, so Anthony had hopes she would be allowed to stay. I did too, however much I suspected he had actually sent her here to be sure I had a second chaperone besides Alice.

Blond and blue-eyed with a pert face and charming laugh, Mabel had cheered me immensely. Like me, she came from a large family, though, in her instance, that meant she had seven older brothers and two older sisters. If I ever wed Anthony Browne, I could not fathom being suddenly stepmother to so many, most older than I.

Although I had told Mabel much of my family and of Ireland, I had omitted the passion for justice and righteous revenge that drove me, and that I knew of Cat Howard's secret, illicit passions. If Mabel told her father, that might be just like telling the king. Not only had I seen the wisdom of not ensnaring myself in the king's wrath, but I didn't want her involved in any dangerous scandals. Edward Clinton had warned me that he expected a large-scale investigation, with the queen's lovers perhaps even being tortured for information when everything exploded.

Although Mabel was petite, lively, and, compared to me, looked delicate, she loved nothing more than to take brisk walks with me along the Thames (once my leg was "healed"), hallooing at passing crafts and picking late wildflowers.

When — if — I wed Anthony, I would think of Mabel not as a stepdaughter but as a younger sister, and I knew she would get on famously with Margaret when she came to live with me, and with Cecily if she visited too.

Ignoring her father's warning for silence, Mabel whispered to me, "Cat Howard is like a cat indeed, sleek and preening, almost purring."

Everyone hushed as the king seated the queen. Then, legs apart like a behemoth bestriding the world, leaning on his carved, bejeweled cane, Henry Tudor turned to address his assembled courtiers. This was not a normal Sabbath service but a hastily assembled thanksgiving gathering on a Sunday evening. Four-year-old Prince Edward, living with his household in the countryside, had just recovered from a bout of quatrain fever so severe that the king had panicked he might not survive.

I slanted a glance at Mary Tudor's profile. Would the king let a woman rule if he lost his heir? Rumors said that, since his young queen was not yet with child after an eighteen-month marriage, he might reinstate Mary and Elizabeth in the line of succession.

But it turned out that the king also meant to give public thanks for something else too. I recall almost precisely what he said that day, for the irony of it struck me so hard I did not know whether to cry silently or scream aloud. I pictured myself standing in the rapt congregation and naysaying what he claimed about the queen — with proof of what I had seen — but I sat like the rest of them, staring at the massive man before us who commanded all our fates.

"Lord High God," he began. I bowed my head with the rest, but peeked at my enemy through slitted eyelids. He stood, not with bowed head, but gazing upward toward the ornate blue ceiling with its golden stars and gilt angels. "We are grateful for the salvation of our dear Prince of Wales, Edward Tudor, beloved by all. And for safe journey on our progress to the north of our realm to calm the once ruffled waters there. And I render thanks to Thee, O Lord, that after so many strange accidents that have befallen my marriages, Thou hast been pleased to give me a wife so entirely conformed to my inclinations as her I now have."

I closed my eyes tight and bit my lower lip hard. He did deserve this wife, but not for the reasons he believed. The murderer of the Fitzgerald men was also a bedswerver with a gargantuan appetite for women and wives, and he had met his match in Cat Howard. Justice for his own adulteries, at least, if not for his persecution of the Geraldines.

I was not only partly appeased but also astounded he did not yet know of his queen's betrayal. Had no one yet discovered it, or had he not been told? Edward Clinton had been so sure the queen would be found out. What a spider's web, one that I yet longed to tear apart. I told myself that if it didn't come out soon, I would somehow send a note to the Privy Council. It would have to be anonymous, since the day Edward and I parted at the royal dockyard in London, I had made several promises to him.

I pictured that scene again as Thomas

Cranmer, Archbishop of Canterbury, the king's chief cleric and close confidant, began his sermon. In my mind's eye I sat not here, but stood clasping Edward Clinton's hands in farewell at the top of the gangplank of the *Defiance* a fortnight ago. Then, I was trying to ignore Alice's hovering rather than the closeness of Anthony Browne as he now reached over onto my lap to hold my hand.

"I have missed you, Gera," Anthony murmured, but I heard other words, another voice.

"I shall miss you, Irish," Edward had said that day on the deck of his ship.

"I could almost say the same, English."

We shared a quick smile. "Gera," he plunged on, turning his back to Alice and speaking quickly, "you promised me the night you tried to steal my papers from the king that you would tell me all the truth next time we met. This isn't really the next time, but I want your promise you will not be the one to betray the queen, whatever her sins."

"I do promise that — as long as it comes out another way, and soon."

"It will. You must learn patience."

"I have been forced to learn that and so much more."

"And about Sir Anthony. A union with him would be a protection to you, the best that you could have, except to wed some country lord who could keep you under lock and key in his castle."

It was a tease, of course, yet he looked most serious. No other privy moments so intense had passed between us beyond that precious day we visited his new manor house and I had wished that he were building it for me. Without putting it into words or actions, we had somehow acknowledged our mutual passion that day, then kept it at bay thereafter. Though I hated to admit it, I had come to see that Edward, however loyal to his damned mentor, Dudley, and his horrible king, was a man of honor.

"You believe I need protection?" I had asked him. "Have you heard something else of late that may endanger me or mine?"

"Only that I have seen your strong backbone and manly courage."

"Manly courage?"

"Ay. I know the heir to the Fitzgerald earldom is in hiding, but you have the heart and stomach for the fight — perhaps with words and not weapons — that you have vowed to make for the Geraldines someday."

I was awestruck at first. This man understood me. He saw the fallen battle banner I must resurrect. "But my brother Gerald has the dedication and courage too!" I protested, before I realized Edward might be leading up to inquiring whether I knew where Gerald was. Had all of this rescuing of me been too smooth? Had he — Ursula too — befriended me to learn Gerald's location and plans? No, no, I could not help but believe the best of him.

He held up a hand to halt the rest of my protest. "Back to my point. I worry that if you wed Sir Anthony, it could be your shield and buckler but your downfall too. Once you are that close to His Majesty through one of his most trusted, intimate friends, you must not think you can get away with something rash or dangerous, even if you ferret out some weakness of the king you can exploit through your connections or your allure. Promise me you will not take risks that way."

"You mean, once I am in his inner circle, try to seduce the king — at least to trust me — so I can bring him down?"

Edward's grip on my hands tightened. "When the queen falls, he will be furious, then crushed. Despite his age and failing health, he will be looking quickly elsewhere for a wife or a mistress to assuage his grief. He's taken mistresses before from among his friends' wives, clear back to Mary Boleyn when she was wed to his friend Will Carey. I loyally serve my king and country, but I know what it is to be a royal ward with a father dead and be dependent on those in power. I know what it is to yearn for place and position, and for someone to truly trust and love —"

"He certainly loves her, and she's so pretty!" Mabel whispered, knocking me out of my daydream as she elbowed me. She sighed so heartily that Anthony leaned into me, over me, and rapped his daughter on her knee with another, "Hush!"

At least all that covered my own sigh, one of exasperation that the so-called King of Ireland could be such a dolt, standing on the precipice of shame and grief he did not see coming. And I sighed inwardly, shamed and grieved by my fierce longing for the man I missed and would never have.

But soon the storm clouds at court gathered, full to bursting. The king, they said, had suddenly gone hunting. The queen, informed of that, was surprised and kept to her chambers, most annoyed. The royal party — Anthony Browne was one who supposedly went hunting with him — was gone nigh on three days. Henry Howard, Earl of

Surrey, came to visit the queen and tried to lure her from her foot-stomping frets with chatter, compliments, and sweet sonnets, but to no avail. As he left her suite of rooms, he snagged me and pulled me aside, looking in quite a foul mood himself.

"Something's afoot," he muttered. "I know your hoary-headed suitor rode out with the king, but do you know where they went or what's going on?"

"I believe each time you have come to court since I have lived here, you are the one who knew the inner workings of it all. Are you surprised you could not cheer your royal cousin, then?"

"They must have had a spat, but she can't recall over what, the silly chit. And after such a triumph on the great northern progress. Strange, for I heard His Majesty made a pretty speech before the court and God himself — the heavenly God, not the earthly one we must put up with —"

"Surrey," I interrupted, "the walls have ears here. You'd best watch your mouth."

"I'd rather watch yours —"

"Because there's been talk you have been overbearing about your Howard family claims to the throne if the Prince of Wales would have died —"

"Ha! The rebel Fitzgerald pot calling the

rebel Surrey kettle black. I only — Now what in heaven's name are those guards here for?" he muttered as eight yeomen marched down the long gallery past us with their halberds held at the ready.

I spotted Mabel and saw her father had returned from the long hunt with the king to parts unknown. I excused myself from the distraught Surrey and hurried toward them.

"Ah, my dear," Anthony greeted me, with a quick kiss on my mouth.

"Is the king back?" I asked. "But why the show of his yeomen guards?"

"Disaster has struck His Majesty — and the queen," he told us, pulling both Mabel and me back into a windowed alcove. "The queen is going to be arrested for the worst of crimes to her royal lord, for we have solid evidence she's been unfaithful to him."

"No!" Mabel cried in disbelief, wide-eyed as she clapped both hands over her mouth.

Afraid to show my expression — a mingling of relief and sadness yet joy that the king would suffer — I put both hands over my face as if I would cry.

"Gera, Gera," Anthony crooned, and pulled me close with one arm, Mabel with the other. I saw he had not even removed his riding cape, which was covered with road dust and made me want to sneeze. "Now listen, my dears. All the evidence against the queen for her licentious past — even as a young maid reared by her Howard grandmother — has been laid out before the king through an anonymous note sent to the council."

I started at that: It was as if I had wished it done. Evidently thinking I was just shocked at his news, he plunged on. "Even since she's been wed, she has been unfaithful to her lord with at least two men, her privy secretary, Dereham, and the king's own favored Thomas Culpeper. I cannot bear to relay to you maidens the rest of it. I am to conduct more of the investigation and help bring the charges."

"He will put her away?" Mabel asked.

"Permanently. We talk treason here, for, adultery aside, she could have got herself with child, and the king could be led to believe it was his own. He was seduced by her youth and beauty, the vile, plotting little whore."

The vile, seducing, plotting, unfaithful whore — that was what they had said of Anne Boleyn. I pulled away from Anthony's embrace as the huge impact of what had happened assailed me. My desire to see the king suffer — it came with a huge price for a young woman, however foolish, and the young men who must have loved her. In my mind's eye, I saw Thomas Culpeper return to Cat Howard for yet another quick kiss and recalled how he twirled her so happily in his arms. . . .

"Gera, I believe we should find you a chair," Anthony said. "You look ashen, my dearest."

"No need," I assured him. "Just the shock, the shame of it all."

"I am sending both of you away from court on the morrow to Mary Tudor's household for a while — with His Majesty's permission," he told us. "Gera, I know you have served the queen, but I am one of four men the king has entrusted with the examinations of the queen's ladies, and since you left the northern progress early and could know naught of all this, I am taking you out of this hornets' nest."

Hornets' nest, yes, that was what it was. But so easily accomplished to escape all this?

In a quick, quiet voice, Anthony went on. "The queen and her accomplice Rochford are to be sent to Syon House on the Thames eight miles from London, where they will be kept close confined and questioned, then mayhap to the Tower."

"The Tower . . ." I said, feeling sicker by the minute. Of course, that would be anyone's fate — even a young woman's — for crossing this king. My father languishing there, my uncles taken from there to their terrible deaths . . .

When shrieks shredded the air, I almost thought they could be mine.

We heard men's voices down the way near the entrance to the queen's rooms, then a woman's strident tones, arguing, cursing, wailing.

"The king's praying in the Chapel Royal," Anthony told us. "Go to your rooms, both of you, and keep your heads down until I fetch you early on the morrow." He pushed us in the direction we should go and vaulted away, shoving courtiers back to reach the ruckus.

Standing shoulder-to-shoulder — though I think Mabel was too short to see it all over the heads of others — we watched as Catherine Howard, queen of England, ran screaming from her presence chamber and careened down the long gallery toward the Chapel Royal, where the king had publicly blessed their union but three days ago. Her frenzied words were hard to discern amidst her cries of terror as Anthony and several of the king's guards ran after her.

"He will see me! My husband will see me! He'll forgive me, save me — no, no, unhand me; I am the queen, the quee-eeeeen!"

I could not catch another glimpse of her as she was dragged back into her chambers amidst the horrified courtiers. Some of her ladies burst into tears. For once, I did not see Jane Rochford. Surrey shoved past us, running down the hall, perhaps to report that another Howard family queen was on the royal road to destruction, with all his family's hopes destroyed as surely as the Fitzgeralds' had once been.

CHAPTER THE SEVENTEENTH

I was pleased enough to escape the chaos at court with Mary Tudor and Mabel, though I admit I would have liked to have stayed to see the king shamed and suffering. He was in a fierce rage and wildly vindictive to boot, at first screaming that the woman who had defied him should have "torment in her death." Yes, we Fitzgeralds had long known the black heart of the man who was king.

Outside in the clock courtyard, Anthony kissed Mabel and me farewell in much different ways: He gave his daughter a peck on the cheek but bent me back in a long kiss and embrace with whispered words of not being parted ever again "when the king is quite recovered."

Truly, I wished for neither of those things, but I did then get my wish to someday confront John Dudley, Lord Lisle. For, unbeknownst to me, he stood there in the flesh, wrapped in fur and leather on this brisk autumn morn, the man given the charge of seeing we were safely delivered to Ashridge Manor in the countryside.

Anthony introduced me to Dudley before we mounted. "My Lord Lisle, I am pleased to present to you Lady Elizabeth Fitzgerald. My dearest, the king's loyal servant, John Dudley, Lord Lisle."

I gripped my fingers together in my fur muff to keep from leaping at him to claw at his eyes. Shuddering — I warrant they thought it was from the chill wind — I stood my ground without a word. Dudley's hard, dark eyes assessed me; I glared at him, and it was not like me to be tongue-tied.

Anthony looked taken aback and became desperate to fill the brisk air with words. "Lady Elizabeth has served the lady Mary before, and is a special friend to me," he told Dudley, making me realize again how much power Dudley must have, this king's henchman, as he had been called. "She's lived in England for years now, first at Beaumanoir near the Greys. She is guardian and friend of my own daughter Mabel while they are under the aegis of the king's daughter Mary."

I recall not what else he said that day, but I do remember that John Dudley told him, "I know her past, even that she was a guest at the home of my niece Ursula and her husband, Lord Clinton, in Lincolnshire this last summer. I assure you, Sir Anthony, I shall take care of her."

I hoped Ursula had not told her uncle that I had seen the queen with one of her lovers. I still thought, as Anthony helped me mount my horse, that Dudley looked like the very devil, with his pointed beard, sleek, slanted eyebrows, and fiery stare. Perhaps I read too much into his so kindly couched but, to me, ominous words: *I shall take care of her.*

I suppose it was best that John Dudley avoided me like the plague during our sojourn to Ashridge in Hertfordshire, where Mary and her ladies were to stay until the upheaval at court was dealt with, for I am not certain what I would have said to him. I longed for a dagger to stick in his ribs, but he was not my ultimate target. I did, however, glare daggers at his back as he escorted us through the frost-blighted countryside. But I knew I must bide my time, as with the king, and find some worthy way to make him pay.

So I watched him continually, without turning my head, trying to learn his weaknesses and ways. I overheard him speaking in a most polished, ingratiating, entertaining way to the lady Mary. He was obviously proud of his children, especially his five sons, for whom he said he had great plans. When he rode farther back in the entourage with our guards, he had the habit of hawking up phlegm and spitting, of boasting and cursing, as if he were a cruder, different person altogether, a hail-fellow-well-met at their level. He seemed content to avoid me too, yet I felt he also watched me.

We finally dismounted, sad and saddleweary, before a gray stone manor house all clasped in the claws of brown, dead ivy. As I was about to follow Mary and Mabel inside, Dudley appeared suddenly around the front of my horse and put out one arm to stay me.

"I regret," he said, "that I was the one assigned to oversee the sad execution of your half brother and uncles."

I gasped. I had not expected such a direct broaching of that or anything smacking of an apology.

"Is it," I countered, "an excuse for horror and injustice to say you serve the king and so must do the unspeakable in his name?"

"Lady, the Bible says we are to serve those in power, even be loyal to an unjust master — which, of course, this king is not."

"Oh, of course not! Two of my uncles did

274

not so much as lift a hand against him! And my father and his sires kept Ireland calm for years for this king and his father before him, so —"

"Enough!"

"It is not!"

"It had better be, or you will drag yourself and those Fitzgeralds left down with you. Fair warning now," he said, shaking a gloved finger nearly in my face. "Best marry Anthony Browne and breed English children who will learn where their loyalty must lie."

Mabel's voice called out from the doorway, "Gera, are you coming in?"

"She'll be there soon!" Dudley answered for me, then turned back to where he had me hemmed in between my horse and his. "You know," he went on, "I understand your loyalty to your family, for I am building a dynasty, and I regret to see your male lineage decimated, though you yet have two brothers, one hiding on the continent, one easily available — he is a ward of the Greys, I believe."

"Are you threatening me to behave so that my brothers will be safe?"

"Not threatening you at all. Your beauty, cleverness, and passion will take you far if they are not used amiss. Take that as advice, not a threat, Lady Fitzgerald, a Geraldine called Gera. And — oh, yes — one more thing," he said as he took a step away, then turned back. "I couldn't place where I had seen you, but your fierce spirit just now and your unforgettable face have reminded me. We'd never met, and yet your image was burned in my brain. You dared to be there that day in High Holborn on the way to Tyburn, didn't you? A young woman, wild with courage and rage, shouted out that battle cry that caused such chaos. I wondered for years, but it was you. And, to a man, your uncles and half brother shouted that same thing — on the scaffold before their ends."

I lifted my chin and stared up at him unflinching, unblinking. "A Geraldine will rule again someday in Ireland, but no longer for this king," I told him. "A Geraldine," I said, not raising my voice. "A Geraldine."

His jaw fell open at my audacity. Even as he shoved his horse's flank to open up an exit for me and I moved toward the manor door, I heard him say, "Then perhaps, Irish she-wolf, the Geraldines will rule for a Dudley heir someday."

I did not so much as look back as I heard him hawk and spit. I was tempted to stride back and spit at him in turn. Though I wanted to both flee and fight him, I walked slowly to join Mary Tudor's ladies in our exile at Ashridge. I hoped my father would have been proud of me for such restraint and for walking regally, head high, as the princess of Ireland he once vowed that I would be.

We passed dreary weeks at Ashridge, all of us feeling on the brink of some deep, dark chasm. I wondered how the queen's other ladies, who had not been spirited away from harsh examinations, were faring. Mary Tudor was tense and always tired, and, as the daylight fled early in December, she kept to her bed. Sir Anthony sent messages that the queen had been stripped of her entourage, jewels, and gifts and removed to Syon House, a former nunnery, in the city. Her lovers were examined under duress — that is, tortured — for information and to obtain confessions. Her promiscuous past was paraded before a tribunal, and she, with Jane Rochford, her panderer, was adjudged guilty, taken to the Tower, and condemned to die.

I did not wish that on anyone, except the king himself, and Dudley, of course, but no longer Edward Clinton, whom I missed fiercely. Thank God, Dudley had ridden back to London after delivering us here and posting guards. And I was so wrapped up in my own agonizing that I did not realize until she told me that Alice, too, had her own fears.

"Lady Gera," she said one day, when the two of us were sitting in the bedchamber, now deserted, that I shared with Mabel, "I realize Jane Rochford deserves to die with her mistress for what she has done, but it sets a dangerous precedent, does it not?"

"What do you mean?" I asked her, poking my needle through a piece of embroidery. I was bored to death and had to do something to keep myself busy.

"That the queen's companion and confidante — her closest ally in all that, who no doubt took her orders and kept her secrets — should fall with her, even to death by beheading. I know you do not like to even think of beheadings, but . . ."

"Indeed, I do not. Both of us have lost loved ones to that dreadful fate. But what are you suggesting? You and I have become good and honest companions, I believe, so tell me plain."

She lowered her voice and glanced at the closed door. "If you wed Sir Anthony, you must let go all other loves. I will keep your past secrets, but, once you are wed, there must be no others. . . ."

"Lord Clinton, you mean? Night and day to this Cat Howard mess. I care for him not — not that way."

She rolled her eyes. "I know you have not been with him that way, and I do not mean to speak out of turn. Only," she said with a shudder, "to think they are questioning and torturing people who have information on her lovers, even her closest friends and servants . . ."

"Enough!" I said, standing so fast my embroidery hoop rolled off my lap. "I said there is no comparison. Sir Anthony may be a longtime boon companion to the king, but he is not the king, and punishment for adultery would hardly be beheading. I'll not be lectured to. I have no lovers and never will. Saint Brigid, I don't even want a husband!"

"I'm back," Mabel cried as she swept open the door, for she had just run to the jakes. Behind her came Lady Susan, Mary Tudor's closest confidante, and I prayed neither of them had heard my hasty words.

Susan said, "We're all to assemble in the solar downstairs to hear of the queen's demise. Lady Gera, your lover, Sir Anthony, just rode in to tell us all the sad news."

I knew she meant *suitor* when she said

lover. I also knew I'd lied to Alice, if no longer to myself, that I cared not for Edward Clinton.

Sir Anthony spared us no detail of the tragic story of the king's fifth wife. How she had been a wanton from her early years, Dereham's lover, loose with her body and morals. How she had to be manhandled to get her into the barge that took her to the Tower. How she finally accepted her fate and called for the beheading block so she could practice laying her neck upon it the night before she and Rochford met their fates. How the queen's own cousin, the Earl of Surrey, was ordered to attend her beheading both as proof of the Howards' loyalty to the king and — perhaps, I thought — as a warning to Surrey himself not to overstep.

Many of Mary's ladies wept. Mary looked pale and ill. I knew she had not liked Cat Howard and that she planned to ask her father if she could be his hostess at court now that he had no queen, but she looked sincerely grieved. Who would not, hearing that her sire, whose blood ran in her veins, had brutally set aside yet another wife? Mary's beloved mother, cruelly divorced; Anne Boleyn, beheaded on what many yet whispered were trumped-up charges; Anne of Cleves, bought off and set aside; and foolish, frivolous Cat Howard, however unfaithful, beheaded too. May God help, I thought, the next woman Henry Tudor turned his amorous, amoral attentions upon.

Though sitting stoic through it all — perhaps newly sobered by Anthony's news or Alice's fears I would wed him but loved another — I finally shed my own tears when I heard where the queen had been hastily buried. Her once pretty, plump body and head lay beneath the paving stones of the same small church in the Tower precincts where they had put my father.

After supper that evening and some privy time he spent with Mary Tudor, Anthony sought me out and walked me off alone from the others. Talk was muted that evening; the winter wind howling as if in mourning and the crackle of the fire in the huge hearth were enough to drown out the mostly female voices.

"My dearest," he said, seating us on a padded bench under a frosty oriel window and taking my cold hands in his big, warm ones, "I know this has been hard for you to hear, and I pray you will not think what befell the king's marriage is a bad omen for another young woman wedding an older man. I mean in my own suit for your favors and hand, of course."

"You have my assurance there were no privy secretaries or fond fellows about my chambers while I was growing up — only my brothers, to whom I am still loyal."

"Yes, yes, of course, as I would expect you to be. That is, unless they gainsay the king. But, I assure you, if Gerald, in Italy or France, would come home here —"

"Ireland is his home."

"I mean, of course, to England, to throw himself upon the king's mercy . . ."

I could not help it. I yanked my hands back and stood, crossing my arms over my chest and thrusting my fists under my armpits. "The king's mercy?" I cried, much too loudly. "Forgive me, my lord, but I have seen little of that."

"Gera, on the scaffold, Cat Howard made a speech that she sinned grievously against him, that she deserved her fate. And so did others."

I sat down beside him again so hard my skirts whooshed out air. "Be that as it may," I insisted, "I know some he has executed did naught but belong to a large family where one member rebelled and took the rest down with him."

"I know, my dearest, I know it is bitter yet for you. And you know that I am full loyal to my longtime friend Henry Tudor. So I must have your word that, should we wed, you would treat him with proper deference and loyalty, else it could be my downfall too, for through me you would be drawn into his closest circle."

Edward Clinton had been right to warn me. Marriage to Anthony Browne meant easy access to the king. Why must Edward see everything so clearly when it came to me? But perhaps he had studied me as I had him.

"Gera? I am not yet asking for your hand, but I am asking if I should continue to court you in the most serious and passionate way."

"You told us this evening that the king commanded Surrey to attend his cousin's bloody death."

"Yes, but what has that to do with us?"

"I have seen even kin betray others in my own family, no doubt at the bequest of the king, your dear friend, just as he forced Surrey to appear to approve his cousin's death."

"Gera, you think too deeply for a woman. Besides, Leonard Grey paid the price for his high-handed ways and other missteps."

"More than missteps. But I would never do that — betray my family, whether it be my brother Gerald, the rightful Eleventh Earl of Fitzgerald, or my deaf and dumb sister — or you, if I wed you, my lord."

His eyes shone glassy with tears as he pulled me to him, sliding our thighs together on the alcove seat in a hard hug. "Then you will get on with the king for me — not like you treated John Dudley, with cold disdain? As for your brother Gerald, if he returns, I will do my best to see he is reconciled with the king, for he was yet young, as were you, at the time of the Fitzgerald rebellion. And your deaf and dumb sister is welcome to come to live in my household, a new, united family, I pray, with children of our own."

Children of our own — that would bind us, make me care for him more; surely it would. But my children would be as much Fitzgerald as Browne, as much Irish as English, I swore to myself that night, as I composed myself to make the answer I knew would seal my future with this man — and get me closer to the king.

"I swear I will get on with the king in any public occasion and keep my secrets to myself, my lord."

"Then I shall formally sue for your hand when you return to court, when the rough times are smoothed there again!" he cried, and took my chin in his big hand to position me for a devouring kiss. Strange, but it did not make me feel I rode wild waves, as the merest look or touch from Edward did. But that was best. I must keep my cause and my head clear, not be swamped by desires I could not control.

So that night, I yielded to Sir Anthony Browne, king's man, my lips but not my heart. The die, as Caesar said when he crossed the Rubicon River into enemy territory he wanted to invade, was cast. Yes, I would wed this man. I would not only get on with Henry Tudor but ingratiate myself with him. But had not Anthony heard that I would keep my secrets to myself? And that meant I would still stoke my hatred of his king and find a way to bring him Fitzgerald justice, albeit, of necessity now, in secret too.

With all the talk of the queen's beheading, I should have known I would have my nightmare again. That very night it came to haunt me. Trapped in the cellars of Maynooth while bombardment exploded overhead, I tried to hold *The Red Book of Kildare* to me, to keep it dry above the water streaming past with the heads in it . . . tried to find Gerald in the flood, to tell him to flee, to beware the betrayal of the Tudor king. My father's face, my uncles', and Silken Thomas's went past, all shouting, "A Geraldine!

A Geraldine!" Then foolish Cat Howard's head spun by as she clutched the ruby red necklace around her neck, screaming at me, "Do not wed for power and fame. . . . Wed the one you love, the one you love. . . ."

I thought I screamed aloud as I awoke, but no one else in our bedchamber stirred. When my heartbeat slowed, I heard gentle breathing. Mabel had the covers clutched tight around her like a little tent, my dear friend and future stepdaughter.

I lay there, perspiring, and tried to calm myself. My once vague plans were coming together now. I would wed a wealthy man who had easy access to the king. We would live at court, where I could find an unguarded privy moment to stop this king's cruelties — and the dreadful nightmare that had stalked me for years. Surely it would go away when I made Henry Tudor pay for his sins against my family, when I got Gerald home and back to Maynooth — someday, somehow. Anthony had said I could have Margaret with me, at least when we were at our own properties, though not at court, which would have disturbed her anyway.

Disturbed . . . that dream always disturbed me. Why could I not forget it when I awoke, or even the next day, like other dreams that fled at dawn? Why could I not forget Edward

Clinton, whom I knew cared for me too, though we were ships passing in the night? Wed to others, we would never again steer a ship together, let alone our lives.

Tears ran from the corners of my eyes into my hairline and my ears. Suddenly I longed for them all — not only Edward, but also Father and Mother, so in love with each other, Gerald, Margaret, my brother Edward, Cecily, Magheen, still mourning the separation from her Collum, who had stayed with Gerald these long years. Uncle James, all my uncles. My dear pet, Wynne. How I missed Maynooth of Kildare!

I stayed awake till the dim dawn, afraid the dreadful dream would return if I slept. Yet in a semisleep, to comfort myself, I danced through memories of two places precious in my heart, Edward's Lincolnshire and my Ireland.

CHAPTER THE EIGHTEENTH

Whitehall Palace, London
March 1542

"His Majesty wishes a privy interview, Lady Gera," Charles Brandon, Duke of Suffolk, whispered in my ear, startling me, since I had not noted his approach. I looked up from the cards on the table and saw the king beckoning me from across the room, where he sat alone.

Henry Tudor, to my delight, had seemed a broken man when we had first returned to court a fortnight ago. He had gained even more weight, his leg abscess pained him and stank, and he hobbled about on his cane. The once great warrior and jouster had to be winched up by a machine to sit on a horse. His daughter and hostess, my mistress Mary, had tried to placate him, but to no avail. He was bitter, mean-spirited, and seething with fury.

So was all that enough to slake my thirst

for revenge? No, never, so I bided my time, learning all I could, including following Anthony one evening after he had kissed me good-night at my chamber door. He had been hastily summoned to the king, and my hunch was correct: He went into the king's rooms — perhaps to his hidden rooms I had heard of — from the narrow back servants' hall through a door with no knob or visible hinges that simply looked to be another wainscoted panel. I had not dared to try it, lest Anthony or another should meet me on my way in. But there would be a time for it, I vowed.

Since I had decided to act in secret against the king, what better way than a secret passage into his presence? When I confronted him, I must not simply surprise him — strike from behind — for he must know the reason for my retribution. Yet I was haunted with the thought that I would be stooping to his level to try to ruin him and grieve his family.

The night Henry Tudor summoned me to his table, all his closest courtiers, now including me, were gaming in the king's presence chamber. I had been winning wildly at Gleek again, this time with Anthony's money, so I assumed the king would tease or berate me for that, as he had before.

"Yes, sire?" I said as I approached where he sat at a black velvet-covered table slightly separate from the rest of us. He had been playing with his three closest favorites, my betrothed, master of the king's horse, whom I would soon wed; Sir Anthony Denny, chief gentleman of the privy chamber, who also controlled access to the king and organized his finances through control of the privy purse; and Charles Brandon, Duke of Suffolk, who had fetched me. All three of them had left the table for some reason and were now nowhere in sight.

"Winning again, Lady Gera?" Henry Tudor asked, snagging my wrist to pull me up from my curtsy and seat me in the chair next to and facing him. I resented calling him anything but *tyrant,* bowing my knee to him, and his calling me Gera, but I forced a smile and addressed him properly.

"Fortune seems to fall my way, Your Grace, but only when I am at the gaming tables."

"Not pleased with your betrothal, you mean?" he challenged, pulling me forward in my chair so my skirt bumped his knees. He was getting hard of hearing, and I had seen him wear German-made spectacles when he read, though he was too vain to use them in public. Why did Anthony not

290

come back to the table? I was so close to this man, the bane of us Geraldines, that I could smell his leg pus soaking through his stocking and hear him rasp to breathe. I was so close I could have clawed his eyes out.

"Of course I am pleased with my betrothed, Your Grace. It is only that once someone said to me when I won a pot of coins that it was 'the luck of the Irish,' and the Irish — my Irish — have had little of that."

"Ah, yes, the sad fate of the Geraldines," he said, as if he were not at all mindful of my past, when I knew he and Anthony had recently discussed it. "But you uphold their honor, very prettily too, if I do say so."

With his hand that did not hold my wrist, he reached over and turned my face one way to the side and then the other in the most intimate of scrutinies. "Tudor coloring — much like my girl Elizabeth's — but a most unique face. Surrey may speak and write drivel much of the time, but he was right about 'The Fair Geraldine.' Hell's gates, girl, if you were a bit older, and I a bit younger — and you did not have the Browne brand on you, of course — we would dance a pretty tune in more ways than one."

He dared to ogle me, down, up, the lewd-ster. I felt frozen in horror and revulsion. Was this how blatantly he had examined Edward's first wife, Bessie Blount, then the Boleyn sisters, poor Cat Howard, and countless others before bedding or wedding them? And I was stunned to realize that, if such a clandestine tryst would give me the time and place to kill him, I would consider it.

Thank God, he did not ask me if I would have liked such attention from him, for I feared I would be sick to my stomach and my very soul. Or could he be testing my loyalty to his longtime friend Anthony? Could that be why they had all cleared this table so he could speak with me privily? Surely they had not been placing wagers on what I would say!

I stared at his hand snaring my wrist. That square, freckled hand with reddish hairs was the very one that had signed the Act of Attainder, which still stood against my family. That hand had approved with the stroke of a pen my father's imprisonment and the cruel public deaths of my half brother and uncles and the despoiling of Maynooth and Fitzgerald holdings.

Lest I say what I was really thinking, I managed to get out, "I hope I will bring good fortune not only to my lord Anthony but also to both of us as we serve you together over the years, Your Grace."

Henry nodded, and his mouth crimped in the slightest hint of a smile. "Will you summon your brother Gerald home for your wedding then?"

That shocked me anew. "I have been told he moves about a great deal, seeking a fine education, so I would not know where to send to invite him."

"Ah, a pity. Well, do your best with that, for we would like to meet him, and what more auspicious occasion than a wedding linking his sister to a dear friend of the king of Ireland."

I almost screamed out, *You murderer! You are not the king of Ireland!* But I repeated what was sadly the truth. "Your Grace, I'm not certain how to send him word, though I would love to have him here on my special day."

He didn't believe me the first time or the second, of course. He almost look amused at our little joust as he said, "Tell him, should you get some inkling of his wanderings, that he should bring *The Red Book of Kildare* with him and much will be forgiven. My Irish representatives need the names in it for proper taxation; that is all."

I knew he lied, just as Uncle Leonard had

when he invited my uncles to Dublin to forge a truce. At last the king loosed my wrist. My hand tingled as blood rushed back into it. I thanked God and Saint Brigid that distant Beaumanoir had that precious heirloom book buried under a hedge. The manor had been forfeit to the crown, so my sisters had moved into Bradgate to be reared with Lady Jane Grey and her sisters. After all these years, only I and Magheen, who detested Henry Tudor too, knew where *The Red Book of Kildare* lay.

"Well," the king said as I rose and curtsied, "Sir Anthony is a lucky man. Lady Gera, I would like you to stay on at court to serve a special woman who is coming to live among us at my bequest, Lady Latimer, Katherine Parr, a lovely and proper widow. She has said she would like to have both my daughters with us too. You, of course, know the Lady Mary well, but resemble more the Lady Elizabeth, flibbertigibbet that she is, so perhaps I will put you in my youngest girl's household."

"Yes, Your Grace. I would be happy to serve the lady Elizabeth."

Elizabeth of England, the unloved Anne Boleyn's girl, was beloved by the masses. And though I'd heard the king mistrusted Elizabeth's demeanor because her mother, so he claimed, had been a flirt and a whore, Mary had expressed some affection and admiration for her half sister. She had told me that the girl was a serious scholar, hardly a ninnyhammer like Cat Howard, however much the king now seemed to trust no young woman.

As for Lady Latimer, Katherine Parr, the rumors I had silently scoffed at could be true: The king intended to take a sixth wife. But I had also heard she had beseeched him to make her his mistress and not his wife, just the opposite ploy of the two Howard family queens. Wise woman, Katherine Parr, I thought, not wanting to take on such a dangerous marriage, but perhaps there was a second reason, so court tittle-tattle said. She had been courted by and was quite smitten with the roguish, handsome Tom Seymour, a naval man too, one of Queen Jane Seymour's brothers, the uncles of Prince Edward.

How stupid and arrogant of Henry Tudor to think that any woman could want him for himself now, I fumed, gazing at the bruise on my wrist as I curtsied again and walked away. Without knowing Katherine Parr, I forthwith felt a certain sisterhood with her. She too knew to tread carefully at this court. And if she wed an old man but loved a dashing, younger sea captain, I understood her to the very depths of my being.

On July 12, 1543, Henry Tudor wed Kathrine Parr, Lady Latimer, at Hampton Court Palace. The king's three children were in attendance, and I could see each from the side pew in which I sat next to Anthony. Prince Edward, for once without his long-faced, bearded uncle Edward Seymour hovering over him, perched proudly in the front pew. Needless to say, his other uncle, Thomas Seymour, who had avidly courted today's bride, was at sea and not expected back to court for a good long time.

Edward Clinton was also busy making a reputation for himself in the fleet. Or, when not at sea, visiting his family at Kyme and getting more children on Ursula. I heaved a silent sigh and forced my attention back to Bishop Gardiner's reciting of the marriage vows I soon enough would exchange with my betrothed. The king had decreed our marriage would be at court also, with himself in attendance, but I still could not quite fathom it all.

I watched Mary Tudor, now aged twenty-seven and sad she had no suitor, who sat beside the five-year-old Edward. Next to

Mary, Elizabeth, now nine, was obviously excited not only to be here but also to be in the king's good graces, for she, like Mary, had suffered her ups and downs through various stepmothers and their sire's royal whims of who was legitimate issue and who was not. I had heard the girl was never to speak of her mother before the king, and I pitied her, for I knew better than to bring up my father or family at court too.

My eyes returned to the bride, petite and fair, with stunning hazel eyes that dominated her kind face. Twice widowed by the death of elderly husbands and with no children of her own, she was thirty-one and an heiress, one, they said, who like Anne Boleyn before her favored the new learning in religion. Anthony and his family were staunch old-school Catholics like the king, despite Henry Tudor's having taken the ultimate power from the pope. Dudley and the Clintons, I had seen, were more middle-of-the-road in their religious beliefs, which suited me, for however Catholic I was reared, I thought that believers — even women — ought to be able to read the Holy Writ for themselves and express opinions about it too. Why, even Brigid of Kildare, however pious, had stood up to the old ways when she must.

All that aside, I thought it so admirable that the new queen insisted on the Tudors being a family. It had been announced in a new Act of Succession that the king would reinstate Mary and Elizabeth as princesses in line to rule behind their young brother and his future heirs. I was happy for the king's daughters, for I liked them both, yet I was tormented again with the question of whether my revenge must extend to them too. The king's son and daughters had done nothing against the Fitzgeralds, yet their father's vengeance against my family had not stopped at the death of our sire but had been visited upon his kin and heirs. I was grateful, at least, that my Irish aunts and many cousins had been left alone at home, as long as they kept out of contention for power.

Speaking of heirs, I had recently met the other seven of Anthony's children, who were all adults. The Browne brood had acted kindly enough toward me, but I believe they tolerated me as something to amuse their father in his later years, like a new pet dog. Out of earshot of his father, Anthony, my lord's namesake and heir, had told me, "If you bear him children, they will be the same ages as my own, but I warrant they will be good-looking. Just remember, if you hope for a large inheritance someday, the Browne properties will be split many ways, most going to me and my heirs."

I darted a glance at Elizabeth again, sitting alert, wide-eyed on the edge of the pew. Her household, which I was to be part of when she was here at court, but not if she left for the country again, was meager. Her governess, Katherine Ashley, sat off to the side, her gaze watchful both on the ceremony and her lively young charge.

With the king's hearty, possessive kiss of the bride, the wedding service ended, and we all repaired to the great hall for the marriage banquet. There was to be dancing too, though probably after the newly married couple took their leave, for the king who had once danced till dawn could barely get up on the dais where the bridal pair sat.

You might know that Surrey, who was strangely not even here, managed to throw a pall over the party. Word came and was whispered down the tables that he had slapped one of the king's men for disparaging the Howard name and had been sent to Fleet Prison in London. If the king didn't personally pardon him this time, the law said, he could have the offending hand cut off.

"Haven't the Howards had enough of losing face and losing heads to not start losing hands — a writer's hands?" Anthony had groused.

Sitting next to him, I had ended up across a table from Elizabeth, who was so excited she could barely sit still.

"I love weddings, though it's really my first one," she told me. "But I shall see many more, and wish I could be at yours, Lady Gera."

"I would be honored."

"If you would ask the king, it might help, though I warrant our new mother will put in a plea for me too," she said, giving me, I thought, a soft-gloved but direct command. She seemed to pick at her food, seeming most enamored of the sweet dishes, especially the jelly fritters and sugary suckets. "So what are weddings like in Ireland?" she asked.

So she knew more than my name and marital status. I wondered what else she had overheard as I said, "I must tell you, Your Grace, as in this country, Irish weddings are of two kinds, the courtly kind and the country kind."

"And have you seen both?"

"I have. Though my family had many friends in our village and attended weddings — and funerals — there, our own family weddings were more like formal ones here, but with jigs danced afterward, as well as stately pavanes or gay galliards."

"Jigs? I never heard of such, but I would like to see one."

"I shall teach you," I whispered to her as Anthony leaned the other way to speak with his friend Lord Denny. "This very night, off in the corner if they let you stay up, for I have not danced a jig in too long. Then, someday, you can decree that an Irish jig be danced at your own wedding."

She gave a slight shake of her head, then mouthed so quietly I am sure not even her watchful governess, two seats down, could have heard: "I shall never wed."

My eyes widened. My lower lip dropped. This sprightly young girl — though at age nine, I too had had harsh womanhood thrust upon me — had gone from light-hearted to sober and sad in one moment.

I nodded and changed the subject. She talked that night of loving to ride ponies and loving to read about Caesar's conquest of Gaul — because she wished that England could conquer the French too, and she thought her father might actually lead the next French expedition. She spoke of the first pretty dress she'd had in months and of translating the book of First Corinthians from Latin into Greek. Of playing leapfrog with her brother and learning to play the virginals.

I was in awe of her. And it answered one thing I'd been agonizing over: I still intended to kill the king, but if I survived that, I would try to work with his heirs through logic and loyalty, to somehow get Gerald home to Ireland.

After the bridal couple had gone off to their marriage bed that night and Sir Anthony decided to sit down following a lively galliard where he'd partnered me, I did teach Elizabeth the Irish jig off in the back corner of the hall, even to the shout of, *"Erin go bragh!"* that Magheen had always added at the end. We giggled through it all, hands on our hips, clicking our heels and spinning about. It made me miss my loved ones again, especially when she gave me a quick hug before she darted off. I wanted to go back to the dancing, but I wasn't sure what Anthony would say if I partnered someone else, so I just watched from where I was. And heard a voice behind me that almost knocked me to the floor.

"I would ask you to dance, but I'd rather take you sailing."

I spun to face Edward Clinton. I had

forgotten he was so tall, but not that he was so darkly handsome.

"I . . . I had no idea you were here."

"The weather in the channel was rough, so I arrived late, near the end of the meal. Will you be serving Elizabeth now, or just teaching her rebellious dances and phrases? Imagine, the should-have-been Irish princess daring to teach the off-and-on-again English princess. At least you did not have her shouting, 'A Geraldine!' "

"Would you keep your voice down? And you have been watching me."

"A favorite pastime. Gera, I am going to sea again, to the north, where we are going to try to settle down the Scots."

"Better than trying to settle down the Irish, I'd say."

"However fierce the Scots are, I'd not dare to take on the Irish. But, really," he said, taking my hands in his as he had when we'd said farewell on his ship, "I wanted to wish you all the best — happiness, a family, safety — with Anthony Browne. I promise I won't be appearing at your wedding. . . ."

I could tell he had more to say but couldn't find the words. His eyes glistened with unshed tears. I could have and should have asked about Ursula and his family, but

I too went tongue-tied, savoring the moment.

Finally, he said, "I'm being given a command in the fleet."

"Still on the *Defiance,* I hope."

"The same. Shall I take you captive so you can steer her clear to Edinburgh for us?"

"Do not . . . do not tease. And Sempringham — how is the manor coming along?"

"I don't get to see it as much as I want to," he said, his gaze suddenly devouring me. "But it's as beautiful as ever."

"I'd best get back."

"Ay. Then here's a kiss for the future bride." Before I could react, he bent and slanted his mouth over mine in a soft kiss that turned hard and demanding. He did not touch me otherwise but to press my hands he held between my breasts, which tingled. I wanted to leap at him, grapple him to me. I did not care if Anthony, the raving king, and the entire court screamed at us; I wanted to hold him, keep him.

He pulled back, both lips and hands. "God bless you, Irish, and have a care for your safety — always."

Damn the man if he thought this memory would be a comfort and not a torment, but he turned and was gone.

■ ■ ■ ■

PART III

■ ■ ■ ■

My Womanhood

In ship, freight with remembrance
Of thoughts and pleasures past,
He sails that has in governance
My life, while it will last . . .
When other lovers in arms across
Rejoice their chief delight.
Drowned in tears, to mourn my loss,
I stand the bitter night,
In my window, where I may see,
Before the winds how the clouds flee.
Lo! what a mariner love hath made of
   me . . .

Thus is my wealth mingled with woe,
And of each thought a doubt doth grow;
"Now he comes! Will he come? Alas, no,
  no!"
    — HENRY HOWARD, EARL OF SURREY

CHAPTER THE NINETEENTH

Whitehall Palace
December 12, 1543

My betrothed held my hand as our wedding service was recited in the presence chamber at Whitehall Palace with the king and court looking on. Bishop Ridley's voice droned on, and my thoughts jumped hither and yon.

"Dearly beloved, we are gathered together here in the sight of God, and in the face of this congregation, to join together this man and this woman in holy matrimony, which is an honorable estate, instituted of God in the time of man's innocence . . ."

Although I thought Elizabeth Tudor quite innocent of evil intent, she was not at my wedding and had written me how "mournful" she was to miss it. The poor girl had been banished to the countryside by her father for wearing a ring with her mother's portrait hidden within and for standing up to him over it. I admired her for her loyalty

and pluck, to champion her mother who —
like too many others — had been cruelly
dispatched by the Tudor tyrant. I would
rather have had Elizabeth here even than
Mary, and certainly rather than the king,
though I had nothing but praise for Queen
Katherine for putting up with her irascible,
demanding husband.

". . . therefore marriage is not by any to
be enterprised, nor taken in hand, unadvis-
edly, lightly, or wantonly, to satisfy men's
carnal lusts and appetites, like brute beasts
that have no understanding. . . ."

Henry Tudor was a beast. Because his wife
read the Bible in English and had dared to
discuss points of religion with him, he had
nearly let Dudley arrest her for questioning.
But I knew another reason the king had
almost turned on her too, however much
she nursed him and put up with his bitter,
quicksilver moods. From Fleet Prison,
where the king had allowed Surrey to keep
his hand but had supposedly forbidden him
pen and paper, someone had smuggled a
Surrey poem to the queen, which the king
had found under a bed pillow. I knew that
poem well, for Anthony showed it to me the
night before our wedding, for obvious
reasons. Although, like the queen's true
love, Tom Seymour, my dear Edward Clin-

ton was kept at sea, someone had told Anthony of our kiss on the king's wedding day.

"It was a kiss for the bride — that's what Lord Clinton said, and he left immediately for the sea and Scotland," I answered back. More than once I had stood up to Anthony, though he liked it not.

"I hear it was quite a kiss," he had raved. "Elizabeth Fitzgerald, I will brook no complications with you! God knows, there are enough of those without Clinton sailing through your head — or heart, like . . . like this mariner mentioned in the poem Surrey dared to have smuggled to the queen! 'S blood, with all I've done for you, plan to share with you, I'll not have doubts about where my wife's loyalty — and her beautiful body — lies! The poetic wretch once wrote another poem about you, I recall, so how do I know this one isn't for you as much as for the queen?" he'd demanded, ripping the paper in half and tossing it on the floor, from which I retrieved it later.

"Anthony," I'd replied, trying to rein in my panic — not that he would cast me off but at how the poem struck home with me — "Surrey did not write it for me or send it to me. Nor should he have so presumed with our loyal, loving queen. The king should not have lost his temper at Her Majesty, nor should you berate me. She has not seen Seymour for months and is likely not to again," I'd insisted, hands on hips, my voice rising. "Don't wed me then if you cannot trust me."

Though I was a mere twenty years to his sixty-four, I could tell he was abashed at my defiance. My Irish temper, he'd called it more than once.

"I-I didn't mean that," he stammered, then cleared his throat. "You've charmed the king — me too, of course. I'm sure the queen's quite safe from arrest now, and I simply wanted to make myself clear. I'm so very possessive of you, my sweet; that is all. Besides, however important Seymour and Clinton are to the king's growing navy, I know if they overstepped in any way with our wives, there would be hell to pay. . . ."

Hell to pay . . . I knew the only way to keep Queen Katherine and myself — let alone the realm of Ireland — safe from this vile monarch was to get rid of him. And now that I lived at court and was about to move into quarters even closer to the king, I must strike soon.

"First, marriage was ordained for the procreation of children . . ."

If I bore Anthony children, I must act

circumspectly to protect them. Could he have children in his old age? Must I take John Dudley's advice to rear children loyal only to the English crown? And if I got with child, would my husband send me away from court during my pregnancy to his new country house at Byfleet in the shire of Surrey, or to his favorite, Battle Abbey in the sweet countryside of Kent? All seemed sunny and soft at those sites, when I still longed for the wild, windy reaches of Kildare, or — yes — Lincolnshire.

". . . therefore, if any man can show any just cause why they may not lawfully be joined together, let him now speak, or else hereafter forever hold his peace."

I wanted to scream, *I cannot wed this man! For he is a friend of my enemy and wants me to be loyal. My heart belongs to another I can never have but will ever love. . . .*

"I require and charge you both, as ye will answer at the dreadful day of judgment when the secrets of all hearts shall be disclosed, that if either of you knows any impediment why ye may not be lawfully joined together in matrimony, ye do now confess it."

I do confess as I took my vows, I also promised myself to be as good a wife to my lord as I could be. That is, considering that

I still wanted to kill his best friend, the king of England.

But one other thing haunted me too. On our wedding night, when my husband, who had amorous skills I had not imagined, took my virginity, and rocked over and inside me, I thought of the waves of the sea. And even when my body responded to his arts, I did not feel that he touched me at all.

The next years, I must confess, spun out of my control and sometimes blurred to blackness. Mostly, it was time spent away from court, for I was with child almost immediately. I became quickly ill, sicker each morn than poor Magheen, who helped tend me now, had been at sea when we left Ireland. To visit me and yet keep his court duties, Anthony rode back and forth to London from our country house at Byfleet.

When I could keep food down, I liked nothing more than to sit in my bedroom window, with my beloved old Wynne at my side, looking out over the Fleet River to watch rowboats or small sailboats pass by. My memories "freight with remembrance of thoughts and pleasures past," as Surrey's poem had said, made me yearn to see my long-lost brother Gerald and Edward Clinton, whose names I never spoke. I was like to go mad from my confinement. Sometimes, even when the windows were tight shut against a storm, I was certain I could smell the sea.

The birth was a horror, and my son was born dead. That is all I can bear to write even to this day: My beloved little son, Gerald Fitzgerald Browne, was born dead and was buried at our larger country seat, Battle Abbey, and I was racked with fever and regrets. Was the Lord punishing me for my lust to kill the king? The Bible said kings were put on their thrones by God, but surely He could not approve of evil ones like Henry Tudor.

I put the pieces of myself back together and returned to court, attending the queen or Elizabeth, living in Anthony's comfortable suite of rooms there, ironically just down the hall from the hidden door to the king's back chambers. Both men were away, for despite his age and increasing physical ills, the king led his troops to war in France in the spring of 1544, while Queen Katherine, who became increasingly dear to me, served as regent in his stead. My lord went with the king, as did Surrey, who had been pardoned and released. The Howards were always good soldiers, even though they were dreadful diplomats.

One evening late, when I knew no one was about, I took a candle and tried the hidden door in the narrow servants' hall through which I had seen Anthony disappear months ago. After two false starts, the panel pushed inward, and I traversed a dark, dim corridor, much narrower than the one I had escaped through at Maynooth. With the king's gargantuan girth, I doubted he could fit through it at all. Pushing aside the door at the other end — I was amazed it was not locked — I peeked into a windowless bedchamber dwarfed by a massive oaken bedstead, then tiptoed to a door to view a small adjoining library with a table and two chairs beyond.

An unseen current made my candle flicker, and I panicked that it would leave me in utter darkness. Solid shadows leaned and loomed from corners, under the table, even from the heavy folds of the velvet bed hangings. My heart thudded so hard it seemed drums echoed in the suite. So this was where the king of England slept and worked when fears assailed him, like an animal seeking its hidden den. Now I knew where to leave poison or take my chance with a knife for his assassination.

But when Henry Tudor returned from France, claiming a triumph at Boulogne, bringing my lord with him, I was soon with child, ill again. Must my babies poison me when they were in the womb? Was it another warning to me from on high?

I spent hours on my knees in prayer, trying to make bargains with the Almighty God about this babe I carried: that if the child lived, I would not try to kill the king but would reason with future monarchs to restore the Geraldines to Ireland. My little coterie of Mabel, Magheen, Margaret, and Alice kept me sane until I bore my second son, named, much to my chagrin, but at my husband's insistence, Henry.

It was another dreadful delivery — how had my mother done this five times? The attending physician, brought by Anthony from London, told me he believed I was so torn from the birth that I would never conceive another child. I mourned that and yet felt some relief too.

Though I kept the child in the country, where the air was better, he lived but one year and was lost to quatrain fever, and I was inconsolable again. The Fitzgeralds must be cursed. One way or the other, we could not keep our males alive. Even my beloved wolfhound, Wynne, had died. If only Gerald would come back and fight for Ireland with me.

No matter that Anthony vowed he had not wed me to sire a family, for he had that. Nothing got me through those deeply dark days. Nothing, that is, but a nosegay delivered to me by messenger from the princess Elizabeth, for she and Mary had been reinstated in the line of succession then. The note with the fragrant nosegay simply read,

Dear friend, Lady Gera. We all suffer tragedies and must learn to bear up under them by helping each other. I have learned this the hard way and can only pray the path ahead will be smoother for both of us. I should like for you to return to my household at court you so briefly graced.

Elizabeth Tudor, Princess

Whether Katherine Parr had put the girl up to that, I know not. I yet have the beautifully scripted note and several of the roses pressed from the nosegay. To my husband's relief and the delight of my coterie of female friends — including the Tudor queen and two Tudor princesses — I returned to court, much chastened and changed, yet still, in the very marrow of my bones, above all else, an Irish Geraldine.

■ ■ ■ ■

I was astounded at the change in the king when I returned. Though it had been boasted he was hale and hearty while he had waged war in France, he had become a cripple. He had to use a special chair some called a tram, with shafts back and front, and to be carried from room to room by six men. Sometimes he was rolled about on a chaired cart covered with quilted, tawny velvet. If the court progressed to a new palace, he had to be winched up in a leather harness and swung onto his horse, a massive destrier so it could bear his weight. Most were not allowed to see him being so handled, but I watched it from a window more than once.

I served the queen, who tried so hard to tend her husband. When Mary or Elizabeth came to court, I spent much time with them, carefully planting seeds about how I loved Ireland and how my family had ruled there for the Tudors over the years. I talked of my love for my exiled brother whenever the opportunity presented itself, for I knew that especially Elizabeth loved and missed her half brother, Edward, Prince of Wales. He was usually away from court to keep him in the salubrious country air, though I knew that was no sure protection from young children being struck down.

Then, as well as his own declining health, two more of the king's cruel acts to two very different people with far varying ranks and means made me see that I could wait no longer for my revenge, whatever the price. For one thing, he ordered a young country woman, Anne Askew, the daughter of a knight from lovely Lincolnshire, to be tortured for her Protestant beliefs. Though I was Catholic, were we not all protestants over some personal belief? John Dudley, Lord Lisle, urged the poor girl while she was on the rack to confess to error, but she would not, so His Gracious Majesty ordered her burned alive at Smithfield in London.

Then in December the year of our Lord 1546, when the Earl of Surrey dared to quarter the royal arms with his own Howard arms, the king had Surrey and his sire, the Duke of Norfolk, arrested and tried for treason. I had no great love for the Howards, and Surrey tended to be an arrogant blackguard, but I could not bear the thought of another family who had well served this tyrant king being brought low — perhaps unjustly executed, as my people had been. It was, for me, the straw that broke the proverbial camel's back, and I did something quite heedless. I was still seething over the loss of my sons and full of festering vengeance against the king.

So when I heard that Henry Tudor had ordered Surrey shamed by making him walk from Fleet Prison to the Tower, however well he had acquitted himself in his trial for treason, I took a plain, hooded cloak from Magheen's clothing chest along with a handful of coins I was saving for Christmas gifts and sneaked out of the palace.

With my bundled goods under one arm, wearing my own fur-lined cloak against the bitter wind, I walked to the Holbein Gate outside Whitehall on King Street. Since the royal mews were near Charing Cross, when I wanted to ride or fuss over my horse, Kildare, a beautiful blond palfrey Anthony had given me as a wedding gift, I always sent word she was to be brought to the courtyard by one of my lord's men. But not today. No good, with what I had planned, to be seen mounting — quite alone — by courtiers gazing out their chamber windows or by my lord's men, so I had sent a lad I trusted to fetch Kildare. The public street outside the palace would have to do for a mounting site.

"Milady, where's the rest of the party

then?" the lad, Ross, asked when he'd given me a boost up with his clasped hands under my foot.

"Just down the street," I told him. "Come back here for Kildare by midafternoon."

"Brrr, 'tis cold," he said, no doubt worried about me more than himself. "You should not ride out."

At those words from a mere lad, I nearly turned back, for if my lord heard I'd ridden out alone, would he think I'd gone to meet someone secretly? Well, he was busy with the king today, and this could not be helped. Besides, Edward Clinton — now Sir Edward Clinton, knighted for seagoing prowess and bravery in battle — was chasing pirates hither and yon, so Anthony could hardly accuse me of meeting him. I warrant pirates harried English ships as sorely as they raided Irish ones.

I dropped the lad one of the many groats I'd brought along to grease palms and turned Kildare away through the crowded street. How I hoped Edward's old mentor John Dudley was not overseeing Surrey's march to the Tower today.

You might know that damned Dudley was rising fast too, and had climbed to the position of Lord High Admiral and Earl of Warwick from his service in France with the king. Earl, no less, though he still did much of the king's dirty work, including haranguing poor Anne Askew as her limbs were stretched and broken upon the rack. And I — though I might be wed to one of the king's two best friends — was still a Fitzgerald under an Act of Attainder against my family, as the earl had reminded me just the other day.

The thought of that made me bold. If they dubbed me yet a rebel and traitor, so be it — and I would act that way.

I reined in so that I could change cloaks. No good to look like a wealthy lady out in London's streets, though I knew the leather-and-brass trappings on Kildare might give me away too. How I wished I had a Geraldine battle banner, and how dared the king arrest the Howards for theirs!

I rode eastward toward Fleet Prison, a noisome place where debtors and non-noble crown prisoners were usually sent — another insult to Surrey. He would have quite a walk through London's streets on this cold day to reach the Tower, where his father was already imprisoned. And he, like I, knew so few emerged from there alive. Like my father, brother, and uncles, he would meet his fate there, another man who had helped the king but had now gainsaid him or threatened his great pride. Surrey's wife and children would be left to mourn. Their goods would be forfeit and parceled out to bootlickers. I would not stand for that, never again.

Tying my plain cloak at the neck to keep the hood from slipping off, I rode down the Strand, then through Temple Bar to the prison. Even in the winter, the Fleet River, so clean near our country home, stank like a very sewer, worse than the summer Thames. Guards in Tudor livery stood outside, forming up in ranks, so I assumed Surrey was yet to emerge. At least another man was in charge; I did not see Dudley. I circled around them to get ahead. From the people lining the route, I could tell which way he would go.

I dismounted near an ordinary, a tavern that served meals, and waited a few moments until a woman laden with loaves of bread in a basket started inside. "I need your help and will pay," I told her. "A friend of the Earl of Surrey wants people along his way to shout out, 'A Howard! A Howard! Bless the Howards!' but then to melt away."

Red-faced from the wind, with her nose running, she nodded, but said, "No one gonna melt much in this cold today, mistress." But she eyed the groats I showed her.

"I need you or someone you can trust to spread these coins along the way to men who will start the cries, then move away — ahead along the earl's route to do the same again."

"And you'd trust me with your coins?"

"Goodwife, cannot a woman trust another woman? Keep several for yourself, send your friends — and then forget you ever saw me."

"Hard to forget a face like yourn. The earl dear to you then?"

"It is only that those who seek his life are not dear to me."

"Aye, I'll do it then, swear I will. Got two braw lads at home. Soon's I deliver this bread, then, I'll have them on their way."

"Two braw lads at home," I repeated, my voice catching. How I envied this poor, plain woman. I could say no more but gave her the coins, praying I could trust her. After the woman came back outside and scurried off, I waited, holding Kildare's reins, tears in my eyes, cloaked and hooded as Surrey was marched past. No cries for the Howards yet, but he walked with his head up, his shoulders back, and his eyes straight ahead. What was it about these Tudor times that made families — the Boleyns, the Howards, even the Fitzgeralds —

proud and powerful, only to be pulled down by this terrible monarch?

Tears froze on my cheeks as I heard the first shouts up ahead, "A Howard! A Howard! G'bless ye, milord!" The cries for Surrey seemed to swell. But, in truth, I saw and heard again that dreadful day my half brother and my uncles were taken to their deaths from the Tower to Tyburn.

As I mounted and rode Kildare back toward the palace, the streets were less crowded, so I assumed some London folk had followed Surrey all the way across town. "Good girl, my Kildare," I said, patting her neck as her hoofs beat a poem of their own in my ears and brain. *Clomp, clomp. Kildare. Kildare, Kill dare* — yes, I would dare to kill the king.

CHAPTER THE TWENTIETH

Whitehall
January 1547

At last, I was going to kill the king. He was already dying, but I was going to kill him anyway.

At the bottom of a coffer full of stomachers and shawls, I had hidden a dagger that could not be traced. I had found it in a box in the stables at Battle Abbey, though I wished I had one that had belonged to my family to do the deed. Anthony kept several about with his various dress swords, but I dared not use one that could be linked to him or to me. Men of means oft had their names or initials or family mottoes engraved upon their weapons.

The ailing king kept much to his rooms, at night to his secret chambers, Anthony had once let slip, as the status of the royal health careened up and down. At times, my lord said, His Grace was quite lucid; other times, he lived in the past, raving about how Queen Jane Seymour was the only woman he really loved — Jane, the beloved mother of his son who would rule after him. He even hallucinated she was with him, had imagined conversations with her, then went to wailing that she had died.

Only the royal physicians and the king's closest friends — especially Lord Denny and my husband — had easy access to him as he rewrote his will and planned his son's investiture as Prince of Wales.

Although the queen had returned to Whitehall a fortnight ago, the king had sent her away to Greenwich for yuletide. She had been regent for him while he was in France, but now he wanted to send a clear message that she would not be regent for his son until he reached his majority. As dearly as Her Majesty had tended him, it seemed the only woman on his mind now was dead Queen Jane.

Surrey was scheduled to die in a few days, on January 21; his father, the Duke of Norfolk, who before the birth of Prince Edward had been discussed as a possible heir to the throne, had not yet been given a death date. So, if my opportunity came soon to confront the king alone in his secret rooms, I might not only avenge the lost lives of the Fitzgeralds, but save Surrey and his sire's to boot.

Truth be told, I eavesdropped on my husband and Lord Denny, gleaning everything I could about when the king insisted on being alone — he needed to "cleanse his soul," Anthony said — and when he summoned others. Guards stood in the main corridor outside his chambers, where many nobles waited, hoping for a final audience, a last bequest of monastery lands or money. But when the time was right, I knew the back way in.

The day before Surrey was to die, I saw John Dudley hovering about in the corridor outside the royal suite like a spider watching his web. He accosted me as I tried to pass by. "Ah, Lady Browne. You know," he said, blocking my way as he had five years ago when I'd first met him, "I heard reports of the strangest occurrence in the streets when the Earl of Surrey was moved from Fleet Prison to the Tower."

My stomach cartwheeled, and I tried to face him down without blinking or flinching. "Really? Such as?"

"I wasn't there, but I have it on good authority that people along the route dared to shout out in the streets for him, 'A Howard! A Howard!' or some such. It reminds me of like tumult for a treasonous family I once was in charge of — much to my regret."

"I find it hard to believe you regretted that. Anything for king and country — and your family. Even destroying another family."

"I will ignore your sharp tongue for now. We are on the same side — the same side, I daresay, that Edward Clinton is on."

My eyes widened. Had Dudley seen us together at the king's wedding banquet? Could Dudley have been the one who told Anthony of that? Surely Edward himself would not have spoken of me, so perhaps Dudley's niece Ursula had. Were our unrequited desires so obvious then? Alice's fears that I cared for Edward were one thing, but it dirtied my desires if this man knew of my feelings for his man Clinton.

When I gave Dudley no rejoinder, he plunged on. "I have not told anyone of your continued rebellious female nature, for you seem to be handling loyalty to your husband well. But sometimes what 'seems' is not what 'is,' especially with a beautiful woman to distract one from her true purpose."

Despite the chill in the hall, I began to perspire. There was no way under heaven this man could know of my plans, for I had not even told Magheen. I decided not to protest or argue but continued to stare him down. That obviously disconcerted him, for he shifted from foot to foot and hit his leather gloves repeatedly in the palm of one hand as he went on. "Lest it — by some far stretch of circumstance — could have been you — again — behind such defiance to urge the common people to cry out for enemies of the king, I am warning you to stay in line."

"Stay in line? Stay in line to be the next person to be dealt with cruelly and unfairly?"

"You speak treason to criticize the king, however enfeebled he is now."

I cared not that this man was supposedly my better. I shook my finger in his face. "Best, my lord, you too heed what happens to families on the rise, lest your precious Dudley family should overstep in Tudor times and pay the price."

He grabbed me by the upper arm and gave me a little shake, speaking now through gritted teeth. "You'll not threaten me, girl. My father died on the block for treason charges under this king's father, and I have been fighting my way, my family's way, back for years. I — Ah, Sir Anthony," he said, loosing me and changing his expression and tone in a trice as my husband emerged from the king's suite and the yeomen guards quickly closed the door behind him.

"Gera, dear, were you waiting for me?" Anthony asked as he came over to us. Now that someone had emerged from the inner sanctum, people shifted closer, trying to overhear what my lord would say.

"Just passing by when the lord admiral wished me well," I said, praying that Dudley would not want him to know of our conversation any more than I did.

"I must go back in to His Grace," Anthony told me rather loudly, perhaps so others heard him. He turned to Dudley. "His Majesty will see you briefly. Since the middle of the month, he has swerved in and out of reason, but he is in good form right now, his old self."

His old self, I thought. That was the self I must censure and attack and make pay. Meanwhile, like anyone given leave to enter the royal rooms, Dudley quickly divested himself of his sword and dagger, placing them on a long table in the hall that held several others. Anthony squeezed my shoulder and kissed my cheek, then motioned to the guards to open the doors again before he led Dudley inside.

Garments rustled and whispers hissed as the onlookers shifted their attention back to the double doors again. Several of the same people had approached me earlier, hoping I would speak to my husband to arrange admittance to the king for them. Now no one looked my way. Although I had been a part of the Tudor courts for years, I was yet viewed as something of an outsider.

As a new thought struck me, I lingered for a moment near the array of weapons, including my own husband's. I had decided against poisoning the king, for I knew naught of such and would have to trust someone else to obtain some. I planned to use a dagger to stab him or cut his throat, then leave it in the king's own hand, as if he had decided to take his own life, burdened, broken, unable to suffer more. But, lest someone decided to investigate, unable to accept that the king would imperil his soul by suicide — when, in truth, as far as I could see, he had burdened his soul with sins his entire brutal life — I would take Dudley's dagger and use that.

In one quick move, I seized Dudley's fine, shiny dagger clearly marked with the inscription *Lord High Admiral,* hid it in the folds of my skirt, and strolled away.

As if my confrontation with Dudley weren't enough to stoke my courage, hearing sections of the king's will that day urged me on too. "The crown and the realms of England, Ireland, and the title of France will go directly to Prince Edward — you understand that, of course," Anthony explained to me as he hurriedly changed clothes in our chambers without summoning his tiring servant. Before I could say aught, he added, "I know you had hopes for an independent Ireland, dearest, but it's best for it to be under the English ruler's aegis *ad aeternam*. As for the throne, only in default will it go to Mary and her heirs, or lastly be settled upon Elizabeth."

He was in a rush to return to the king's side. Though he had said the monarch hardly slept for long, still plunging from alert periods to strange, waking dreams, my lord was exhausted and on edge too. Yet I think he was bolstered by his own self-importance to be so near and dear to the king.

"The navy now numbers nearly seventy ships, and is in good hands under the Earl of Warwick as Lord High Admiral, as well as others, sea captains like Thomas Seymour — and others," he repeated, evidently, I thought, so he did not have to use Edward Clinton's name. "And I," he said, thrusting out his chest as I helped him don his padded velvet doublet, "am a beneficiary in the will, to inherit three hundred pounds, which I shall use to build myself a fine tomb at Battle Abbey. The king has great plans and designs for his own resting place at Windsor next to Queen Jane. Queen Jane, Queen Jane — when he plunges into one of his non compos mentis stages, he continues to speak to her as if she were alive, the only wife he's ever deeply loved; he raves on and on."

"I cannot believe he did not once feel deeply for the other wives he so brutally set aside," I argued. "He surely loved Catherine of Aragon in his youth, and Anne Boleyn too, to wait all those years to wed her, to ruin the holy houses and break with the pope. Anne of Cleves was a mistake and poor Cat Howard a disaster, but our current queen has been a loving nurse and loyal helpmeet to him."

"The thing is," he went on, "it's long been treason to predict or so much as speak of the sovereign's death, but Anthony Denny plans to broach it to him soon, mayhap on the morrow. He must prepare himself, call in Bishop Cranmer for the last rites. It would be a horror for our liege lord to die unshriven."

My husband shuddered as he spoke a torrent of words. I wondered if he saw his future fate in the king's present predicament. Despite his self-importance, he seemed shattered by his friend's approaching death. I felt so much the opposite that I had to keep my mouth — mostly — shut.

"His Majesty can't even sign his name to documents now," Anthony went on, "and there are a raft of them. We use the dry stamp, which impresses his signature on the parchment, then is inked in and witnessed by as many of us are in the room."

How, I thought, I'd love to get my Irish hands on that dry stamp, on his will in general, and free Ireland from English rule, *ad aeternam,* as Anthony had put it.

"Well, I must go back to him, my dear. He wants peace and quiet — only one man at a time before he sleeps this evening, and we've even moved him to his back rooms, where he's retreated for years when he wants to really be alone."

"As if," I whispered, half to myself, "death could not find him there."

"What's that?"

"Nothing. My woman's whims are of no account when it comes to the import of your service at this extraordinary time."

"Just so. I shall be off then, for I must ask if His Grace meant to leave Bishop Gardiner out of the will. Oh, so many details, so many requests. After all, Gardiner performed the marriage service for the king and queen. I'm sure His Majesty will reinstate him. I don't see why it always has to be Bishop Cranmer he turns to, except that Cranmer's been ever willing to go along with any shift in the royal winds. He is still at his house at Croydon, not allowed to so much as come to the palace yet to give the last rites."

He pecked a kiss on my cheek and was out the door. When he returned, I knew he would fall into a deep sleep, but I could not even spare the time to wait for that. I wrote him a note saying I had gone out for a walk in the winter gardens. I did that whatever the weather, just to escape the suffocating feel of this place. But I would be waiting on the other side of the secret door to the king's back bedchamber, listening for when he was alone and all was silent. In their pride of being the king's closest friends, neither Anthony nor the king's other cronies had used the secret door lately, but always the public one. I guessed that few others even knew of the back way in, and Anthony had no notion I was aware of it and had once been inside the royal inner sanctum.

I gripped my hands together and pressed them to my lips with my eyes tight shut to steel myself for what was to come. After years of longing for justice and revenge for the Fitzgeralds and Ireland, it was finally time to risk all, to risk my very life. I had no children to leave motherless. Even if I were discovered and arrested for regicide, Anthony would be protected by his position. I had my sister Cecily's promise that she would take Margaret and Magheen into her and her husband's household should anything happen to me, a vow she'd made when my life was nearly lost during my first son's birth. Dear Mabel would have to do without me, and my brother find a way to return to Ireland on his own.

I could bear up to it if I were caught, I told myself. I would speak out for Ireland and the Fitzgeralds much as Surrey had defended his own cause so eloquently at his trial. If I must, I could die the way he would on the morrow, the way my uncles had. I could face the Tower, that very place my father had passed from this world. And Edward . . . My regrets would go no further. He was far away and would not warn or rescue or stop me this time from doing what I must. But how I would have loved to see him and Ireland again.

I pulled a shawl of finest lawn from my coffer and laid Dudley's dagger in a pocket

I had sewn for my own weapon. I wrapped the shawl around me, then over that my warmer furred one. I sniffed hard and shook my head to cast off self-pity and stepped out into our withdrawing room. I had told Magheen and Alice I intended to wait up alone for my lord this night. I could carry no candle, no lantern. Surely there would be a light in the king's bedchamber at the end of the dark passage.

But I was barely two steps from our chamber door when Anthony came running toward me. "He snapped at me to get out!" he cried, and pulled me back into our rooms. Tears tracked clear down to his trembling jowls. "He told me, 'Hold your peace!' He said, 'I remembered Bishop Gardiner well enough and of good purpose left him out my will for his lately troublesome nature.' Oh, I am undone! What if His Grace never summons me again, after all these years as boon companions? What if he cuts me out of his will and the elaborate plans for his state funeral too?"

"Be calm, my lord," I urged as he closed the door behind us and began to pace. "He knows of your friendship and good service to the crown. He sounds astute — in his own mind tonight."

"He yet comes and goes, but I was appalled. I . . . I am so exhausted."

"You must rest. You said the next day he oft forgets what came before. All will be well if you just get some rest yourself, my lord."

I coerced him to lie down and, despite his agitated state, he was soon snoring. I left the note to him that he had not seen and tiptoed out again. It was barely dusk: It seemed we all lost track of hours and days, waiting for the king to die. This was Surrey's last night on earth, hopefully the king's too.

I hurried down the silent, darkening corridor and turned into the narrow servants' hall. I put my ear to the panel entrance but heard no voice, no movement, so I pushed it inward. Silence. I gathered my skirts close and stepped into its dark depths, closing the panel behind.

The air in the passage was stale, so it must not have been used recently. It was black as the pit of hell, my fearful flight from besieged Maynooth as a child all over again. But no Magheen this time, no salvation by boat at the end of the tunnel.

A cobweb wove itself across my sweating face and snagged in my eyelashes. No matter if I kept my eyes open or closed, it was the same deep darkness.

I went slower, one hand along the wooden

wall, one out ahead so I would not bump into the door at the end. A sliver jabbed into my finger, but I ignored it. My hand touched the door.

I froze, straining to hear. Yes, some strange sound on the other side, like a rhythmic hissing. I pictured a fat, coiled serpent within, the king of England I had so long detested. Snoring — that was it. He slept.

I pictured the arrangement of the two rooms I had walked through nearly three years ago, the shadows, the silence. Not silent now. As I pushed the panel inward but a crack, I saw wan light, though it nearly blinded me at first. If I were caught inside, I had a new plan, an excuse: My lord was so distressed that the king had scolded him over Bishop Gardiner that I had come in the back way to beg that my husband be forgiven.

As I took a silent step into the king's bedchamber, I felt the cold tip of Dudley's dagger prick my elbow. Truth be told, I had come to kill the king for my people and my country, and for all those he had foully murdered while claiming to be the savior of his people. But if my other enemy's dagger did the deed and was discovered, let John Dudley suffer for it.

I moved silently, giving my eyes time to

adjust, though there was little enough to bump into but the bed, which dwarfed everything. Finally, I saw that an ornate, lighted lantern stood on a small table across the room. I felt I'd opened a long-sealed tomb: No air stirred, and the stench of the king's abscessed leg, the very smell of death, sat heavy here.

He had gone quiet now. What if he were dead already? It would not be enough if he escaped me after all this time! But no, though the snoring had ceased, a sharp rasping for breath resounded from the big, curtained bed. Had he hidden out here like a wounded animal, or was he ashamed to let others see him as he was? Did he really want to cleanse his soul and risk dying alone? *Ah, well,* a little voice in my head seemed to say, *at the end, cobbler or king, we all must die alone.*

Though I knew the king was hard of hearing and curtains closed off most of the huge oaken bedstead, I tiptoed into the small adjoining room to be certain no servant or guard slept there. No one. Just shadows, like dark ghosts from Henry Tudor's past and mine, those who had been murdered, those who needed justice, even from the grave.

A single, fat candle burned on the small

table here, illumining a short stack of parchment. The candle diffused the sweet scent of expensive ambergris and threw flickering light on the rows of rich parchment-and-leather-scented books shelved on all four walls. Hoping no one would wonder how the obese, crippled king could rise from his bed to lock the door to his more public chambers, I went to it, listened with my ear to the ornately carved and gilded wood, then twisted the key in the lock.

As I passed the table again, I bent to look at the documents lying there and gasped. In fine script, the king's will! How I longed to burn it all, at least the parts about the Tudor heirs being bequeathed my Ireland. I pushed the papers aside to get to the back of the document. He had signed it already, or, at least, it had been impressed with what Anthony had called the dry stamp and someone had inked it in.

I could barely keep myself from taking out the dagger and slashing the king's precious will into pieces. Instead, I fished out Dudley's dagger and, as carefully as I could, cut off the bottom inch of the last page that bore the signature. Let them think the king had done that before he did away with himself.

I bent to stuff the narrow piece of parchment in my shoe, where it crinkled in protest. A thought hit me then with stunning force: Should I be taken and executed, no one would ever know my reasons, my story, my legacy. I should have made a will, or at least a recording of my life's events. If I survived the day and the king was buried, I would not let my life and loves and reasons for my deeds be buried too. I would write my story.

I restacked the papers, tamping them into place. Keeping the dagger out, I trod as quietly as I could back into the bedchamber.

The king was breathing easier now. I took off my heavy outer shawl and tied it around my waist, lest I would need to flee, for I must leave nothing behind that could be traced. I unwrapped the thin lawn shawl with its pocket now empty of the dagger, for I gripped the steel handle, warm from my own body heat. I pulled the gauzy material of the shawl over my head like a scarf, again in case I must flee, so I would leave naught behind but the dagger and the king's corpse.

The bed was not only huge but high. At least it had a three-step mounting stair, which the king, no doubt, or those who lifted him up, had needed. I stepped on the first step and knelt upon the third. I hoped to wake the king, so he knew why he would die. But if he called out for help, would his voice carry clear to his guards or to someone who might be just beyond in his formal bedchamber? Was this gigantic but ill man yet strong enough to stop me? Should I try to gag or bind him with my shawl?

I parted the bed curtains so I could see within. At first, I thought I saw only a pile of pillows, but the king was propped upon them. I cleared my throat to see if he would move or react. Now or never, I told myself. Let him die in peace, some would say, but I would never have peace that way. Silently, I heard the shouted, futile, but bold words, *A Geraldine! A Geraldine!*

I knelt upon the mattress, dragging my skirts and the shawl around my waist. I crawled closer, my fingers gripping the dagger handle so hard that my entire frame shook as I began to lift it. Granted, the smells made me want to flee — his infected leg, sweat, urine, the very scent of death. Anthony had whispered that his skin was turning yellow as old parchment with inner poisons, but all was shades of gray shadows here.

I held my breath and positioned myself to strike. Then a voice, soft, wheezing, said from the depths of the black bed and the huge, fleshy frame, "You've come to bed at last, my dearest love, my angel."

CHAPTER THE TWENTY-FIRST

In the depths of the royal bed, a huge, familiar hand clamped my wrist and yanked me close. "Jane, my dear wife, Jane," the king whispered.

I went icy cold. The dagger, clasped in my hand, was trapped near my rib cage, under his huge arm. For a dying man, his grip on my other wrist seemed as strong as it had that night at the gaming table. If I could just free my right hand . . . I must strike now and be away. They said his lucid moments came and went — or what if someone heard him wailing and broke down the locked door to come in? What if, in the morning, he reasoned out who his Jane really was?

I knew my coloring was somewhat similar to Queen Jane's, but he was clearly delusional in one of what Anthony had called the king's non compos mentis states. My lawn shawl had fallen forward over my face, so I peered at him through a scrim. If he thought I was his dead queen Jane Seymour, perhaps that made him think I was an angel or apparition.

"I don't want to die, my love," he went on, sniveling like a child, "but I want to be with you in heaven."

Despite his hallucination, he thought I was a ghost, so he was not in the past but in the here and now to realize Jane was dead.

"You gave me my son," he whispered, "and he will rule after me, but I don't want to die. I'm the king and I don't want to die-eeee. . . ."

"Sh!" I crooned. "Hush now, husband."

"Jane, my love, I know I've changed since you left me, gained much weight. I've become a glutton since your death — my only sin, but for lusts of the eye."

Was that what the king believed and would claim to his confessor on his deathbed? He thought his only sins were gluttony and ogling women! My hand cramped around the dagger, but I fought to calm myself, to say what I must.

"Everyone must die, my lord. But I know you must have many regrets besides losing me."

Drawing out my words, I spoke in a hushed, wispy voice, hoping no hint of my

346

crisp Irish brogue slipped in. I could not believe my daring, but I had naught to lose, snared against him like this. I must talk my way free and finish my deed.

Then a new thought struck me. After all, I wanted this man to suffer for what he had done to my people — to his own people. If I simply stabbed him, it would be over, brutally, though he was dying anyway. But what if he thought his angel Jane had come to prepare him for hell? Torment in the time he had left was better justice than a quick, if bloody, death.

"R-regrets?" he stammered. "You m-mean regrets of dead children with the Spanish princess? But you gave me Prince Edward. You said you loved me."

"For one thing, I am speaking of regrets for the deaths of your first two wives and the callous setting aside of two others after me, not to mention beheading that poor girl Cat Howard. I speak the truth now without fear, since you can no longer hurt me. Oh, yes, I feared you, knew I had to wed you, or you'd bring me and my family down, ruin us as you had others. Love? Love for our son, but only fear for you."

"Jane . . . Jane . . . you cannot mean th—"

"Even now you have turned your affections from Queen Katherine after she has nursed and tended you, even in your vilest moods."

"But . . . b-but you understood about my first two queens. I explained it to you, you above all people. The Boleyn was a whore, and my marriage to Spanish Catherine a sham and sin, and not my fault."

"Princess Mary's mother was loyal and loving to you until the day she died. Anne Boleyn was innocent of the charges against her, my lord; in God's truth, you knew that. Incest? Witchcraft? You pursued her for years, devastated the English Church for her. As you face eternal judgment, surely you know that, and you will admit all at the judgment seat. But you wanted to get her out of your way so you could have me, have the chance of a legitimate son."

He recoiled from me, but I still could not free the dagger from under his arm. The man's weight was amazing.

"You . . . Jane, how can you be so cruel to defend her? The entire Boleyn family betrayed me — incest with her brother. At least his wife, Rochford, died with Cat Howard! And now the Howard men will go down too!"

"How could Cat Howard love you, any more than I, for even then you were a fat old man. And now you'll kill the Howard men? For what, my lord king? Yes, Surrey and Norfolk should have been chastised for their arrogance, but that was nothing compared to your pomposity. They fought England's wars for you and with you over the years. It grieves me greatly — and all the saints of heaven too — that you are so brutal and cruel. You have dragged down and have slaughtered by royal decree families that have helped you, and that shows your weakness, your fear, not your strength and power. 'Tis a great, great sin, huge sins encrusted on your doomed soul."

"No — nooo . . ." Even though I feared I was overdoing my part, he began to gasp for breath, his once-commanding voice a mere whine. "You cannot mean these things!" He shoved feebly at me, but my wrist was still trapped; I could feel my entire arm going numb. He hissed, "Sent from hell, you a demon —"

"Sent from heaven, Henry Tudor! A harbinger from heaven. It is to hell you are going for the way you have destroyed so many innocent and loyal, from your first wife to the brave Fitzgeralds of Ireland who ruled there for you over the years. You could have been the greatest king in Christendom, but now you must pay the price for all eternity."

He began to choke, crying, sniveling with one hand lifted to cover his face. I gave a great tug to free my arm from under him and loosed it — without the dagger.

"It cannot be, cannot be, for I am blessed, beloved of the Lord High God. It cannot be. . . ." His whining trailed off, and he lay back on his pillows, gasping for air. I wished I had the dagger, but I would have had to strike him with my left hand, and that mountain of flesh could well protect his heart or throat. I could only hope his shock and horror might make him senseless or even bring death before his cronies could call for Bishop Cranmer to administer the last rites, offering atonement for his sins. Whatever happened, I had made my point with the dagger of truth.

So I fled the king's bed, of necessity leaving Dudley's dagger behind and finally leaving behind some of my fierce hatred for England's dreadful Tudor.

After my confrontation with the king, I lay shaking all over as if I had the ague, feeling chilled even beneath two coverlets. I was huddled in the truckle bed in the next room, where Magheen slept those days she stayed with me when Anthony was away. He still slept, where I had hastily undressed and scattered my garments in the dark. As I had heard the king's snoring, I could hear my husband's now through the closed door.

I was so undone I could not sleep and was terrified that, if I did, I'd have my nightmare again. Waking reality on the morrow seemed dreadful too. What would happen when Anthony or others found the defaced royal will? I had hidden his signature from it. Perhaps they would discover the dagger in the king's bed and question Dudley. The king might recall what had happened and would surmise who had invaded his inner sanctum and imitated his dead wife. Or would he now send for Bishop Cranmer for the final Church rites to cleanse his black soul? I had thrown the lawn shawl with the pocket for the dagger down the chute of a common jakes, but if I were taken and tortured, what would I admit to? Oh, Saint Brigid, I should not have mentioned the Fitzgeralds with the other families he had ruined. Had Queen Jane known of or cared one whit for the Irish Geraldines?

And the most awesome agony of all: Would I — could I — have really killed the king if it had come to that, committed a murder, what I condemned him for? *Thou shalt not kill. Vengeance is mine, sayeth the Lord.* All the years of hatred that had driven me, eaten at me . . .

In fevered prayer, I thanked the Lord God that he had given me another way — a better way — to punish the king for his cruelties. For, whether he was in his right mind or not, I had tormented him as he had so many others. I had not killed the king, for that was the Lord's doing, and He had given me my just revenge.

Besides, were the king's advisers partly to blame for the massacre of my family, of others? His Privy Council, his secretaries of state, his supporters over the years, even my husband? No, as I look back on it even now, years later, I record here in my life's story that I yet blame the king. His son, Edward VI, the boy king, became a pawn in the hands of the Seymours and Dudley; Mary Tudor, when queen, harkened to her bishops and her Spanish husband; even bold Elizabeth had her Cecils and Walsingham. But the horrid Henry Tudor was a law unto himself, and I believe he was judged in death accordingly.

I would say exactly that in the written reckoning of my Fitzgerald family, those who should have been Ireland's kings but someday, perhaps, at least could rule there again. Yes, I would record my memories soon and, when I could, hide them with the precious *Red Book of Kildare* and pray I could help return my brother Gerald to Ireland someday.

'Round and 'round my frenzied thoughts went. I would never be a poet, but I would author my own words. Pieces of Surrey's poems pranced through my mind: *I weep and sing in joy and woe . . . for my sweet thoughts sometime do pleasure bring . . . gives me a pang that inwardly doth sting, when that I think what grief it is again . . .*

Yes, joy and woe, I would write it all, the memories and motives of the woman who could have been the Irish princess.

That morn, sometime after the late January daylight, a pounding on the door jolted me from sodden sleep. I got up, wrapped a coverlet around myself, and had stumbled nearly to the hall door when Anthony burst from our bedchamber, half-dressed.

"Why are you sleeping in here? You should have wakened me!" he cried, pushing me aside to reach the door himself. Then, more quietly, "What if His Majesty has taken a turn for the worse?"

It was Sir Anthony Denny, concern stamped hard upon his face.

"His Grace became hysterical last night, shrieking he was damned to hell. We broke through a door he had somehow locked, and he soon after went into a sort of trance — a coma," he reported. "Bishop Cranmer has been sent for. Come at once!"

"Gera, bring my leather jerkin and shoes!" Anthony ordered as both men raced down the hall.

I closed the door and wilted against it, my legs shaking. Justice. Victory for me and mine. But what if the king rallied as he had before and remembered too much?

Knocking sounded on the door again; it reverberated through me.

"Gera, 'tis Alice. The palace is astir! The king is truly on his deathbed now, they say!"

"I heard," I said as I opened the door for her. "I must dress quickly and take Anthony some things."

Alice bustled in as Magheen, ever spritely, came in behind her with her usual morning hug. "You know," Alice said, "perhaps facing death, the king will now have a care for how my poor Lord Leonard felt when he was sent to his death, or your menfolk too."

"Yes," I told her as I threw the coverlet off and went barefoot and naked into our bedchamber to dress, "perhaps the king has thought on that a bit."

Quiet chaos reigned in Whitehall Palace the

next two days as the king sank further into death's cold waters. I liked to think of it that way, that my nightmare of all those heads floating past me would haunt him too. Strangely — blessedly — I had not dreamed of such since my nightmare clash with the king.

Anthony said the queen was not allowed to see her husband in his deplorable condition, for he had left orders to that effect. The royal children were at separate rural retreats and were not to be told of the king's approaching death yet. Sadly, the Earl of Surrey had been beheaded on Tower Hill, and his father was to be dispatched on this day, Thursday, January 27.

Everyone knew the king had received communion from his confessor, and finally Bishop Cranmer had been summoned to administer the last rites, as if he were the angel of death himself. Anthony kept muttering that before the king had sunk into a coma, he had suffered "sobbing deliriums as if he were doomed to hell for all his evil deeds." Finally Bishop Cranmer arrived, but the king was in no state to give permission for anything — finally, praise the Lord! I later learned that when Cranmer reached the king, Henry Tudor gave no sign that he "put his trust in the mercy of Christ to forgive his sins." No nod, no gesture — nothing, though Cranmer insisted the king "had wrung his hand as hard as he could" in response, and Anthony agonized that the king's soul had gone to purgatory quite unforgiven.

At least the king's power and life had ended. I thought the very walls of the palace, perhaps all of London and the realm — certainly, I thought, the folk, even the fens and fields of my Ireland — breathed a sigh of relief that his thirty-six-year reign was over. The king, my enemy, at last was dead.

"We have a mess on our hands," Anthony told me the morn after the king died. He looked grief-stricken, yet excited, for he was to play a large part in the royal mourning rituals. He had just sat down for a quick supper in our chamber, more or less perched on the edge of his seat so he could jump up again. "In the midst of all these elaborate funeral arrangements," he explained, "we've discovered the king sliced his own signature off the will we'd struggled so hard over." I strained to hear him, for his mouth was full of powdered beef. "It must have been in one of his confused states, though how he got from his bed to the will on the table in the next room — and locked the door to that room — we cannot fathom. We found the dagger that did the deed, though."

I felt my face heat. I took a slow sip of wine, hiding behind my goblet. I had decided to save, rather than destroy, the signature of the king. I fancied that when I could, I would paste it at the end of *The Red Book of Kildare* as if he had signed it in approval.

"So an unsigned will means what?" I asked.

"Tell no one! We are forging onward, and nothing the king wanted will be changed. By the way, John Dudley has been privily censured too, so that should make you happy. Though he denies it, he dared to secrete that dagger I just mentioned on his person when he went in to see the king the other day. Evidently he meant it as a gift to His Majesty, since the king had it with him in bed when he died."

"How do you know it was Dudley's?"

"My dear, I wish you would properly call him by his title. He'll be a power behind the next throne, and your bitterness toward him must end. His office of Lord High Admiral, you see, was scripted on the dagger plain as day. Well, the king always loved the navy and fancied himself the ultimate

Lord High Admiral, I warrant."

I shuddered at that thought but tried not to show it. No matter, for Anthony plunged on. "The Seymour brothers will no doubt get titles, as they will be advisers of their royal nephew; at least, Edward Seymour will be, as Lord Protector. Tom Seymour's a bit more problematic, a wencher, hotheaded, but then perhaps most sea captains are — and that is their allure, eh?"

He meant to goad me, but I said naught. He jumped up, leaving his meal half-eaten. "I do know something for certain, though," he went on, interrupting my wondering as to, if Dudley resigned from his admiralty position, who would be elevated in his stead.

I reined my wayward thoughts back in. "And what is that, my lord?"

"The Seymours' dead sister, Queen Jane, would be thrilled for her son, proud of her brothers and the glorious, long reign her husband has had, don't you think?"

Going over to open the door for him, I said, I am sure a bit too tartly, "I can hardly speak for a dead woman, my lord, and that is that."

After being embalmed and lying for two days in the room where he had died, Henry Tudor's body was moved from his secret apartments to a heavy, elaborate hearse hastily erected in the Chapel Royal, the very place where the king was praying the day Cat Howard tried to reach him to beg for mercy. The hearse was not a wheeled one but a structure to elevate the coffin, surrounded by nearly a hundred foot-long, square wax tapers. The funeral journey to Windsor, his final resting place next to Queen Jane — though I warrant he would have liked to change his wishes on that now — would take two days. So identical hearses were being constructed, one for Syon House, the midway resting point of the funeral cortege, then a third inside St. George's Chapel at Windsor.

In the Chapel Royal at Whitehall, with the queen leading the way, we all filed past the bulky coffin. Candlelight blazed on the banners depicting the saints, the flags and escutcheons of arms, and the huge canopy of rich cloth of gold draped overhead. The chief mourners were led by Henry Grey, 3rd Marquess of Dorset, the father of Jane Grey, who had been a companion to my sisters when they lived with the Greys at Bradgate Hall after Beaumanoir was lost to us. Continual requiem masses were said and sung for the release of the king's soul from purgatory into heaven. But all the trappings of kingdom and Church aside, I believed that my Queen Jane had told the truth: The soul of Henry Tudor, entrusted with his subjects' well-being, had sorely perverted his power, so was not destined for celestial realms.

The next day, I accompanied Queen Katherine in a separate, heavily guarded entourage of her ladies to Windsor for the funeral, while the much slower cortege made its way behind us out of London. Bells tolled, Anthony told me later, for, as master of the horse, he led the dead king's riderless steed close behind the chariot bearing the coffin. Atop that lay the life-size waxen effigy of the king in all his robed and crowned grandeur. I heard later that onlookers whispered that it vibrated when the chariot clattered over cobblestones, so that it seemed the king would cast off death and rise.

Crowds choked the highway, even as we women and our guards passed ahead of the funeral procession. I was tempted to spread some coin along the way as bribes, and not ones for goodwill cries to be shouted for the king. But most of all, I longed to shout myself, "The tyrant king is finally dead, but the Geraldines live on!"

■ ■ ■ ■

Within St. George's Chapel at Windsor, the king's effigy and coffin rested atop a painted and gilded hearse thirty-five feet high. It was fringed with black silk, the candles flaming around it made from four thousand pounds of the finest wax.

With the queen and her other ladies, I looked down upon it from the elevated queen's closet, a privy second-story viewing area. Like me, Katherine Parr was dry-eyed. How beautiful she looked in her blue velvet robes lined with sarcenet and a purple bodice and kirtle all made especially for the funeral. I wondered if she had thoughts for her true love, Tom Seymour, who had courted her before she caught the king's eye. Like me, did she silently long for her lost mariner? And now that she was widowed yet again, would Tom Seymour come back into her life? I knew she must remain unwed for a time, lest she be with child by the king — fat chance that, I thought.

Below us, the requiem Mass droned on, with Henry Tudor's coat of arms, helmet, shield, and sword laid upon the altar. Ironically, Bishop Gardiner, after being snubbed by the king, gave the funeral sermon, since he was the bishop for the Garter Knights and this was their chapel. He preached from the text, "Blessed are the dead which die in the Lord." Whether or not, like the thief upon the cross, the king had his sins forgiven at the last, I knew I had spoken my piece and he had heard me.

Finally it was over, the pomp, the elaborate trappings and rituals. The floor of the choir was opened. The king had wanted to have his remains rest temporarily in the huge vault below until his ornate tomb was completed nearby. Much of the marble had been pilfered from the expensive stone monument the king's old adviser, Cardinal Wolsey, had planned for his own tomb before the king brought him down. *A betrayer, thief, and murderer,* that was what the inscription on it should say, I thought as I watched sixteen yeomen guards slowly lower the massive coffin into the vault.

"Ashes to ashes, dust to dust, *cinerem cineri et pulverem pulveri,*" echoed in the high-vaulted chapel.

Then a clarion voice rang out: "Almighty God in his infinite goodness, give good life and long to the most high and mighty prince, our sovereign lord King Edward VI, by the grace of God. The king is dead. Long live the king!"

Others took up the echoing cries from below, even the grieving queen and her ladies, though I barely mouthed the words. Then people shouted, "Long live the noble King Edward, ruler of England, France, and Ireland!"

And so, I thought, as those words pierced my ears and tears at last burned my eyes, *my quest begins anew with the next generation of Tudors and their advisers, even that damned Dudley.*

CHAPTER THE TWENTY-SECOND

Chelsea Manor House, Village of Chelsea
May 1548

"Just think, a secret wedding! It must have been so romantic!" Princess Elizabeth said with a sigh. "I think love is so much more exciting when it's forbidden, don't you?"

I certainly had no desire to answer that, but she seemed to be talking to her cousin Lady Jane Grey anyway. As usual of late, Elizabeth looked absolutely transported, moonstruck. And she was the center of attention while her cousin Jane Grey, her governess, Kat Ashley, and I watched her antics. Frowning, Mrs. Ashley shook her head as if she'd heard it all before and did not approve one whit. I had heard her raise her voice to the princess in private but never around others.

"Lord Thomas loved Katherine Parr from afar all the years she was wed to my father," Elizabeth went on. "Then he wed her in secret but five weeks after she was widowed, because he could not wait! I should like to be adored just like that someday, wouldn't you?" she asked Jane more pointedly this time.

"Not I, Your Grace," the girl replied, perched on a turf bench beside me, while Elizabeth paced in the new-budded rose bower where we sat outside Chelsea Manor House. "I'd fancy a wise tutor over an avid suitor."

Ever since Queen Katherine, now called the dowager queen, had moved from court to her dower house, a lovely red-bricked manor on the Thames just southwest of London, her former ladies had been rotated in and out of her service. So I was here for a month while Anthony, pushed aside by the new men surrounding the young king, had mournfully retired from court to our house at Byfleet in Surrey. I preferred it here, for Byfleet was the place my baby boys had died, and that yet haunted my heart.

Elizabeth resided with her stepmother here and, like me, Jane Grey was visiting for a while. Lady Jane, now aged ten, though so serious and learned a child that she seemed much older, looked wistfully down at the book closed in her lap, as if she'd rather read it than listen to such dramatic outbursts from her royal cousin. Thin and plain, Jane reminded me of my sister Cecily when she was young, her nose always in a book, though Cecily's choice would not have been Ovid's *Metamorphoses* in Latin but a courtly romance more suited to Elizabeth's raptures. I knew the princess was also a serious scholar and sat long hours at her lessons, so perhaps it was just spring fever that possessed her today.

Elizabeth had been fidgeting since the four of us had walked out along the velvet lawns that overlooked the Thames. "My parents were wed in secret just like the dowager queen Katherine and Lord Thomas, were they not, my Kat?"

"Indeed they were," Mrs. Ashley said, "though I thought you fancied fine public weddings. I heard you begging Lady Browne for more details about Irish ones."

"I didn't mean public or secret weddings for myself, so I do agree with you on that, Jane," the princess said, and came over to pat her cousin's shoulder, though she smiled at me.

Just yesterday the two of us had shared the memory of my teaching her the Irish jig and even danced it together again. I had also regaled her with happy stories of my Irish childhood, ones I had recently recorded in my new manuscript, tales of rowing our *namhóag* on the River Lyreen with my brothers and sisters, stories of the times my father took us sailing in Dublin Harbor and much more. The recountings of the Fitzgerald tragedies I was saving for the right time, for I wanted Elizabeth on my side before I brought all that up. After all, my new plans to help my family and the Irish did not include direct revenge now that Elizabeth's vile father was dead, but indirect persuasion of any future rulers. That was the way my father had once conducted himself with the Tudors, and I would take a page from that — except for that damned Dudley, whom I hated as much as I had the king.

As for later playing on Elizabeth's sympathies, after all, her mother had been cruelly beheaded in her flush of life as many of my family had been, so I expected to use that tie. Oh, yes, I laid my schemes well for binding her heart to mine before I would ask for her aid. My dear stepdaughter Mabel was not here at Chelsea, but I had been practicing my tales of Irish triumph and tragedy on her for years. Her father didn't know it, but I had turned her into a bit of a sympathetic Irish rebel, and I hoped to do the same with Elizabeth.

But the best thing in my life right now was that, with Henry Tudor gone, my brother and I had finally corresponded after thirteen years apart. Magheen had at last admitted that Collum had sent word to her from time to time over the years. She had not told me so that, if I were questioned under duress, I could truly say I knew naught of Gerald's location. Currently he lived on the fringes of the French court, longing to come to England, and then, like me, to go home!

"Dear Jane, I did not mean to put you on the spot." Elizabeth's voice interrupted my plotting.

Despite her high spirits, at least she always took a care for Jane's shyer and quieter nature. I had heard Jane's parents beat her to their will, so she was no doubt grateful to be invited to Chelsea for a respite. When she arrived here the same day I did, I noted bruise marks on her fair skin, and recalled how rude and overbearing her parents had been when they came upon us during their stag hunt years ago. Like the surrounding orchards and gardens here, Jane seemed to blossom, but compared to her cousin Elizabeth, she was still a pale bloom.

We kept busy at Chelsea, and that helped immensely. It was much a women's household, since Katherine's new husband, recently raised to the title of Baron Sudeley, came and went from duties in London, where he sat on the Privy Council with his brother, now the Earl of Hertford. Seymour had also replaced Dudley as Lord High Admiral, so he was overburdened with duties. As far as I could tell, Tom Seymour stayed at Chelsea only at week's end. I had been in his presence but two days, and this was my sixth day here, so he would be back soon.

And now that Seymour was to relinquish the title of Lord High Admiral, Lord Edward Clinton would soon take that lofty, powerful position! Though I had not heard from him in months — as in Surrey's mariner poem, he probably never gave me a thought — I was so proud of him.

"So, you would like to be adored." The dowager queen repeated Elizabeth's words as she joined us in the shady arbor. I had not seen her lurking nearby. How long she had been eavesdropping? "By whom, pray, dear Bess?" she asked.

"Why, by everyone," Elizabeth answered, blinking in obvious surprise at her stepmother's sudden appearance and her pointed question. "Though I mean not to be selfish about it, I should like to be loved by you, by my friends here, by my dear royal brother and —"

"And by my lord Thomas?"

Jane shrank back as if she'd been slapped, and I started at the unusual edge to the woman's sweet voice. It was no secret in the household that Elizabeth adored the handsome, brazen Tom Seymour. Most women did, but for Kat Ashley and me. I found vulgar his flirtatious nature, his bravado, and the fact that he swore great oaths in nearly each sentence, as if to make his words seem important, but his wife was besotted with him.

Seagoing character though he was, Seymour seemed so different from Edward Clinton, who exuded a smoldering strength rather than a bombastic personality. But what made someone desirable — even to the point of adoration — was in the eye of the beholder.

A few days later, the next Saturday evening, my eyes beheld the real reason for Elizabeth's raptures and the dowager queen's unease. It was twilight, and through a mist coming off the Thames, as I looked out my bedchamber window to watch boats on the river, I gasped.

"Damn him!" I muttered.

"Still fuming over the dead king or the

fact that the Privy Council hasn't yet answered your petitions for your brother Gerald's return?" Magheen asked from near the hearth, where she was using the firelight to sew a snagged hem.

"No — nothing."

But it was something indeed. Elizabeth had run out to meet Seymour in the bower where we women had sat the other day. Even from this height and distance, I knew it was the princess, for she reminded me so of myself in coloring, face, and form. Seymour swept her off her feet, whirled her about, and gave her a huge, back-bending kiss on the mouth, grinding his lips against hers. Why, I felt that kiss in the pit of my stomach.

Rumors of Seymour were that he was ambitious for power, which he felt his brother, Lord Protector of their young royal nephew, hogged for himself. Power, deceit, and betrayal hardly made me blink an eye after the things I'd seen. But I was surprised how much I cared for the English princess. Though she was Tudor through and through, I could not hate her as I had her father. I was dedicated to making her my friend and ally in pleading with her brother to permit my brother to come to England to sue for the return of his rightful place. I needed to protect her, but I needed her goodwill too.

What to do, what to do? I must warn Elizabeth's governess, though I didn't put it past the astute woman to know already of this illicit liaison. From the queen dowager's snide comment a few days ago, I surmised even she must have suspected. I blamed Seymour for the seduction. How far had it gone or would it go? Elizabeth, poor girl, was about to ignite a powder keg here, one I was sitting on, when I could not afford a misstep in my campaign to get Gerald back. Saint Brigid, but this reminded me all too well of glimpsing Cat Howard with her illicit lover. I was not going to turn tail and keep quiet this time.

I saw Elizabeth bolt toward the house, though she went around to a side or back door. Had Seymour sent her in or had he overstepped and she had fled?

I made an excuse to Magheen and hurried out into the hall and down the back servants' stairs, thinking she might come up that way. I heard feet pounding up from below and waited by the small window on the top-floor landing.

"Oh!" she cried, and stopped stone-still when she saw me. "Gera, I thought you were Kat."

"No, but I happened to be looking out a south window just now."

"And thought you saw what in this twilight mist?" she said, defiantly propping her hands on her waist. How quickly her mind worked, I marveled. How she emanated strength even when she was snared.

"Your Grace, I see clearly that your face is flushed —"

"Just from running up three flights of stairs, so —"

"And your hair is in disarray, and your skirts have rose thorn pulls in them."

"From the other day when I paced past the roses."

"It's a different dress, a very pretty, fancy one for a solitary stroll."

"Leave off! Whatever you think, you are wrong."

"I only think I want to be your friend, so I must warn you. I do know about young hearts yearning — I mean not to sound like a poet or a scold, Your Grace. It is just if I saw you with him, others may too, especially your stepmother, dear to us all."

"But you won't tell." She stated a fact, not a question.

"I am only telling you that you are risking much."

"But you do that too, do you not — risk

much? They say if your family had not rebelled, you would be an Irish princess, and there's still an Act of Attainder against your family, so you must walk on eggshells too."

Too, she had said. Then, despite our differences, she saw our similarities. I tried to choose my words very carefully. "You see, Your Grace, people gossip and usually cast the worst light on things. I know that, but you do too."

"You said you understand a young, yearning heart. And you will not tell Kat or my stepmother?" A question this time, a plaintive one.

I held out my hands to her from two stair steps above. She took them in her perspiring ones and came up to my level so we stood eye-to-eye, our petticoats pressed together.

"The English princess and the Irish one have a bargain," she said.

"Yes," was all I could manage, for this was not the bargain I sought, but perhaps it was another step toward mutual trust. I felt then, more strongly than ever, the impact of Elizabeth Tudor's personality, yet how much of a pawn she must be in the clutches of a skilled seducer. As she gave my hands a quick squeeze and passed me to hurry up

374

the last flight of stairs, I leaned in the window, looking out again at the thickening dusk, this time down toward the side door, where the girl had evidently come in.

I saw someone striding up the lawn, two men, Seymour following a cloaked man, tall with broad shoulders. Perhaps that was why Elizabeth had rushed in. Foolish as ever when I glimpsed the back or silhouette of such a one in the street or heard fast hoofbeats as I walked outside or saw a sailboat putting in here or anywhere, my heart — my young, yearning heart — beat harder. But each time, as now, I was disappointed, for I heard Seymour's voice boom out, "Your name, sirrah?"

The man's words were muffled. How I longed to tell Seymour what I had seen and warn him off from Elizabeth, but she would see that as my breaking my vow. Now that I really knew the man, no wonder his own brother and the Privy Council thought him a hotspur, and not only for eloping with the queen five weeks after the king's death. I had once considered getting Seymour on my side in my quest to help Gerald, but I could not trust or stomach the man now.

The stranger who arrived that evening at Chelsea was not the future Lord High Admiral, Edward Clinton, but it meant upheaval for me anyway. He was my son-in-law's man, sent from Byfleet, where my lord Anthony had suffered a stroke, and I was to head home at first light.

What the physician called the palsy paralyzed Anthony's left side, his leg, arm, and face, so he stayed abed and needed tending. He spoke in a slurred way, though I soon could understand him, even when others could not. His son and heir came and went, though Mabel often stayed for weeks. Anthony preferred to be taken care of by his longtime body servant, Clemmet, but he liked to have me sit with him while he mumbled on so much about the past I feared he had merged it with the present. He was his royal master's man to the end indeed.

He was ever in a fret over his being shuffled aside since the king died. Though he was seventy years of age, and the court and times had changed, he found it so hard to let go. Sometimes he said he heard the king calling him. He had nightmares he had received a royal summons but could not find his way to the king through the maze-like corridors of this or that palace.

When word came in the autumn of 1548 that the dowager queen Katherine had died in childbed bearing Seymour a daughter, it was another blow and break with the past for both Anthony and me. "So many gone," he whispered when I told him the sad news. "So much changed . . . and not for the best . . . the old ways and days . . . much better. Why, when the king and I were young . . ."

At least I learned that, through letters to each other, Katherine and Elizabeth had managed a distant reconciliation. My warning to Elizabeth had gone for naught: Katherine had caught her husband kissing the girl and ordered her away. Sadly, on Katherine's deathbed, racked with fever, the dying woman had accused her husband of poisoning her so he could have the princess for his wife.

And so I strove to be a good wife, but, God forgive me, though Byfleet Manor and its grounds comprised the property to be left to me from Anthony's properties in his will, I still hated the place. It was quite new, soundly built and comfortable, near the river with apple orchards and knot gardens, but the memories of losing my sons here and being told by a physician I would never bear another child made the place seem dark and cold to me.

It was in bleak December, nearly a year

after the king died, that our peace there was shattered by a visitor. I had long given up my heart's desire that I would ever see Lord High Admiral Edward Clinton again, especially in what seemed to me to be my endless exile from court and the seats of power. After writing several petitions to the Privy Council asking that the Earl of Kildare, Gerald Fitzgerald, be pardoned and allowed to visit me in England, I had also given up on any important person visiting from London or the court. I feared I would turn into my mother, a rural recluse, writing letter after helpless, hapless letter to save the Fitzgeralds.

So I was especially surprised when Magheen gestured to me from the hallway outside Anthony's room while he slept one mid-December day.

"It's starting to snow, but that didn't stop our visitor," she told me in a whisper, then gestured me farther down the hall.

"It's not news about Gerald and Collum, is it? I'm not sure I shall ever forgive you for keeping word of their whereabouts from me all those years."

We had been over that before, and she ignored it. " 'Tis the Earl of Warwick with two guards," she said.

I gasped. He was always just Dudley to

me, even when he'd risen to be Viscount Lisle and then the Earl of Warwick. "Dudley?" I blurted. "Here? To see my lord? Oh, that will cheer him, that someone of import still cares ab—"

"To see the Lady Browne — in private."

CHAPTER THE TWENTY-THIRD

Byfleet Manor, Surrey
January 20, 1549

"Now, don't fuss," Magheen told me, "but I ordered hot cider and meat pies for his lordship, and not with the poison you probably would have included."

"Not until I find out what he wants, as he's flying high with power these days." I had never told Magheen or anyone that I had tried to kill the king with Dudley's dagger, but she well knew that our visitor was second on my list. "Still," I whispered as we darted into my bedchamber so I could don something more presentable than a plain day gown, "it could be word about Gerald. It must be!"

And it was, though couched in typical Dudley terms as the two of us sat in the solar downstairs and began a verbal wrestling match with holds and turns, feints and flips, the likes of which I'd not seen since my uncles used to show off for all of us in a grassy ring at Maynooth.

Dudley, Earl of Warwick, but no doubt aiming even higher, began with some small talk that set my teeth on edge. I wanted to order the wretch off my property, but I worked the conversation around to asking if he had seen my petitions about a pardon for my brother and permission for him to be granted safe return from France.

"Indeed, I have, well-written letters too, Lady Gera. What is his first name again?"

"Gerald, Eleventh Earl of Kildare," I said, keeping calm, though I knew he was baiting me.

"Since the Act of Attainder against your family, my lady, he is not recognized as earl in this realm. But I have much influence with the council and could see championing your concerns and requests to them."

"I would be very grateful. But at what cost?"

"Ah, a lady who knows how to come to the point. Very well. Let me get to the real reason for this visit. The princess Elizabeth has been placed under house arrest on her rural property of Hatfield House and her closest servants and confidantes, including her governess, taken to the Tower and questioned."

"To the Tower? For what reason?" I asked, trying to keep my voice in check, for I feared I knew the answer to my own question.

"She has been accused of planning to overthrow her brother and his government with the help and firepower of the king's uncle, Thomas Seymour," he said, confirming my worst fears. He stopped and took a slow sip of heated cider, then put the mug down on the small table between us as if we were yet talking about the Byfleet River icing up. I tried to stay calm, but I fear my voice betrayed my agitation.

"She's but fifteen," I said, "and he is . . . how old?"

"Old enough to defy his brother, the Lord Protector, and the Privy Council, old enough to wed the dowager queen with reckless abandon, old enough to store up arms for no good purpose in Seymour House in the heart of London, and certainly old enough to be arrested for treason four days ago when, fully armed, he tried to take the young king as his prisoner. I do take your point about who would be mostly to blame for their liaison. But my point is that, since you were sent to the Chelsea household at the time Elizabeth and Seymour were there together —"

"I was there barely a week, until my lord

took sick."

"But, I hear from a good source, long enough to become quite a favorite with the princess — perhaps a confidante, eh?"

I stared him down as I had before. I suppose I should have presented a more hospitable disposition to him, but would he not have thought I was putting on a show? Yet that was exactly what I decided to do. Years ago, before I knew Elizabeth, I would have leaped at the chance to bring a Tudor down, but not now, not her. Like me, she had enemies at court, and this vile opportunist was obviously one of them, this man who would be ecstatic to ruin both Elizabeth and me if it suited his own ambition. I had no doubt that, if Dudley knew I was aware of her passion for Seymour and that I had spoken to her about it but had told no one else, he would have had me in the Tower for questioning.

"My lord," I said, still not blinking an eye, "all I can tell you is that Tom Seymour was an affectionate host to everyone, and it is true, as you no doubt know, that he cuts a swashbuckling figure with the ladies. But I have heard the princess say more than once that she does not wish to ever wed, so I cannot help you with damning evidence against her. I even heard her say she wanted her royal brother's approval, and I am certain she was loyal to him."

"Loyal to her brother as you are to yours?"

"Blood is thicker than water, they say. Yes, of course I am yet loyal to my brother — both of them — and to my sisters too."

"Let us not have another go-round on all this. Perhaps I have not made my position plain enough, a position which can help or harm, irreparably, your brother Gerald's position with the council and the king. I need you to testify that Elizabeth Tudor, young though she is, was in collusion with Seymour to bring her brother down, push her sister Mary out of the line of succession, and rule England with Seymour as her consort."

"Ridiculous! I know not what Seymour had in his head, but I know nothing of the kind about Her Grace."

"Even though I would be willing to lend my full weight to help bring your brother Gerald back to England under, shall we say, a truce for things past?"

I supposed I wavered a long moment then. My deepest desire was to return Gerald to Ireland, and this would be a huge step in that direction. But to be championed by John Dudley? And to have to trust him? I knew he was mentor to the man I would always secretly love, so there must be some good in him. But I saw much good in Elizabeth. God help me, I saw myself in Elizabeth of England.

"Well?" he prompted, leaning forward across the small table toward me. "Even if you know very little, that could seem much if presented with persuasive words."

"I regret I cannot help you and seem therefore unable to help my very innocent and deserving brother, my lord, at least at this time."

"Then I must tell you that you are in luck anyway, Lady Browne, a Geraldine! a Geraldine! to your very core. The council has decided to consider a pass for Gerald Fitzgerald to come for a visit, though when I cannot say."

"Oh, that is wonderful news!" I cried — and almost cried indeed as tears welled up in my eyes. But I realized that this man had misled me too. What he had tried to bargain for my help was already going to happen. I was so tempted to tear into him, but I had been around enough to know to play the game for Gerald's advantage, and for poor Anthony's too.

"I ask one small favor, my lord," I dared, fighting to keep my tone civil. "Not for me or my brother but for my lord Anthony, who, as you know, served our king's father faithfully for years."

"Say on," he said as he stood.

"He much misses being about the court, all the heady events from the days he served his king. If you would be so kind as to spend a few moments with him, bring him news of the day — even if it is about Seymour's foolhardiness — I would be grateful. I believe you counseled me once to be loyal to my English family, and we spoke about how family matters to both of us."

"I would be honored and could do no less for an old soldier and servant of the crown — and for a woman with a backbone of steel — steel like in a dagger I once had," he said, and bowed stiffly to me. "I would swear I left it on a table outside the dying king's chambers, but somehow it ended up in his bed. If you would lead the way to your husband's bedside, Lady Gera."

So he would not see the surprise on my face, I quickly turned away to lead him from the room. "Perhaps you were so distressed that day, my lord, you did not realize what you did or didn't do," I threw over my shoulder.

Did he know? How much? A formidable foe indeed. I wanted to slap him, to push him down the stairs as he followed me up to our second floor. But I was now doubly afraid of him, and — I must admit — a bit in awe of him too. The snake beckoning to Eve in the Garden of Eden, that was what he was, charming, clever, but deadly.

At least he did me a favor that day, spending an hour with my lord, as if an earl and member of the Privy Council had been sent purposefully to report to him.

I made certain Dudley and his men were fed a hot meal again before they set out, grateful he did not ask for them to spend the night under my roof. Donning a cloak and gloves against the cold, I went out to see them off from our small, cobbled courtyard slick with snow.

He surprised me by taking my hand before he mounted. I was grateful for my gloves and his, for I could not bear for him to touch me. It frightened me how he read my mind at that moment, for I had told myself not to ask about Edward's family or his new position as Lord High Admiral, but he said, "I recall you visited the home of my niece Ursula and her husband during the great northern progress. She's been quite ill with breathing problems, you know, a sort of lung fever."

"No, I didn't know. I am sorry to hear of that."

A corner of his mouth quirked. "Her husband is often at sea, of course, acquitting himself well for king and country. Edward Clinton is my protégé, you know, and as loyal to me . . . as others should learn to be."

My eyes widened; I knew not what to reply. It was obviously a command or threat that I should not struggle against nor gainsay him. He kissed my gloved hand before I could protest and mounted. "I have no doubt we shall meet again soon, Gera Fitzgerald," he said, and spurred his horse away with his two men close behind him.

Anthony rallied a bit after that, but his health sank as spring burst with new life outside. He slept longer each day, and mumbled when he was awake about past times and pastimes with the king he'd loved and I'd detested.

"He said you were a wench after his own heart — that is, the way we were in the old days, when we used to run about after women," he told me.

"You must rest now, Anthony. Save your strength, for Mabel's coming, and your other children too."

"I shall be buried next to my wife, Alys, but I shall take good memories of you with me, my dear."

"I am happy to know I pleased you, my lord."

"You pleased me but never loved me; I know that. In love with your Ireland, in love with . . ."

He choked and gasped. His face contorted, his body convulsed; then he went quite still. Dead before my eyes, before his children arrived, before he could finish his last thought. Was he going to mention my brother — or Edward Clinton?

I was a widow at age twenty-six. We buried him with great pomp in a fine tomb at Battle Abbey, where his armored effigy already lay carved next to that of his first wife. I must record here that Anthony has a far better memorial than Henry Tudor to this very day, for, with all the twists and turns that were soon to come, the former king's plans for an elaborate monument were somehow shuffled aside and ignored. The Lord High God works in wondrous ways; that's all I have to say on that.

Although I would have loved to sell Byfleet, I had nowhere else to go in my widowhood, so I made that my home. Of course, I would have liked to sail for Ireland straightaway, but I dared not, as the Act of Attainder against my family was still in effect and I dared not jeopardize Gerald's chances with misbehavior. Besides, I was awaiting word of when he would arrive in England, so I hoped to return home with him later — if that was permitted.

A fortnight after the funeral, the bluff, kindly Mason Haverhill rode up to the house and delivered to me a condolence note from Edward Clinton, Lord High Admiral. It bore a red wax seal imprinted with an anchor. I broke the seal and read the missive as I escorted the stocky man into the house and saw that he was well fed. I have that note to this day, pressed in the pages I was then writing of my life's story, next to the note and pressed posies Elizabeth sent when I lost my boys.

Aboard the Defiance, Deptford in the Thames, this day of our Lord September 4, 1549. Dearest Lady Browne — Gera. My heartfelt condolences in the loss of your husband. I have been at sea, chasing pirates and at war with the Scots, when I would prefer to make peace with the Irish. I do know and share from afar, on rocky waters, the pains of one's spouse being ill unto death. Keep your spirits up and keep your head, Irish.

Always, Edward

Mason Haverhill, the ship's master who oft sailed with Edward, told me much about their seagoing adventures, making me long to be a sailor and not a land-bound soul staring only at the little Byfleet River. My fingers yet tremble at the emotion and longing that leaped off the page as I read the note that day and as I stroke the folded parchment now. There was a hint of flirtation in his desire to make peace with the Irish, wasn't there? And "keep your head"? That too could be taken two ways, so perhaps he was scolding me to behave again. And Ursula must still be ill. Edward's man's visit . . . the note . . . it was all I'd had of him for years.

Magheen and I made a trip to visit Jane Grey, back in her home at Bradgate, to renew our abruptly truncated acquaintanceship and put in a good word for Gerald with her father. We two Irish colleens also went for a walk on the grounds and covertly dug up *The Red Book of Kildare.* I intended to entrust it to Gerald when it was safe to do so. Magheen, of course, was as excited as I, for her dear Collum would be coming home with Gerald — someday, we prayed. We took our Irish treasure back to Byfleet House with us, and I buried it in a metal box in my own garden this time. And waited and waited for my life to begin again.

Though I felt far distant from important events those early months of my widow-hood, I had learned a great deal in the few days I was at Bradgate, for Jane's parents stayed abreast of significant happenings. Elizabeth and her confidantes, including her governess, had been exonerated. Yet people whispered that the princess's reputation was besmirched by Seymour, who was beheaded for treason in May of 1549, the very month Anthony died.

I must record here — especially in light of what happened later — that during our short visit to Bradgate, I saw how terrified Jane was of her parents. I asked that the girl be permitted to visit me at Byfleet when I saw how they abused her, but they brusquely turned that offer down. I know they buffeted Jane about and I heard her mother screeching at her more than once. Poor Lady Jane Grey.

Another thing I learned during our few days there was that the Greys were close friends with John Dudley, Earl of Warwick. There was talk that Jane would wed one of his sons to bond the two families, so perhaps that was what all the discord was about, for Jane had whispered to me that, like Elizabeth, she wished not to wed. I thought anything Dudley had his hand in — except, of course, his championing of Edward Clinton, and possibly expediting my brother's return — seemed pure poison.

I also learned at Bradgate that Edward's career, under the young king — with a push from Dudley, no doubt — was on a meteoric rise. His prowess at sea with the fleet, especially his part in the Scottish Battle of Pinkie, led to his receiving lands and being named to the honored position of Garter Knight. How I wish I could have attended his garter ceremony at St. George's Chapel, Windsor, the very place where King Henry lay rotting in his tomb. Edward was also named a Privy Council member, which would keep him more in London, despite his sea duties. As if he were a man who could be in three places at once, he was also given grants of land and orders to build a power base in Lincolnshire for the crown. And, I'd overheard, something that was not meant for my ears but pricked them up — all these honors were bittersweet, because his wife, Ursula, the Earl of Warwick's niece, was ailing so sore with lung fever she could not even get out of bed.

Speaking of the devil — Dudley, alias Warwick — I heard that not only was Tom Seymour out of the way on his path to power, but Edward Seymour, King Edward's other uncle, who had served as Lord Protector, was out of favor for his strict, rough handling of the king, and the Earl of Warwick was riding high in the boy king's favor. Jane Grey had told me with a sigh, "How wonderful that Warwick permits the young king to have a childhood and not just study day and night. I am so happy my royal cousin is allowed to play at arms and parade through London's streets, and not just be so strictly confined and handled."

As I said, poor Jane Grey — and the rest of us, even those of us who knew not to trust Dudley but still did not see what was coming.

My life truly began again on May 6 of 1550, when I received a second missive from Edward Clinton, Lord High Admiral, delivered yet again by his ship's master, Mason Haverhill:

To the Lady Gera Fitzgerald Browne, Byfleet House, Surrey, from the hand of the

Lord High Admiral, Edward Clinton, G.K., London.

I will be staging a water festival at Deptford for the king on the Thames next month. Although it will be a military display, we need two lovely ladies to grace the scene as water nymphs, so if you and your stepdaughter Mabel would be willing, there will be a chamber assigned to you at Greenwich Palace. . . .

"Mabel! Mabel!" I shouted, for she was visiting me that week from London. Though I was twenty-seven years of age, I tore out in the garden to find her. I felt I was a child again, as if I had been told I could go to visit the sights and shops of distant Dublin. "We're going to London! I'm going back with you! And whatever is a water nymph?"

CHAPTER THE TWENTY-FOURTH

Deptford on the River Thames
June 1550

Though I thought the twelve-year-old king looked rather pale, even in the warm spring sun, color came to his cheeks, and his eyes sparkled at the excitement of the river tournament.

Watching from behind a gold brocade curtain, I sympathized entirely, for I was thrilled to be back even temporarily at court, where I could do some good for Gerald. He had been invited to come to London but was still reluctant to trust the Tudors, so was biding his time in Paris a bit longer. I had written to advise him that to put too much confidence in John Dudley, Earl of Warwick, who had extended the invitation to him, could be a two-edged sword. If Dudley thought it would help him and his family, he might be of aid — otherwise, I wrote, beware.

And, oh, yes, I must admit that day of the river tournament, I also sympathized with the English boy king's exhilaration because I was so thrilled to be near Edward Clinton that I could hardly keep my mind on my coming histrionics.

Shortly after our arrival at the palace, the Lord High Admiral of England had come calling on me and Mabel, giving us both a hearty greeting and a quick kiss on both cheeks. "In the French fashion," he had said, though his eyes watched my mouth. His stylish, close-cut beard enhanced his dark eyebrows as his gaze went thoroughly — possessively, I thought — over me. We stared too long at each other, I warrant, for Mabel had to clear her throat to break the spell.

"So," he said, clapping his big hands together, "there will be a rehearsal dockside at Deptford on the morrow, and I will send horses for both of you. You will have short parts to learn in rhyme about the mock battle, the king's forces against the powers of evil."

"Scotland?" I asked. "France or even Ireland?"

"We're keeping this all in the realm of allegory," he told me. He touched my arm, sending a tingle up it as if I were some green girl who had never been wedded and bedded. "You'll both recite some high-flying rhetoric, which the king loves, the sort that would have made the Earl of Surrey proud. It will be such a fine show that I have my two sons here for it — wait until you see how little Henry, whom you bounced once on your knee, has grown. He's thirteen now and his brother Edward is eight, but the two girls and young Thomas are home tending their mother. . . ."

Cold reality smacked me in the face. Edward had two sons here in London. He had five children by Ursula to add to his three daughters by his first wife. And I . . . I was barren and would always be bereft for my losses.

I blinked back tears as he told us more about the performance of the so-called water nymphs, but I remember naught else about his visit that day but that I adored him, much to my shame and peril, and he belonged to everyone but me.

"Gera, you look strange." Mabel's voice interrupted my agonizing as we waited for our cue to caper out from behind the curtain to begin the pageant. I was quite certain I had picked out Edward's two boys, seated in the crowd directly behind the king.

All five of Dudley's healthy sons were also in that second row. "Are you quite all right?" she asked. "Are you ready to go on?"

"Yes," I told her, told myself too, "I am ready to go on." I took her hand for our entry at the edge of the dock, where the king and his court were assembled under a golden canopy. I kept glancing at Edward's *Defiance* approaching on the Thames to take on the other ship.

In our pure white satin gowns trimmed with golden ribbons with long, trailing trains and with our hair flying free, the two of us flitted out before the assembled king and court and began to speak our piece. Wishing Elizabeth or even Princess Mary were here — but seeing Dudley in the front row right next to the king — I began my lines first, gesturing grandly:

On the bright, broad Thames, see the
    vessel of the king.
Who shall dare attack it, for the Lord High
    God will bring
Victory to England, peace and bounty to
    our land.
But now, we view in battle the power of
    royal command.

Mabel began her four lines as the brisk

breeze flipped our tresses in our faces and flapped our skirts almost as smartly as the battle banners above the king's pavilion. He smiled and clapped, even cutting off Mabel's last words. Dudley dared to wink at me as if we were in collusion for something.

Behind us, as we scurried out of the way, both ships — the *Defiance*, all bedecked with Tudor bunting and banners, and a smaller ship — came closer to each other in the curve of the river. Sailors aloft in ratlines or clinging to furled shrouds began to gesture and shout at one another. "For England and Saint George! For England and King Edward!" echoed across the stretch of river. Cannon shots boomed and echoed as cannonballs flopped in the river with great white splashes.

As Mabel and I darted off, out of the observers' line of view, I turned to look at the *Defiance.* What a lovely, exciting time I had enjoyed on it. Pure show though all this was, I delighted to see Edward standing near the prow with sword upraised as if to spur the royal sailors onward. The two ships began to pass with a great fray and two more cannon blasts. As they barely missed each other, men leaped from deck to deck, fighting with clanging swords or in mock hand-to-hand battles as some sailors grappled the two ships tight. My eyes stayed on Edward, all clad in Tudor green, as he began a sword fight with the black-clad captain of the other ship. And then it happened.

I tripped on my train, tumbled off the dock, and fell bum-first into the Thames with a splash equal to that from a cannonball. I heard Mabel shriek just before the cold water smacked me, and I went under, all wrapped in strangling skirts and train. I did not know how to swim but shoved the sodden satin away and instinctively clawed upward through the roiling current.

I choked and sputtered as my head broke the surface, unable to kick, but flailing hard to stay afloat. I heard voices — shouts as I was dragged away by the river current. I bumped into a dock post, slippery and slimy, though it was at low tide, and clung. I held on for my very life.

"Rope! Ropes or a ladder!" someone shouted from above, followed by a huge splash near me. Had they thrown down a ladder?

No, a man had jumped in feetfirst. Despite the water and hair in my eyes and my frenzy to keep my head up, I recalled Edward's note, *Keep your head up, Irish.* How I wished my rescuer would be him, but I knew it could not be.

John Dudley surfaced near me with a huge gasp for air. With two powerful strokes, he swam over and seized both the dock post and me. "Must you always . . . be so much . . . trouble?" he demanded as two ropes made of fine, twisted Tudor bunting dropped next to us, then a third. "Hell's gates, girl — don't struggle. I've wanted to tell you all along that . . . you and I can help each other . . . if you just don't . . . fight me!"

He was the last man on earth I wanted to touch me or help me, but I had no choice. And I heard what he said, though I had no breath to answer. I warranted I looked like a drowned cat when I was ignominiously pulled up and applauded by the king and court — or perhaps Dudley's rescue of me was. So I made a mess of things that day. The incident enhanced Dudley's reputation as hero and savior. And, sadly, a Fitzgerald once again became the talk of the court instead of Sir Edward Clinton, Lord High Admiral, for the water festival he had worked so very hard on.

Back in our chambers in the palace, Mabel insisted I go to bed to get warm, but she soon shocked me by bringing Edward Clinton right into my bedroom when he came to see me, and then, though she left the door open, she went out into the other room.

"Gera, are you all right?" he asked, bending to take my hand, then perching on the side of the bed, which sagged under his weight and almost toppled me into him. "I saw what happened, but couldn't get in to help."

"To help me *again,* you mean, as you have before. But, from where you were, you saw me fall? You were fighting that other captain."

"I should have been, as I was to be the victor," he told me, looking a bit sheepish as he loosed my hand and rolled up his sleeve to show me a black-and-blue mark on his wrist. "I had Mason Haverhill cast as the villain, and we'd practiced our duel. But I should not have been trying to watch a water nymph — which hardly fit the tenor of a military battle, anyway, but which I added to the plans just to see you — and then you turned into a mermaid, fortunately one Warwick rescued."

"He did. I actually thanked him."

"So he told me. He rather thought it was some sort of victory."

"But you added our parts just to get me here to court?"

"Guilty. Of that and much more. Mermaids oft lure sailors to their destruction, you know."

"I am so sorry I made a mess of things."

"You did, but what is new about that?" he asked with a sigh. "That's what I expect from my Geraldine, but she's still worth the cost."

He was regarding me so intently I began to blush. I'd been freezing since I fell in that river, but I felt warm now. "I thank you too for putting up with a bitter woman all these years," I added.

"Bitter — not you. The taste you leave in my mouth is of spice, which I quite favor over sugar." I could tell he wanted to seize me, and here I lay in bed with him so close.

"But . . ." he said, shaking his head and frowning as his voice trailed off.

"But you need to take your sons and head home to tend your ill wife."

"Yes."

"Dudley — I mean Warwick — told me. You must take care of her. I did see your sons — very handsome. Your heir looks a good deal like you, and the other boy more like your wife."

As if for the first time he realized he sat

on my bed, he stood suddenly. "They say, Gera — that is, Warwick says — your brother Gerald will be guaranteed safe passage home soon, since the invitation to return was evidently not enough for him, or someone he harkens to, who must not trust Warwick and the council — on which I sit too, remember. If I can — if I don't have family commitments — I will try to see that Gerald stays safe. I will hold the Privy Council to it."

"I would be so grateful. You have risen far, Edward, perhaps as far as I fell today. Oh, I pray that wasn't a prophecy or warning for the Fitzgeralds' future, not after what we've all been through!"

He nodded and started to say something else, but then just bit his lower lip for a moment. He had crossed his arms and thrust his fists under his armpits as if to keep his hands controlled. But the intensity of his gaze made me feel he could see through my covers, as if he ripped them from me and touched me everywhere.

"Take a care not only for your brother but for yourself too, Irish," he said, and suddenly uncrossed his arms and bent to tip my face up for a kiss — quick, strong. "And don't do something foolish, like confront Warwick or the king — or marry in haste."

"As the princess Elizabeth and Jane Grey always say, I shall not wed."

"There are negotiations going on right now to marry the princess Elizabeth to a foreign prince, and Jane Grey may well wed one of Warwick's sons, so that's the way of it. Arranged marriages for them when the other sort would be so much more agreeable . . . enjoyable . . . worth waiting for."

He turned away abruptly and strode for the door. I meant to tell him I would pray for his wife, but he was gone in a trice without looking back.

The Lord giveth and the Lord taketh away, my mother used to say. In the autumn of 1551, nearly a year after my infamous swim in the Thames before the king's court, so much was given and taken.

In September of 1551, I was stunned to hear that Ursula Clinton had died of her lung malady. I sent Edward a condolence note by messenger to Westminster, where the Privy Council most often met, but I heard nothing in return.

I should not have been surprised to hear that the king had given the Earl of Warwick the vaunted title of Duke of Northumberland, one of the highest peerage positions in the land. King Henry's death had spared

the life of Surrey's father, the Duke of Norfolk, but he was wasting away in the Tower.
The last of the Seymour brothers was
dishonored and no longer Lord Protector,
so Dudley was now the most important
power in the realm, with great influence
over the young king. At last I came to realize I might have to deal with the devil
Dudley, because the Lord gave me a miracle
at last: My brother Gerald was coming
home.

We received word from France that he
would be sailing to England and, thanks to
Dudley, alias Northumberland, I was permitted to come to London to greet Gerald
when he landed at Deptford, where the
water pageant had been staged.

Of course, I took Magheen. I invited
Cecily but she was in childbed; my other
brother, Edward, was on duty for the Greys
nearly on the Scottish border; Margaret
didn't want to go out into public "with all
those big people" she didn't know, she
signaled to me with a flurry of hand gestures. So Mabel went with Magheen and
me. We stayed with Mabel's friends in town,
then went down to the royal docks at Deptford on a sunny, warm-for-November day
in 1551.

We had been told the name of the ship we

were awaiting was the *Goodspeed.* I regretted it was not the Lord High Admiral's *Defiance,* but I vowed to let nothing ruin this triumphant day. My family was still under an Act of Attainder, and Gerald might not be recognized as an earl, but once we were together we would find our way back to prominence in Ireland!

At last, as they say, my ship came in. With its sails all furled, but for on the mainmast, it picked its way through smaller traffic in the busy Thames and put in at the dock, where we women awaited while our guards and horses were back on the bustling wharf. The *Goodspeed* was bigger and bulkier than the *Defiance* and boasted a figurehead that looked like an etching I'd seen of Aeolus, Roman god of the winds, with his hair and robes blown back.

My eyes skimmed the railing for a man who could be Gerald, sixteen years away, sixteen years more grown. Magheen began to screech and jump up and down. Yes, yes, I saw Collum, leaning over, waving madly. Why, he had gray hair and looked a bit stooped, and he was finely dressed. And that tall young man beside him. Of course — it was Gerald, smiling, pointing at us. I was so overwhelmed at first, no words would come.

"Welcome, welcome to England!" Mabel

called out as the ship bumped the dock and sailors swarmed down ratlines.

Gerald leaned over the railing, smiling at me — or was it at Mabel? No matter. I shouted up my greetings to him in Irish, and he yelled right back in the best brogue I had heard in years, calling me, "Gerabeth! Gerabeth!" to which I answered, "A Geraldine! A Geraldine!"

I began to cry. Chains rattled, the gangplank slammed down, and we rushed up it. Gerald hugged me so hard I thought my ribs would break. He spun me about as Collum and Magheen huddled together, arms entwined amid the bustle of the crew securing the ship. My brother's face was no longer thin, but angular. He sported a small beard. And his voice was so low, a man's voice — well, of course it was, I told myself.

"Oh, Gerald, now we'll be able to fight for Ireland together!" I cried when he set me down.

"But carefully, warily. I must make allies here besides my own family, dear Gerabeth!"

My eyes teared up again to hear the pet name he and Father had called me by when we were young. I introduced Gerald to Mabel, who was blushing madly as he looked her over. So there we stood,

Magheen and her beloved, loyal Collum; Gerald, who could not take his eyes off Mabel and she him; and I, suddenly, strangely alone for one moment amidst the ado of the crew setting things to rights.

Alone, that is, until I saw the man striding toward us on the deck, whose gaze snagged mine and burned into me to, as ever, make me feel I was at sea with racing, rocking waves shaking me to my very core, my hair and gown blown back with abandon like the figurehead of the ship.

"I did not expect . . . expect you to be here," I said as Edward Clinton took my hand and raised it to his lips for a long kiss.

"This vessel had to do, as the *Defiance* needed a bit of patching up."

"Don't we all?"

"Gera, when I heard your brother was to be brought here from France, I pulled rank and brought him home myself. I knew how much it could mean to you and your Ireland."

"I am sorry to hear about Ursula, that the children lost their mother."

"Thank you. My two oldest boys are in the service of Northumberland's household, and the others are with my cousins at Kyme Castle."

"Is your new Sempringham Manor not

finished?"

"It is, but I thought it best not to move Ursula or the children there from Kyme. I wanted Sempringham to . . . to start over."

"To start over," I repeated as if I were a parrot.

"It seems everyone out here is momentarily distracted," he said. "Would you have a glass of wine in my cabin, and then we'll pour for everyone and have a toast to a fine future?"

I nodded, and we turned away.

"Gerabeth," Gerald called to me as I started down the steps into the companion-way, "why did you not tell me that England has maids far fairer than those in France and our Ireland?"

"Because," I called back over my shoulder, "I wanted you to come back and meet my dear friend for yourself."

"I could have told him just the opposite," Edward said below in the dim companion-way as he pushed his cabin door ajar. "However beautiful and alluring English maids are, there's nothing like an Irish rebel lass — if you're game for high adventure." His voice was raspy; he seemed suddenly out of breath.

He closed the door to his small captain's cabin behind us, and I was instantly in his arms, crushed in his embrace, our mouths moving together, drinking each other in. I know not which one of us had moved first to the wild embrace and kisses and explosion from years of longing, our own reunion. I only know it was as inevitable as it was impossible, the Irish Geraldine girl and the English lord, the man I had met the very day I'd left my Ireland.

But now there was no past, almost no future. Only the now as Edward and I leaned against his cabin wall, pressing together. I could not breathe, did not want to breathe apart from him ever again. Linking my arms around his neck while he grappled me to him with hard hands on my waist and bottom, I returned his wild, deep kisses, until his mouth roamed lower, trailing fire down my throat. He pulled the ties of my cape awry and kissed and licked the dark hollows between my breasts, tugging one of my sleeves off my shoulder as if he would undress me there. My skirts flattened out between his body and the wall. As he nipped at my bared shoulder, his knee thrust between my legs nearly lifted me from my feet. If he had claimed me there, standing, I would have welcomed it.

"This — and more — is what I've always wanted from you," he said in a gasp as he looked dazedly into my eyes, my head thrown back against the wall, my hair tumbling loose. "But I want to savor every moment of our first time — in a bed, not in a rush, not when we have guests hovering. We have to . . . to both keep our heads — Damn, I didn't mean to say it like that."

"I adore you," was all I could manage in the whirl of my desires.

"That's all I need to know — for now," he rasped, still panting, and looking as flushed as I felt.

"For now," I whispered, reaching out to smooth his hair I had mussed. For the first time in all the years I'd been in England, in a strange way, I almost felt I had come home.

CHAPTER THE TWENTY-FIFTH

Edward escorted Mabel and me back to Byfleet, for Gerald was to reside in quarters in
London that Dudley had arranged for him.
I was grieved Gerald was not staying in the
palace, where he might have access to the
king and his council, but was relieved he
was not assigned to Dudley's household. I
also was thrilled to hear that the deed of
Maynooth was restored to Gerald, though
he was not to go there and did not have his
title returned — yet.

Gerald and I had decided that Magheen
and Collum were never to be parted again,
so Collum came home with me, though
should Gerald be permitted to return to
Ireland, they would both go with him. I was
happy for the reunion of our two Fitzgerald
servants, so faithful all these years. And I
was ecstatic to have Edward with me for
several days when we had previously had to
snatch at minutes and hours.

The two of us dawdled over goblets of wine and a late dinner when everyone else had gone to bed. Never one to go 'round Robin's barn, Edward pulled me onto his lap as we sat near the fire and said, "I hope you agree that, like Magheen and Collum, we need to make plans never to be parted again, that is, when I am not at sea."

"Is that a proposal, Lord High Admiral?"

"It is, if you can abide a sea captain. I think, my Gera, you will not be jealous of my mistresses, ships and the sea, for you love them too."

"I do."

"Then will you say with me 'I do' in public?"

"Not at court again."

"No, not at court. At Sempringham, then to repeat our vows someday at your Maynooth."

"You have been talking to Gerald to know that name."

"No, I was at the council meeting where the deed was restored to him and his future heirs. But all the way across the channel, I was questioning Gerald and Collum about your past in Ireland. I did not know all of you had suffered so much. I wager they suspected from the first that my interest in the fair Geraldine was very personal."

"But there is something I must tell you before we — I — can make plans."

"Say on, but we cannot live in Ireland, and, I'm afraid, neither can Gerald yet, though we can work on that together — with the Duke of Northumberland, whom you must at least get on with, if not obey."

I looked down at our hands with fingers intertwined in my lap. His hand rested heavily on the juncture of my thighs through the thickness of my gown. But I must keep my mind on what I would say.

"Gera, what?" he prompted, lifting my chin with his free hand. "Is there some impediment, some arrangement with another? If there is, I'm afraid I will have to kill him."

"I am barren, Edward. When I lost my second son . . ." My lower lip quivered and tears blinded me. For a moment I could not go on.

"It's all right, sweetheart," he whispered.

"It isn't! The physician told me he was quite certain I would never bear another child, and you have such fine families. I may be yet of childbearing age, but you need to know I cannot bear you a child."

He pulled me into his embrace. Always, I felt lost in his arms, and yet there I also seemed to find myself.

"Gera," he crooned, rocking me a bit, "I did not know, but that's not really what I want from you. You won't have my children then, but you will always have my heart. I wed Bessie to please the king and Ursula to please John Dudley. But you please me for myself. I am asking you to be my wife, till death us do part."

I sat up, lifted my head, and looked at him straight in the eyes. "You want me to wife despite the fact that the people you must yet please surely think I'm a flaming rebel?"

"You are a flaming rebel, my love, and I wouldn't have you any other way — and I long to have you in every possible way."

"Is that a lewd offer, my Edward?" I asked, sitting up and smiling through my tears. I wiggled my hips on his lap a bit and saw dark fires light in both his eyes.

"It is, Irish, for I think much deeper relations — foreign affairs, in effect — should be fostered between the Irish and the English, beginning right now — and evermore."

To that proposal and proposition, I simply said, "Amen!"

I was to wed Sir Edward Fiennes Clinton, Garter Knight and Lord High Admiral, Privy Council member — also governor of the Tower of London, I'm afraid — at his manor of Sempringham in Lincolnshire almost a year after Gerald came to England. We would have married much sooner, but Edward was sent to sea again. Meanwhile, I sold Byfleet and moved with Margaret, Alice, Magheen, and Collum to Sempringham.

I became acquainted with the Clinton children, especially the three youngest: Anne, who was five; Thomas, four; and little Frances, but a toddler. I had them moved from Kyme to Sempringham and spent hours with them each day, also making friends with their caretakers, Edward's cousins, Lettice and Neville Clinton, who were a good ten years older than I but had no offspring of their own. I vowed to rear Edward's youngest three when we were in Lincolnshire, where they would live until we found a suitable home in or near London.

Though I longed for Edward at my side the months he was at sea, with a small entourage of servants I rode Kildare about the area, taking small gifts to folk who owed my lord allegiance, something I had learned long ago from watching my parents visit their people. I took some pretty pewter pieces to the shepherd and his wife who had helped us the night we fled King Henry's great northern progress, and I stood as sponsor to their twins when they were baptized in the church.

I read and reread Edward's barrage of notes to me, sent by ship and horse as if he were afraid I would forget him or change my mind. I used the purse of money he had given me and my profits from Byfleet to buy manor furnishings from Lincoln and London. As best I could, missing Edward as I did, I enjoyed the wild beauties of the area that reminded me so much of my own home, taking Margaret, Magheen, and Alice to pick fresh flowers and walk the shady lanes. And I waited for my mariner to come home to me.

Finally, on October 1, 1552, we married in the small chapel at the manor, all bedecked in autumn flowers, and had a wedding banquet with Mason Haverhill and Edward's most important local liege men and all his — now our — children. Through his three daughters by Bessie Blount, Edward was a grandfather, and I had to laugh to be introduced to the little ones as *Grandmother.* I, who had no children of my own and, but for Mabel, whom I missed terribly, had no lasting bonds of affection with Anthony's brood, was of a sudden not only

Mama to Edward's three youngest, but also a grandmother!

Most important of all, I was Lady Clinton, lost in a whirl of love and laughter. I savored each moment with my husband — a month he had promised me for a honeymoon — and quite forgot, for once, the dangerous demons who lurked in the real world. I even set our table with the etched and gilded Venetian goblets John Dudley sent us for a gift. Gerald, who was avidly courting Mabel in London, had sent us a French tapestry, when I had longed for good stout Irish linen, but then, how would he get that?

Oh, yes, Edward taught me to swim in our fishpond, too, so that, as he said, "The next time you take a dive into the Thames or the Irish Sea, no one will have to fish you out."

"I have two more gifts for you," Edward whispered to me in our big bed the morning after the service and celebration. "One of them just arrived this morning — I hope."

"Mm," I said, cuddling back against his strong, naked body, never wanting to get up even for more gifts. He had already given me a triple-strand pearl necklace and a new saddle for Kildare, as well as a white satin night robe embroidered with green shamrocks. "Let's just be slugabeds and stay here all day," I said, exhausted but utterly sated from our wild night of lovemaking.

"I'm starved," he said, and tickled me. "But you will like these things, I promise."

"I like everything you give me," I said, turning toward him and holding tight.

"Well, perhaps later, then, for the gifts . . ."

He chuckled and began to nibble at me again, his tongue wetting a hot streak down my throat. I had never fathomed wedded love could be like this: mutual, consuming. And then I heard a dog bark.

"Ah," he said, pulling back, which spilled chill air into our little cocoon of covers, "I believe the gifts are here, one of them, at least. Haverhill rode to meet a ship to fetch them."

"Oh, a pet dog? Well, I shall need all the company I can get when you go to sea, since you cannot take me with you — or will not."

"Let's not have our first argument, love. And yes, it is a pet dog, the kind Magheen said you would like so —"

"A wolfhound? Did she tell you about my dear old boy Wynne?"

"Yes, but this is a female straight from Ireland, one named Erin, I understand, but if you wish to change her na—"

"Oh, Edward, my love!" I leaped from the bed, dragging the top coverlet around my nakedness and rushing to open the bedchamber door. Collum and Magheen stood there, a small wolfhound in Collum's arms. I shocked myself by bursting into tears as I cuddled the little mite. All those years I had to leave Wynne behind, and then my uncle Leonard brought him to Beaumanoir, perhaps to make up for his betrayal of our family. The night I had to flee Maynooth and leave Wynne behind . . . all I had to leave behind . . .

"Oh, my love, I can never thank you enough," I cried, turning to hug my husband with one arm as he appeared in the hall wrapped in yet another coverlet.

"Best tell her the other, Collum," Edward said.

"Ay, milord. Besides this pup, his lordship sent to Dublin for an Irish *namhóag,* much like the one you and Gerald used to row on the Lyreen," he said as Magheen beamed at his side and I cuddled Erin in my arms. "It's a big one, though, with a mast and a sail. 'Tis out on dry land in the courtyard, but —"

"But we will put it in the river here and go for a sail," Edward said as he reached in to scratch the puppy behind her ears.

"You've given me so much," I told him as I swiped at my happy tears.

"And maybe, someday," he said, reaching

out to cup my wet cheek in a big hand, "a trip to Ireland to find Erin a mate and find the past you Fitzgeralds left behind."

But, as ever, my happy times were so fragile. The next summer, just when Edward had returned yet again from sea to spend several weeks with all of us at Sempringham, word came that the young king, who had been ailing, was sick unto death. We hastened back to London, where I rented rooms for us while Edward attended crisis council meetings.

I could tell that even Edward was now doubting the morality of Dudley's tight hold on the king, for he allowed few admittance to the king's chambers at Greenwich. I wondered perversely if he had moved the king into the secret, small rooms behind every royal chamber that the boy's father had built.

"Gera! Gera!" Edward called to me, bursting back into our bedroom after he'd been gone only several hours this time. He sailed back and forth between London and Greenwich, where the council had hunkered down for now. I sat at a small desk with Erin asleep on my lap, writing a note to go with gifts for our three youngest children back in Lincolnshire. My husband nearly shouted,

"King Edward has signed a document setting the succession of his sisters aside!"

I jolted so hard, I bent the nib of my quill and splattered ink on the page. Erin jumped to the floor and began to yip, running in circles. For once we ignored the pet we both fussed over. I saw Edward was truly distraught as he began to pace with Erin at his heels. He had been worried that his longtime mentor would lose his power when Mary became queen, but if Mary — and Elizabeth — were set aside, did that not mean civil war?

"Set the princesses aside in favor of whom?" I demanded, jumping up and hurrying to him. "Dudley himself?"

"Not exactly. Hell's gates, now I know why he arranged for his son Guildford to wed Jane Grey." He threw his hat on the bed and raked his fingers through his hair. "The ailing king — he's in great distress and pain — has signed a document leaving the realm to Guildford and Jane, since Jane is of Tudor blood. The new will completely cuts out the Tudor sisters."

I sucked in a huge sob. My husband, usually so stalwart and strong, was shaking and looked stricken to his very soul. I sympathized with him in his betrayal by someone he trusted — oh, yes, I knew how that felt.

Years ago I would not have believed I could be in anguish over King Henry's children being set aside, but this was wrong, so wrong.

"Then Dudley plans to rule through his son and Jane," I whispered, my mind racing.

"I fear so. I told him I don't like it, but he said to stay in line, or he'd revoke my admiralty command and ruin your brother's chances to regain his title. He's . . . he's stepped over his own line of sanity, morality."

I bit my lip to keep from screaming, *I told you so! Years ago, I could have told you so!*

"I've been so loyal to him all these years," Edward plunged on, "and owe him so much. He's been almost like the father I lost so young. At least this will keep England from a half-Spanish queen rumored to want to wed Spanish royalty."

"And it overturns King Henry's will."

"A will Dudley claims was never legally signed — or rather that the king cut his signature off later when he reconsidered the succession of mere women."

"Mere women!" I muttered, hating Dudley even more. I collapsed on the coffer at the foot of the bed and put my head in my hands, not picking up Erin, who pawed at my slippers. I broke out into a sweat. I had that royal signature, but it had been dug up yet again with *The Red Book of Kildare* and hidden under floorboards in the corner of this very bedroom. I planned to give the book into Gerald's care and knowledge only when and if he sailed for Ireland, for I knew he had been questioned about its location and contents already. But the king's signature had been made by what was called a dry stamp and then inked in by someone. Dudley could claim it was a forgery, and he already suspected that I had done something amiss with his dagger the night the king died. What if he reasoned that I could have the signature he did not want found?

"You cannot support this," I said, looking up at Edward. "What are we going to do?"

"I have orders to fortify the Tower, in case it comes to a fight. Jane and Guildford are being moved there soon for their safety, and because monarchs always stay there before coronations. Northumberland —"

"I knew he was a very devil," I shouted, leaping to my feet. "Mayhap you will go back to just calling him Dudley now. You cannot play his game. Fortify the Tower? And be prepared to fight there, I suppose, against Mary Tudor and those rightfully loyal to her?" I knew I was losing control, but I could not help it. I sounded like a fishmonger's wife. Whining, Erin had retreated under the bed.

"Gera, I need you to swear you will be loyal to whatever I must do through this. I know you have hated Dudley for years, even transferred your wish for revenge to him when King Henry died, but he did save your life."

"Saved the life of a mere woman, after aiding and abetting the immoral, brutal, and publicly shameful deaths of my half brother, the Earl of Kildare, and my uncles — all of them. After my father died in that very hellhole of the Tower which you are willing to go to fortify!"

"I can't help all that. I want your solemn vow you will do nothing to endanger your position or mine in this! We will have to find our way through this crisis, all of us, the kingdom, Northumberland, you and I, the former princesses Mary and Elizabeth."

"Former? Dudley may be able to coerce the king to that, but not the kingdom! I don't put it past Dudley to have signed the so-called will himself for that poor, sick boy!"

"How nice that you are now standing up for the current Tudor ruler and his Tudor sisters! I'm going now, Gera. Stay here and stay safe if the streets become dangerous. There are crowds and factions forming. Promise me!" he repeated, and seized my shoulders hard to give me a little shake.

"I promise you I will do what I must — what I should — as you should."

"Don't make me lock you in here, Irish."

"Why not, Dudley's man? The English have locked up the Fitzgeralds for years, locked them out of their properties and homeland!"

"I am leaving two guards downstairs. Gera, please don't let this come between us. It has been my greatest — my only — fear for us."

"You might know Dudley would threaten Gerald while he claws his way to power over the body of a sick boy and the rightful royal heritage of two *mere women!*"

Edward went out and slammed the door. I heard his voice, but not what he said, as he spoke to someone.

I threw myself on our bed and beat the mattress with my fists and sobbed so hard I could barely breathe. I could not believe I had defied and screamed at the man I loved. Everything I had closed up inside so long had come pouring out. And what else shocked me was that, though I had hated Henry Tudor and his henchman Dudley all these years, I, whom my father once called the Irish princess, and who had been deprived of my birthright, was firmly for the Tudor women in their claim to the English throne.

CHAPTER THE TWENTY-SIXTH

London
July 6, 1553

I made myself stop sobbing and sat up on the bed. Erin came out from underneath it with her head cocked, as if to ask me what all that had been about. I patted the mattress and she jumped up, using the mounting stool we had placed there for her.

As I hugged the dog, I detested myself for losing my Irish temper with Edward, especially when he needed my support and advice, albeit more calmly, cleverly couched. I had shouted like a shrew. Perhaps he was staying loyal to Dudley partly because that bastard had threatened both his admiralty position and Gerald, which, of course, would have hurt me too. Whatever Edward's reasons, I refused to stay here while events that affected me and my family went on. I was no longer a girl who could merely watch a parade go by, taking my dear ones to their

430

deaths. I would go to Edward and find some way we could help Mary and Elizabeth. What I saw happening to them had happened to me in Ireland — dispossession and defeat.

When I peeked out through the keyhole, I saw a guard I did not know, sitting on the floor across the hall. Collum would not have stood for this, but he had gone out with Magheen and Alice to market. Saint Brigid, but an Englishman — even one I loved — was not going to hold a Geraldine prisoner in her own bedroom, not even a second-story one.

Hurrying lest they send Magheen or Alice in to sit with me when they returned, I rummaged in Edward's clothing chest for breeches, a jerkin, shirt, and cloak. The July weather was warm and muggy; I hardly needed the outer garments, but they would help to disguise me. They all hung huge on me, but I belted and gartered them around my waist and knees. I yanked my hair back, tied it in a horsetail knot, and shoved it up under an old cap of his.

I knelt to cuddle Erin, but it reminded me so much of tragic farewells with Wynne that I could only whisper, "Stay." Immediately minding me — did Edward think a wife should be that obedient? — the dog settled down on her cushion in the corner, as if she were guarding where I'd hidden *The Red Book of Kildare.*

Taking a goodly amount of coin, I climbed out through the window set ajar to catch the summer breeze and closed it behind me lest Erin would try to follow. After crawling across the span of tiled roof, I dropped onto a thatched one, then another, until I could dangle my feet to the edge of a watering trough. In a trice, I darted down the street to a livery stable where our horses were boarded.

There I saw another guard — this man of Edward's I did recognize — sitting on Kildare's stall rail! But my husband, naval hero or not, would not surround or embargo me. After all, this was for his good as well as mine.

Trying not to draw undue attention, I hied myself down the street to another stable and leased a sturdy enough looking mare. The man who saddled her eyed me strangely, probably thinking I was a pretty boy, but I was soon on my way, down to the water gate to take a horse barge. It was then on the Thames as London seemed to float by that I realized where I was determined to go. To the Tower, where my father had died and from which members of my family were carted to their deaths. To the place Elizabeth's mother and Cat Howard had lost their heads. I prayed I had not lost mine already, in mad love with one of Dudley's key men and daring to insist we must stand up to this deceit and evil.

All too soon, the stony skirts of the Tower loomed over us. I paid the bargemen and, sitting astride like a lad, rode my horse around to the only gate I saw open. "Gotta message for the Lord High Admiral," I muttered to the guard, and, to my relief, was let right in.

Within, I felt the very weight of the walls pressing on me. Gray, all was gray here; the lofty stone towers melded with the summer sky starting to spit rain. Above on the battlements, cannon sprouted like black teeth, and armed guards gathered. Thunder rumbled distantly, so it seemed cannon shots echoed within, as if I faced the nightmare of the siege of Maynooth again.

Men marched; some rolled huge guns here and there. Quite a troop of soldiers had assembled off to one side, with mounts saddled for riding. I stopped a running lad and repeated, "Gotta message for the Lord High Admiral." The boy jerked his hand toward the central, square building, its walls whiter than the others in this vast royal armory and prison. Which tower had my family languished in? Where had my father died? I tied my horse amidst four others, including my husband's, which I recognized, and hurried inside the building that dominated this cobbled courtyard and green.

Edward might be angry with me for coming here, but he would be glad to see me too, I tried to buck myself up. We could discuss things, make peace, even in the midst of this martial madness. I wanted to assure him of my love, to support him, but convince him he must not trust his future to John Dudley, whatever the man's promises or threats.

I saw the ground floor of this central white building was a cluttered armory, with swords and lances, halberds, and pieces of armor laid out on the floor being counted and sorted. I found the stairs and started up, passing a washerwoman hefting a pail of water and rags. She did not look at me, and no one seemed to notice her — an invisible woman. How I wished I could be the same until I found my lord.

It was dimly lit here, especially between the well-spaced torches, which sputtered as gusts of wind reached inside. As I came to a landing with halls cutting off in two directions, I heard a familiar voice, but not the one I sought. It was Dudley's! The thick wooden door at the end of one short corridor stood ajar.

He was saying, "You must capture Mary before it is announced that the king is dead."

I gasped, pressing both palms over my mouth. Young Edward Tudor was already dead, but Dudley was keeping it secret? Otherwise, would there not have been a hubbub in the streets or on the river? And who was Dudley sending to capture the princess Mary? Surely not my lord!

"I'll bring her back safe and sound, Father."

"If a stray bullet or fall from a horse should occur, Robert, do not let it worry you. It will save us time and trouble with her later."

Robert Dudley, one of his sons. The one, I'd heard, who had been a childhood companion not only of Prince Edward Tudor but also of his sister Elizabeth. Deceit, treachery, and betrayal. Dudley's vaunted family loyalty had turned into the rank, raw pursuit of power. So he had one son set to take the Tudor throne with Jane Grey and one set to capture Mary.

"Just so you understand, I'm depending on you," Dudley's voice cracked out. "This is of the essence for our plan."

"Thank heavens she's fled from Huddleston to Sawston Hall, as it is but fifteen miles due north. That will be no protection for her. Would that I were chasing Elizabeth, though."

"Sharp little minx that she is, she's taken to her bed at Hatfield, claiming illness, so we'll worry about her later. If we all play our cards right, perhaps you can join her in that bed someday, eh? Queen Jane and King Guildford on the throne, with you and Elizabeth standing in the wings."

"Are you forgetting I'm wed?"

"Are you forgetting that kings can call for divorces in this land? Be off with you now. Your men are waiting."

I darted down the other hall and, from the shadows, watched the young, handsome Robert Dudley stride away, spurs jangling, his chest armor reflecting the sconces. The washerwoman flattened herself against the wall, but he did not so much as glance her way.

At the other end of the hall, I too stayed pressed against the cold stone, fearing Dudley might emerge. All I needed was for him to find me here and stop what I now knew I must do. I could not risk the time or the chance I would be caught searching for my husband, for I had to warn the princess

Mary. I could not — nor could Edward — trust the Dudleys to rule England. They would never help Gerald and me but would see us as threats, as had King Henry. Dudley, Duke of Northumberland, who planned to rule through his son, could also ruin Edward, who would surely see the wretch he was and defy him. But Mary might help the Fitzgeralds someday, and, I prayed, Elizabeth might too.

I fled down the hall and down the stairs. Outside, Robert Dudley was rallying his men, the group of assembled riders I had seen earlier. I found my horse but walked her slowly around the troop of men, at least fifty, I reckoned. Once out into the street, I mounted and headed north. Our servants and Edward would be worried and furious when they saw that I had fled, but Robert Dudley had said Sawston Hall was only fifteen miles to the north. I would have to ask my way once I got on the Great North Road, but I must keep ahead of those men.

Just as it started to rain, I risked looking back, only to see the main gate of the Tower spew forth Robert Dudley and his hard-riding armed troop.

The ride itself was a wet, gray blur. Twice I shouted at carters or farmers for directions. It was nearly dusk when I pounded with both fists on the heavy oaken door of Sawston Hall.

"Open! Open at once!" I shouted. What, I feared, if the princess Mary was not here? What if she'd gone on? If so, I must hide until Dudley's men rode away.

When the door swung inward, I darted in and slammed it behind me, despite the two armed men who stood there with drawn swords. They stared aghast at me, sodden and frantic in men's garb. "I am Lady Gera Clinton," I gasped out. "If the princess is here, she must flee now. Northumberland's sent his son and an armed band to seize her, and they can't be far behind."

One man ran off down the hall shouting for his master, Sir John Huddleston. The old man appeared instantly; then, to his dismay though he tried to motion her back, the princess Mary came right behind. "Gera!" she cried, squinting to see me better. "It's been so long!"

I curtsied, but my legs almost buckled. "Your Grace, your royal brother is dead, and Northumberland means to put his son and Jane Grey on the throne. Men led by his son Robert are right behind me to take you prisoner."

Chaos erupted in the hall as several other

men and ladies appeared, arguing with one another, urging the princess to stay or flee. In their midst, garbed all in black, Mary Tudor grasped her large gold crucifix and gazed upward as though she heard none of their babble.

"Silence!" her unmistakable voice quieted them. "I vouch for this woman's honesty. Though her lord is a man greatly deluded by Northumberland, I believe her. Prepare the horses at the back. Listen! God has quieted the storm outside for us. We shall flee!"

Everyone seemed to forget me as I leaned exhausted against the staircase balustrade, but old Lord Huddleston in his riding cloak came up to me. "I've ordered a fresh horse and food packed for you too, dear lady. You'll come with us, of course."

"You've no time to pack food! I must turn back to London. I had to tell her, that's all —"

A crash nearly sundered the front door. "Open in the name of the king!" Robert Dudley's voice shredded the sudden lull. Something huge battered the door a second time.

"Liar!" Mary spit out low. "My brother, the king, is dead, and you know it well, may

God rest his poor soul. And *I* am queen now."

"Out, out the back!" Sir John cried. "Lady Clinton, please!"

I ran behind the others as the front door smashed inward with a grinding crunch. Outside, I caught a glimpse of the princess's mounted party melting into the black forest behind the lawns. Yes, there was a fresh horse for me. I mounted and raced after Mary's party, out into a little valley. From the crest of a distant, forested hill, we reined in and turned back to watch Robert Dudley's men force Sir John's servants outside and put the torch to stately Sawston Hall. Sir John watched it burn with tears tracking down his wrinkled cheeks.

"Do not grieve, my loyal friend," Mary declared, "for, by the Holy Virgin, I shall build you a greater Sawston when the throne is mine." Her crucifix glinted blood-red in the reflected inferno. She turned my way. "Gera, you have saved my life. I shall reward you, too. I only hope your lord husband sees the error of his ways and comes to my banners." She raised her low-pitched voice like a battle cry: "Do not look back, only ahead to a brighter future for England! On to Framlingham Castle, where we shall make our stand. Come!"

Like homeless Gypsies in the night, our bedraggled band turned our horses away from the raging holocaust toward Framlingham — and farther from my lord Edward, to whom I longed so desperately to return.

July 16, 1553

From rural towns and hamlets, thousands of peasants, tenant farmers, and gentry knights poured toward Mary Tudor's banners at massive old Framlingham Castle, which King Henry had taken from the Norfolk family, but which King Edward had given to his sister Mary. Outside the triple moat, fortified bastions, vast battlements, and thirteen watchtowers, Tudor loyalists camped and awaited Northumberland's army, rumored to be approaching from the south. Carts of bread, beer, and meat rumbled in from obscure towns in Norfolk and Suffolk to feed the rough soldiers of Mary's makeshift army. Woodsmen cut down trees and used the trunks to block the possible approach of seasoned, trained fighters under the banners of Queen Jane Grey and led by her father-in-law, the Duke of Northumberland. In defiance of the overwhelming odds against her, over it all fluttered Queen Mary Tudor's blue-and-green pennants. It reminded me of how Maynooth had been provisioned and protected against the English forces — and we had lost.

"Gera, look you," Princess Mary said as she pointed from the tallest tower, where we stood overlooking the sprawling scene. "Golden iris growing in the inner moat like another sign from heaven that I shall prevail!"

On our frenzied ride to Framlingham, Mary's little band had seen the numerous crudely lettered signs along the rural roadsides, where word of the Tudor king's death and Jane Grey's insurrection had finally spread: *Vox Populi, Vox Dei* — "the voice of the people is the voice of God." Many of the faithful who flocked to Mary's aid believed she was the new Virgin Mary, come to do God's righteous avenging work against those who had imposed King Henry's new religion on the people of England. But Mary too believed she was a savior, and that terrified me. Each tiny event became to her a momentous sign that she must stamp out the new Protestant religion as well as those who opposed her under Northumberland — and that, I feared, included my husband.

With Mary's permission, I had sent him a carefully worded note by messenger two days ago, telling him I was safe and with Mary's forces. I begged him to join us. I had no word that he had received my plea, but informants said that Northumberland, with three thousand mounted men and foot soldiers, thirty cannon from the Tower of London, and thirty cartloads of ammunition, was camped at Cambridge and set to do battle. Hearing that, I almost fled, for I had no doubt that John Dudley would have me arrested or worse when he found I had betrayed him. And my Edward — was he helping Dudley? Would he ever forgive me for casting my fate with Mary's forces?

"The flowers are beautiful, Your Grace, but my heart is still heavy," I said, choosing my words carefully. "Instead of rewarding me as you have kindly offered, the favor I would ask is that you promise pardon to my lord Clinton."

"By the Holy Virgin, the choice is his, and he has evidently made it! If he came to me as you did, or brought his navy over to me, of course I would consider pardon. But as England's rightful monarch now," she declared loudly so others could hear, "I cannot be ruled by my heart in anything. Though," she said, half to herself, "when I choose a husband, I pray he will love me as a woman as well as a queen."

As her entourage walked on with her, I stood there alone on the windswept heights, looking in the direction that Edward's help or Dudley's hell must come.

Word spread through the castle and among Mary's army like wildfire: The Privy Council had abandoned Jane Grey and declared for Mary in London. They were sending emissaries to sue for her forgiveness and favor.

I had been living in borrowed gowns from some of her ladies, and I donned the best I had, Irish green, I told myself. Would my lord be with the men from the council? Had he gone over to Mary's cause? And what of Dudley and his army — would they still attack? Even the stout stone and flint walls of mighty Framlingham seemed to hold their breath.

Boldly, the uncrowned queen walked among her people, making brief speeches. Helmets flew in the air; caps and coins tossed for the cause made a carpet under her feet. I stayed as close to her as I could, waiting for news, praying I would be close if my husband came with the others from London.

Pikes and swords gleamed in the hot July sun, as everyone broke into cries of, "God save the queen!" Several of the local folk, addressing me as the princess Elizabeth, curtsied to me too, but I was thankful Mary did not see or hear that, as rapt as she was in her own joy.

And then, from beyond the crowd, heading for the crest on which the massive castle stood, came a single, fast rider whose horse made puffs of dust as it parted the jostling throngs.

Queen Mary squinted to better see the rider. "An emissary from the council or a messenger with news of Northumberland's approach?" she said. "Gera, you're so tall — your eyes. Who is it?"

A cheer rose in my throat, then dissolved in the bile of stark fear. It was Edward, riding hell-bent straight for us. I almost fell at Mary's feet, but I locked my knees and stood. "Your Grace, it is Lord High Admiral Clinton, come to your banners," I cried, and prayed that was the truth.

Mary's closest comrades cheered as Edward reined in at the outside ring of guards and approached on foot, extending his drawn sword, hilt first, toward the queen in the universal sign of surrender. Murmurs lifted from the crowd. Many recognized him and whispered his name. As word spread, hundreds of his own sailors and soldiers who had come to Mary shouted his name in a chant. I stood stock-still, too terrified to pray. His narrowed eyes met my gaze but briefly; I could not read the emotion there. He swept off his helmet and dropped immediately to one knee before the queen. He bowed his head — his hair was mussed — while the queen took his sword and passed it to the man behind her. So brave, so proud, my Edward.

"My gracious queen, I have come to cast myself upon your mercy for past errors of misplaced loyalty." His strong voice rang out in the expectant hush. When she said nothing, he lifted his head to stare up into her stern face. I breathed for the first time when Mary thrust out her stiff hand and he bent over it in a brief kiss of homage.

"Is not your master Northumberland hard on your tail, then, Lord Clinton?" the royal voice challenged. I edged closer. Surely this move of abject loyalty would appease Mary Tudor.

"To tell true, Your Majesty, I hear he is near Cambridge, holed up there, his ranks riddled by desertions to your just cause."

"Are you one of those deserters?"

"I come directly from the Tower in London, Your Majesty. I was ordered to secure it and protect the usurper Lady Jane Grey and her husband there, but I deserted that duty as soon as I heard you were here — and my beloved wife with you."

My heart thudded in my throat when I saw Mary's yet flinty expression. Why was she not relieved and ready to rejoice as I and the others close around her were? I knew she had been casting about to get a devoted Dudley man in her grasp to make an example of. Saint Brigid, no, not Edward! Not after what I had done for her, and yet I dared not argue with her before her people.

"Arrest this man for treason against the God-given queen of England!" Mary cried as guards leaped forward to take Edward's arms. I gasped and threw myself at my husband, clinging to him as he dared to speak again.

"I was hoping you would have need of England's Lord High Admiral for your God-given cause, Your Majesty," he said calmly.

"Lord High Admiral no more! I must show no mercy to John Dudley and his minions!"

Finally I spoke. "Please, Your Majesty. Send me with him then —"

"Gera, no," Edward muttered amidst the chaos as he was pulled away. "Stay with her; try to reason —"

"Very well then, your lady wife will go with you!" the queen cried. "My people

447

must make their choices to whom they will be loyal. For England and Saint George!" she urged the common cry.

"For England and Saint George. Long live the queen!" a man's voice behind us shouted, and the crowd roared as the shout spread. I clung hard to Edward's hand as he was hustled toward the castle. Mary had made me choose between her and my husband, and so I had. I should have known to trust no one who held ultimate power, English power. "For England and long live the queen"? No, until the day I died, my cry must be for Ireland and the Geraldines!

CHAPTER THE
TWENTY-SEVENTH

At first I could not fathom that we were actually being sent to the dungeon, but down we went on a twisting staircase into the depths of the old castle. It was dark and dank, much worse than Maynooth's cellar. Our guards hurried us along a narrow stone hall lined with wooden doors with small, square iron grates. One man had a lantern, but I could hardly see down here and I stubbed my toe against rough paving stones. With a hard hand on my upper arm, Edward held me up.

"Are there lights for the cells?" I dared to ask. I could not tell whether Edward was not speaking because he was resigned or enraged — and at the queen or me?

"Not with straw on the floors, milady. Can't have a fire here."

Keys jingled as the man with the lantern took an interminable time unlocking the door while the two armed guards hovered.

Edward gripped my hand harder than I had held to his and pulled me in after him. Before I could try to read his face, the door slammed behind us, plunging us into blackness. The men outside shuffled away; silence reigned.

To my relief, Edward clamped me to him, my head under his chin, his arms around me tight, grappled chest to breast. "Thank God you are all right," he whispered, his breath hot in my ear. "Despite their show of leaving, we must whisper," he added as he pulled me away from the door until we bumped into a stone wall.

"I came to the Tower to find you," I explained in a rush, "but I overheard Dudley tell his son Robert that the king was dead and to arrest Mary and get rid of her in the process if he could."

"I didn't know the king was dead until I faced Dudley down at the Tower, after Robert left with his men. I was furious he would dare to keep that from me — from the kingdom. By then, Collum had come to find me to say you'd gone out the window. You could have broken your neck, and at that point, I wanted to break it for you."

"I just didn't want us to argue. I wanted us to work together to help Mary and protect ourselves. I guess I did the wrong thing."

"You didn't. We both should have followed Mary's banners, but I thought I could reason with Dudley. He's gone mad with power — and now, at last, I think he knows he's going to pay for it."

"Poor Jane Grey."

"Queen Mary's cousin or not, I warrant she'll never leave the Tower alive, or her young husband either. They say her parents beat her until she agreed to wed him."

I shuddered in his arms. "I believe that. I've seen the marks on her before and now whatev—"

In midword, his lips covered mine, a possessive, demanding kiss, full of pent-up anger but of passion too. He leaned against the damp wall, and we clung in our mutual embrace and hungry kisses. When we at last came up for air, breathing hard in unison, time flew as we told each other all that had happened since we'd been parted. Finally, exhausted, shivering, we slid down the wall and sat on the stone floor with me in his lap, still holding tight.

"I will beg her to just send us into exile," I told him. "We'll go to Ireland and hide out there."

"Fugitives and rebels, my love? Put to the

horn and hunted as your brothers once were? Never that. Our new queen used the word *treason* to me and obviously wants a scapegoat. I'm hoping when she gets her hands on Dudley, that will be enough for her. But if not, our lands and my life could be forfeit."

"No! No, that cannot be, not more of this. Not after everything with my first family!"

He held me tight again, then whispered, "Is there a light in the hall?"

I turned to look and had to squint at the sudden brightness. Could the setting sun slant in like this so far below the ground?

Voices. Among the men's, one commanding, low voice I knew.

"Down here — the queen!" I whispered, and we scrambled to our feet, dusting ourselves off, I shaking out my skirts and tugging back my loosened hair as if being in a dungeon did not give us some excuse for how we looked.

The key scraped in the lock. The queen's stocky silhouette filled the doorway. Mary Tudor stepped in behind two men, each holding lanterns. Until I saw that she held a scented pomander to her nose, I had not realized the rank smell of mildew and worse down here.

We bowed and curtsied and stayed down.

"Rise," she said.

We faced her, holding hands.

"I perhaps owe my very life to your wife, Lord Clinton. And now you owe her yours too. The admiralty must go to someone I can truly trust, but I am not so vindictive — or foolish — that I will rid England of a brave sea captain. On the morrow, you will be given two horses and provisions and be sent home to Lincoln — is that your northern seat?"

"Near there, Your Majesty. Kyme and Sempringham."

"Then there you will stay until I have need of your service. I expect you to shore up support for me there. I have been reminded by Lord Jerningham that you once helped put down the rebellion against the Tudors in the north."

"Yes, Your Grace. I carried letters from your father commanding others to hold the area."

As he said that, he gripped my hand so hard I flinched. Did he think I would not hold my tongue through this? Did he think I would tell her I tried to deface or ruin those orders?

"Though I intend to show humility and forgiveness," the queen continued, "even as our Lord Christ did to those who betrayed him, your former master will meet his doom. And I will not see your face, my lord — or that of your wife, since she has chosen to share your fate — until and if I send for you for further loyal service. Do you understand?"

"I do with gratitude, Your Majesty," he said, and bowed again, pulling me down with him.

"Gera, I have a boon for you too. Partly because John Dudley wanted to keep your brother Gerald under his thumb, I shall return his title of Earl of Kildare to him when I settle all else, and mayhap I shall send him home to Ireland to help keep the peace there."

"Oh, Your gracious Majesty, that would be such . . . such a brilliant strategy!"

"I am going now and will send someone to see you are brought upstairs to be fed and properly clothed before you set out on the morrow. Do not go back to London and do not make a show of your leaving here."

Still with our heads down, we did not see her depart but heard the swish of her skirts and the scrape of her booted heels, then her low-voiced orders to someone in the hall. Such bounty from a Tudor, for Edward, Gerald, and me! From the darkness of despair to the light of hope, despite the loss of Edward's admiralty and his place on the Privy Council. Our lands and lives — our future — not only spared, but a brave new beginning bestowed.

"I can't bear for the *Defiance* to go to someone else," Edward muttered through gritted teeth, "but we're both damned good at earning our way back. And you have ties not only to Mary but also to Elizabeth."

As we started to climb the narrow dungeon stairs, I told him, forcing a cheerful tone, "After all, most of my life, there's been nowhere to go but up."

London
January 1554
Despite our second honeymoon, we worked hard to, as Her Majesty had said, shore up support for her in Lincolnshire. And it had given us solid family time with the children. But we were, thank the Lord, recalled much sooner than we had expected, for London was under attack by a peasant and Protestant rebel group and the queen wanted every good military man she could find to aid her. Though this rebellion was a dryland one, Edward was summoned to protect the palace, and I went with him. I was grateful for the excuse to return to some influence near the throne but was agonizing over

455

several things.

For one, the queen planned to marry Prince Philip of Spain this coming summer, and few Englishmen wanted our realm — yes, I must admit I saw England as my home as well as Ireland now — to become, in effect, a Spanish colony. Also, rumors were rampant that the queen had hearkened to her bishops and Spanish allies about persecuting — that is, burning at the stake — everyone who would not publicly declare for certain Catholic rites that the Protestants detested.

Although the queen had immediately released the Earl of Surrey's father, the Duke of Norfolk, who had been incarcerated in the Tower during Edward's brief reign, Jane Grey and her young husband still languished there. As for that devil Dudley, he had been beheaded on Tower Green a month after his rebellion. Because I knew my husband had conflicting emotions over that, only in private had I lifted a congratulatory drink to Dudley's demise. King Henry and John Dudley, dead at last, though there was much yet to do to return the Fitzgeralds to their proper fortunes. For that was the only way we could help lift our people from poverty, superstition, and the oppression of cruel English rule. I must do all I could to support not only my husband but the cause of my kin and home country, dear Ireland.

Other woes that assailed those I cared for at that time included that Parliament had once again declared the marriage of King Henry and Anne Boleyn null and void, so "the lady" Elizabeth was a bastard once again. I had corresponded with her during our exile in the north, and I was certain she was innocent of something else: The queen believed her half sister had instigated or at least sanctioned this so-called current Wyatt Rebellion. It was true that the rebels wanted the darling of the Protestants to have the throne in place of her sister, but that hardly meant Elizabeth was to blame. Yet I knew that, since the queen was still considering beheading her cousin Jane, what might she do with Elizabeth if she could prove — or concoct — treason against her?

"I cannot abide the queen's younger sister being blamed for all this," I told Gerald and Mabel as we sat together in Mabel's rooms at Whitehall Palace, where we awaited Edward's return from a royal audience. "She was not to blame for the Thomas Seymour mess, except for youthful bad judgment, and I am certain she would not have given her support to this revolt."

Gerald held Mabel's hand and trailed little circles on her palm with his index finger. They were betrothed but were delaying their wedding until the queen restored his title — Gerald's idea, not Mabel's. "Gerabeth," he said, turning toward me and frowning, "I cannot believe you are always standing up for Anne Boleyn's girl. Queen Mary will wed and have children, and Elizabeth will never get the throne."

"I don't care; I admire her. Sometimes she reminds me of myself."

Gerald gave a snort, which quite annoyed me. "Just because you look a bit alike or have the same first name, my lady Elizabeth?" he goaded. He rose and walked to the window and scraped a small circle of frost off with his ring, for the winter winds were bitter cold. I forgave his rude manners at once. He was frustrated by waiting and felt penned in, and I understood that. He peered out toward the nearly frozen Thames. "I'll go with Her Grace's forces if they face Wyatt's rebels, of course," he told us, "but they should do what our people used to — fight in good weather and hunker down before a fire with a beautiful maid in the winter."

He winked at Mabel and she smiled at him, lost in love. I recognized the feeling.

Besides, they were suited. I had begun to turn her into an Irish rebel, and Gerald had completed the transformation. If — and when — she went home as Gerald's bride, Countess of Kildare, I'd wager Mabel could match me for standing up to and for the Irish.

The hall door opened with a whoosh of chill air, and Edward rushed in. "You might know the queen has no standing army. She has tried to parley with Wyatt, but he replied with insolence, demanding her surrender instead of his. Her Majesty has ordered that men in the streets arm themselves. She is placing me in charge of protecting the palace, and the old Duke of Norfolk in charge of the city, but we must protect the city to save the palace. Gerald, with me. Ladies, keep close here. And, my love," he said, pulling me to him and tipping my chin up, "that means no going out windows or tunnels to join the fray. Swear to me."

"Yes. I'll stay near the queen to remind her that you and Gerald fight for her cause. But Elizabeth cannot have given this rebellion her blessing. She's too smart, too —"

"But she's still young and has proven that she can make mistakes." He kissed me once, soundly, as we old married folks, wed all of fifteen months, tried to ignore Gerald's very fond farewell to his betrothed.

That was the last I saw of my husband for two days.

Even from Whitehall, we could hear the beating of distant drums, for men were being mustered as close as St. James's Palace. Most of the foreign diplomats had fled, but, unfortunately, ferret-faced Simon Renard, the Spanish ambassador, stayed behind to spew his poison in the queen's ear.

"Your Majesty, are you certain you can trust these men who have turned on the Tudors before?" I was told he had said. "The Howards would have taken the Tudor throne. Granted, the Earl of Surrey paid the price, but why did you free his father, Norfolk, from the Tower and give him a command? And Captain Clinton, once a rebel, always dangerous, wed to that rabble-rousing female Geraldine who wants her family to rule Ireland."

If I had heard that firsthand, I would have scratched his Spanish eyes out. Instead, I kept near the queen, where I could keep my Irish eyes on him.

Tense hours followed, for Mary ordered her army not to fire the opening salvo. Short-tempered, she paced the long gallery overlooking the Thames. I had to wonder if

I was cursed, for this could be the third siege of a castle I had faced in my thirty-one years on this earth, and I was a hapless pawn in all of them. How I wished I could hoist a battle banner, take a sword, and fight beside the men!

My lord's former sailors moved all barges and boats from the Thames so that Wyatt's forces could not use them to cross, but that merely delayed the rebels. They marched to Kingston and crossed the Thames at night to approach the capital from the west through Knightsbridge. All too soon, the four hundred men under Edward's command, some civilians and some trained, were engaged in fighting, some of it hand-to-hand. What if Edward were wounded or killed, let alone what if he failed to hold his defensive line? Had the queen recalled him only for his military prowess in the past, or because he must save her to save himself?

As I chewed my lower lip and tried to ignore the roiling of my stomach, I saw Ambassador Renard sidle up to the queen again. He unrolled a piece of parchment I recognized: the drawing Edward had made to show the queen his defensive plan. I moved closer, shifting my way through the cluster of her ladies, as if we females could protect her if Wyatt's forces breached the palace walls.

"Your most gracious Majesty," Renard said, unrolling the parchment and frowning at it as if he had been bidden to criticize it, "will you not allow me to send for aid from Spain? Can we truly trust those who have served not only your enemy Dudley but the Protestant cause before? And as I have urged, not only your royal sister but Lady Jane Grey are becoming a touchstone for such rebels, *sí*. Best they both be kept under lock and key, if not sent far away."

"Exile, Ambassador?" she replied. "Then my enemies would surely rally to their cause."

"A permanent exile," I heard him whisper. "Not only from England, but from this earth."

"Your Grace," I said, "forgive me, but this foreign ambassador is counseling you to do what, thank God, was not done to you. Outside forces hoped to use you for their purposes, but your loyalty to your family, even in difficult times, kept you faithful. I believe your sister is fully loyal and stake my life on my husband's loyalty, and worry only about advice you get from foreign quarters!"

Mary listened intently, but Renard looked livid. "Your husband," he cracked out, pointing at me, "is betting his life on his success today, *sí,* I tell you that!"

"Ambassador! Gera!" Queen Mary interrupted my next retort. "Both of you, leave my presence until you can calm yourselves and speak only of my God-given rights as queen. I do not need fighting of any sort in or near this palace! The Virgin Mary is with this royal Mary, and we shall prevail!"

I curtsied and went huffily from her presence, only to realize she might not prevail. I could hear the fighting coming closer, the sounds of guns and drums — even men's shouts. Had my lord's forces not held their defensive lines? As I paced in the corridor above the courtyard facing King Street, I managed to stop a messenger only because I recognized him, and called out, "Haverhill! How does my lord Clinton?"

Out of breath, he gestured to me but kept going. I lifted my skirts and ran to keep up as he gasped out his words. "We met the rebels with cannon shot and arms. Bloody fighting now. No one has taken Wyatt yet. But he's sent a splinter group of men — around another way — and the queen must take cover. . . ."

Even as he spoke, chaos erupted outside. Everyone ran to the windows to look down. The rabble of guards in the courtyard shouted as a hailstorm of arrows from Wyatt's approaching forces thudded against the windows. Several panes shattered and sprayed inward. Lurching toward him, keeping low, I grabbed Haverhill's arm.

"The palace can hold out a while," I shouted, "but Edward must be told they made it here!"

"I have orders to warn the queen! Then I'll go back. Streets blocked — gotta take a roundabout way."

"That will take too long. Consider her warned with this noise outside and broken windows. You must go back to Edward and bring him and some men here — attack them from the outside too. I've seen it done — years ago in Ireland before my home castle was taken by deceit. He'll know what to do. Go. Go!"

"He told me to tell the queen first, and then we'll go, or I'll send someone else!" he shouted. "His lordship was adamant that the queen be warned while she could still flee!"

"I'll tell the queen! You get back to my lord with word of this, and tell him to bring troops here, even if it weakens the line of the main onslaught. Now, or I will ride there myself!"

He finally obeyed, muttering something

about women captains. I looked out the windows again. Below, the men my lord had left at the palace were holding their own. Could I risk that Edward would be warned and arrive in time with reinforcements? Could I delay telling the queen that all might be lost and she should flee?

But I did not have to go to her, as she, Renard, and six yeomen guards, all trailed by her ladies, came rushing along the corridor to view the fighting below, as if there were some fine joust being played out for them.

"Whatever are we to do?" Mary was saying, wringing her hands with her big crucifix clasped between. "I will not leave my palace and my capital, not to a rabble who want to put my sister on the throne!"

"Your Grace," I said, rushing up to her and curtsying low, "I can assure you more help is on the way."

"Assure me how?"

"Not only do I know my husband's loyalty and zeal to protect you, but I just spoke with one of his lieutenants, who said this splinter group will be dealt with."

"She lies," Renard said.

"Gera Clinton's fault is that she dares to say things she should not," the queen clipped out. It was, perhaps, the biggest gamble of my life, but then both King Henry and Queen Mary had remarked upon the luck of the Irish. Within a half hour, thank God, before Wyatt's forces could batter their way into Whitehall, his soldiers were penned in and cut down by my husband's men. With Wyatt himself taken, the upheaval was over — that is, the military upheaval, for the queen's blood was now up and she — with thanks to my lord for bringing the extra troops, and her ear unfortunately still tuned to Ambassador Renard — moved with swift vengeance.

Scores of rebels' bodies swung from gibbets throughout the city. Townsmen who had turned traitor were hanged from their own shop signs, while wives and children cowered and wailed inside. Rebel leaders' heads on pikes studded London Bridge. Thomas Wyatt himself was hanged, drawn, and quartered. Jane Grey and Guildford Dudley, whom Mary had once insisted would be spared with Christ's tender mercy, were beheaded. And Elizabeth Tudor was brought by force to London and imprisoned in a suite at Whitehall and questioned endlessly about her treachery and treason to have secretly spurred on this unholy rebellion.

CHAPTER THE TWENTY-EIGHTH

Whitehall Palace
March 18, 1554

"I cannot believe the queen won't let anyone see Elizabeth," I complained to Mabel, my arms folded over my chest as I paced in Edward's and my rooms at court. Though command of the royal navy had been given to a doddering old man, Lord Effingham, at least Edward had been given a commission at sea and captained the *Defiance* again. He was sailing somewhere south of England right now, when he should be here.

"She's not only been held as a prisoner," I went on, "but I just heard the queen is sending her to the Tower! The Tower, where her mother — and my family — met their deaths. Elizabeth has consistently insisted she had naught to do with Wyatt's rebellion, they can prove nothing but that she had a letter from him, they have no reply from her, but she is being suspected of treason.

Treason! The Tudors did always see treason behind every tree!"

"I hear you, Gera, and half the palace will too if you don't calm down," Mabel said, looking up from her embroidery of the Fitzgerald crest.

"If I don't speak up, who will? Besides, I can barely hear myself over the ceaseless rain battering the windows. You shouldn't be so calm either. Gerald's title was promised; he fought bravely with Edward during the rebellion, and nothing — not so much as a word about the return of his earldom!"

"I am angry about that. Her Majesty is planning her own wedding, but — stubborn man that Gerald is — certainly *so* different from you," she added, her voice dripping sarcasm, "she's delaying mine."

"Yes, I'm stubborn. The Fitzgeralds are, so best get used to that." I stopped pacing so quickly my skirts belled around me. I sighed and went over to the window smeared with rain. The queen had given us fine rooms overlooking the Thames, perhaps a nod to Edward's love of the sea. Saint Brigid, but how I would love to be at sea with him. I'd even help him chase the pirates that dared to interfere with English — and Irish — shipping.

I saw someone was braving the elements

on this bleak, wet mid-March day: A six-oared boat, not a royal one, had pulled up to the royal wharf. Someone fully guarded was being taken toward that bobbing boat. I held my breath so I wouldn't steam up the pane and wiped the inside moisture away.

Elizabeth! I had sensed it was her, known it was her, just as when I had looked down to see her running to a tryst with Tom Seymour years ago. But now she looked slumped and sick, swaying slightly on her feet. Her steps dragged, and her hood barely covered her red head that I could just make out through the wash of rain. She had no female companion, only two cloaked men and six bulky guards — perhaps the oarsmen. I began to pray that, if someone else looked out a palace window, the rain I had been cursing would obscure the fact that I was going with her.

"I'll feel better if I take a walk," I told Mabel, and grabbed my warmest cloak.

"Surely not in this downpour."

I was out the door before she could say another word, swirling the cape around my gown, yanking up the hood, and thudding down the stairs. Poor Elizabeth was going to face the Tower alone and, no doubt, afraid. They said she had been ill, though the Spanish ambassador had told the queen her sister was counterfeiting her aches and pains. Ha! I write now what I could not have admitted years ago: If I had Mary Tudor for a queen and also for a sister, I would have been ill too. She hearkened to the most hateful advice and was becoming more suspicious and vengeful every day. Her father had tortured and murdered those who would not accept him as the head of the English Church. Now Mary planned to do the same to those who would not return to the Catholic Church her father had ruined.

As I rushed outside on that rain-swept Sabbath, the city bells began to clang, summoning the faithful to Mass. As if they tolled her doom, Elizabeth, bedraggled and bereft, walked toward the boat bobbing in the Thames. I immediately recognized her escorts, the old Earl of Sussex and the tall, thin Marquess of Winchester. Elizabeth did not see me: She looked straight ahead. No pomp and circumstance, hardly the center of attention she once admitted she longed to be.

As she was helped into the boat, I rushed down the wharf. The drumming of the rain on the wooden boards and its patter into the river nearly deafened me.

"Halt, there!" Lord Winchester shouted at

me. "What's amiss?"

I could have replied much as to what was amiss, but I said only, "I am sorry I was delayed. I'm going with you, my lords, just to the Tower; then you will return me here. You did not think Her Majesty would send her sister away without at least one woman along, did you?"

There, I thought, I hadn't exactly lied. I tilted my head and stared down both the marquess and the Earl of Sussex, though I was aware Elizabeth gaped up at me. Both courtiers knew me, so I did not bother to introduce myself.

Winchester looked flustered and Sussex skeptical. I prayed they would not send someone to confirm my words. "Well, wouldn't be proper without one woman, milady," Sussex muttered.

Not risking another word, I climbed unaided into the rocking boat and perched next to Elizabeth, who gladly made room. Once we cast off upriver, she leaned heavily against me, and we held hands, her right with my left. Now I blessed the rattle of rain because it cloaked our words.

"I'll never be able to thank you enough for daring this," she told me, a bit hunched over as if she would indeed be sick. I prayed she did not suffer from the mal de mer that dear Magheen did on the sea, for the river was rough.

"I've been through so much over the years; what else can they do to me?" I muttered.

"My thoughts for myself exactly, but to the Tower on possible treason charges . . . I am terrified."

"I know you are innocent."

"And I know to trust you, because I heard you were once given the opportunity to say I had plotted with Seymour to overthrow my brother. But you declined, because, you said, you knew nothing untoward about him and me. Except you really did."

"We made a bargain that night on the stairs at Chelsea Manor. Besides, it was John Dudley interrogating me, and he can go to hell."

"And mayhap did," she said, and then was sick over the side of the boat.

I took out my damp handkerchief and wiped her face. I put one arm around her shoulders the rest of the way as London slipped past; then the bridge and the Tower itself loomed.

"Your father died here, so I heard," she said.

Once I would have screamed that her father had killed mine, but I said only, "Yes,

Your Grace, sadly so."

"It's not Your Grace, just plain Lady Elizabeth again, you know."

"Not to me."

"Dear Irish princess," she whispered, "at this moment I tell you, blood ties aside, you and I are more sisters than Mary and I shall ever be, dispossessed as you and I both have been by the Tudors."

At that, I marveled so I could not reply. Besides, as we neared London Bridge, the tide and rain combined to make the current in the narrow passage between the arches deeper and faster. I wondered if Mary Tudor had actually thought that Elizabeth might perish here in a so-called accident, much as John Dudley had meant to happen to Mary herself. Skilled bargemen knew just how to shoot the bridge's supports on the rapids, but a whirlpool swung us around, while Sussex and Winchester shouted at the oarsmen to go on, and they pulled at their oars to right our prow. White as bleached Irish linen, with her eyes pinched closed, Elizabeth leaned against me and clung to my hand. At least she did not see the gruesome rotting heads of executed rebels leering down from the bridge above.

Once we survived that, the bottom of the boat scraped a stony shore. The great iron jaws of a portcullis to the Tower loomed over us.

"No," Elizabeth said, raising her voice at last to her guardians and guards, "I will not go in this way. Not through what they call Traitor's Gate, for I am no traitor to my queen or country!"

"My lady, we have our orders," Sussex insisted.

She loosed my hand and stood in the boat, bracing her knees against mine. Her white face flushed; her quivering lips tightened. The constable and six warders of the Tower now assembled on the steps, waiting for her to disembark.

"No!" she said again, clenching her fists at her sides, her furious face running with rain. "Never!"

Old Sussex looked frantic. "Queen's orders, my lady, that you must get out here."

"Well, then," she said, "all good subjects obey their queen." With one heavy touch on my shoulder, she climbed unaided from the boat and leveled one long, thin finger at the men. "Tell her this! Here lands as true a subject, being prisoner unjustly, as ever stepped on these stairs!" She dropped her arms to her sides and stared up into the driving rain. "Before You, O God, I say this, having no other friend but You alone!"

And there, on the top step, she sat. I scrambled out and stood behind her, then realized I must sit in her presence. I sat next to her on the step, still awed at the royal outburst of temper, deeply moved by her defiant stand. Yet it was exactly what, as an Irish princess, I would have done if I had been sent hapless and accused to a prison in old Dublin town.

Elizabeth ignored the pleas of her escorts, and they were quite afraid to physically force her to go in. Soaked to the bone, we both shivered until our teeth chattered. Did she intend to die of catching her death of cold or ague out here? No, I knew and trusted Elizabeth Tudor.

At last, when she realized they were about to carry her, she turned and whispered to me, "I did not mean it about having no other friend but God. I have loved Kat Ashley as the mother I never knew, and I shall not forget my Irish friend. We shall meet again some fairer day and dance a fine jig together," she concluded, but her voice broke on a sob. She cleared her throat.

Elizabeth of England stood with her feet still in the puddles of rainwater at the edge of the cold Thames. She lifted her drenched skirts and stomped up the steps without a look back.

"I will go in now," she informed the Tower constable and warders, as if she had never refused. I heard her inquire of the nervous constable, a man we had entertained in our home, "Ah, are all these guards for me, and I just one frail, weak woman?"

I stepped back into the boat and huddled in the rain as I watched her disappear with shoulders back and head held high. The rain ran down my face so fast I could not tell that I was crying.

Evidently the queen never heard what I had done — she never mentioned it, and I told only Edward, weeks later. Or else perhaps Her Majesty said naught because she needed my husband's goodwill to keep England's coasts clear of smugglers and pirates. At any rate, she at last — at last! — granted Gerald his earldom on the momentous date of May 13, 1554. We Clintons and Fitzgeralds had a big celebration with a feast and dancing for our whole family; the next day Mabel and I began to plan her wedding.

Only fifteen days later, the twenty-eighth of May, Gerald and Mabel were married. Standing before the altar as a sponsor to them in a church near Westminster, I could not help but be proud of how lovely the old place looked. The crucifix gleamed upon the altar, and I had hired a washerwoman to scrub the very stones under our feet. Which reminded me of my two surreptitious visits to Elizabeth during the three months she spent incarcerated in the Bell Tower within the Tower of London before she was finally released, just nine days before this wedding. I would have loved to have her here as a special guest, but she had been sent, once again, into rural exile.

I bit back a smile — joy for this day but also for recalling that the washerwoman I'd seen in the Tower during Jane Grey's brief reign had seemed invisible to everyone. So I had gone garbed as such with my red tresses under a cap, hefting a heavy bucket of water and rags, and no one paid me heed. No one but my friend Elizabeth, who actually smiled when she saw it was I the first time. But the last time I went so disguised, we had a bit of a spat.

"I promise you, dear Gera," she had whispered through the grate in her cell door as I pretended to swab the hall floor, "if you and your lord ever serve in my household, it won't be scrubbing floors. You have made my day — my week — my month, for I was fearful at first that scaffold standing in the courtyard was for me."

"It was left over from Jane and Guildford, poor souls."

"So they finally told me. Be careful, Gera, for the guards may be back soon. But yes, I know how it was for Jane, buffeted about by her parents, and I don't blame her for what happened. But there's another who has cheered me here besides you, a friend from my youth, Robert Dudley, still imprisoned here."

I slopped water on the floor and nearly slipped in it. "John Dudley's son?" I demanded, forgetting for a moment to keep scrubbing. "But he went to arrest your sister. He —"

"No one understands him. I pray that, like me, he will be freed. He sent me posies once, had to bribe a guard to deliver them to me." She gave such a windy, heartfelt sigh that I felt it through the grate.

"Forgive me, Your Grace, but I . . ." I hesitated because I did not want to deflate her joy. I knew young, yearning love, yes. I'd told her that before when she made such a misstep with Tom Seymour. I could not bear to tell her that the Dudleys had joked about Robert getting into her bed.

"But what?" she prompted.

"I'm far too plainspoken, Your Grace, but you do know he is wed?"

"Something else arranged by his father, that is all."

I also recalled that the Dudley men had joked about marriages being put aside, about divorces. Before I could say worse, I blurted, "I heard he wed her against his father's wishes because it was a love match."

"See — you know nothing of it," she clipped out. "It is not at all like the thing with Seymour."

"I guess I'd trust the likes of shifty Seymour before I'd fall for a son of John Dudley!"

I could see her only from nose to eyebrows through the grate in her door, but I could tell I'd overstepped. "So, are you saying the sire ruins the son? Not true, Gera, else I'd have an Irish washerwoman I know blamed for being the child of a traitor, and I would never do that."

"You'd best not, for my father was not a traitor, just judged and executed as one by your father!"

"You'll not lecture me. I —"

We heard sharp whistling down the corridor. Was someone close enough to overhear us? I had learned that sounds echoed strangely in these labyrinthine corridors. Without another word, I hefted my bucket and moved away, down the stairs and back out into the streets to the livery stable where I'd left my horse. I was saddened that the Tudor temper and the Irish temper had tangled.

I must admit that such disputes between us have happened many a time since over the years, so severely that once, when the throne was finally hers, I was actually committed to the Tower for "plain-speaking to the queen," though she sent to have me released the very next day. We made up over wine, stuffing ourselves with comfits, and even danced a jig together, our privy jest for when we were alone. Yes, we were friends many years, but too much alike and, especially after Kat Ashley died, Elizabeth of England could brook no woman who gave her bold advice, had a dashing husband — and was a red-haired beauty too.

England's people began to call their queen Bloody Mary for her religious persecutions and the fact that she and her Spanish husband, Prince Philip, spent much English blood on Philip's war against France, one that my husband was forced to help fight and came out of quite the hero. But through all the things I detested Mary for, there is something for which I praised her. She permitted Gerald and Mabel, now the Earl and Countess of Kildare, to return to Ireland in the autumn of 1555. I was distraught to see them sail away without me, especially since Magheen and Collum went too, planning to live the rest of their years there. Gerald took with him the precious *Red Book of Kildare,* for the lists of loyalists and properties within would serve him well.

Edward, home on a brief leave, put his arm around me as we waved their ship out of London harbor and out of sight. "I swear to you, we will go too, as soon as we can manage," he promised.

I wiped my tears and sighed. "I've been saying and praying that for over twenty years now, but it may never be. I vow, but the queen means to keep me a hostage here for Gerald's good behavior. I must see Kildare and Maynooth again! Gerald and Mabel will need material goods and funding to rebuild and refurbish there, and I could help with that."

"Patience, Gera. After the queen bears this child she carries, she will be so happy she will let you go and me with you."

But there was no child for the queen. Twice she suffered false pregnancies as her health plummeted. Prince Philip, by then King of Spain at his father's death, left and returned, then left again — for good. Mary's heart as well as her health was broken, for she adored him.

During the rest of Queen Mary's reign, Elizabeth and I corresponded again, for we had long patched up our quarrel in the Tower. *How dare a mere prisoner in the Tower argue with a visiting washerwoman?* — she had recently written from her refuge at Hatfield House in the country.

When Mabel and Gerald had been gone two years, he sent Mabel back to court to ask the queen for funds to help rebuild his lands and power base, but Mary was heeding no one then. Ill, morose over Philip's desertion, shamed by her two false pregnancies and the loss of Calais in France, the last European foothold the English had held for years, Mary was in no mood to help the Geraldines or the Irish. But I had not given up on returning my family to leadership there, so we could help our poor people who had been ridden roughshod over. Gerald and the Irish needed not only funds but hope for the future. With no help from Queen Mary, and with Gerald's weak position, I would have to find a way.

CHAPTER THE TWENTY-NINTH

The Naval Docks on the Thames
April 1559

The queen was dead, and this time, "Long live the queen!" Elizabeth of England, my friend, took the Tudor throne when Mary died of stomach tumors in November of 1558. Edward was again Lord High Admiral, and I became one of the twenty-five-year-old queen's ladies. But still I was passionate above all else to return to Ireland, at least for a visit, for things were difficult there. In the void left by the Fitzgerald absence, other families had taken over some of our lands, people, and power.

At last, I saw the way to help not only Elizabeth but also the Fitzgeralds. Queen Mary's former, elderly Lord High Admiral, Lord Effingham, had not had the experience nor the stamina to chase pirates from our coasts, but Edward and his captains did. The only problem was that he was stretched too thin, building up the queen's navy, which had been greatly ignored since King Henry's death and which might be needed if the Spanish came calling. Meanwhile, the tricky French had to be kept appeased and literally at bay.

So one time when my lord was at sea, along the Scottish coast aboard a new ship, and when one particular pirate dared to defy the queen's and Privy Council's orders to cease and desist taking French ships as personal prizes, I went down to the royal docks at Wapping to speak with Mason Haverhill, who had been ill but was now much recovered. He was aboard the *Defiance,* which, despite being overhauled and patched up, was beginning to show her age, but then, weren't we all?

"You don't mean it!" he cried when I told him my plan and presented him with the piece of parchment signed by Elizabeth R. herself, and a second paper granting me permission to use the admiral's old ship — the latter missive I must admit I had cobbled together myself from another document Edward had signed. Before I could answer, Master Haverhill added, "Forgive me, milady, but I almost forgot whom I was speaking to. Of course you mean it."

"As the Lord High Admiral's wife?"

"Ah, no, I mean I almost forgot I was talking to the Irish Geraldine, who has done so much for the Tudor queens and ruler of Kildare County from afar, so the admiral says."

"Does he now? Then let's put out early on the morrow — and, if you don't mind moving your things out of the captain's cabin for me . . . The *Defiance* is still seaworthy, is she not?"

"Oh, aye, milady. Seaworthy and ready as ever, only you're not meaning to commandeer her like a pirate yourself and steer her home to Ireland, are you?"

"No, Master Haverhill, not yet, at least. I suppose my husband warned you of that."

He shrugged and grinned crookedly. He'd lost weight in his illness, but his ruddy color was returning from when I'd seen him last at our London house when he had come for dinner. He actually saluted as I turned and started down the gangplank, for I had much to do — for my husband and for Ireland.

In the English Channel off Plymouth Harbor
I knew a screaming scandal would ensue when word reached my enemies at court about my plan — perfectly legal — to use what was called the Lord High Admiral's prerogative, that is, his power to catch and

claim for himself any pirate's prize. I kept telling myself that Edward was stretched too thin trying to catch pirate ships, so he could use my help. And the queen was especially bent on stopping Englishman Martin Frobisher, whose attacks on French ships were playing havoc with Her Majesty's attempts to maintain peace with France. Years later, Elizabeth ignored and abetted English privateering vessels that harassed our Spanish enemies, but the time was ripe for what I dared. The only problem would be dealing with my husband, a fact I did not share with Master Haverhill, for Edward would be no doubt livid I had done this without his express permission and risked my limb and life to do so.

I wore no hairpins, proper hood, or pretty female cowl today. My long russet hair streamed free like a Fitzgerald battle banner. Despite how it shocked Haverhill and the crew, I had donned men's hose and trunks for climbing the ship's rail and had thrust a matchlock pistol in my belt. This particular pirate had given Elizabeth fits for months, so she had actually signed the paper I had shown Haverhill. Despite our spats, we mutually admired each other. She knew I was up to the task.

The *Defiance* bucked the channel wind

and tidal current as we patrolled the coast prowling for our prey, the pirate Martin Frobisher, who was out for nothing but his own profit, and at great cost to the queen's reputation, as if she could not control her own seamen. He had caused lawsuits and diplomatic chaos, though, God knows, no love was lost between England and France any more than between England and Spain. But the queen wanted peace with France, so I was hoping, so to speak, to kill two birds with one stone: please the queen and help gather funding for my family in Ireland.

"Milady, you needn't stand out in the elements," Haverhill called to me as I stood amidships, peering into the devil-black dawn. I could barely make him out near the beakhead as the ship lumbered up and down. "I can summon you from the cap'n's cabin if we espy them," he assured me. "Our intelligence on Frobisher's movements may be wrong. The sea spray will turn you to a pillar of salt like Lot's wife."

That comparison perversely amused me, because she had been punished for looking back. I wanted to look not only back but forward to Ireland, and Edward had promised more than once that we would go there. If I could pull this off without getting his ship — or his wife — damaged or destroyed, he would have to plead with the queen to let us go for a visit, because Elizabeth would owe me a favor — again.

"Would the Lord High Admiral be huddled in his cabin now?" I scolded Haverhill, ruing my sharp tone the moment the words were out of my mouth.

"Point taken. Aye-aye, milady!" he replied crisply, and turned away with his spyglass again, though it must do him little good in the low-lying pall of fog.

Despite the rocking deck, I stood steadily, legs spread like a man, but with a knot in my stomach at what I dared. Overhead the sails strained, pregnant with the wind. The rigging thrummed a dissonant sound, like phantom Irish harpers tuning their strings.

The heady feel of command coursed through me, for at last, whatever my duty to others, I finally steered the helm of my life. Surely, naught worse than what I'd survived could happen to me now.

"There, port side, Master Haverhill!" one of the sailors aloft shouted. "Could be Frobisher's privateer! Ay, the *Gerfalcon,* the *Gerfalcon* for a certain!"

As I turned to squint through the thinning fog, the ship's name echoed in my head. I heard again the Fitzgerald battle cry the day my people fought for their very lives, for Ireland's freedom: *"A Geraldine! A Geraldine!"*

I pushed the past away and ran to the leeward rail. Our ship had cut the *Gerfalcon* off, taken its crew by surprise as they tried to slink into the harbor with their booty — yes, towing the bare-masted prize of a French merchantman behind them. That, I wanted too. If I took Frobisher, his booty was mine by queen's command and Lord High Admiral's prerogative.

I had told Haverhill to use no deceptions, no promises of pardons or counterfeit invitations to a parley. Use the truth, lay it on the line, then fight if one must — that had always been my privy motto, for I'd seen the horror and havoc that deceits and lies could breed. So he used his voice trumpet, his tinny words echoing over the human hubbub from both vessels.

"Halt and be boarded! In the name of the queen of England and Lord Admiral, stow sail and be boarded or be damned by firepower!"

They began to slow; unless tricks or treachery were in store, they were ours now. Frobisher's crew no doubt carried small firearms, but why should he order them to fight? He'd been to prison twice for privateering and had been merely fined and soon released. No Execution Dock at Wapping for him, for the queen knew raw talent and courage when she saw it, lowborn or high-bred. It was what had saved me more than once.

The *Defiance* thudded into the privateer's hull; our men grappled it to us with hooks and ropes. The Lord High Admiral's armed sailors clung to the shrouds and lined the deck for boarding the captured vessel. I was suddenly reminded of the river festival Edward had presented on the Thames for the young king, and I told myself to be careful I did not fall in.

On both English ships, canvas flapped like cannon shots as men shortened sail. The mainsail directly over my head rattled and thundered as it sheeted home. Only then did Master Haverhill say to me, with a little bow, "If you'll wait right here, milady, I'll have Frobisher disarmed, bound, and brought to you."

"I will give him a chance to surrender first," I told him. "I've seen too many fine fighting men bound and shamed. I came not only to capture the privateer, but to board it." Holding to a rope with my free hand, I climbed lithely over both rails to the *Gerfalcon*'s main deck. It was easier than mounting an Irish palfrey.

Frobisher looked exactly as he'd been described to me, brawny and a bit wild. With size, swagger, and stance, he dominated the men around him. At least he'd had the sense to sheathe his sword, and I saw he and his crew had put their pistols on the deck.

"You! You, here?" He gasped and pointed rudely as I faced him down, hands on my hips. He glared at me. When I did not so much as blink — such disarming stares from the queen oft made someone blurt out his guilt — he plunged on: "Oh, for a moment, I thought it was the queen herself, but I know who you are. Had it not been an admiralty ship, I would have fought to the last man," he boasted, crossing his arms over his chest and rocking back cockily on his heels.

"You are an unlicensed privateer and freebooter, Master Martin Frobisher," I accused in my strongest voice, intentionally not addressing him as captain. "After being twice warned by the crown to cease and desist, you are yet causing discord with the sovereign nation of France, which endangers English royal policy. I arrest you in the name of the Lord High Admiral, the council, and the queen."

"I have papers — a license — a commission to capture French prizes," he protested. "The Frenchies are the ones up to no good, not me."

"I expected you to cobble up an excuse. A license signed by whom?" I demanded, my dander up now at his thinking he could hoodwink a woman — although one who had forged a paper of her own but yesterday. "Your blackguard first mate? A tosspot in a tavern? Some poor doxy from the Plymouth stews?" I shouted.

"In faith, you're wide of the mark. 'Tis a pass signed by a Huguenot leader," he blustered, knowing full well, I warrant, that he had not one sea leg to stand on.

"Didn't you learn your lesson from being captured and imprisoned twice before?" I goaded. I could tell he wanted to insult me in return. At least now that Elizabeth ruled England, no one dared say — to my face, at least — that I was but a feeble female, a fallen Fitzgerald, or an untamed shrew. I was full thirty-six years of age and had swallowed a bellyful of such taunts, though I reckon my fair face and fair sex had saved me once or twice.

"Martin Frobisher, you are my prisoner, and your ship and the captured merchant-man are forfeit," I declared as my ship's crew cheered and whistled as if I'd doubled their wages.

"You're all privateers too!" Frobisher railed as our men seized him. His face went red as a Kildare pippin; veins stood out on his temple, and spittle flecked his lips. I'd been warned he had a temper by someone who had never seen an Irish temper. "Poxy legal privateers you are, too, that's all!" he ranted. "You and the queen, peas in a pod, two clever, flame-haired freebooters; I don't give a fig if you wear masculine garb and sport a pistol today! Unwomanly, brash, and brazen, both of you — and you an Irish wench at that, and they're pirates to the core and —"

"I shall be certain," I outshouted him, "to tell Her Majesty that she has been wrong — wrong to not send you to Execution Dock instead of England's jails, which you all too soon buy or bribe your way out of, you flap-mouth, base-court cur!"

I slapped his face and boxed his ears. He tried to kick at me, but two of our men pulled him back. When I nodded, they dragged him toward our vessel to be kept secured. A moment of shocked silence followed from both crews. I stood stunned too. I had actually arrested and struck a man who had defied Tudor might, for doing the very thing that had been my passion for years.

"Now, won't that be something to tell the Lord High Admiral when he returns from Scotland!" Haverhill broke the silence. With a gap-toothed grin, he displayed a bottle of wine and a bolt of cloth. As his men hustled back to work, securing our captured vessel and its crew, he made a little bow. He flapped open and draped a length of robin's-egg blue velvet over my shoulders like a royal robe.

"I take it your men have already surveyed Frobisher's booty in the hold of my formerly French ship?" I asked. With a flourish, I flung the end of the velvet up and around my shoulders. At the very least, it was a heady feeling to win for once, to be the one giving instead of taking orders.

"Silks too," he assured me, "and ginger and nutmeg, by the smell of the hold, milady. Crates of wine, not even in barrels, all of it in glass bottles, can you believe? And it's all yours, since you stand today in the stead of the Lord High Admiral for his rightful perquisites and in high favor with the queen — so's I hear, that is."

"You heard true, Captain, but one never knows which way the wind blows with Her Majesty. That bottle and more are yours, for your fine service, but not until we have all three ships safely in the Thames. The queen, of course, must have Frobisher's privateer ship for her navy. His crew you may release later, if they are willing to sign onto legally licensed vessels, but the captured French one is mine."

I didn't say so, but much of the wine and the sumptuous French fabrics was not destined for London but for Ireland, or at least the profits from their sales were. And my ship, the captured French prize, I would rename the *Pride of Kildare,* and sail her home with Edward someday soon.

Dublin Harbor
May 6, 1559

When I had sailed away from Ireland twenty-four years ago, I had met Edward Clinton on the ship. And today, going home, I stood shoulder-to-shoulder with him, steering my own ship, the *Pride of Kildare.* We were laden with money and goods to help rebuild Maynooth and help the Irish recover from years of persecution. I was laden, as Surrey had once put it, *In ship, freight with remembrance. Of thoughts and pleasures past . . .* And of so much grief and pain. But not today. Today was just for joy.

Our puppy, Erin, was full-grown now, pacing on deck as if she were excited to be back too. Alice and Margaret had come along, but they were still belowdecks. Dawn was barely breaking, and we'd made better time than we'd expected. Though I'd gone to bed for a few hours, I had hardly slept at all. Now Edward moved to stand behind me, his hands over mine on the spokes of the great wheel as we guided the ship together into the crowded harbor.

"Do not think," he whispered in my ear, "that your punishment for forging my name on that admiralty document is over."

"Punishment, my lord? You call my being at your beck and call in our bed punishment? In that case, I shall board and capture many more ships."

"Hell's gates, Irish, that's exactly what worries me. At least Her Majesty was happy enough to have Frobisher locked up again and to be given his privateer for our fledgling navy. Thank heavens she's a Tudor who prefers peace to war."

"Her Grace is so besotted with Robert Dudley's deceitful, seductive courting of her, she would be happy with anything. But she's in for a fall, Edward; I know she is, and I've told her so."

"You said she mentioned to you more than once she would never wed, but she needs the adoration from him."

"Yes, I know."

"Then since she hearkens yet to you, best you not get in arguments with her — or me. Master Haverhill, come and cozy us up to the wharf!" he called out. "I'd best arm myself lest more wild Irish come on board and take me prisoner as this one has."

"Aye, Admiral," he said with a grin so wide it nearly split his face in half. "And aye-aye, Cap'n Lady Clinton."

I ignored their chuckles and leaned on the rail to take in the view. Erin leaned against my legs, but I only patted her head, for she was too big for me to pick up anymore. Amidst the larger ships like ours, I watched the darting cockle boats and even fisherfolk in a little *namhóag*. I saw where the River Liffey poured in, fed by Kildare's own River Lyreen that had been Magheen's and my road to freedom the day we fled. Right up that stream was Uncle James's Leixlip Castle. Amidst the rooftops of Dublin town, I spotted the hulking Kilmainham Castle, where Uncle Leonard had betrayed the Geraldines and I had first met Alice.

That very morn we oversaw the packing of the carts we'd hired, piled high with furnishings and foodstuffs for Maynooth Castle and the village. We took guards with us, since we carried a goodly amount of coin for rebuilding the castle and Fitzgerald power. At last, ahorse with the carts rumbling behind us until they fell farther and farther back, we set out for Kildare.

I was drunk with all I saw. Glimpses of golden dandelions and marsh marigold in the wet spring meadows so green — a thousand shades of Irish green. The familiar frogs I'd never heard the like of since I'd left croaked from ditches. Little leprechauns, Magheen used to call them. I could not wait to see her again, and Collum too.

Late that afternoon, as we neared the old Fitzgerald town of Maynooth, rebuilt from its burning, people came out upon the roads to greet us. A young colleen, about my age when I left, curtsied and extended to me a makeshift bouquet of shamrocks and bluebells, no doubt fresh-picked from the woodland floor. She was nervous in her little speech of welcome, but it was so good to hear the Irish brogue about me everywhere again. I dismounted and hugged her, walking my horse the last half mile — Edward did the like — smiling and waving at the greetings and cheers of those who lined our way as if I were the queen of England herself. Or better yet, an Irish princess.

Then someone began the chant, the very one I'd called out for my family on their way to execution, the very one I'd shouted on the day Gerald came back from Europe, the cry of my heart. For those few moments, as much as I loved and treasured my husband, I was not a Clinton but a Fitzgerald again.

"A Geraldine! A Geraldine! A Geraldine!" the people cried, as Erin barked in unison as if she knew the chant.

Through my smiles, I burst into tears, and Edward put his arm around me.

But where was the tall tower of Maynooth? As we walked arm in arm, I tried to catch a glimpse of it through the spring beech forest.

There it was! Tall and proud despite its wounds from cannonballs, sturdy and solid with Fitzgerald banners flapping from its parapets.

I handed Edward my bouquet, dropped my reins, and began to run. Erin loped along easily beside me, just as Wynne used to do. Margaret appeared from back in our entourage, laughing, barefooted like we once ran in the springs and summers of our youth before everything went so wrong. I kicked off both shoes and started up the lawn with her beside me.

She was signaling, *House! Home!* I seized her hand and stretched our strides, pulling her along. Near the castle entry, waving wildly, awaited Gerald and Mabel, Earl and Countess of Kildare, so regal-looking compared to us, but I could not contain myself. Ah, yes, tears glistened on Mabel's cheeks too. Just behind them stood Collum and my Magheen, their wrinkled faces wreathed in smiles. Magheen lifted her skirt hems and did a few steps of a jig, which, I must admit, despite the glory of the day and this place, made me miss Elizabeth Tudor just a bit.

Like a silly child, I loosed Margaret's hand and, raising my arms to the blue sky, twirled about once before hugging everyone. For one mad moment, in their arms, welcomed home, it was as if Mother and Father were here to greet me again with the young Irish couple who had served us so faithfully and so well. But there was my handsome husband, shaking hands, smiling, clapping Gerald on the shoulder, even though he still had my posies in his hand — and held my future happiness too, whatever the coming years would bring to Ireland.

"Welcome back! Welcome home, Gerabeth!" Gerald cried as he pulled me away a step or two, his arm around my shoulders as he lowered his voice. "I'm hoping you can write to the queen about several things. . . . I'm so glad you're here, for I need your advice and help."

"And you shall have it!" I told him, and hugged him hard.

That night they spoiled us with all my old favorites: soused herring, cockles from County Kerry, and prawns from Dublin Bay, braised woodcock, carrot pudding, and ale cake. The men drank themselves silly with *usquebaugh,* which the English called whiskey.

Edward was sleeping heavily in the early morn when I got up in my night rail and wrapped myself in his big robe to stare out the window at the dark lawn encircled by the silver ribbon of the Lyreen. I stood there until dawn, when my husband and all the world began to stir. The eastern sky went from lilac to rose to yellow sunlight on my face. In that golden moment, for perhaps the first time in my life, though I had much to do, I was at last, for now, content.

AUTHOR'S NOTE

First, a defense of the foundation for this novel: that the Fitzgeralds were considered the royal family of Ireland. Two of the many sources that present and defend this fact are these: Padraic O'Farrell writes in his *A History of County Kildare* (Dublin: Gill & Macmillan Ltd., 2003, p. 256), "From 1454 until 1534, the Fitzgeralds were the 'uncrowned kings' of Ireland." In her book *Ireland* (Northampton, MA: Interlink Pub Group, Inc., 2006, p. 519), Catharina Day says much the same: "[The Fitzgerald Earls of Kildare, known as the Geraldines] were so powerful and wealthy that they were the uncrowned kings of Ireland."

Most books on Irish history also claim that the slaughter of the Fitzgeralds began the split between medieval and modern Ireland. One of these is *The Geraldines: An Experiment in Irish Government* by Brian FitzGerald (Maryknoll, NY: Orbis, 1986).

(Interesting author last name; he no doubt had a special interest in his subject matter. And on that point, we can assume one reason President John Fitzgerald Kennedy was proud of his middle name. Even in America, there are many famous Fitzgerald descendants, from Ella Fitzgerald to F. Scott Fitzgerald.)

Other books of interest for more information on Elizabeth Gera Fitzgerald and her family can be found in these references: Gillian Kenny, *Anglo-Irish and Gaelic Women in Ireland c.1170–1540* (Dublin: Four Courts, 2007); Mary Ann Lyons, *Gearoid Og Fitzgerald* (Historical Association of Ireland, Dundalk, Co. Louth, Ireland: Dundalgan Press, 1998); and William Nolan and Thomas McGrath (eds.), *Kildare History and Society* (Dublin: Geographic Publications, 2006).

The rest of Gera's story, after this novel ends, would have made a thousand-page book had I pursued it all. Despite the novel's happy ending, tough times lay ahead for the Fitzgeralds and Ireland. Gerald, 11th Earl of Kildare, struggled for the next thirty years to get back to "the old days." The Act of Attainder against the family was not lifted until 1569, because Ireland (as any person familiar with past or recent history knows) was not ready to bow to English rule. As late as 1574, Gerald, Earl of Kildare, was blamed for a scheme to raise armed men. The next year he was arrested and imprisoned in Dublin Castle and was eventually sent to the Tower of London for ten months. (Yes, Irish history repeats itself.)

The fact that he was released may be tied to Gera's continual relationship with Queen Elizabeth, for historians agree that, unlike her father, this queen never sought the elimination of the house of Kildare. Some courtiers and councilors were furious at the queen's temperate handling of the family, including the fact that, during Gerald's stay in the Tower, his wife and sister had visitation rights and Mabel (who became increasingly pro-Irish) was allowed to go back to Kildare to see to their business affairs. In May of 1580, Gerald defiantly declared, "All you Englishmen are joined in one and an Irishman can have no right or justice at your hands." Yet Queen Elizabeth had Gerald released from the Tower; he was spared a traitor's death and simply banished from court. He died in London. And so, despite Gera's dreams, there was no return to Geraldine rule in Ireland.

As for Gera and Edward Clinton's lives after the book ends, they had a very successful thirty-three-year marriage. His will and other documents show how much he trusted and protected his wife. As well as serving as Elizabeth's Lord High Admiral, Clinton often served the queen on diplomatic missions to France. Like the queen herself, the Lord High Admiral was heavily invested in privateering against England's enemies and had a stake in Drake's around-the-world voyage of 1577–1580. On May 4, 1572, Edward was created Earl of Lincoln, which made Gera Countess of Lincoln.

They both remained influential at Elizabeth's court until their deaths. An early indication of Gera's influence is that, in the days just before Elizabeth was declared queen, Gera was with her at rural Hatfield House and helped to broker a meeting between the soon-to-be queen and the Duke of Feria, a friend of King Philip of Spain. More than one source calls Gera a confidante of the queen. Years later, they continued to have their fallings-out, but seemed to patch things up quickly.

The Earl of Lincoln died in London on January 16, 1585, and, because he was a Garter Knight, had chosen to be buried in St. George's Chapel, Windsor, where his resting place is marked by a highly ornate monument of porphyry and alabaster that Gera had built for him. She died in March of 1589 at a good age for that time. Her sister Margaret was her chief mourner, and Gera was buried next to her beloved husband. Visitors to Windsor can, of course, view the plain floor stones over the resting place of King Henry VIII. (He never did get the elaborate tomb he wanted and had pilfered from Cardinal Wolsey; it is now in the crypt of St. Paul's Cathedral and honors Lord Admiral Nelson!) However, visitors to Windsor may see the effigies of the Earl and Countess of Lincoln at the southeast end of St. George's Chapel, for they have by far a finer memorial than King Henry.

As ever, I must note that in Tudor-era research, dating events exactly can be a real problem, as their calendar could be confusing and writers obviously remembered things different ways. For examples of this, I found that in reading for this novel:

- Gera's birth dates vary, as does the order in which she and her siblings were born. According to *The Dictionary of National Biography,* her birthdate is uncertain. I have selected a date of 1523 from among the possible choices. It makes no sense to me that Surrey would have written his laudatory sonnet to Gera (either in 1537 or 1538 —

I saw both dates) when she was much younger than sixteen. Also, as noted in the story, extremely young girls did not become companions to royalty in Tudor courts.

- Gera wed Sir Anthony Browne in either 1542 or 1543.
- John Dudley was named Earl of Warwick in 1546 or 1547.
- The date of the Fitzgerald men's executions at Tyburn was either February 1537 or July 1537.

When possible, I have tried to stick to historical records, but I did move one event. It was actually 1569 rather than 1559 when Gera captured Martin Frobisher's pirate vessel. It was such a bold, feminist endeavor that I had to include it in this portrait of her. At that time it was recorded that she had "a remarkable business head, [and was] much occupied with Admiralty matters, especially wreck or pirates' goods or Lord Admiral's perquisites (what we today call perks) and was in high favor with the queen." (Quote from *The Expansion of Elizabethan England,* A. L. Rowse [Madison: University of Wisconsin Press, 2003, p. 256])

Other random matters of Tudor trivia I found interesting:

- King Henry VIII did not sign his will and did have secret back rooms at Whitehall and other palaces. A fascinating book on all this is Robert Hutchinson's *The Last Days of Henry VIII* (New York: HarperCollins, 2005).
- For those who believe in ghosts — and what self-respecting castle in the British Isles doesn't have a resident ghost? — Queen Catherine Howard is reputed to be "seen" yet today, running and screaming down the long gallery of Hampton Court Palace toward the Chapel Royal, begging King Henry not to have her arrested. Although I saw the site in broad daylight, the tour guide was most convincing, insisting that experts in the paranormal have recorded those very screams.
- From the time Gera's half brother, "Silken Thomas," was held in the Tower of London yet remain these letters he carved into a stone in his cell: THOMAS FITZ G.
- Maynooth Castle, eleven miles from Dublin, may be visited today in County Kildare, but it is much changed from

Gera's time. The keep and newer manor house are available to tour. At the time this book was printed, more about it online with pictures can be found at this Web site: http://www .heritageireland.ie/en/midlandseast coast /MaynoothCastle/

My thanks to the following people who helped with background information for the novel:

- Catherine O'Connor at the Office of Public Works, Maynooth Castle, for her kind correspondence and suggestions for research. Although I have visited Ireland, I did not have the Fitzgeralds in mind for a book until after I left, so Ms. O'Connor helped a great deal.
- Joseph Templeman, clerk of the Sempringham Parish Council, for information on and a drawing of historic Sempringham. Of Kyme Castle, only its tower yet remains, and it looks much like what Maynooth's must once have been.
- Kathy Lynn Emerson, who writes Tudor-era historicals as Kate Emerson. I appreciated her loan of a book about Gera's brother Gerald, called

510

Surviving the Tudors: The "Wizard" Earl of Kildare and English Rule in Ireland 1537–1586, by Vincent P. Carey (Dublin: Four Courts Press, 2002), and enjoy her excellent Web site on Tudor-era women. See www.kate emersonhistoricals.com/TudorWomen F.htm

There are two extant portraits of Elizabeth Fitzgerald Clinton, Countess of Lincoln, although, some argue that the one painted more close-up might be Mabel Browne Fitzgerald. The more formal 1560 portrait is by Steven van der Meulen and can be viewed most easily at http:// en.wikipedia.org/wiki/File:Elizabeth_ Fitzgerald.jpg and the one by an unknown artist at http://www.tudorplace.com.ar/Bios/ ElizabethFitzgerald(CLincoln).htm.

At least two portraits of Edward Clinton are extant, a youthful one drawn by Holbein, labeled *Clinton,* and one painted much later by an unknown artist — perhaps the same anonymous artist who painted the one of Gera. The best links to view these are found by Googling "Edward Fiennes Clinton + portrait."

As ever, thanks to my husband, Don, for being such a patient traveling companion

on our journeys around the British Isles.
And for proofreading my manuscripts and
acting as my business manager.

Karen Harper
November 2009

ABOUT THE AUTHOR

A former college instructor and high school English teacher, **Karen Harper** writes contemporary suspense as well as historical novels. Karen and her husband love to travel both in the United States and abroad and, when at home, divide their time between Columbus, Ohio, and Naples, Florida. For additional information, please visit www .KarenHarperAuthor.com.

■ ■ ■ ■

READERS GUIDE
THE IRISH PRINCESS
KAREN HARPER

■ ■ ■ ■

A CONVERSATION WITH
KAREN HARPER

Q. What about Gera Fitzgerald especially interested you and made you want to write a whole book about her?

A. I can't recall exactly where I first discovered Gera, but I believe it was in reading about women who served Queen Elizabeth I during her long reign. Gera stood out to me — Irish (unusual); rebel; red-haired, like the queen, but unlike the queen, a noted beauty. I knew Bess Tudor liked to be the most beautiful woman around. So why would she keep a striking woman like Gera with her over the years? Evidently, not just to keep an eye on someone suspicious, as the Tudors were wont to do. Gera was very intriguing, and as I researched her, I learned the tragedy of her family. I must also admit, I'm always looking for main characters who have a good love story of their own. I, like Gera, am a sucker for swashbuckling sea captains. Also, I had recently been to Ireland and thought the country was lovely; settings are important to me.

Q. You take the stance that the Fitzgeralds were considered the royal family of Ireland and suggest that their downfall marked a profound change in Ireland. What were some advances made under the Fitzgeralds, and how did they affect the lives of ordinary people? How did that change after the Fitzgeralds lost power?

A. As I detail in my Author's Note at the end of the novel, historians pretty much agree that the "reign" of the Fitzgeralds marked the division between medieval and modern Ireland. The military and political strength of Gera's family gave the warring factions of Ireland a period of peace during which villages, agriculture, and trade flourished, despite the deep divisions that remained between the "haves" and the "have-nots." Gera's father began the University of Maynooth in 1518 and managed to keep the English at bay from conquering Ireland earlier than they did. I wonder how long the Irish could have remained fairly independent of English rule, taxation, and interference if Gera's half brother, Silken Thomas, had not blatantly provoked the English king.

Q. It's interesting that both Gera Fitzgerald, in The Irish Princess, *and Katherine Ashley, the focus of your novel* The Queen's Governess, *married late in life and ultimately had no children. How common was that among women who spent time at the Tudor royal court? How do you think their childlessness shaped their lives?*

A. It was rather rare that married women, let alone those at the Tudor court, were childless in this era, although there are plenty of examples of women, like Gera, whose children did not live to adulthood. Actually, I think that having and losing one's babies (Catherine of Aragon is a prime example) was even more tragic than being childless. In Kat Ashley's case, I think her childlessness was sad because she was such an excellent caretaker of children. However, if she'd had her own, perhaps she would not have poured as much love into the young Bess Tudor. In Gera's case, her lifelong care for her disabled sister Margaret, as well as for her younger stepchildren, probably helped fill that void in her life.

Q. How much about Gera is documented in the historical record and how much did you

embellish? And can you tell us more about
The Red Book of Kildare?

A. The first part of this question is huge. I
am writing faction; that is, I take the facts I
can find and fictionalize only the parts of
the plot I cannot research. Naturally, this
means conversations and some sections of
the story are made up, but I try to stay with
what logically could have happened from
the research. In this novel, the part I could
find the least about, and therefore fictional-
ized, is Gera's escape from Maynooth
Castle. It is unclear where she was between
when her mother left for England and when
Gera joined her at Beaumanoir. Maybe
Gera went with her mother when she ini-
tially left for England, but I could not have
Gera miss the great initial adventure of her
life during the castle siege. However, once
her life began to intertwine with the Tudor
princesses', and when she married the quite
well-documented Edward Clinton, she
became much easier to track.

The Red Book of Kildare is still extant and
is housed in the British Museum. Therefore,
I must admit that the English finally got
their hands on it, though I am not sure
when or how. Its most recent translation
from Latin, as far as I know, was edited and

explained by Mac Niocaill in the 1964 publication *The Red Book of the Earls of Kildare*. Originally, it was compiled by the scholar Philip Flatsbury for Gera's father. Records in it begin from around 1503 and include maps, lists of important people, title deeds, and the wealth of the Kildares: pewter plates, silver saltcellars, etc. It was also a rental book with names of those loyal to the family, which is why the Tudors wanted it. I do not know that Gera kept and hid it during her life, but I do know it strangely disappeared around the time of the siege of Maynooth, then reappeared approximately when Gera's brother Gerald returned to Ireland as earl. *The Red Book of Kildare* is not to be confused with the legendary lost Book of Kildare from the 1100s in Ireland, which was supposedly dictated by an angel.

Q. You present Gera Fitzgerald as a passionate, strong-willed woman who was able to express herself even within the strictures of the Tudor court. How unusual was she?

A. Much of Gera's character I took from the very telling detail that she was once sent to the Tower for "plain-speaking to the queen." It reveals so much about her and about the queen that Gera was soon released and back in Elizabeth's good graces. In my years of studying and writing about Elizabeth Tudor, I find that she was wise and clever enough to listen to and be advised by others. Despite some of the things that could have made Elizabeth angry at or jealous of Gera, the queen must have seen their similarities — including, perhaps, their childlessness. I believe Elizabeth leaned for advice on both Lord High Admiral Clinton and the Irish Fitzgerald.

Q. Was Edward Clinton really as dashing as you portray him? It's wonderful to hear that he and Gera had a long, happy marriage, but if he was frequently off on the queen's business, how much time did they really get to spend together?

A. Evidently, with Edward and Gera Clinton, absence did make the heart grow fonder. To draw from my own family history, my great-grandfather was a pilot on Great Lakes vessels, was gone much of the year, yet he and my great-grandmother had a good marriage. It is true that Edward Clinton was absent a great deal and Gera was at court with the queen for long periods of time, but they seem to have been a very happy couple. Perhaps the fact that they had both been wed before — in arranged marriages — made their marriage of choice really work. As far as I can tell, their marriage to each other was set up by no one but themselves. And, maybe it's just me, but as I mentioned before, sea captains — and the Lord High Admiral of the navy, no less — seem very dashing. My own love of the sea and ships is probably reflected in Gera.

Q. I've read other novels about Elizabeth I in which Robert Dudley is presented in a more positive light than you present him here and in your other novels. Do you really believe he was a blackguard who cared more for his own advancement than for Elizabeth? Did she love him more than he loved her?

A. I used to have a much rosier, more romantic view of Robert Dudley, the queen's "dear Robin," than I do now. (The same can be said about my changing view over time of Henry VIII.) I do believe Robert was more in love with the princess and queen than with the woman. But that's a question she could never answer; nor can I. That is the price one must pay for fame and fortune — just exactly what is the lover in love with? I am, however, continually amazed by the crazed ambition of the Dudleys, as with other Tudor-era families — including the Tudors. I keep coming back to the quote, "Absolute power corrupts absolutely," which, sadly, seems as true today as in the Tudor era.

Q. Was Henry VIII's treatment of the Fitzgeralds typical of his treatment of other powerful families? Was he harsher toward families of his outlying kingdoms, such as Ireland, Scotland, and Wales?

A. I've recently been reading a great deal about Henry VIII's father, King Henry VII. Under him, the Tudors took the English throne in battle, although they had some royal blood in their veins. The horrors of the War of the Roses were only one generation back from Henry VIII, so the Tudors were paranoid about others threatening their claim to the throne. Henry VIII's consistent but unspoken policy was to get rid of anyone who challenged his power, usually by charging him or her with treason. This could include his English relatives (such as the Earl of Surrey and his father, Norfolk), leaders of rebellions foreign or domestic, or even just severe critics. He also turned on once-intimate friends such as Sir Thomas More. In short, Henry VIII was an equal-opportunity destroyer.

Q. You have obviously done a tremendous amount of in-depth research on the Tudor period. Can you describe the process you use? How do you keep track of all your sources and make choices when your sources provide contradictory information? And when do you know it's time to stop researching and start writing the book?

A. All good questions. I have studied the Tudors and their times for about thirty years and have a good-size library about them. However, each new novel demands additional research, which I keep filed in folders with headings such as — for this book — Ireland, Characters, Culture, Ships, etc. Sources do often disagree: Sometimes I'm forced to take my best guess by relying on surrounding evidence. When I hear the characters start "talking to one another," I know it's time to actually begin to write. I always look for a grabber beginning to propel the plot, but I like to deal briefly with my heroine's early life, because I feel we can usually understand a personality best if we see the family from which that person came. When I was teaching school and had a problem student, I always tried to schedule a parent conference. How often, the moment I met one or both of the parents, I said to myself, *Oh, now I get why their child acts that way!*

Q. Was there any fascinating new information you uncovered during your research for this book that never made it into the story?

A. Fascinating, yes, but no real bombshells. As I mention in the Author's Note, Gera and Edward had a long marriage and she served the queen far into her reign, so their story does not end where I end it. But this book needed to conclude when Gerald and Gera finally returned to Maynooth and their beloved Irish people. Of course, her hopes for Ireland's independence from England under her family's guidance were not realized. I will add one thing about this question that interested me and seemed so modern. When Edward Clinton's will was read, so much of his property and decision making was passed on to Gera that her stepson, Ursula Dudley's son, was pretty upset about it.

Q. Have any comments about your work from reviewers and readers particularly surprised you?

A. Of course, all authors love good reviews.

Just last week I spoke to two readers' groups at the Toledo Public Library in Toledo, Ohio, who had read *Mistress Shakespeare*. I was really touched to hear several of the women say that the novel had inspired them to take a look at Shakespeare again — as a person as well as a writer. And, as a former university instructor and high school English teacher of British literature, I'm always thrilled when a reviewer or reader says something like, "I hated history in high school, but your book made it really come alive." That is always a double payoff for me besides someone just liking the love story or the adventure.

Q. You also write contemporary suspense for another publisher. What are the challenges and rewards of combining historical and contemporary writing? And how do you remain so incredibly prolific?

A. The challenges include keeping the two very different narrative voices for modern and historical stories separate. The sentence structure, as well as word choice, of course, is quite unique to each era. That said, all good writing is suspense writing and needs in-depth character development, so there are many similarities. As for being prolific — I love being a storyteller and having my readers learn something while they are entertained and challenged. I try to take my readers into a different world, even in my contemporary books. Drawing a reader into the Elizabethan world is not so very different from drawing him or her into the unique world of the Amish, Appalachia, or the Everglades.

Q. You also divide the year into time in Ohio and time in Florida. Does that change in setting have an effect on your work?

A. I can manage to lose myself in writing a book whether there are maple trees or palm trees outside my office window. However, I always write my historical novels in Ohio, because that's where my Elizabethan-era library is. Still, my husband is continually appalled by the books and stacks of research I take to Florida each year so I can work on a contemporary book. Fortunately, I'm an early riser and can get some writing done before the business or beauty of the day takes time or tempts me to go outside.

QUESTIONS FOR DISCUSSION

1. Even in the early scenes of this novel, it is obvious that female children are valued less than male children. How is Gerald treated differently from Gera during the threat to their family? Are there hints that Gera might have made a better leader for the family than her brother? And is this pro-male bent still evident in modern families?

2. Gera is forced to leave her homeland and live in a country whose king she despises. What do you think keeps her desire for revenge alive for so long?

3. In some ways, Gera is a typical Irish rebel. Is she just lucky not to get caught in her rebellion, or does she choose her rebellions wisely?

4. Gera feels a connection to Elizabeth Tudor that goes beyond the similarity in their appearance. What do you think they have in common, and how are they different?

5. Can you think of a modern-day equivalent to the autocratic power Henry VIII wielded over his subjects, who were vulnerable to made-up charges of treason and summarily executed?

6. Gera falls in love with and weds Edward Clinton, a man she detests earlier. Does she really hate him for a while, or is she lying to herself? Is it a good idea to marry a man who has family ties, loyalties, or interests that are at odds with yours?

7. Some of the best novels have a central character who has a strong story arc; that is, the person learns and changes a great deal during the novel. Is Gera's swing from hater of the Tudors to friend of Mary and Elizabeth believable? Should the sins of the fathers be visited upon their children, or will those children be completely free from

the errors and prejudices of their parents and other family members?

8. If you've read other novels set during this period, how does Karen Harper's portrait of well-known figures differ from the way they're depicted in other novels, and even plays and movies? For example, compare Robert Dudley, Jane Grey, Mary Tudor, Elizabeth Tudor, Thomas Seymour, and Henry VIII's many wives.

9. Discuss Gera's response to her inability to have children as compared to the attitudes of other childless women in the novel. At a time when a woman's worth was often based on her ability to produce healthy children, especially males, and when child mortality remained high, discuss what impact childlessness might have had on these women's lives. How have attitudes changed since then?

10. In wartime even today, many married couples face long periods of separation. What effect does this have on a relationship, especially if the woman is the one left behind? What do Gera and Edward do —

and what can modern couples do — to keep their relationships vital and strong?

11. Gera was recorded as being sent by Elizabeth Tudor to the Tower for "plain-speaking to the queen," but she was quickly recalled. As much as both of these women must have hated and dreaded the Tower of London, this says a lot about them. Gera, when she does lie, for example about the location of *The Red Book of Kildare,* words her answer so "it wasn't quite a lie." Are we sometimes Geras in that respect today? Where is the line between always telling the truth and softening it or bending it a bit in relationships with family and friends? Is telling the blatant truth always the best way to go?

12. It is interesting in historical novels to see a woman who desperately wants to do something she cannot, because of the strictures of that day. For example, Gera would obviously love to command a ship of her own, or to step in to represent and run her family. Women became shopkeepers or printers at this time, for instance, only because they were widowed or orphaned and had to keep the business going after

being left it by a male family member. Are there any such barriers left today, now that we have women soldiers, pilots — even sailors on submarines? Are there still no-females-allowed-or-approved careers in our modern world?

13. Gera has a deep love of Ireland and, later, Lincolnshire and Sempringham. What makes people feel passionately attached to certain locations? Is it just because we were born or reared there? What memories and ties to places (not just where you were raised) emotionally bind you to particular locations? Happy memories? Beautiful scenery? Some deep, inner longing?